PIPER PRINCE

Forbidden Forest 2

AMBER ARGYLE

Book Cover Design by Melissa Williams Design

First Edition: April 2019
Library of Congress Cataloging-in-Publication Data
LCCN: 2019903471

Argyle, Amber
Piper Prince (Forbidden Forest) – 1st ed
ISBN-13: 978-0-9976390-4-9

For My Little Knight,

You were the best friend a girl could ask for.

Your gentleness, loyalty, and heart exceeded that of all other men,

Even if you were a horse.

CHAPTER 1

MEMORIES AND MAGIC

Wearing a torn and bloody wedding dress of deepest red, Larkin stepped into a vast cathedral made of trees gilded by early morning light. A single, luminous column shone on Larkin's little sister, alighting her puff of strawberry-blonde hair.

"What did you say?" Larkin panted, her bruised ribs aching.

"The trees are our friends," Sela repeated. The first words she'd spoken in weeks—oh, how Larkin had missed her lisp. But something about her words pricked at Larkin's memory. She'd heard Sela say that before, but when?

Was it possible Sela knew something about the magic of the trees? But that was impossible. She was a child of four, and she had no idea of the sacred tree in the heart of the Forbidden Forest, thanks to the druids' lies and superstitions.

Larkin crossed the meadow to kneel before her sister. "Promise me, promise you'll stop running off! Mama is worried sick!"

1

Instead of answering, Sela's big eyes grew round with concern. She touched the scrape on Larkin's cheek, the deep ache testifying to the swelling and bruise. "You have an owie."

A scratched cheek, bruised ribs, and a bloody wound on Larkin's palm from a sliver. She'd been lucky to escape the druids at all. She tugged Sela's hand down. "I'm all right."

Sela noted the bandaged hand holding hers. Her brow furrowed, she looked from Larkin back the way they'd come—toward the encampment of hundreds, perhaps thousands, of pipers.

Three days ago, Sela had escaped their town under the pipers' enchantment. All she would remember was Larkin being forced to a wedding to Bane under the cover of night and then waking in the forest. She wouldn't know about Denan breaking up the wedding but failing to rescue Larkin. About the blood and death of that night. About the fear during the days following.

Even now, Larkin's heart quickened with memories, her magic buzzing in her sigils, aching to be released. She shoved down memories and magic and the betrayals of Nesha and Bane. How could he try to force her like that? And then ... And then the next night, he'd singlehandedly held back the druids so she could escape with Denan.

Love or hate—Larkin wasn't sure which emotion was stronger when it came to the man she'd once considered her best friend. Probably both.

"I want Bane." Sela's voice wavered. He'd always been like a big brother to her.

But Bane had been captured by the very druids he'd been working for. Larkin shuddered to think what the Black Druid Garrot would do to him.

"Denan is going to fetch him for us." He'd promised he would.

The brilliance around them faded. The temperature dropped. Sela looked around and nervously stepped closer to Larkin, who glanced at the sky. No clouds. Her eyes burned and stung, forcing her to look away. But in the after-vision, the sun was not whole, but pitted on one side, as if a chunk had been bitten off.

Uneasy, Larkin took her sister's hand in her uninjured one and rose to her feet. "We should get back. Mama will be worried."

Sela dug her heels in. "No!"

Larkin tugged harder, dragging her a couple of steps. "It's safer at the encampment." The piper army was back that way. And Denan. The mere thought of him awoke the brush of butterfly wings in her chest.

That warm, fluttery feeling snuffed out as darkness spread across the daylight like poison.

"What is this?" Larkin whispered. Darkness meant wraiths. The only safety from wraiths was the trees. Primal fear had Larkin moving before the thought had fully formed. She grabbed Sela under her arms and boosted her into the tree. "Climb high as you can. Quick."

Sela didn't question. She grabbed a branch and scrambled up. Larkin jumped for the same branch. Her fingers didn't so much as scrape it. She circled the tree, sick waves of fear making her skin damp beneath her corset.

There was another, lower branch. She made a running leap. Her fingers caught it, but her momentum threw her forward. She slipped and landed hard on her backside, yelping at the pain in her ribs.

The golden brilliance of morning had shifted to the silver of twilight. And the sky—the sun was gone, streamers of light snaking across the firmament. Stars winked into existence.

Day had become night. How was that possible?

Sela was already so high up in the tree, Larkin could barely make out one eye and a pale hand against the brown bark. No time for her to come down.

"Stay there," Larkin said reassuringly. "I'll find another

tree."

Sela whimpered.

"Quiet now. Quiet as a baby bird when the hawk circles."

"Don't leave the ring," Sela whispered so softly it might have been the breeze playing tricks on Larkin's ears.

Larkin searched the outer ring of trees, their branches interwoven to form a dense canopy, with the massive tree in the center. She jogged toward one of those trees, eyeing a low-hanging branch. Ribbons of light snaked on the ground at her feet, startling her. Unnatural. This was all so unnatural. She staggered. Were her eyes playing tricks on her?

She knew the moment the wraiths came; cloying rot inundated her senses, and wrongness settled under her skin. If not for the rush of adrenaline that coursed through her, she would have gagged. Her body needed to run. Ached to run.

Instead, she pulled out the whistle hanging from a cord around her neck and blew three sharp blasts. Denan had promised help would come if she blew it. She prayed it would come soon enough. Then she called for her magic. It flowed into her, steadying her. Her sigils gleamed a faint gold, the buzzing under her skin like angry bees. A concave shield of golden light formed on her left arm, a glowing sword in her right.

Larkin crouched behind her shield, eyeing the torn shadows that coalesced into a hooded form, its cloak undulating on a nonexistent breeze. Ramass, king of the wraiths, came into being before her, his pointed crown sharp enough to cut.

Beside Ramass, the other three wraiths formed from the shadows. To his right, the only female, Hagath, formed at his side. Larkin did not know the names of the other two. One wore a mantle like the ceremonial mantles the pipers wore. The other hung back from the rest, his gaze on the forest.

She braced for them to attack. They outnumbered her four to one, but none stepped past the center line of trees.

Ramass held out a mail-covered hand. "You are mine." His

voice came out a cross between a screech and a dry rasp. She recoiled—she hadn't known the wraiths could form human words. But then, they had been men once.

Larkin licked her dry lips. "My—" She caught herself a second before giving her sister away. "You can't come in the ring." She tried to declare it like an irrefutable truth. It came out more like a question.

Still, they made no move to attack her. Larkin didn't let her guard down. She'd seen them throw their poisoned blades. Seen the forked lines of ruin crawl through the victim's skin. Her friend Venna had been one of those victims. She'd gone mad before throwing herself from a cliff.

"Blood of my heart, marrow my bone." The Wraith King beckoned her. "Come."

She brushed away the hauntingly familiar words. Clenching her teeth, she refused to look into his treacherous eyes. Her gaze flicked toward the sky—still darkness where there should have been light. "Never!"

The wraith reached into his robes. "You will." He took out a sparkling black flute and played.

No. The wraiths couldn't possess the same magic as the pipers. Larkin stumbled back. It was already too late. The music awakened something dark and hungry inside her that wanted what it should never have. Against her will, she took a step forward. And then another. And another. Until she reached the edge of the ring of trees. One more step would be her last.

His words, the darkness clawing for purchase inside her, fear and loss and betrayal—it all combined into a heedless rage. She gripped her shield with both hands and opened her connection to magic wide. So wide it burned through her and tugged a ragged scream from her lips. Her shield pulsed, a ripple of golden-white energy pealing outward.

She staggered back, her sigils raw. Her legs buckled beneath her, and she fell to her knees. Her sword and shield winked out. Her vision went dark.

She came around flat on her stomach and blinked as the world swirled sickeningly around her. She forced her head up. Through the dim haze, the wraiths appeared fickle and moth-eaten. The pulse had hurt them, but it hadn't banished them.

Ramass stretched toward her pale, freckled hand. It had fallen outside the line formed by the ring of trees. She jerked back, but not before he snatched her wrist.

An oily sea of rage and hatred poured into her, eating her up from the outside in. She twisted her wrist, trying to break free. He hauled her to her feet. Dizzy, she kicked feebly. He wrenched her into his crushing embrace. The feel of his chest against her back—like death and cold and serrated shadows. She reached desperately for her magic, but the connection had gone dry.

She screamed.

"No!" a voice cried.

She knew that voice. "Denan!"

Time slowed as thorned shadow-vines edged around her, sucking her into Ramass, into his cold nothingness.

Arrows made from branches of the White Tree cut through Hagath. Already wounded, she dissipated like smoke on a clean breeze.

"Vicil!" Ramass shouted for aid from the other wraith.

Leaping through Hagath's outline of drifting ash, Denan swung his gleaming white ax. The blow meant for Ramass slammed into one of the other wraith's shield—the one Ramass had called for. Vicil stepped between them and cut at Denan from the right. Denan shifted his shield and braced against the blow, his ax chopping down.

The thorned shadows snatched at Larkin. She slipped into Ramass and the darkness that lived deep beneath the roots of the trees. Ramass was taking her somewhere. Transposed over Denan, a black, thorn-covered tree appeared. With every moment, Denan seemed farther away. Fading. He wouldn't be able to reach her. Not in time.

Behind Denan, Tam stepped into view. He pulled back his bow, aiming not for the fourth wraith bearing down on him, but for Ramass. He let fly. Half a beat later, Ramass screeched, the sound making Larkin's ears ring and her soul scream. The cold bite of the shadows sucking at her lessened. The view of the dark tree wavered. Ramass's bone-crushing hold weakened.

She jerked one arm free, wrenched out the gleaming arrow sticking from his shoulder, and slammed it into his chest. It tore through flesh and skittered over his ribs. Black blood sprayed across her face, blinding her.

With another scream, Ramass exploded into ash. Time slowed as Larkin fell upward and through shadow. No sooner had she emerged into the light than she hit the ground with a thump, the arrow coated in black ichor still gripped in her fist.

She pushed herself up, broken leaves raining down from her chest. Her watery arms gave out. Too weak to stand, she rolled to her side. Feet and hands digging into the loam, she dragged herself away from the battle.

Ten paces away, Denan's ax scythed through the coiling shadows of Vicil that faded to nothing. He pivoted on the same swing and launched his ax. It slammed into the wraith standing over Tam, which imploded into writhing shadows.

Following his throw, Denan picked up his ax. "Tam?"

"Nasty, stinking corpse would have to work a lot harder to best me," Tam said in a shaky voice. He spat into the fading outline. "Gah! Rature is the worst of them."

Rature. The fourth wraith's name was Rature.

Denan came to kneel beside her, his gaze searching the Forbidden Forest. "Larkin?"

The oily sea of shadows clung to her. Hatred roiled through her. Desperate to scrub away the violation, she crossed her arms over her chest and scoured her back. Her arms. All the places Ramass had touched her.

"Larkin." Denan rested a hand on her arm. She recoiled—even that gentle touch too much for her senses. She rocked in time to her head shaking over and over.

"We need to get her back to the encampment," Tam said from above her.

Expression grim, Denan tried to take the arrow from her bloody grip. No. She needed it. She—

"Larkin," Denan said softly. "Give me the sacred arrow." Sacred. Because it was made of the White Tree. "The wraiths are gone. The eclipse is over. You're safe."

"Eclipse?" she managed through chattering teeth.

"The moon moved over the sun."

Tam held out his hand. She put the arrow in his grasp. He tucked it into the sheath of arrows tied to his leg.

"So the darkness and the strange lights?" she asked.

Denan pointed at the sky. She followed the gesture, the sun blinding her. When she blinked, she could see a red outline, a chunk out of one side. The moon blocking the sun. It made sense.

Denan gripped her arm and tried to pull her up. She scraped his hand off. "No! Sela—"

"We'll find her, Larkin, I—"

"She's there!" Larkin pointed to the tall tree just visible beyond the trees.

Both men followed her gesture.

Tam nodded. Blood soaked his shirtsleeve. "I'll fetch her."

"You're bleeding." Ancestors, if the wraiths' poisoned blades had touched him ...

Tam glanced at his arm. "Old wound, from Hamel."

She flinched at the memories of just last night. Old wound, indeed. *At least it isn't from a wraith blade,* she reminded herself.

The ground beneath Denan rasped as he pivoted and looked around him. "First, check for mulgars. Leave me your water gourd."

Tossing it to Denan, Tam took off at a jog, bow and arrows in hand.

"Your corset," Denan said to her. "Take it off."

The ghost of the wraith's hands still gripped her. His body flush against hers. The hollow nothingness and the writhing anger boiled inside her. She choked back a scream.

Denan swore and knelt beside her. "I need you to trust me, Larkin. His blood is poisoning you."

Taking out his knife, he cut and ripped away the wedding dress. Corset, overdress, and shift piled around her, leaving her exposed from the waist up. He removed the stopper and held the waterskin over her.

Clean water gushed along her skin. Instinctively, she tipped up her face and scrubbed at the drying blood. With the blood went the anger and nothingness. Denan pulled out his own water gourd and poured it over her as well. Too soon, the water was gone.

Murmuring reassurances, Denan removed his shirt and tugged it over her head. She pushed her arms through while he wrapped his green, mottled cloak around her shoulders. Shirtless, he hauled her into his arms and settled against a tree, her rich red skirts flaring around them.

She buried her face in his neck, breathing in his familiar scent of woods and smoke and sunlight. She splayed her fingers across the raised sigil—the White Tree that took up most of his chest and proclaimed him the future king of the Alamant.

The tension and fear left her in increments, her body losing its rigidity only to succumb to teeth-rattling shivers.

He took her pale, thickly freckled hand in his bronze one, pushed the copper tendrils of her hair away from her face, and kissed her temple. "Better?"

She'd missed this man. This husband of hers. Missed the safety of his arms and his ability to wield the ax and shield lying within easy reach.

"I will be."

Denan rubbed her arm, seeming to need the reassurance of touch as much as she did. "The effects won't last. Just ride it out. It will be all right."

"Denan, if you hadn't come for me ..." Ramass would have taken her with him. Somewhere she wouldn't want to survive.

"But I did. I will always come for you."

There was a time when those words terrified Larkin; now, they gave immeasurable comfort.

"'Blood of my heart, marrow my bone.' Ramass said that to me, called me his. What does it mean?"

Denan's grip tightened around her. He didn't say anything for so long that she thought he wouldn't answer. "It's what they say to their slaves before they take them back to Valynthia."

Valynthia, the ruined city the wraiths had corrupted, the heart of the curse that enslaved them all. He would have made her his slave. As Maisy had been. No wonder she'd gone mad.

"You're safe," Denan murmured.

For now.

The shivers lost some of their bite. She sagged, exhausted, in his arms. From her left, footsteps sloshed through a hollow of leaves. Sela ran toward them. She stopped short at the sight of Larkin, her wide eyes taking in the half of Larkin's ruined, bloody dress that lay in tatters on the ground.

Larkin forced herself to stand, to give a watery smile. "We scared them away."

Sela clamped her lips shut. Larkin's heart fell. Somehow, she knew her sister was done talking for a long while.

Larkin wanted to curse the wraiths and cry at the injustice; the wraiths had no right to hurt any of them, least of all her sister. Instead, she took Sela's hand.

Tam tipped his head back the way he'd come, his spring-blue eyes flashing. "Denan, you need to see this."

Denan grabbed his weapons and motioned for Larkin and Sela to walk between him and Tam. They strode into the ring of trees.

Denan looked about in awe. "I thought all the arbor rings had fallen."

"What's an arbor ring?" Larkin asked.

"A place where the White Tree's magic flares. They're surrounded by an enchantment that renders them nearly impossible to find." Denan studied her with pride. He clearly thought she'd found it.

She should tell him the truth—that Sela had been the one—but she needed the warmth of his gaze. Needed his approval. The truth congealed in her throat.

"The light is back," Tam said.

A crescent of sunlight stamped out the black sky, washing the world in blessed light—light that would keep them safe from the wraiths.

Until night fell.

CHAPTER 2

FLEE TO THE ALAMANT

Tam and Denan led the way for Larkin and Sela through the press of pipers—all wearing leather armor and mottled clothing like dappled sunlight on the forest floor. The men bowed to Denan, their prince, but their eyes followed Larkin—some with curiosity, some with disapproval, some with reverence. But they were all looking.

Larkin kept her head down. Apparently, the rumors of her being the first woman with magic in nearly three centuries had spread. As had her escaping with Bane. She'd been trying to save him—how could she not try to save the boy who had saved her so many times?

But the pipers wouldn't know that. All they would know is that she had escaped. Men had died to rescue her from the druids. Some of those men would have friends here.

At least Denan had managed to find her a tunic and trousers, so she didn't have the embarrassment of wearing the stained skirt with his overlarge tunic. Larkin almost missed the corset—it had held in her bruised ribs, which ached fiercely.

Larkin heard the stream before she saw it—the singing of water slipping over moss-covered stones. Three piper guards watched her mother pace back and forth. She turned as Larkin and her friends came into view.

"Sela!" Mama cried, startling baby Brenna in her arms so she flailed. Mama pushed the baby at Larkin and scooped up Sela, scolding and crying at the same time. "You're going to kill me if you don't stop running off."

Her brown eyes offered Larkin thanks. Warmth built in Larkin at the love behind those eyes. She may have inherited her freckles and bright copper hair from her father—curse his drunken hide—but her brown eyes were all her mother's.

Larkin laid her infant sister on one shoulder, patting her bottom and shushing her. "She was talking before."

Mama made a cry of relief. "Oh, Sela, sweetness, can you talk for Mama?"

Fat tears rolling down her cheeks, Sela adamantly shook her head and pulled back her sleeve, revealing a bloody scrape. Even at four, Sela knew the power of distraction. Larkin hadn't even known her sister was hurt.

Mama sniffed and turned over her arm. "We need to wash it." She carried Sela to the stream and settled her next to it. Sela squirmed, but Mama held fast, poured water, and rubbed at the scrape.

"What happened?" Mama asked.

The curse bound the tongue of any who knew the truth from explaining it to another. Mama knew about the pipers and Larkin's magic. She didn't know about the wraiths or the curse.

"Tam and Denan fought off a beast." It was all the curse allowed Larkin to say.

Mama tugged Sela's sleeve over the cut. "Oh, my girl, it will be all right in the end. You'll see."

Larkin remembered when she was a child of no more than

ten. It had been so hot and dry that even the weeds were wilted. A sudden rainstorm had gusted over them. Larkin and Nesha had whooped and shrieked and slid down the muddy hill until Larkin had sprained her ankle.

Nesha had ducked under Larkin's arm and helped her to their father. He'd scooped Larkin up in his arms and taken her to Mama, who wrapped her ankle with torn rags and gave her bitter, willow-bark tea.

Larkin was achingly aware of her older sister's absence, of her father's descent into drunkenness. That awareness came with a stab of pain; both had betrayed Larkin so thoroughly she could never forgive either.

Brenna arched her back and yawned, her gums and pink tongue visible. The baby would never know her father or oldest sister. Pity welled in Larkin—pity where relief should be.

Pushing her confusing emotions away, Larkin looked for Denan and found him huddled in conversation with Tam and Talox, who must have arrived while she was busy with her mother and sisters. Talox and Tam could not be more different. Tam reminded her of a fox—if a fox had curly hair, blue eyes, and a constant, impish grin. Talox reminded her of a huge, sleepy bull—gentle and soft-spoken until he stepped into battle.

Tam shifted, and she caught sight of a fourth man—Denan's uncle, Demry. With their dark features and similar builds, uncle and nephew looked quite a lot alike. Demry had guarded her after the arson attempt on Denan's family—a blaze set by Bane. She breathed out in frustration. Both the pipers and the druids wanted Bane dead. It made it awfully hard to keep him alive.

She snuck up behind the men and strained to listen.

"Can we make Ryttan before nightfall?" Denan asked.

Demry's dark eyes glanced at the sky. "Not this late in the day."

"Best make for the waterfall, then," Talox said in his rumbling voice.

Denan nodded to his group of pages. The young men were always rotating in and out of duty, making it impossible for Larkin to keep them straight. "Give the signal. Our armies move out now."

One of the boys lifted his flute to his lips and played a set of sharp notes. The pipers shifted into motion, packing up their sleeping pods and camps.

Denan pointed to one of his pages. "Engineers to take the lead. I want pikes and a trench dug." Another page broke into a run, his too-big shirt flapping. "Captain Demry, you march next, arrow pattern."

Demry gave a sharp nod and started off. He caught sight of Larkin and stopped in his tracks, his face shifting from determination to disapproval. "Princess." He gave a curt bow and marched past her.

Larkin's cheeks burned. As far as Demry knew, she'd run away from her husband with an attempted murderer. She awkwardly shifted the baby in her arms and approached Denan.

"We can't leave," Larkin said in disbelief.

"I have to see to my men," Denan said. "Talox will take you to the center of our two armies. You'll be safe. I promise."

Larkin stepped in front of Denan, blocking him. "Bane and Maisy are still out there." Maisy had disappeared in the night. And Bane—Denan had promised they'd rescue him from the druids.

Denan ground his teeth. "No one has seen Maisy."

"We can't just leave the poor girl." Mama came up from behind Larkin, Sela gripping her hand.

"She's the one who left the encampment," Tam muttered.

Talox shot him a look. "Maisy knows the dangers of this forest better than most."

"My men know who she is," Denan said. "If she's smart, she'll follow. There's not much else I can do."

"Perhaps she went back to the Idelmarch?" Mama said.

"She's been branded a traitor," Tam said. "To return would mean death."

"As I was branded a traitor," Larkin ground out. "As was Bane when he saved our lives."

Sela began to cry.

Denan shot Talox a look. "Pennice, Larkin, go with Talox."

Larkin wasn't going anywhere.

Not meeting her seething gaze, Talox took Brenna from Larkin's arms. "Come along, Pennice."

Mama planted her fists on her hips. "What's wrong?" she demanded.

Denan shot a glance at Sela and stepped closer to Pennice, his voice dropping. "You've seen Larkin's magic?" Mama nodded. "There is another kind of magic, as dark as Larkin's is light. When night falls, they'll attack. We need to reach a defensible position before then."

Mama paled. "I left my home because I was promised my family would be safer with you than with the druids."

"I swear by my life," Denan said, "I will protect you and your daughters, Pennice."

Tam leaned against his bow. "They won't even get close."

She looked at the three men, then at the pipers shifting through the forest around her. She addressed Denan, "You stole my daughter from me. Why?"

"He can't tell you, Mama," Larkin said. "Magic prevents it."

Sela tugged on Mama's skirts, begged to be picked up, and then buried her face in Mama's shoulder. "The light magic or the dark?" Mama asked.

"Dark," Larkin said. "You have to figure out the truth, as I did."

Mama looked at Denan. "Perhaps you had a good reason for kidnapping my daughter and forcing her to marry you. Perhaps you didn't. Either way, you have wronged us both."

He bowed his head. "I will make it up to you."

Mama stepped back. "You better."

Talox motioned for Larkin and her mother to follow them while Denan headed off.

"Go on ahead, Mama. I'll catch up." Larkin hurried after Denan.

Lips pursed, Mama trailed after Talox.

"You promised we would go back for Bane," Larkin said when she caught up to Denan.

Tam took one look at her and jogged ahead, out of earshot.

"I never said that."

She rounded in front of him. "We can't leave him to die!"

"What do you want me to do?"

"Rescue him."

Denan let out a long breath. "How many men would it take to overpower the druid-led army inside Hamel's fortifications?"

Hamel had been quiet, unimportant. She still didn't understand why the army had come, why they'd built a fortified wall on the outskirts of her hometown. "I don't ... I don't know."

"Five hundred Idelmarchians with access to dampeners and defensive superiority." Dampeners, made from the sacred tree, that rendered the pipers' magic useless. "Even with my two thousand pipers, a prolonged siege would expose us to retaliation from Landra." The Idelmarch's capital city and the seat of the druids' power. "We would have to take the city by force within two days. I estimate at least five hundred casualties. Perhaps a thousand."

Bitter cold washed over her despite the rising heat. She wrapped her arms around herself.

Denan's voice gentled. "Are you willing to face the mothers, wives, and children of the men who die to save your friend? And what about the men of Idelmarch? How many of them will perish?"

"Could we sneak in, like you did to rescue me?"

"Before the dampeners, yes." He shook his head. "But not now."

"So you're telling me Bane is going to die and there's nothing we can do about it?"

He sighed. "I can try to ransom him. Perhaps the druids would trade him for gold ... but I don't want you to get your hopes up."

Ancestors. She rubbed at the ache in her chest. "How will we ever tell Caelia we left her brother behind?" Bane's sister had been taken to the Alamant nearly a decade before.

Denan's gaze dropped, his hands fisting at his sides. "Are you so eager to save him because he's your friend, or is it something more?"

"Denan ..." She trailed off.

"Why, Larkin? Why did you choose him over me?"

The pain in Denan's eyes ... She hadn't meant to choose Bane. Not like that. But she supposed, in the end, she had. She reached toward Denan, but he flinched away from her touch. She hadn't realized how badly she'd hurt him.

"He wouldn't leave the Alamant without me," she whispered. "I couldn't let him die—not after everything we'd been through. I planned to take him home to Hamel, see my family one more time, then return to you." Her eyes fluttered closed. Unless Denan managed to ransom him, Bane was going to die, and there was nothing she could do to help him. "You must think me very foolish."

"No. Young, perhaps. Inexperienced in warfare, certainly." He sighed. "We expect resistance from the taken—how could we not? But I thought ... I thought you were growing to care for me. And when you escaped with the boy you had claimed to love so many times, I almost didn't come after you, Larkin. If not for my promise that I always would ..."

She swallowed at the lump in her throat. "I meant it when I said I chose you."

He finally met her eyes. "No more running and no more secrets, Larkin. I can't bear it."

"No more running. No more secrets." She risked reaching for his hand. He stared at her palm before taking it in his. "I will send a messenger to the druids, offering a ransom for him. Will that do?"

She nodded, relieved. "Bane isn't an enemy of the Idelmarch. The wraiths are the real enemy. Surely we can make the druids see that."

"I wish it were that simple," Denan said.

Still chilled from the wraith's touch, Larkin shivered. "The druids can't want the wraiths to win. There has to be a way."

"If there is, we'll find it." He squeezed her hand. "Stay with Talox until I come for you." He took off at a jog, caught up to Tam, and called out orders to his men by name.

Larkin glanced in the direction of her village. The ransom would work. It had to. She hurried to catch up to Talox. Through the heavy forest, Larkin caught glimpses of hundreds of pipers, their pied cloaks rendering them blurs of movement out of the corners of her eyes.

It was shocking how fast the Alamantians cleared out, how completely they melted into the Forbidden Forest.

WIFE

The ancient, enormous trees of the forest blocked out the sun, leaving the pipers in cool shadows. They pressed through the leaf litter from the previous fall. The meat of the leaves had long since rotted away, leaving behind the skeletal traces of veins, delicate and lovely as a moth wing.

The forest smelled of death and life—the spiciness of green rot and the sweetness of new growth. But deep beneath the rich colors and smells, an undercurrent flowed—an undercurrent that gently buzzed against Larkin's sigils as if it recognized her.

The White Tree was hundreds of miles away, seated deep within a lake inside a fortified city of trees. And yet it was here too. How had she not sensed it before?

Larkin heard the gentle rush of the spring long before she saw it. The smell came next—clean, cold water and moss. The spring bubbled up between black rocks before rushing into the forest.

It was the same spring she, Alorica, and Venna had stopped

beside that first day in the forest. Alorica had convinced Venna to make a run for it. She'd been darted with gilgad venom for her trouble and carried for the rest of the day.

Venna was dead now.

Much of the army paused to drink, crushing the bright green moss against the rocks. Larkin took her turn drinking from the headwaters. She refilled her water bladder while Sela lay on her belly and drank straight from the source.

They moved downstream to let someone else have a turn. They found Mama leaning against a tree, nursing Brenna. Larkin handed her the waterskin. Her mother drained it in one go.

Larkin directed Sela to kneel beside her on the bank. Together, they washed the sweat and dirt from their hands and face—the midspring day had turned hot.

Crouched beside her, Talox shifted, water dripping from his chin. "I've my own needs to attend to. I'll refill that waterskin and be right back."

Mama watched until he was out of sight. "Tell me the truth, Larkin. Has Denan enchanted you? Because if so—"

"Did the druids tell you that?" Larkin shook out her tousled braid and rewove it. "You've felt the pipers' enchantment. Their influence disappears with their music."

Mama unlatched the baby and shifted her to the other breast. "And how do you feel about Denan?"

Avoiding her mother's gaze, Larkin tied the end of the braid with a cord of leather. "He's the best man I've ever met."

"You don't really know him."

Larkin wet the corner of her borrowed tunic and wiped a patch of dust Sela had missed on her temple. "There now," Larkin said.

Clearly exhausted from walking all morning, Sela lay down on the moss and watched the water slip past.

Larkin sat beside her mother. She dropped her voice to a whisper so Sela wouldn't hear. "I thought I knew Bane." His name felt like an ember on her tongue. "He was my best friend for years. But I never guessed he and Nesha were together, that she was carrying his child." Before Nesha, he'd been sleeping with Alorica. Larkin hadn't known that either.

Mama winced and pretended to be interested in something to her left.

Larkin's gaze narrowed. "You knew?"

Mama shifted nervously. "I tried to get Daydon to allow them to marry. But with her club foot ... He offered Bane for you instead. It was the only way I could save you from the forest."

Larkin rubbed her face and tried to stem her rising anger. "Nesha believes I knowingly stole Bane away from her."

Mama raised an eyebrow. "She said you saw them kissing."

Apparently, Mama believed that too. "Why are you both so quick to think so little of me? I saw Nesha kissing someone; I never saw his face, never guessed it was Bane."

"Maybe we never really know a person." Mama wiped her cheeks. "Do you remember when your father would chase you around our hut on all fours and tickle you until you cried?"

"I hate him."

"He wasn't always awful."

Why was she defending him? He'd betrayed Mama most of all.

"He saved me from my brute of a father and coward of a mother," Mama went on. "Took me where they couldn't find me, even with all their money. Bought land and built me a house with his own hands."

Larkin had never heard these stories before. Mama never spoke of her past. So why start now?

Mama chuckled. "Neither of us knew anything about farming. We worked until our fingers bled."

Yet it had all changed that afternoon he'd overheard Mama telling them she would have another daughter. "Why was he so angry when he found out Sela was a girl?"

Mama shrugged. "He never told me. All he would do was drink."

He was mean when he drank. "I'll never forgive him. Nesha either."

"They're your family."

"And both of them nearly got me killed."

"Larkin," Mama said, her voice chiding.

Huffing in disgust, Larkin left her mother's side to lay beside Sela on the mossy rocks, watching the light highlight the ribbons of water. She reached in and pulled out a smooth, mauve stone. "Pretty."

Sela looked at the rock, stood, and walked away. Heart aching, Larkin watched her go.

Over the tops of the trees, the massive cliffs loomed larger and larger. The waterfall split the cliffs in half, the roar discernable even at this distance. Beneath that roar, the thwack of axes sounded. They turned a corner, their view opening to the base of the gully.

Pipers built a pike wall—sharpened sticks lashed to fences at the perfect angle for impaling a rushing horde. Beyond that, sleeping pods had been set up in trees and cook fires let off lazy smoke.

"Nearly there," Talox said. Sela slept on his massive shoulder, her arms curled tight even in sleep.

Larkin breathed a sigh of relief—her arms ached from holding Brenna. It had been a long time since their lunch of dried meat and fruit.

"Thank the ancestors," Mama murmured. Between giving birth not long before, nursing, and lack of sleep, she was clearly struggling to put one foot in front of the other.

Talox pointed ahead. Larkin shaded her eyes and caught sight of Denan at a break in the pike line. Bracing Brenna's head, Larkin hurried forward.

Unstringing his bow, Denan strode out to meet her. He embraced her, squeezing her too hard. Brenna squirmed and squawked. He pulled back and chuckled. He rested a hand on Brenna's downy head. "Sorry, little one."

Larkin peered up at him. "What's going on?"

"You must be tired. Let me have a turn carrying her." Without meeting her gaze, he tugged Brenna from her arms and started past the pike line.

Unease caught fire in her belly. "What aren't you telling me?"

Denan glanced at her askance and then away again.

The situation reminded her of the first time they'd pushed through the forest. Only that time, he'd been bound from telling her the truth by a curse—a curse that no longer applied to her. "Denan—"

He glanced back at Talox, Mama, and Sela. He dropped his voice. "The wraiths don't just take slaves. They fixate on certain girls. And they don't stop until they have them."

Horror washed through Larkin. She could feel the wraith around her again. His smell invaded her body. His shadows ate away all warmth and goodness. The vision of the Black Tree superimposed over reality. She couldn't catch her breath. Couldn't catch it.

Denan pulled Larkin behind the shelter of a massive tree. "This is why I didn't want to tell you."

"Why?"

"Maybe ..." Brenna fussed, and Denan patted her back. "Maybe all this time they've been looking for the girl meant to break the curse."

Dizzy, Larkin pressed her hand against the bark. The steady, faint tingle in her sigils increased. Calm washed through her. She breathed out in relief.

"Don't tell my mama." It was bad enough that she knew.

Denan's jaw set with fury or determination or both. "Ramass would have to go through both my army and Demry's to touch you, Larkin. You're safe."

Two thousand against the mulgar horde. Would it be enough? "How long until we reach the Alamant?"

Brenna's fussing increased, and he bounced her in his arms. "If we force march, two days. Maybe three."

Men were going to die. Tonight.

This was happening too fast. She couldn't take it all in. "My family?" She choked, thinking of the terror Sela would endure, and so soon after she'd just started opening up again.

Brenna had settled in his arms. He laid her over his shoulder and rubbed her back. "We'll enchant them and hide them high in the trees. They'll sleep through the worst of it and wake up with no memory of what happened."

"And if the mulgars break through?"

"They won't."

"But if they do—"

"We have the advantage of choosing our location and building fortifications. And we only have to hold them off until morning."

"Mulgars don't fight during the day?"

"Oh, they will. They're opportunistic—driven by instinct and hatred. They go for the easy kill, the taste of blood. But without the wraiths to drive them, they won't keep throwing themselves on our spears. They'll retreat." He cupped the side of her face. "Where's my warrior wife? The one who braved the forest twice to protect those she loved? The first female warrior in three centuries?"

"Not that I've done anything with that magic," she grumbled.

"You saved me. And your magic will only grow stronger as

your sigils do. Someday, you'll do more. I know you will."

The weight of his words settled around her heart. "How can you know that?"

Shifting Brenna to his other arm, he pulled up his sleeve, revealing the ahlea sigil—the sigil for women's magic on his wrist. "I was meant to find the one who would break the curse. I found you."

He rested his palm on her uninjured cheek. "The Idelmarch lost magic and memory; the Alamant faces barrenness and shadow. Part of that curse was broken with you. I think you can break it for others."

Larkin heard her mother's labored steps long before she reached them.

"Start with your mother." He pulled back. "See if you can remove the curse from her."

Mama huffed into view. She stiffened at the sight of Brenna in Denan's arms. Then her gaze went to Larkin, and she stilled. "What's wrong?"

Denan gave a bright smile. "There's a lovely pool below the waterfall to wash up in, Pennice. Ancestors know the baby needs changing." He grinned down at her. "Don't you, sweet girl?"

Kicking her feet, Brenna stared up at him with eyes that still straddled the line between brown and blue. They reminded Larkin so much of Nesha's violet eyes that she had to turn away for a moment. Mama took the baby from him and stepped back.

Pretending he hadn't noticed her mistrust, Denan strode out ahead of them. "This way."

Larkin felt her mother's questioning gaze on her, but she kept her head down and followed Denan. She paused at the base of the pool ringed with stones. Water plunged from the steep cliffs covered in ferns into a turquoise pool.

Pipers stood on the shore, bows in hand as they fished for their supper. Others sat around campfires, sleeping or eating. Even with the masses of soldiers, it was still a beautiful place.

The mist kissed her sweaty face and felt like a cool caress on her exposed neck.

But that tranquility and beauty seemed far away. All Larkin could feel was sorrow. The first time she'd been here with Alorica and Venna. They'd been so determined to escape, so united in their hatred of the pipers.

The second time, Larkin had been escaping with Bane. They'd plunged over the waterfall in their small boat. Larkin could still feel the grit against her cheek. Still feel the shock at the sight of hundreds of mulgars standing just inside the tree line, watching, but not attacking.

Why hadn't they attacked?

"Larkin?" She started out of her memories to find her mother watching her with concern. "What is it?"

Mama wouldn't be brushed off—not a second time. "I was here with Venna and Bane." Venna was dead. If Denan's ransom went wrong, Bane would be too. She choked, any other words she might have said sticking fast to her throat.

Mama reached for her.

From the pool, Tam crowed as he held up two fish on the same arrow. The men around him slapped him on the back and cheered.

"Looks like Tam has our supper." She pushed past her mother.

Bellies full of fish and foraged greens, Larkin spent the last remaining moments of sunlight washing out Brenna's swaddling—even with mulgars and wraiths hunting them, such things must be done. Mama wrung them out and hung them on bushes to dry while Sela stared at the waterfall as if entranced.

Scrubbing her hands clean, Larkin caught sight of her reflection in her cupped hands. The wraith's blood had left splattered burns across her cheek and neck amid the freckles—the stinging, one of many small hurts. She shivered and let the water fall.

A dozen steps from the shore, a boulder jutted out—the same boulder she and Denan had shared her first time through the forest. She'd just discovered he meant to make her his wife, whether she wanted it or not. She'd been so angry with him. So confused and hurt and lost.

It was also the first time she had a name for the strange things she'd been able to do since he'd given her the amulet. She touched it through her tunic, feeling the outline of a tree imprinting against her skin. Like the sacred arrows and the pipers' weapons, it was made of the sacred wood of the White Tree and had its own kind of magic.

Just like the magic pulsing in her four sigils. She opened them to the magic, marveling as they gleamed iridescent, their shapes geometric and floral. They were still growing in size and strength. The one on the back of her hand called up her sword. The one on her left forearm called up her shield. The final two were on the nape of her neck and a band around her upper arm. She didn't know what they did.

She opened the one on her arm to the magic, to the familiar, almost painful buzzing. She focused on herself and her mother, trying to see what was different between them—why one of them was cursed and one wasn't.

Nothing.

She tried again with the sigil on her neck. Still nothing. She rubbed her hand over her head in frustration. It would help if she knew how her curse had been broken. Perhaps she'd been born this way?

No. She rubbed her thumb across the faint scar on her palm. Everything had changed with the sliver. Her first thorn. Imperfect and quickly lost. The first time she'd gone through the forest, the barrier—or stirring, as her people called it—had attacked her, rendering her a blubbering mess of terror. It hadn't the second time. But then it had again the third.

But what had allowed her to receive her thorn in the first place? It was almost like the White Tree had reached out through the ordinary trees, infusing it with just enough magic for her to use. Like the tree had cared about her even then. Like a friend might.

"The trees are our friends."

The words Sela had spoken in the arbor ring and then before, when she and Larkin had been running for their lives from the beast. The enchantment made the trees look like melting candles, their wicked, burning branches snatching at Larkin.

Until her sister's cool hands had touched Larkin's shoulders. The enchantment had faded. Something had broken free inside Larkin—a light where before there had been only darkness. And then Larkin had noticed Denan, who'd been watching Sela, keeping her safe from a distance.

Could it be? Was Sela the one Denan had been meant to find—the one who'd broken the curse? Larkin gasped and rose to her feet, her gaze landing on her sister, who stacked stones into precarious towers.

"Larkin." Denan came up behind her. He wore his armor of boiled, studded leather. Strapped across his back were his ax and shield, both made of the impenetrable wood of the White Tree—it would send anything with dark magic back to the shadow until night came again.

The way he looked at her, almost reverently. What if that reverence was just because he thought her a curse breaker—the savior of his people?

No. Sela was a child. She couldn't have been the one to break the curse. She just couldn't.

Denan's gaze fixed on Larkin—open and vulnerable and so full of need.

"What's wrong?" Her voice cracked on the question. A stupid thing to ask. He could die this night, protecting her and her family. She might never see him again.

"Come with me?" he asked.

Mama laid out the last of the swaddling over a bush. "She needs to stay with me."

"I'll be right back, Mama." Larkin pushed to her feet and took Denan's warm hand in her cold one. Larkin felt Mama's eyes on her. She clearly didn't approve. How could she? But Larkin didn't pull away. She couldn't.

She followed Denan wordlessly along the pool of water. He looked around once before pulling her into an alcove tucked behind a tree. The waterfall spray misted her skin, and the roar of it filled her ears.

The space was tight, her back against the moss-covered rock face, ferns draped across her hair. His body a mere breath away; the heat between them became a living thing. His hands braced on either side of her head. The muscles in his arms locked as if it took a great deal of strength to keep from touching her.

"Denan, what's wrong?"

"I almost lost you today." He sounded almost angry. He rested his forehead against hers. "Larkin, if the wraiths had …" Unable to bear his pain, she reached up, taking his beardless face between her palms.

The forest take her, she could lose him too. "I'm here."

"May I kiss you?" He still hadn't met her gaze. He seemed almost … shy. She heard the question he wasn't asking. Did she want this? Did she want him—forever?

"We've already kissed twice," she reminded him breathlessly.

"But you've always kissed me." The backs of his fingers shifted down her cheek, along her neck, before skimming across her collarbone, trailing fire wherever they touched. "This time, I want to kiss you."

"Yes." Please.

A trace of a smile ghosted across his full lips. And then finally, finally, his gaze met hers. The depth of feeling in his obsidian eyes made her heart kick in her chest. Was that feeling based on a lie? Ancestors, it couldn't be. She couldn't have tasted this only to lose it so soon.

She wanted to rise up, wrap her arms around him, and kiss him. But she forced herself to wait, to let him set the pace. The pad of his thumb rubbed her bottom lip. His hand slid along her jaw and into her hair. He tilted her jaw back. She wet her lips, eyes slipping closed. Their mouths met, his lips soft and tender.

She took his face in her hands, the pockmarks rough under her fingers. She wound her arms around his neck and rose up on her toes. His palms skimmed down her back before settling around her waist.

He was holding back. Being patient. Considerate. The forest take him, he was always so patient and considerate. She took his bottom lip in her teeth, nipping before sucking gently. He moaned—a moan that sparked through Larkin, turning to a molten heat that spread through her torso and then her limbs.

He deepened their kiss, his arms wrapping around her so tight he lifted her from the ground, her toes scraping the mossy ground.

"Denan," Tam called from out of sight.

She let out a frustrated breath and rested her forehead in the crook of his neck.

"Denan," he called again. "It's almost sunset." She heard the apology in Tam's voice.

Denan growled low in his throat—she could feel the vibrations against her lips. "I don't start a battle I can't win. No harm will come to you, Larkin. I swear it on my life."

"And who will protect you?" Emotion choked her voice.

"I will always come for you."

Tears clogged her throat. She clutched the words that had once felt like a curse; now, they were a promise to keep her afloat in a sea of turmoil.

He squeezed her. "I love you."

The words shocked her. Before she could decide if she should say them back, he strode away. Her fingertips covered her mouth. She could still taste him, still feel his body against hers. What if he never came back to her?

He'd come to prepare her, she realized. To make sure he hadn't left any words unspoken before battle. She hurried after him, arms reaching, but by the time she left the alcove, he was already striding past Tam and Talox, his gaze fierce and dark.

Damp from the waterfall spray, she shivered. The two pipers faced her. Tam had the gall to wink.

Talox rolled his eyes at his friend. "Can you be serious for even a moment?"

Tam shoved him.

Talox barely shifted. "Denan has gone to battle a hundred times, Larkin."

For half a moment, she wondered why they hadn't started after Denan yet. After all, they were his personal body guards. Then she realized the truth—he'd left them to guard her.

"No," she said. "Go with Denan. I'll be all right."

"I am," Tam said. "Only Talox is staying. But I couldn't miss the opportunity to tease you before I go."

Talox smacked the back of Tam's head. "His men love him, Larkin. They will not let him fall."

Tam made a face. "I wouldn't say *love*. A certain fondness, maybe."

Larkin rubbed her throat. "You can't know that. No one can."

Talox didn't disagree.

"He won't be on the front lines." Tam flipped his dagger, catching it by the hilt. "He'll be directing his commanders and the reserves." He cursed as he timed it wrong and sliced his finger. Sucking on the thin line of blood, he picked up the dagger.

"After all, can't have our prince dying."

She flared her sigils, a blade and shield of golden light appearing in her hands. Tam dropped his dagger again.

Talox looked more determined than ever. "You haven't been trained to use them."

He was right. She'd only be in the way. She reluctantly dismissed them. "What can I do?"

Talox tugged his pipes out from beneath his shirt. "I could enchant you. When you wake, he'll be there."

She considered the gleaming flute. "No. If he can fight, I can wait for him."

Talox tucked it back in his shirt. "Then I will wait with you."

Tam turned on his heel. "Have fun guarding the women and children, Tal! I'm off to kill mulgars."

She opened her mouth to berate him for being so flippant, but Talox rested his heavy palm on her shoulder, his eyes flashing as he called, "They stick you in a tree because you're too short to reach over the shields."

Tam spread his arms in challenge. "Why hide behind a shield when you can rain fire from above?" He started whistling.

Talox leaned over her. "Humor is how Tam deals with the fear and pain."

"How can you stand it?" Larkin mumbled.

"You should try it. It helps."

He led her downstream. Mama nursed the baby by the river while Sela curled against a gnarled root, her ear pressed to the bark and her expression dreamy. Talox guided them to a tall tree, where three men waited. He introduced them as Dayne, Ulrin, and Tyer. Dayne was tall and broad, dwarfing all the other men. Ulrin had a unibrow, the curve of which matched his mustache. Judging by his long hair, Tyer was married.

Ulrin and Dayne took the children and started up the tree Sela had been under. Tyer assisted Mama.

When Larkin moved to follow, Talox held up a hand. "Your family will be safer separated from you."

Her mouth fell open in wordless protest. "But—" She stopped herself from saying she needed to protect them. Talox was right. If the wraiths were after Larkin, her family was safer away from her.

Mama hopped down from the tree. "We will stay together."

Talox's expression gentled. "The dark magic is after Larkin specifically. Your little ones need you. I will look after Larkin."

Larkin's eyes slipped closed. She hadn't wanted Mama to know the wraiths hunted her.

Tears welled in Mama's eyes. "How is this safer than the Idelmarch, Larkin? We would have been better off with the druids, and you know how much I hate the druids and that worthless queen."

It was easy to forget that the Idelmarch had a queen. Iniya Rothsberd had lost her power to the druids decades before Larkin had been born. They'd even kicked her out of her own castle.

"There are two thousand men between me and the—" *Wraiths.* Larkin choked, the curse stopping her mouth. "The dark magic. This is just a precaution."

Mama wrapped her arms around herself. "We've all been cursed, haven't we?"

Larkin blinked in surprise. Her mother was a smart, brave woman. "Yes, Mama. And I'm going to break it." Certainty burned in her chest. But then her gaze shifted to Sela, resentment flaring. Larkin shook herself. Sela was her sister. She loved her.

Mama wiped her cheeks and shot Talox a fierce look. "You bring her back safe."

He bowed. "On my life."

Mama turned without a word and took Tyer's hand. Larkin watched as the three soldiers helped her family up the tree.

Talox touched Larkin's arm. "This way."

She looked toward where the sun had been cleaved in half

by the horizon. With one last glance at her mother and sisters, Larkin climbed another tree far enough away she couldn't make out her family through the forest between them. There, she settled in to watch the last of the daylight die.

CHAPTER 4

WARRIOR

The sun had long since disappeared beneath the horizon, and still the mulgars had not come. Inside the camp, guards patrolled the shadows beneath the trees. Archers had strapped themselves to the perimeter trees. Foot soldiers waited taut beneath them.

Beyond, the engineers had chopped down a line of trees—the trunks of which had been strategically piled in the center and alighted, while the branches had been lashed together to create rows of pikes before a shallow trench.

The forest was eerily quiet; even the wind had died. Larkin had slept so little and been so worried over the last few weeks that her body felt wrung out. Her eyes burned whenever she blinked. Despite her declaration that she would wait and watch, she fell asleep in a pod stretched tight between two branches.

It was the smell that woke her first. A pervasive decay of rotting flesh. Heart thudding in her throat, she sat up, eyes shifting to where Denan had been last, near the center of the line, behind the soldiers. He wasn't there. She climbed out of the pod. The edge caught her foot. She grabbed a branch to steady herself; the drop to the forest floor seemed very far away.

"There." Talox pointed to the right. Denan's shield gleamed in the firelight as he called to his men and gave orders to his captains. One of the archers called a warning. Pipers moved into battle formation two rows deep. The first row held short swords and huge shields. The second carried spears.

She sat in her pod, legs dangling. "Wraiths?"

He shook his head. "They'll be far back from the sacred arrows, driving the mulgars forward."

"But I can smell them."

He shook his head. "It's not as old or as oily."

She sniffed. Talox was right. The smell was that of a fresh corpse just starting to turn. Not that of old rot and the grave. "What is it, then?"

"Mulgars. Thousands of them."

No sooner had he spoken than the first mulgar broke away from the line of trees. She wore what was once a fine dress. Black lines etched her face and disappeared into mismatched armor. She hadn't managed two steps before she fell, body bristling with arrows.

Hundreds of mulgars burst from the forest's shadows, the firelight etching their faces with darkness. Aside from the pounding of hundreds of feet, they didn't make a sound. Not as arrows bristled from their flesh, black blood dripping. Not as the first dozen fell upon the pikes or the dozens and dozens after them. Bodies piled up two and three deep. Still, they kept coming, leaping over their fallen without pause.

"Do they not feel pain?" Larkin asked.

"They know only the will of their masters."

More and more poured from the trees. "Where did they all come from?"

"The Valynthian side of the Forbidden Forest."

The first few reached the Alamantian line. Spears stabbed from above, swords from between shields. More mulgars fell, dying without a sound. Limping on leg stumps or stepping on their own spilling entrails, they fought until death. Their faces remained blank, empty.

They had been human once. They were not anymore.

"Are my mother and sisters watching this?" Larkin asked in a choked voice.

"Their guards will keep them asleep," Talox said. "As I should be doing." Yet he made no move to his flute.

She shifted to look at him, the pod swaying beneath her. "Then why are you allowing me to watch?"

"You have been chosen as a warrior, Larkin. This will be your life someday."

Pipers called up and down the line. The first man fell, his hands gripping his side. A reserve soldier moved to replace him, while a pair of healers lifted the man on a stretcher and carried him to the healers' tent.

"How can I be a warrior if I'm a wife and mother?" Most women alternated between pregnant or nursing well into their forties.

"There are herbs to prevent children—or to limit them, if you chose."

"Such things are myths." Mama had always said so. As the town midwife, she should know.

"Perhaps for the Idelmarch," Talox said.

If such a thing were possible, Larkin could live whatever kind of life she wanted. She could choose. "Am I not also chosen to be queen? To break the curse?"

"A queen is a warrior of necessity in times like these."

She gripped the edges of her pod. "I'm not sure I would choose it."

Talox shrugged. "Sometimes it's not what we choose, but what chooses us."

His words niggled at the doubt buried deep inside her. What if she hadn't been chosen at all?

Denan rotated his front line out. Carrying their injured, they retreated to safety. They rested, drank water, and bound up flesh wounds. Some lay down, but most kept their eyes on the mulgars.

Talox rubbed his head. "Own your destiny, Larkin. Whatever it may be."

"What if I'm not any good as a warrior?" What if she was nothing more than the first woman with magic? A coincidence of timing and nothing more?

"You were chosen by the White Tree. She can see things inside us that we can't see on our own."

In the healers' tent, a soldier started screaming—screams that sounded eerily similar to the ones Venna had made. Larkin closed her eyes against the memories assaulting her. Venna fevering in her arms. The black lines climbing her skin, bleeding into her eyes. The madness that had taken her before she'd tried to kill Larkin.

Larkin started to rise. "I should assist the healers."

Talox's hand closed over her shoulder. "The wraiths can't sense you in the trees."

"But the wards ..."

"We don't want the wraiths to have a handle on where you might be—they can sense you sometimes, if you leave the trees."

Even surrounded by water, fire, and two thousand men, she wasn't safe. Larkin gritted her teeth. If she was to be a warrior, she would defeat the wraiths, once and for all. "Will you teach me? To kill them?"

Talox gripped a knife, as if merely talking of the wraiths made him anxious. "Wraiths cannot die. They can only be sent back to the shadow."

If the curse could be defeated, even in part, surely there was a way to defeat the wraiths. "Then teach me that."

He watched the battle. "Four wraiths with three centuries of experience. They are the greatest warriors to have ever existed and wily as a pack of wolves. You do not defeat the wraiths—not alone."

The day before, Denan had charged the wraiths while Tam loosed from a distance. "Archers. You use archers."

Talox nodded to the front line. "That's why you don't see any of the wraiths now. One arrow will weaken a wraith. Two or three will send them back to the shadow. If you must fight them hand to hand, keep an archer nearby to end them the moment there is a clear line of sight."

"Does no one ever defeat them hand to hand?"

"Not often. Not when the merest cut of their blades turns one into a mulgar."

"But I have an advantage." When the wraiths had been waiting outside the arbor ring and she'd been certain she was doomed, she'd flared her shield and nearly sent all of them back to the shadow. "I can pulse."

A wicked smile curved his lips. "Can you imagine what a dozen women with magic could do?"

It would change everything.

She flared her sword—a curved, cutting blade with a tip for thrusting. It gleamed with a faint gold light in the pitch dark.

Talox plucked a leaf and ran it against the edge. It sheared in half with the merest pressure. "A blade this sharp can be as dangerous to the person wielding it as their enemy. Not to mention that the light draws attention. Lore has it the ancients could shift between weapons. Even vary the sharpness and brightness of the blade. You need to figure out how before you end up in trouble."

"Perhaps if I lessen the flow of magic." Larkin constricted her sigils, and the blade dimmed to the faintest outline of light, like the reflection of moonlight across glossy leaves.

Talox tested another leaf. It didn't cut at all. He ran his

thumb across the edge and then pressed harder. "Good. Much safer for you, anyway."

And it would use up less magic.

"Now," Talox went on. "See if you can change the shape." With a thought, she made it into a knife. Then a dagger. A two-handed blade. Awed, she flared her shield and changed it from round to square.

Below them, a man was screaming. Two soldiers dragged him between them toward the healers' tent, blood gushing from his leg. She rubbed at the lump in her throat. "How do you bear it? How do any of you bear it?"

"That's enough for tonight." Talox tugged out his pipes and played—the music full of drowsy sunshine and droning bees. Larkin tried to stand, but her legs didn't want to move. Come to think of it, she didn't want them to move either. She was too comfortable and sleepy. Her horror melted away into contented dreaminess.

"But I have on a dampener," she protested, though she didn't want him to stop playing. Denan had given it to her when he'd tried to rescue her. It made her resistant to piper enchantment.

Talox held up her chain with the amulet and dampener, which was shaped like a curving leaf.

The lying cheat. "I'm staying awake for Denan." Why was she staying awake for Denan? Sleeping was a better idea. She couldn't keep her eyes open anymore.

The branch shifted. Her legs were lifted into her pod, a blanket tugged over her. "You aren't doing yourself any favors by being too exhausted to march tomorrow," Talox said. "And none of us will be in any kind of shape to carry you."

Without his constant enchantment, she nearly succeeded in opening her eyes. She should get up. But she could no longer remember why. He began to play again, and sleep stole her away.

The sun was a distant sliver on the horizon. The last of the daylight swallowed up by darkness. Her fingers were locked tight around a hand. Bane's hand. Though she didn't dare turn around to look, she recognized the size and shape. Even the callouses were familiar to her.

Her head whipped from side to side, desperately searching for a tree to hide in. It was too late. The wraiths were behind her—though for once she couldn't smell them. They chased her and Bane. She tugged hard on his hand, trying to get him to run faster.

Then his hand was gone.

The sleeping pod shifted, freeing Larkin from the nightmare.

Cold arms wrapped around her, cinching her tight against an equally cold—and very bare—chest. Shifting, she curled into Denan, breathing deep the scent of his soap to chase away the last of the fear.

Suddenly, she remembered the battle from the night before. Her eyes flew open to find Denan watching her, early morning light softening the scars on his cheeks. Light that would keep them safe from wraiths. She examined his face, searching for signs of pain or injury. "Are you all right?" she asked breathlessly.

"The mulgars broke away before dawn. Demry's army is pursuing them."

The branch beneath her shifted. Talox slipped down the tree. Her eyes narrowed to a glare.

"Talox did me a favor," Denan said. "You too, if you'd admit it."

"Denan ..."

He traced the planes of her face with his fingertips. "Your freckles remind me of stars. I wonder if I could map out constellations to guide my way to your mouth." He bent down and kissed her, lips soft. Then he pulled her tight to his side. "I need a few hours of sleep while the reserves pack up the camp and start transporting the wounded."

He flung the other arm over his face. His dark lashes brushed against his cheeks. The dark gold of his skin gleamed. His hair had grown longer, a bristling that felt soft and prickly at once beneath her fingers.

"You're looking at me. I can tell." He peeked at her through one slitted eye. "What is it?"

He'd kidnapped her, stolen her from her life and her family. And yet, from the first moment they'd met, he'd been willing to die to protect her. In every moment since, he'd proven he would live for her too. And just now, he'd called her freckles stars.

Warmth swelled in her chest, filling her until she thought she would burst. She leaned forward, pressing her lips gently to his before pulling back.

He tried to blink the sleepiness from his eyes. "What was that for?"

Emotion clogged her throat. She wanted to push it down, force it away, but he'd gone to battle last night. He'd said the things he needed to say. She had not.

"Little bird?" he prompted when she remained silent.

She forced herself to meet his gaze. "I love you too."

His eyes widened, nostrils flaring. Joy seeped around his mouth. He bit his bottom lip, as if to keep the emotion from showing. "But?"

But ... So many mistakes. So many wrongs. Their two nations bound as enemies. The war she felt sure was coming. The curse pulsing in the forest around them—a curse she was no longer sure she was meant to break. But in this moment, they were safe and together. In this moment, that was enough.

She took his face in her hands and kissed him again. His lips were soft, pliant beneath hers. He let her set the pace. She explored his mouth, the taste of him. The feel of his smooth beardless cheeks beneath her hands.

Something shifted inside her. She would no longer run from Denan, no longer push him away. From now on, he would be the place she ran to. He would be her home.

Denan had been right all along. He was her heartsong. And it was more than a little terrifying. When she pulled back, she was shaking.

"Larkin?" he whispered.

"It's just … It's a lot. To love you. To let go of all that happened before. To move away from everything I knew into nothing I do." She chuckled nervously. "Am I making any sense?"

He brushed her cheek. "No," he teased.

She chuckled. They held each other until his breathing deepened and steadied. His arms slackened around her. She wanted to stay with him, but she desperately needed to empty her bladder. And she should check on her mother and sisters and help with the injured.

Denan didn't stir as she eased from his arms. She slipped down the tree. Talox waited below. The engineers, who had also been held in reserve and so had some sleep, trekked out, packs of equipment on their backs or carried between them. They started toward her mother's tree while eating a quick breakfast of dried fruit and cheese.

"There you are." Larkin turned at her mother's call. Pennice came from the direction of the healer's tent, which was overflowing. She pushed the baby into her arms along with a bag filled with bloody bandages. "Take Sela to the river. Start a fire, boil the used bandages, and pack the baby's dried swaddling."

"I can help with the healing." *I've decided to love Denan. To never leave him.* Why couldn't she say it out loud?

Mama stepped closer. "I'm the one with medical knowledge, and this is no place for a four-year-old. We need clean bandages as much as anything, and it will be a while before they've packed up the rest of the camp."

Was Larkin no more use than as a babysitter and laundress? Still, she held the baby close, took Sela's hand, and led her to the edge of the pool. The waterfall sparkled golden in the morning light.

Larkin wrapped Brenna in Denan's cloak. Lighting the end of a stick in a nearby campfire, she pressed the smoking end into the leaf detritus she'd gathered and blew until she had a cheery little flame that fought back the early morning chill.

Sela crouched beside it, dumped out a pile of little sticks, and began arranging them into people with leaves for clothes and hair. Six people. And next to it, she built a little hut of stones.

Their family at home. While their father had betrayed them all, Nesha had never betrayed Sela. Had only ever tried to protect her. Sela was only four. She couldn't understand all the reasons Nesha and Harben were no longer with them. But she clearly missed them.

In contrast, Larkin had been fighting resentment and uncertainty of Nesha. Ashamed of herself, she touched each one and tried to guess which was which. Sela would shake her head or nod. By the end, she was almost smiling.

Larkin pulled her in close, tucking her under her arm. "I love you."

Sela nested against her.

Larkin kissed her head. "Sela, what did you mean when you said the trees were our friends?"

Sela shifted and looked up at her, lips sealed.

Larkin tried to keep her frustration at bay. "Please, Sela. Talk to me."

Sela turned back to the fire. Talox set a heavy pot of water to boil and left again.

"Did you remove the curse?" Larkin asked in a whisper. "Are you the one Denan was meant to find?"

Sela blinked up at her.

Larkin laughed nervously. "You don't even understand what I'm talking about." She passed a hand down her face. "Of course you don't. Come on. You're going to help with the washing."

Larkin scrubbed out the bloody rags on the shore. Sela hauled them into the pot to boil. Brenna wiggled and stared at the leaves and birds above her head.

Larkin felt a presence behind her and turned to find Sela, her face pale. She pointed to the other side of the river. Larkin followed the gesture but saw nothing.

"Sela? What's the matter?"

Sela motioned frantically for Larkin to follow. Scooping up the baby, Larkin grabbed Sela's hand and hustled up the bank.

Talox rushed toward them, ax and shield in hand. "What is it?"

Heart hammering, Larkin shook her head. "I don't—"

A scream pierced the air. Sela ducked behind Talox and buried her head in his legs. Putting himself between them and the river, Talox ushered them deeper into camp.

Pipers rushed past them, weapons out.

Larkin glanced over her shoulder at the opposite side of the mouth of the river. Bushes shifted. Someone crashed through, landing on his back with a mulgar on top of him. The two rolled. A knife flashed, black blood dripping. The man staggered to his feet. Only it wasn't a man.

It was Maisy.

CHAPTER 5

RESCUE

B loody knife in hand, Maisy stabbed the mulgar again and again, though it was clearly already dead. Black blood dripping down her face, she fixed her blue eyes on Larkin before she noted the pipers taking up defensive positions. Her expression wild, she retreated, the bush she'd emerged from half swallowing her.

Sela whimpered. Somehow, she'd known. There wasn't time to consider how.

Larkin pushed Brenna into Talox's arms. "Maisy!"

"Larkin—" Talox began.

Larkin forced Sela's hand into his. "Take them to my mother!"

He stiffened. "My orders are—"

"Then find someone else to do it." She shoved between the soldiers, ran past the mouth of the river, and stood on the riverbank.

"Maisy," Larkin called over the river rushing between them.

"It's not safe on that side."

Half hidden behind the bush, Maisy's gaze shifted to the dozens of armed men lining the top of the embankment. "I will not be the plaything of pipers. I will never be a plaything of anyone ever again."

Larkin held out her hand. "I swear that won't happen." Maisy considered Larkin's empty palm. "Are you hungry? I'm sure we can find you some breakfast."

Maisy started at something behind her, something Larkin couldn't see. More mulgars? She darted to her feet and ran along the embankment.

Pushing past pipers, Larkin tried to keep pace with her. "Maisy! Maisy, come here before it's too late." She bumped into another solid piper. "Move!"

To her surprise, he jumped to obey.

Behind Maisy, mulgars breached the tree line. The pipers loosed arrows. Talox's tree trunk of an arm snaked around Larkin's waist and hauled her behind the line of soldiers.

"Where are my sisters?" Larkin cried. He was supposed to be looking after them.

"The same place you're going."

He'd come back too soon to have given them to her mother. He must have passed them on to someone else. She tried to pry his arms off her, but they were like iron bands. "Put me down! Maisy won't trust anyone else."

"Maisy's well-being isn't my priority. Yours is." Having reached safety, he released her.

She made to march back to the river, but Talox blocked her. "Don't."

She glared at him. "You said last night I had been chosen as a warrior. Start treating me like it."

"You're not ready."

She flared her sword and shield. "I am. For this, I am." She would not let another person down—not one more.

He considered her before giving a tight-lipped nod.

Relieved, Larkin released her weapons and hurried downstream and pushed through pipers. When they didn't move fast enough, she barked, "Move!" Just like before, they did.

On the other side of the river, the mulgars had taken cover from the pipers' relentless arrows behind the trees. Occasionally, one would try to loose an arrow in the direction of the pipers, but their arrows never made it past the halfway mark of the river.

Maisy crouched along the bank, a fallen tree trunk between her and the mulgars.

A mulgar stood, drew his ugly bow, and loosed an arrow at her. It thunked into the trunk. Arrows from the pipers rained down on him as he ducked out of sight. Maisy hunched down lower, her arms over her head. She was going to get herself killed if she stayed over there.

"Swim, Maisy!" Larkin demanded.

Across the distance, their gazes met. Maisy hesitated, expression conflicted. She winced, touched her leg, glared at the pipers, then bolted straight at the mulgars.

"What are you doing?" Larkin cried.

"Which of you tried to dart her?" Talox thundered.

Maisy's wince—someone had darted her. She would be unconscious in moments—unconscious and helpless at the hands of mulgars. Larkin gasped in outrage.

From Maisy's right, a mulgar darted into the open, his path aimed at intercepting her. Instead of veering in the opposite direction, Maisy kept on. Could she not see him bearing down on her?

"Maisy!" Larkin cried. The fool girl wasn't listening. "Bring him down!" she cried to the pipers. A hundred arrows rained. One punctured his wrist. He dropped the club but didn't fall.

Half a dozen steps before the two would have collided, Maisy launched herself toward a branch. She hooked her foot around it and pulled herself up a wide tree. The mulgar grabbed her other foot and yanked. She managed to hold on by her fingertips. The mulgar bared his stained teeth, his mouth gaping wide over her exposed calf.

Another half dozen arrows bloomed from his back. Still trying to hold on, the creature staggered back. Maisy kicked him in the face. He dropped hard. She hauled herself up and climbed, the thin tree shaking and wavering under her weight.

"You fool!" one of the pipers cried. "Lie down before the venom makes you fall!"

Talox grabbed the man's leather breastplate and shook him. "What were you thinking, putting her at risk like that? Did you hit her?"

The man, who was impossibly handsome, paled at the sight of Talox towering over him. "I might have nicked her," he admitted.

Envenomed and halfway up a tree surrounded by mulgars.

"Talox," Larkin said. "We can't let her die."

Their gazes met. The memory of Venna's death hung heavy between them. Even when she lay dying, they had both refused to leave her behind.

"I'll shield us," Larkin said. "We'll be safe enough."

He passed a hand down his face. "If we go with a contingent of pipers—"

"She won't come, and I can't shield an entire contingent."

He stared her down. "Denan is going to kill me."

Her insides felt watery. "I'll protect you."

"Can you swim?"

Ancestors, she was not going to throw up, but the mere thought of going in the river that had nearly taken her life as a girl … And then she had to face mulgars on the other side.

Mute, she nodded.

Talox stripped off his armor and gave orders for a dozen pipers to lash their shields together to create a kind of raft. While they worked, Talox took Larkin's hand. Together, they waded into the river. The cold was a shock against Larkin's skin, and she gasped.

When the water reached their waists, Talox laid out his shield and rested his ax atop it. "Hold on. That way we won't be separated."

She nodded, too terrified to speak and glad she could blame her chattering on the cold. Perhaps seeing an easy target, one of the mulgars popped up and loosed a black arrow. It speared into the water a dozen feet in front of them.

"Now would be the time for the shield," Talox said.

She flared her magic, stretching the shield wide enough that it covered both of them. Talox nodded, and they pushed forward and started kicking and swimming with one hand.

Emboldened, more mulgars left cover to fire at Maisy, the pipers on the other side, or Larkin and Talox. Their crude arrows glanced off her shield, which rippled. She felt each blow—a twinge in her magic—but her shield held beautifully.

She could do this. She *was* doing it.

A couple of mulgars positioned themselves behind Maisy's tree and chopped at the trunk with their axes. The branches shuddered with each blow. Halfway up, Maisy wavered like a woman deep in her cups. The forest take her, she was going to get herself killed before Larkin could rescue her.

"Maisy, lie down before you collapse!"

Maisy obeyed, slumping across two branches, and didn't move again.

Talox found purchase first and pushed to his feet, hauling his shield and Larkin with him. Out of breath, careful to keep her shield up, she scrambled to get her feet under her in the sticky mud. Mulgars charged from the cover of trees. The pipers on the other side put them down just as quickly.

Talox hefted his ax and shield into position. "Flare your sword. Stay behind me. Keep the shield up."

He rushed up the embankment. She struggled to keep up with him. The mulgars left cover to charge them, their eyes glazed with frantic hunger. The pipers loosed at any that emerged, dropping one after another.

There were too many to stop them all. The closer they came, the more details Larkin could see—broken fingers, missing teeth, bald spots on their heads. And the smell—filth and rot.

When Larkin and Talox were halfway to Maisy, the first mulgar slammed into her shield and bounced back, the impact shuddering through her connection. It didn't hurt so much as vibrate uncomfortably.

Another hit her shield. And another. And another. She gritted her teeth, forcing herself to hold it. Three mulgars rose to their feet and circled around. She tried to make it bigger but didn't dare expend any more energy.

The first reached Talox.

"Talox," she cried in warning.

He was already swinging. He blocked its spiked mace with his shield and chopped its shoulder. The creature staggered back, what remained of its arm dangling. Oblivious to the pain, it charged him again. Talox kicked it down and ended the creature with his ax in its chest.

He barely pulled it out in time to meet the next mulgar.

The third veered toward Larkin. Remembering her lesson with Talox the night before, she lengthened her sword and drove it into the creature's chest. She felt the weight of the mulgar shift and sag, like her sword was a line tethering them.

The mulgar's eyes focused, locked with hers. Then it dropped to the ground. Dead. Her sword flickered and faded.

"Larkin!" Talox barked.

She started and felt her connection to the magic wavering. She opened her sigils wide, unintentionally pulsing, which threw a dozen mulgars back.

The tree holding Maisy groaned and tilted—the mulgars had

managed to chop through half the trunk. The mulgars charging Larkin and Talox didn't notice as it turned in place like a dancer, leaves fluttering. It tipped, slowly at first, and then faster and faster.

It was going to land on Talox and Larkin.

"Larkin!" Talox shouted. He barreled into her, pushing her under him, his body a shield over her. Flat on her back, she watched the tree rush toward them. Holding her hand out, she held her shield in place and shut her eyes.

Her shield sigil shuddered but held as the tree crashed down on them. She opened her eyes to find them surrounded by branches in the bubble of safety.

Talox blinked. "That's handy."

"Maisy," she cried. Ancestors, she'd been in the tree when it had fallen.

"Stay here." Talox pushed off her and passed through the shield as if it somehow recognized friend from foe.

"Talox!" Larkin pushed shakily to her feet.

Ignoring her, he waded and climbed through branches, his ax swinging on mulgars rising to their feet. He bent, plucking Maisy from the green.

Not far from Larkin, a mulgar struggled free. Before she could raise her sword, the pipers ended him.

Maisy over his shoulder, Talox struggled through branches toward her. Larkin channeled more magic into her sword, making the edge razor sharp, then she blazed a path out of the tree. Three swipes, and they were free.

Huffing, Talox ran beside her. The way to the river was clear. Larkin formed the shield behind them to protect from any arrows. The pipers who'd made a makeshift raft out of shields were halfway across the river. Larkin wasn't sure what it was for until Talox settled Maisy inside.

Larkin hadn't even considered how they would drag an unconscious Maisy through the river. Relief that Talox had at least thought ahead, she sloshed back into the river, which now felt warm against her chilled skin.

"Hold on and worry about that shield," Talox said.

As the pipers pushed the raft into the current, Larkin forced her hand through a strap on the back of a shield and looked back. Mulgars rushed them. The piper archers loosed arrows, dropping mulgars by the dozens, yet still they came.

Larkin opened her sigils wide, flaring her shield as wide as it would go. It formed a dome over them. Mulgars paused at the side of the river, careful not to let a drop touch them, and loosed their own arrows. They rained down on the shield, which rippled and danced. It stung, as if Larkin's sigils were raw from multiple hits.

Mulgars crumpled by the dozens as the pipers filled their bodies with arrows. Lying on his back, one mulgar raised his bow, sighting beneath the shield. Then his arrow was gone, and Talox hissed, a line of blood sheeting down his arm.

"Talox!" she cried.

"I'm all right," he said through clenched teeth.

Helpless to assist him, Larkin concentrated on holding on. The strap dug into her forearm painfully. Pipers waded out, grasping the raft and hauling them in. Not sure if she could release her shield, she glanced back to the shore. The mulgars were all dead.

Two pipers gripped Larkin's arms. She struggled to pull her arm from the wet leather. Finally, she had it free, and the men helped her slosh through the water to the other side. When she was steady, she nodded her thanks, and they released her.

"Talox?" She searched for him among gasping pipers.

"What?" He lay panting on the rocky bank.

She as she knelt beside him and parted his torn sleeve. The cut didn't appear too deep.

She sagged beside him. "My mother's going to kill me."

"Not if Denan kills us first."

They locked gazes and laughed, the sudden release of tension making her giddy.

She spotted Maisy being lifted from the raft by the handsome man who'd darted her. Larkin rushed to the girl's side as she moaned, her head lolling to the side. Her skin was deathly pale—but then, it was always deathly pale.

"Set her down." Maisy would hate being in any man's arms. The piper eased her onto the grassy slope above the embankment and pulled out the antidote.

"No." Talox heaved himself over to Maisy and held out his hand. The handsome piper glared and refused to give it up.

"Captain," Talox barked. A man hustled over to them. "This man put a girl in further danger by darting her. See that he has ten lashes and another fifty once we return to the Alamant."

The handsome man gestured wildly. "She's mine."

He thought darting her gave him rights to be her husband! "The forest take you," Larkin spat.

Talox glared at the man. "You overstepped and you know it."

The handsome man glared. "You've had your chance, sir."

Wait, the two were fighting. Over Maisy? Larkin considered her. She'd always been the ratty, filthy, mad girl. But Larkin had to admit, washed clean by the river, the woman was striking—with her pale skin, blue eyes, and black hair.

Now Larkin was shouting at both of them. "She's not your slave!"

Talox held out his palm toward Larkin, who bit back her cutting remarks and decided to trust Talox. For a minute.

"Seventy-five lashes," Talox said.

The piper slapped the vial into Talox's hand. Clapping his hand on the back of the handsome man's neck, the captain marched the man away.

"I get that you need children to keep back the mulgar horde," Larkin said through clenched teeth, "but the pipers don't take broken women." She understood the necessity of that. Women needed to be strong of body and mind to survive the Forbidden Forest.

Talox bit off the cork and motioned for Larkin to hold Maisy's head. She lifted the woman's head onto her lap and tugged Maisy's stringy black hair away from her lips. He tried to pour the antidote into Maisy's mouth, but she screwed her lips shut.

Larkin took the vial from him. "It's the antidote," she said. "It will counteract the poison."

Maisy fixed Talox with a glare.

"Take it or die," Larkin said, sick to death of Maisy's stubborn idiocy.

Grudgingly, Maisy opened her mouth.

Larkin poured the liquid down. "How is she even moving?"

Talox started to pull up the hem of her trousers on the leg the piper had struck. Maisy made a sound of alarm.

"She hates being touched by men," Larkin said.

"I need to see her dart wound," Talox said.

"My leg," Maisy slurred.

"I'll do it." Larkin found a welt with the smallest of scratches in the center on Maisy's thigh. Sunken scars in the shape of forked lines marred Maisy's legs, marking her as a former wraith slave.

Talox nodded in understanding. "She wasn't dosed with enough venom for it to take full effect."

A healer jogged over to them and knelt beside Talox. "You need a few stitches."

"Make it quick," Talox said.

The healer set to work. Maisy shot Larkin a pleading look.

"The venom will wear off," Larkin said to Maisy. "You won't be like this forever."

"You didn't stop him," Maisy said.

No, Larkin hadn't stopped that man from darting her. She

wasn't all-powerful. "You're welcome for saving your moronic life simply because you wouldn't cross that blasted river."

Maisy had the gall to look hurt. Larkin growled in frustration and reeled in her temper. When Maisy looked at a person, she saw a monster waiting to be unleashed. Larkin couldn't blame her. Rimoth's corpse-pale skin had caressed Larkin once. To think of him touching his own daughter like that … She shuddered.

Finished, the healer bandaged Talox's arm. "Give it a week to heal, if you can."

Talox grunted—they all knew a week wasn't something any of them had. He pushed to his feet and made to pick Maisy up. She writhed and scowled at him. "I will never marry you."

Even if Maisy wasn't mad, rescuing a woman was no way to pick a wife. "Talox," she said, a warning note in her voice.

He wouldn't look at her. "The law is clear. She's my responsibility."

Larkin's own twinning marriage thorns pulsed in sympathy.

"Dead bed. You'll be dead in your bed," Maisy sang. Her singing usually precipitated her descent into utter madness.

Larkin gripped his arm and pulled him out of earshot.

"Ow," he complained—she'd grabbed his injured arm by mistake.

"Maisy is terrified of men. For good reason. And she's mad as a headless chicken."

"I know the wraiths had her," Talox said.

"It's worse than just that. Her own father … touched her."

His gaze shifted from stubbornness to pity. "I won't let harm come to her, Larkin, especially not by me."

"That's what I'm trying to explain. Forcing her to be yoked to any man in any way *is* harming her."

Maisy continued to slur lullabies with a morbid twist.

"You think I want this—to yoke myself to a madwoman?" He choked. "My heartsong is dead."

Venna. Ancestors save her, Larkin hadn't realized just how much she'd asked of him.

He passed his hand over his shaved head. "Someone has to be responsible for her. She's dangerous."

Larkin threw her hands into the air in frustration. "So you're what? Her guardian?"

"Yes!"

"I have been to the wraith city," Maisy interrupted in a dreamy voice. She stared at them with her vivid blue eyes. "I have seen things—things I will trade for my freedom."

"What kinds of things?" Talox breathed.

Maisy sang.

Blood of my heart, marrow my bone,
Come hear the saddest story e'er known.
A cursed queen and her lover lost,
A forbidden magic and what it cost.

With more words to remind her, Larkin recognized where she'd heard this song—it was an old lullaby. "That first line— the wraith said it to me only yesterday." But why would a wraith repeat the line of a lullaby to her? It didn't make any sense.

Talox pointed to one of the pipers. "Wake Denan."

The man took off at a jog toward Denan's tree.

CHAPTER 6

MAISY

Denan's eyes were bloodshot, but his sharp gaze caught on Larkin. "Why are you wet?" He looked at Talox, who was also wet and sporting a bloody bandage around his arm. Then he saw Maisy, also wet and clearly drugged. His expression hardened. His fists clenched. He shifted to Talox. "Tell me you didn't let her save this girl?"

Talox folded his arms. "She has to learn sometime."

Denan took a step toward him, violence in his gaze.

Larkin stepped between them, her hands out. "What good are my weapons if I never use them?"

His sharp glance cut her to the quick. "You learn to use them in the practice field, not surrounded by mulgars." He pointed at Talox. "And you know the wraiths want her! You know she's our best chance at defeating this curse!"

"I—" Talox began.

"No!" Denan shouted over him. "You think with your heart and not your head. It's what got you demoted." Demoted because he'd disobeyed Denan's explicit orders to leave Venna behind, mortally wounded as she was by a wraith blade—something Talox would never do.

"It was Larkin's decision," Talox said.

Denan swore and took another step toward him. Larkin pushed him back. Pipers were gathering. One of the pages took off at a run. "Larkin's decision? This isn't about Larkin. It's about breaking the curse—our best hope in nearly three centuries! You don't put that at risk to save one fool girl!"

More and more pipers were gathering, watching the exchange. Though Talox's face remained stoic, he had to feel the humiliation of Denan berating him in public.

"Stop it, Denan," Larkin said. "If you want to blame someone, blame me. I'm the one who insisted we go."

"Ancestors, Larkin, you should know better!"

Tears smarted in her eyes. She swallowed them back. "I couldn't lose someone else."

"Stop being selfish," he snapped.

She flinched. But Denan was right. Saving Maisy had been selfish. Larkin's life wasn't a currency she could afford to spend—not when so much was at stake.

"Don't, Denan." Talox's voice rumbled with a hint of anger.

"Don't?" Denan said. "Don't?"

"We're fine," she said. "It turned out fine."

Tam ran up, looking between them and seeming to guess what had happened just as Denan had. "Easy, both of you. Everyone's watching."

Denan paced, his furious gaze fixed on Talox. "Your orders were clear. You disobeyed them. Twenty lashings. Fifty when we reach the Alamant. And you're demoted to a common foot soldier. Get out of my sight."

Expressionless, Talox bowed, turned on his heel, and strode away without looking back.

Heart aching, Larkin watched him go. She rounded on Denan, her own fists clenched. "You didn't need to do that. Especially not in front of everyone."

Denan turned his back to her and crouched beside Maisy. Her gaze locked on his. "I will never marry a piper."

"I heard." His expression turned shrewd. "That will cost you."

Remaining single in a kingdom where every woman was a priceless commodity was a steep price, indeed. Bitterness flooded Larkin's mouth.

"The forest take you," Maisy hissed.

Denan didn't react to the insult. "Our people fight the wraiths and mulgars, keeping both the Alamant and the Idelmarch safe. For that, we need sons. To have sons, we must first have wives. Because of the curse, our women never bear daughters. We must take them from elsewhere. Talox caught you. So you are his."

Maisy ground her teeth. "I know all about your curse, Alamantian. I lived with the wraiths."

"Denan," Larkin warned. She knew Talox would never hurt anyone, even if Denan would allow it. But Maisy did not.

"I would kill him in his bed first," Maisy said.

Denan ignored Larkin and fiddled with his flute. "We have ways of ensuring you do not."

Maisy bared her teeth at him.

He leaned toward her. "If you wish to escape this fate, the information you give me must be of greater value than the sons you would bear."

Larkin wanted to rail against Denan for his mercilessness—this wasn't fair or right or just. But then, neither was life. Denan was a hard man. He must be. She wouldn't make his burden any heavier with childish protestations. But when they were alone, she was going to wring him dry.

Maisy looked away. "What do you want?"

"You are the only one to have escaped the wraiths, to break

free of the mulgar curse. I want to know everything about the fallen city of Valynthia, how you escaped, and anything you remember about them."

"You were a mulgar?" Tam gasped.

"I was their slave. They removed my curse so I could serve them."

"That's impossible."

Larkin was grateful Talox wasn't present to hear this part. She couldn't bear the thought of him hoping for something that would never be.

Maisy nodded to Larkin. "Show him."

Larkin tugged up the hem of Maisy's trousers, revealing the telltale fork-tine scars on her legs.

Tam staggered back. "The mulgars could come back from that?"

"Only if the wraiths remove their poison," Maisy said.

Tam's mouth thinned. "Why would they do that?"

Maisy turned to Denan. "And if you don't like my answers?"

"I am a hard man, Maisy, but a fair one."

She hesitated before nodding in agreement.

Denan motioned to Tam, who played a melody that ensured only truths were spoken. It was inescapable and relentless as a migraine.

"Where do the wraiths come from?" Denan asked.

"The curse begot them," Maisy said.

"Why can they only come out at night?" Denan asked. "Why do the trees and water repel them?"

"I don't know," she said.

Denan's lips pursed in frustration. "What do they want?"

"They want us dead," she whispered. "Or like them." Her gaze lingered on Larkin.

A chill tiptoed across Larkin's exposed skin.

"How did they capture you?" Tam asked.

Maisy screwed her eyes shut. Tam's melody shifted, driving and hard.

Sweat appeared on Maisy's upper lip. "I went into the forest one night to escape my father ... I knew it wasn't safe. I knew the beast would hunt me. I hoped it would tear out my throat." She paused, breathing fast. "Instead, something much worse found me."

Larkin's eyes drifted shut. *Wraiths.*

"Why did they choose you?" Denan asked. "Why not some other girl?"

Larkin heard the question he wasn't asking: Why had the wraiths taken an interest in Larkin? "Can you use magic?" Larkin asked.

Maisy huffed. "Do you think my father would be alive if I could?"

"What did they want with you?" Denan asked.

"To hurt me for the pure joy of it. To make me their slave."

The flute lowered in Tam's hand, the song silenced. "How did you escape?"

Maisy chuckled bitterly. "No one escapes the wraiths. They let me go."

Denan motioned for Tam to begin playing again. The song started up again, the notes as precise as marching soldiers.

"Why?" Denan asked.

"I don't know," Maisy said.

Denan's eyes narrowed. "Why do they pursue specific girls so relentlessly? Why not just turn them into mulgars?"

"They're looking for someone they can turn into one of them."

All three of them stiffened. Dark foreboding shivered through Larkin. Tam's playing skipped a beat.

Denan worked his jaw. "Surely you remember something."

"After weeks of torture, the wraith cut me with his shadow blade." Maisy's eyes turned distant, empty. "Pain. Trees and forests and darkness. Always darkness. A ruined city. I lived there. Only, I didn't. And always, the will and voice of the wraiths drove me, stealing my will. My body existed as an extension of theirs. I hated what they hated with an all-consuming need."

"And Valynthia?" Denan asked.

"A city of ruin and shadow," Maisy said. "That wicked, wicked tree in the center."

"I need a map of it," Denan said.

Maisy's eyes widened in disbelief. "You think you can—what? Invade? Kill them?" She laughed. "You can no sooner kill the night."

"The curse is already crumbling," Denan said. "And this war won't end unless we somehow manage to defeat the wraiths."

So much was at stake. They were relying on Larkin, and she had no idea where to even begin trying to break the curse.

"You will draw a map of this city for us." Denan said. It was not a question.

Maisy shook her head in disbelief. "What I can recall."

"And you will tell us anything else you remember?"

"Yes." She regarded Denan. "Is it enough?"

Denan closed his eyes, and when he opened them again, the pain was well masked, but Larkin saw it in the set of his mouth. "I extend the protection of the Alamant to you, Maisy, daughter of druids. You will marry only if you wish.

"But know this," Denan went on. "If you break our laws or become a risk to anyone, including yourself, I will imprison you. Am I clear?"

Her eyes narrowed. "Yes, *Prince*."

Ignoring her impudent tone, Denan motioned for Tam to stop playing, rose to his feet, and called to one of the pages who always followed him at a distance. "Fetch one of the healers' stretchers."

The page started off.

"Send my mother and sisters to me," Larkin called after him.

The boy's eyes cut to Denan, who nodded his assent.

Denan motioned for Tam and Larkin to follow him and took a few steps before pausing and looking back at Maisy. "One more thing: the wraiths—is there a way to kill them?"

Tam began to play again. The song was giving Larkin a headache.

Maisy's expression turned inward, as if she were trying hard to remember—or perhaps fight off—a memory viler than the rest. "During the daylight"—she spoke as if the words were physically painful—"they are vulnerable, weak. I think you could kill them then."

Denan nodded for Tam to stop playing.

Larkin followed Denan a few dozen steps away. "Is there a way to reach the wraiths during the day?"

"In the heart of mulgar-infested lands?" Tam huffed. "It would be suicide to try."

"I don't trust her," Denan said.

"She couldn't lie," Larkin reminded him.

Denan shook his head. "The wraiths have a way of poisoning everything they touch."

Throughout the camp, pipers played a few short, shrill bursts. All at once, the trees came alive with soldiers groaning and pushing out of their pods.

"So you don't believe any of what she says?" Tam said.

Denan pursed his lips. "I think we very, very carefully consider her words and try to find a way to use it to our advantage. In the meantime, I'll order one of my pages to follow her and report to the nearest captain if she causes any trouble."

Pipers descended from the trees. Hundreds of them. A few eyed Maisy with more than a little speculation.

"Will she be safe?" Larkin asked.

Denan followed her gaze. "I doubt anyone would risk their

lives to meddle with her."

Larkin looked at him. "Risk their lives?"

"The penalty for rape is death," Denan said. "The penalty for assault is castration. Jeering would earn them a whipping."

Her mouth fell open. In the Idelmarch, she'd been groped half a dozen times by various town boys and even a couple of the men. She'd never told anyone. What was the point when no one who mattered would have believed her? Instead, she'd learned to be careful where, when, and with whom she went.

"In a place where men outnumber women three to one," Tam said, "we have harsh penalties for harming a female."

And because the pipers could play an enchantment that made it impossible to lie, their guilt or innocence would be known without question.

"All of us have taken classes on how to treat and care for women," Denan said.

"Who teaches these classes?" she asked in surprise.

Tam shot her a confused look. "Our mothers."

The page returned with a stretcher. Tam settled Maisy inside even as she cursed him.

Mama appeared, Brenna in one arm and Sela clutching the other hand. Sela took one look at Maisy and balked.

Mama tugged on her hand. "Come on, Sela, what—"

Sela broke away and scampered up a tree before anyone could stop her. They all gaped at her as she peered down at them between branches.

"She's got good instincts," Tam said approvingly.

Larkin rolled her eyes.

"Sela," Mama said in her best patient voice. "Come down."

Maisy began singing one of her dark songs. Sela ducked into the leaves.

Denan motioned to Tam. "Put her under."

Tam played, the melody thick with the promise of dreams. Maisy's eyes grew heavy, her song slurring to silence. Larkin gripped the dampener, grateful they had some protection against the pipers' indiscriminate magic.

"There now," Denan said to Sela. "She'll sleep for hours."

Sela peered at him. What did she see? The man who'd saved them from the gilgad and then tried to kidnap them? The man who'd kidnapped Larkin?

Larkin gestured for Denan to boost her up. She settled next to her sister, who clutched the trunk in a death grip. "Come on, Sela."

Her sister shook her head.

Larkin took a breath, calling upon her patience. "What will make you come down?"

Sela's gaze flicked to Maisy, and she trembled, her little body damp with sweat.

"Tam," Larkin called. "Take Maisy on ahead."

He looked to Denan, which stirred the embers of Larkin's anger. Denan nodded his approval. Tam motioned for one of the soldiers to help him. Together, they picked up Maisy and carted her away. As they disappeared, Sela relaxed, slumping one backbone at a time.

"Now will you come?" Larkin asked.

Sela let Larkin help her down.

Mama waited below, her foot tapping, but her ire wasn't for Sela. "How could you leave your sisters alone like that?"

Sela's eyes were red-rimmed as Larkin deposited her into Mama's arms. Mama held the baby out to Larkin. Brenna's body was limp with sleep.

"I was trying to save Maisy," Larkin said.

"At the risk of your sisters?" Mama said incredulously.

"Talox left them with my men," Denan said. "They were perfectly safe."

Mama glared at him. "And how do I know your men are trustworthy?"

Denan considered her. "I suppose you would have to trust

me."

"You—the man who kidnapped my daughter and married her against her will?"

Larkin stiffened.

"I have done my best to make that up to her," Denan said softly.

"That doesn't discount the wrong you have done her," Mama said. "Or me."

An hour ago, Larkin would have tried to intervene, to soften her mother. After what had happened with Talox, Denan had earned his own tongue-lashing.

His shoulders slumped. "No, it doesn't."

She appraised him. "In my experience—and I have more than most—power corrupts all men and women. Just look what you have done with your magic."

He frowned. "I will earn your trust, Pennice."

Larkin sighed. The more powerful a person became, the less Mama trusted them. Larkin couldn't really blame her suspicion of Denan. It had taken Larkin a long time to forgive him, even if she had understood his reasoning.

She rested her hand on Sela's back. "I had to help my friend." Was Maisy her friend? Could anyone be friends with a madwoman, especially one who liked to throw rocks? "And it wasn't safe for you."

Sela glanced toward where Maisy had disappeared. Her lower lip trembled.

"The pipers have put her to sleep," Larkin said. "She won't bother anyone."

Sela ducked her head into Mama's shoulder.

"Give her time, Larkin," Mama sighed.

Larkin didn't know what else she could have done, but there was no reasoning with four-year-olds—or angry mothers, apparently.

Denan stepped up next to Mama with a clean bandage in his

hands. "We need to cover Sela's eyes."

Mama took a step back. "Why?"

He shot a pleading look at Larkin. She didn't understand. Then, all at once, she did. In order to leave, they had to wade through dead mulgars. "We have to go through the battlefield now."

Mama blanched. "Better put her to sleep."

"I can carry her," Denan offered.

Looking bewildered and afraid, Mama looked between Denan and Larkin. "I'll do it."

Lips pursed, Denan nodded. He motioned to his men, who'd been waiting for them. They surrounded Larkin and her mother four men deep. One of them played, sending Sela into a deep sleep. Larkin stared at the large entourage and shot Denan a questioning look.

"Just in case an ardent is pretending," Denan whispered to her.

"A what?" Larkin asked.

"Regular mulgars are all brute force and no finesse," Denan said. "Ardents retain their cunning."

Larkin shuddered at the thought of an intelligent mulgar pretending to be dead while lying in wait for her.

Denan let out a long breath. "Larkin—"

"Don't," she said through clenched teeth. "Not now."

Larkin would never forget moving through the battlefield. Broken mulgars lay in grotesque positions, flies already attacking their faces, birds darting away as they approached. Pipers moved among them, gathering arrows from the bodies.

Larkin tried to keep her eyes locked on Denan's back. To breathe shallowly. To pretend she wasn't stumbling over and stepping on hardened flesh. She almost asked one of the pipers to enchant her too. But if this was the life of a warrior, she'd better get used to it.

As for Mama, she wore the same stoic expression as when she lost a mother or baby. Or both. Thankfully, it didn't take long to pass through the scores of dead. Mulgars like Maisy had been. Mulgars like the one Larkin had killed the day before. There had been a person in there, behind the wraiths' corruption, and Larkin had killed him.

"What are they?" Mama whispered to her.

"Mulgars." She sagged in relief that the word had passed easily through her lips.

"Are they the dark magic that hunts you?" Mama asked.

"No," Larkin said. Something much worse hunted her. "These are just their servants. Men and women turned to mindless monsters after being cut by a corrupted blade."

Had the man beneath the corruption realized he was dying? That she had killed him?

Mama checked to make sure Sela was sound asleep. "I truly believed the druids would kill us if we stayed." Garrot, the Black Druid in charge, had threatened it enough. "Perhaps it would have been better. Cleaner."

"We're safe, Mama. I know it's hard. But when you see how magical and lovely and secure the Alamant is …"

Mouth set in a grim line, Mama nodded.

The other pipers dispersed, their mottled cloaks rendering them invisible within moments. Tam and Denan murmured to each other. Larkin was still furious with him, but now was not the time for a spat.

Denan turned back to them. "Let me carry Sela, Pennice."

Mama sighed in defeat and handed her over. "How many soldiers do you have?"

"We have two armies in this company," Denan answered. "Mine and my uncle Demry's. Each is a thousand men strong."

"And how many mulgars are there?" Mama asked.

Denan hesitated. "Best guess? They outnumber us three to one."

Two thousand men were all that held back the mulgar horde? Larkin shuddered.

"Denan." Tam gestured to one of the pages, who ran through the forest toward them.

Hands braced on his knees, the young man paused before them, panting, "Scouts report the mulgar army lying in wait ahead."

Denan looked to the east. "Alongside the river?"

"Have Demry drive them off," Tam said with a shrug.

The boy shook his head. "They've a bunch of ardents leading them."

Tam and Denan exchanged a loaded glance.

Larkin stepped closer. "I thought the mulgars wouldn't fight your superior numbers without the wraiths to drive them?"

"They don't, usually," Tam murmured. "But if they have enough ardents ..."

"We could cross the river," Larkin said. Wraiths couldn't cross moving water.

"The only place to ford is the pool beneath the waterfall," Tam said.

Which would mean backtracking through the battlefield. Larkin shuddered.

Denan passed his hand down his face. "It's either that or let them drive us farther south—dangerously close to the Mulgar Forest."

"Mulgar Forest?" She didn't like the sound of that.

He looked down at her, a question in his gaze. "I don't want to frighten you. Nor do I want to lie to you."

"I'm already frightened," she whispered.

He breathed out and seemed to come to a decision. "When the Silver Tree became evil, became the Black Tree, so did the forest around him. We do not go there—not if we can help it."

Picturing the magic that hummed through the Forbidden Forest, she could well imagine the opposite in the Mulgar Forest.

She rubbed her sweating palms against her tunic.

Denan turned to the page. "How far north do they extend?"

"Three miles," he said.

Denan was silent, his brows furrowed with thought. "Have Demry turn and guard our rear—I don't want them attacking us while we cross. We'll ford the river here and head for the old road. From there to Ryttan."

The page set off.

"What's Ryttan?" Larkin asked.

"An ancient, fallen city of ruins." Denan didn't look happy about it. "The wall still stands. We'll be safe enough tonight."

"Why didn't we head there before?" Larkin asked.

"It's out of our way. It will add another night to our journey," Denan said.

Two more nights of mulgar attacks. Larkin wasn't sure she could bear it. Not that she had a choice.

CHAPTER 7

RUINS

The river crossing wasn't as arduous as Larkin had anticipated. While most of the pipers swam across the pool, others crossed on lines. The wounded were ferried over on a makeshift raft. Denan had tied Sela to Larkin's middle and enchanted her asleep. Larkin had zipped across the river, Tam catching her on the other side.

She hadn't even gotten wet.

Denan had rigged a pod to wrap the baby around Mama's chest while she crossed over on the ropes. It had been so comfortable Mama left it.

After they'd left the last of the dead mulgars on the north side of the river behind, Denan slipped a dampener around Sela's neck. Larkin crouched down, and Sela climbed on her back. Denan had gone off with his Uncle Demry to work out logistics.

Tam ranged ahead as Larkin and her family trekked through heavy forest. The thick undergrowth took all of Larkin's attention, until suddenly it didn't. Dirt-covered bricks peeked out from beneath her feet.

Larkin glanced up in surprise to find they had come upon an ancient brick road wide enough for two carts to travel abreast. In places, the road was cracked. In others, bricks had shattered. Cut saplings wept thick globs of sap. The pipers obviously kept it cleared.

Stretched out before her was the vanguard of Denan's army. She looked behind her, to where the road shifted out of sight—a road that had once connected two cities. Tired, dusty people had once traveled this road to sell their goods or visit their families. People who were now ashes and dust—forgotten. As Larkin would someday be forgotten.

Standing on that ancient road, Larkin felt small, a gasp of breath in a windstorm.

"Larkin?" Mama paused to look back at her, a question in her gaze.

Larkin let Sela slip from her back. "I think you can walk for a while."

Sela didn't protest. Larkin took her hand. Together, the four of them continued through the day, only pausing at noon to rest and eat a simple meal.

As the day shifted to evening, a hush fell over the entire army. Mounds of tumbled, pitted stones covered with vines flanked the road. At first, Larkin dismissed them as natural, until they approached a standing wall. It had sunk in places, the orderly rows and columns of bricks bulging like once-trim men grown fat.

A utilitarian gate of beams and metal braces stood open to admit them. A jumbled heap of large stones stained black and covered in vines was piled on either side. Giant, carved gilgads stood above them on their hindquarters, tails wrapped around their legs, faces frozen in a snarling rictus.

Larkin's heart raced in her chest. She and Sela had been attacked by a gilgad the first time they'd entered the forest. Denan had saved them. Worried for her sister's reaction, she glanced over her shoulder to check on Sela. She'd fallen asleep again, which explained the damp spot on Larkin's shoulder.

Before they reached the gates, Denan strode out to meet them. Larkin tensed with every step that brought him closer. He glanced at her once and then was careful not to look at her again.

"What is this place?" Mama asked him.

"Ryttan—one of our cities that fell to mulgars after the war."

"What war?" Mama asked.

"The Alamant—my ancestors—was at war with Valynthia—your ancestors—when the curse fell."

"And who began this curse?" Mama asked.

"The ones with the dark magic," Denan said. "They were men once. They are not anymore."

"The real beast of the forest?" Mama asked softly.

"Yes," Larkin said.

Beyond the wall, crumbled domed buildings littered the forest floor like upright, broken eggs. A long line of headless statues lined the path—men with swords and shields and women with some form of flute, each with sigils still visible on their skin.

"Who were they?" Larkin asked.

"Defenders of the city," Denan answered. "There's a hill near the center. We'll spend the night there."

"I thought the pipers only had tree dwellings," Larkin said.

"Not always."

Beyond the statues was an open square, an empty fountain beyond. It was packed with soldiers. Cooks had set up enormous pots of stew that smelled of gilgad meat. As the soldiers passed through, they filled their bowls, ate, and washed the bowls in a nearby stream before returning them to their packs. Captains directed men to the healers' tent or into position along the top of the wall, where they were to rest until sundown.

Denan led them to the shade of a large tree and turned to Mama. "You and the little ones rest. Larkin and I will fetch supper."

He still wasn't looking at her, as if he could sense that her anger had been carefully packed away to come out later. Which it was.

Denan lifted Sela from Larkin. The breeze felt wonderful against her sweaty back. Sela shied away from him to curl up against Mama's side where she'd settled inside the wide roots.

Larkin and Denan hadn't taken two steps toward the crowd when one of the pages came running. "She's awake, sir. And she's mad."

Maisy. Had to be.

Denan frowned and hurried after the man, Larkin on his heels.

"Larkin!" Mama called.

"I'll be right back," Larkin answered without looking back. Not two dozen strides later, Larkin lost Denan in the crowd. She turned about and rose up on her tiptoes, unable to see him over so many tall, bulky men in armor.

A sudden bang, shout, and hiss had her turning to her right. She shoved her way to the opposite side of the fountain. Maisy had backed up to a tree and hissed at Talox like a feral cat. She'd drawn a crowd; easily a hundred soldiers watched with interest.

Working together, Denan and Talox hemmed her in. Maisy was cornered. She would attack for certain. Someone was bound to get hurt. Larkin broke into a run.

Maisy drew her knife. Denan and Talox both took defensive stances, shields out.

Larkin launched herself in front of them. "Maisy," she snapped. "Stop it! All of you, stop it!"

Maisy's mad, accusing glare fell on Larkin.

Larkin forced her voice to calm. "No one is going to hurt you."

"They've already hurt me," Maisy hissed.

"You were scaring Sela."

Maisy ground her teeth. "You abandoned me."

Larkin set her jaw. "I'm sorry, but Sela is terrified of you, and my family needs me." Her family would always, *always* come first. "Do you understand?"

Maisy's voice turned soft, childlike. "Please don't leave me again."

Ancestors. Larkin couldn't be two people. She couldn't be Maisy's keeper. "Maisy, put the knife down."

Maisy's gaze shifted to Denan and Talox, to the pipers surrounding her. A shudder rolled through her, but the knife fell to her side, though she didn't release it.

"I've done all I can for you, Maisy. I'm sorry."

The betrayal and hurt in the other woman's eyes nearly undid Larkin. Maisy's voice darkened.

The beast comes. The beast takes.
That which he takes, he breaks.
That which he breaks, he remakes,
And then a beast like him awakes.

Rhyming usually preceded violence, but Maisy remained calm.

"My page will take you to a supply cart," Denan said to Maisy in what Larkin had come to recognize as his prince voice. "You will be given the same supplies as our soldiers. As long as you hinder no one and stay clear of Sela, you are free to do as you wish."

Guilt eating her from the inside out, Larkin strode to Talox.

"You would abandon me again?" Maisy called to her.

Larkin's steps stuttered. But if she must choose between her sister and Maisy, her sister would win every time. She forced herself to keep going.

Talox met her searching gaze. He didn't seem angry or hurt, simply resigned to his fate. Bandages peeked out from his shirt where he'd been flogged.

She folded her arms in front of her chest. "You're guarding me tonight."

His brows rose, and he glanced over her shoulder. She felt Denan's presence and straightened to her full height.

"I've been demoted," Talox said matter-of-factly.

"Doesn't stop me from hiring you as a personal bodyguard."

The corner of Talox's mouth quirked in amusement.

"Larkin," Denan said in exasperation.

She whirled on him. She'd dealt with enough pain and suffering over the last few weeks to last a lifetime. This was an easy, simple fix. And she was fixing it. "I'm the princess, aren't I?" It wasn't a question. "As your wife, I have access to our funds, do I not?"

"Yes," Denan said.

"Can we not afford a guard?"

"Yes, but—"

"Well then, I can spend those funds how I choose. I'm hiring Talox."

She held her breath and waited. He stared at her, gaze shifting to Talox and back to her again. He nodded once. She'd never taken advantage of her status or his money before. It felt good to do both.

She turned back to Talox, his relief obvious. "Tonight. Before the sun sets."

Talox bowed. "Of course, Princess."

Satisfied with herself, she turned and marched toward the cooks. Pipers watched her in silence, some openly grinning.

Denan stepped up beside her. "That was ... a kind thing you did."

She paused and turned to him. "You're not angry?"

Denan's eyes were sad. "Pipers like our women strong-minded." He stepped closer, his voice dropping. "You understand why I did what I did? Soldiers must obey orders, Larkin. And putting you at risk is not something I'll tolerate."

"I know you were worried about me, but we were fine. I wasn't even hurt."

"This had nothing to do with my feelings and everything to do with my people. They will always come first."

He was lying to himself if he thought this was all about his people. "You didn't have to do it in front of everyone."

"Yes, I did. I can't be seen showing favoritism, even for someone I love like a brother."

"Demoting him would have been enough."

He huffed in frustration. "You don't understand."

"I understand. I just don't agree."

"No, you don't."

She rolled her eyes. They weren't going to agree—not on this.

Neither of them speaking, Larkin and Denan fetched supper for her family. The stew was bland—the bloated grains did nothing for the flavor or texture. The gilgad tasted a little like chicken and a lot like fish, though it was denser than both. But it was filling, and they were all hungry.

Afterward, Larkin and Mama washed up while Denan stretched out to his full length, his hands tucked under the back of his head. He always slept like that, as if even in sleep he refused to take up less space. It was warm enough that they left Brenna naked, with a thin shirt over her to keep the bugs off.

Larkin tried using her unknown sigils to no avail, growing more and more frustrated with each attempt. She didn't even know for sure her sigils would break the curse—they hadn't broken hers.

Once again, her gaze drifted to her sister, who was drawing in the dirt with a stick. Larkin looked away quickly, her hands suddenly clammy for no reason, but her eyes drifted back again.

Her sister looked so lonely and sad. She crouched next to her to see a crude family drawn into the dirt. Only this time, two figures were missing—their father and Nesha.

No matter what they'd done, Larkin would not take them away from Sela. She took her own stick and drew their father, his curling red hair and larger build. Then Nesha, with her long waves.

Sela watched, enraptured.

Larkin looked at her, this little girl who kept losing members of her family. "Should we find leaves for clothes? I bet you could find a pretty one for Nesha's dress."

Sela looked at her as if debating, then she scrambled to obey. Larkin joined her in the hunt, and soon, they had the girls dressed in pretty leaves, flowers in their hair. They tore leaves in half for Harben's trousers and shirt. When Larkin looked up, Mama watched them, tears shining in her eyes. She nodded. Larkin gave a little smile and nodded back.

Tam approached and crouched before them. "Which one am I?"

Sela's blank look turned to one of confusion.

"You're not in our family," Larkin supplied.

Sela nodded.

Tam tugged one of her curls. "Sure I am. I'm your handsome uncle. Didn't you know?"

Sela looked to Larkin, who smiled at her. "Tam is teasing. He's not an uncle, but a very good friend."

"Sometimes, friends can be family too." He rose to his feet and held out his hand. "Time to go. Come on, little one. I saw some lizards in the ruins. Want to try to catch one?"

Sela shot to her feet and took his hand.

He stiffened and looked guiltily at Mama. "That is, if it's all right with you, Pennice."

Mama took one look at Sela's pleading face and waved them away.

With a whoop, Tam swung Sela onto his shoulders and started off. He looked back at Larkin. "Catch up. Denan knows the way. You can get him up. He never snaps at you."

Larkin laughed. "Coward."

Tam grinned. "I just have a strong sense of self-preservation."

Larkin nudged Denan with her foot. He lazily opened his eyes and stretched, back popping. He yawned and held out his hand. She helped him up.

Larkin, Denan, and Mama continued between stone buildings, Tam's excited chatter drifting back to them. Larkin caught sight of Sela and Tam now and then, climbing and exploring the ruins.

Most of the roofs had crumbled, leaving only the exterior walls. One rectangular building was so large her entire town could have fit comfortably inside.

She peered through the lacy, carved arches into the forest growing in the interior. "What was that?"

Denan glanced up the narrow, steep steps. "A library."

Larkin's eyes widened. How much knowledge had vanished when the roof had caved in?

"It must have been beautiful," Mama murmured.

Denan looked about as if he hadn't really noticed. "We don't know how they managed to fit the stones together so perfectly." He shook his head. "Even if the war ended tomorrow, we no longer know how to rebuild what was lost."

They moved on. The sheer size and scope of the city was a testament to the fact that a far greater civilization than Larkin's had gone before.

"Why doesn't anyone live in the buildings?" she asked.

"They're not safe," Denan said. "The city crumbles a little more every year."

A pervasive feeling invaded the place—as if the buildings watched them pass. The cries of the long dead seemed to echo

81

down streets overrun by forest. "Are you sure no mulgars hide in here?" Larkin murmured to Denan.

"It's the gilgads you should worry about. This used to be one of their hibernation nests." At her horrified look, he chuckled. "It's been in our possession for nearly a century."

"Larkin." Mama pointed deeper into the fallen city. Through the trees, conical buildings rose from the ground—buildings that looked like a larger version of Larkin's family hut. And now she understood where the knowledge of how to build them had come from.

She pointed. "What were they?"

"Individual bath houses," Denan said. "Ryttan was a city of leisure and learning. Lots of universities."

Bane would have loved to see this. The two of them would have explored the city for days. Worry made her throat go dry. "Has Bane been ransomed yet?"

Denan stiffened. "It's too soon to have heard from my emissary."

Larkin surreptitiously wiped at the tears that filled her eyes. Denan pretended not to notice.

Mama reached out and grasped her hand. "His father is a resourceful man. Bane will be all right."

Head falling, Larkin nodded.

They approached a conical building with the roof still attached. At the base of the tree at the side of it, Talox slept. Larkin was relieved to see him.

Sitting against the trunk, Tam flipped his knife, catching it by the hilt. It tumbled to the ground. He cursed and rubbed his fingertips into his bloodshot eyes. He was obviously exhausted.

"You should sleep while you can," Larkin said.

He shrugged and rooted around for his dropped knife.

Denan sighed. "Come on, I'll teach you how to tie up your pods."

He helped them climb the tree and tied a rope around Sela's

waist so she couldn't fall. He showed Larkin and Mama how to tie the knot that secured the pods. Sela burrowed into the first one, wrapped her arms around her legs, and stared into the canopy.

Denan monitored as Larkin tied her own pod, his fingers gently correcting hers. He nodded when she had it right and stared at the pod with a look of such longing that she couldn't help but give him a push toward it. "Sunset is only a couple hours away. Rest. Nightfall will come soon enough."

"I won't be able to sleep—not this close to battle. Come. I want to show you something."

Larkin hesitated. She wasn't as angry anymore, but she was still upset.

Hurt flashed across his eyes. She sighed. "All right."

He nodded, clearly relieved.

Mama watched them, her lips pursed. "I don't like the idea of her wandering down there alone."

"She won't be alone," Denan said. "And there's no danger to her. At least until nightfall."

From below, Tam gave them a sly grin.

"Did you find your knife?" Larkin huffed, annoyed at his implication.

He flashed it at her. "I could teach you if you want."

She shot him a dubious look. "Didn't look like you were that good at it."

"You say the nicest things." He started flipping his knife again.

"Why isn't he sleeping?" she whispered to Denan.

"Tam never sleeps much."

"Why?"

"He should probably tell you that himself."

Worried, she looked back at her friend. She'd force an answer out of him later.

Denan led her to a thick cluster of buildings. A compound

really, with the larger building flanked on each side by large, beehive-shaped domes, the interiors too shadowy to make anything out.

"What was this place?" she asked.

"After they drove the gilgads out, Ryttan became a city known for its bathing pools."

But the domes were huge. Much too large for a person or two. "They bathed together?"

Denan pointed to each in turn. "Men on one side, women on the other."

She paused in front of the larger one. "And this one?"

"This one was for swimming. Though when we took it back, it was crawling with gilgads hibernating in the hot water."

Her lip curled at the idea of the heated pools crawling with giant lizards. "Where'd all the water go?"

"The pipes that brought it here from the mineral pools broke. If we have time, I'll show you tomorrow."

They walked beside a short wall that came no higher than her knees, the top lined with broken statues of lithe snakes. Beyond was an overgrown walkway between two deep rectangular depressions.

Denan hopped into one of them, helped her down, and trotted through vines and leaves, a millipede the size of her arm scuttling away. On the far side, they reached a carved fish. From its gaping mouth came a trickle of steaming water that had obviously been a torrent before the pipes broke.

"Waterspouts like this surround the building. Pipe works too. I think they also channeled the water to heat their homes, which explains why they lived on the ground instead of the trees—it would have been a lot warmer."

She ran her fingers through the water and jerked back, hissing at the heat. "It's too hot to bathe in."

"They would have added cold water," Denan said dryly.

She flicked water at him.

He chuckled as he wiped his face. "Want to see the inside?"

She looked up at the towering building. "Aren't you tired?" By her count, he'd had less sleep than all of them save Tam.

"I told you—I won't be able to sleep this close to the battle."

"Is it safe?"

"I'll go ahead. Scare out the monsters." He hauled himself out of the depression and onto a short walkway. After a dozen steps, he disappeared inside the darkened mouth of the middle building.

Swallowing hard, she checked twice for millipedes and climbed after him. Steeling herself, Larkin opened her sigils, sword and shield appearing in her hands, which added a little illumination. Wary of bugs that might drop on her head, she touched her sword to the vines nearly obscuring the entrance. They easily fell away. Easing through, she could just make out the thorned relief carved into the archway.

Inside was pitch black. How was Denan supposed to see a gilgad—or worse, a mulgar—before it ate him? Even fully extended, her sword only showed a step or two in each direction. Denan was lost to her in the darkness. Where had he gone?

"Denan?"

No answer. Before her were four steps that led into the blackness. Feeling safer with her back to the wall, she slipped along the perimeter, steps on her left, wall on her right. A few chunks of white plaster remained on the walls, flakes of golden plating and opal insets outlining what must have once been a beautiful representation of the White Tree.

Something shone at her feet. She kicked at the dirt, trying to see the floor beneath the layers of dirt. She made out the corner of octagonal tiles in brilliant gold.

A sound behind her. She whipped around, something crunching underfoot. Denan trotted up the steps. She breathed, her hand to her chest. "The forest take you."

"You scare easy."

"Of course I do! I grew up thinking the beast would get me."

He kissed her forehead. "I suppose he did."

"Where did you go?"

He frowned. "I wanted to make sure it was safe first."

"What was safe?"

He took her hand and led her down the steps. "I know you're still angry with me."

She stiffened but didn't say anything. It was lighter here. Looking up, she saw a break in the ceiling where tree roots had broken through. Judging by its blackened shell, it had been burned—probably a lightning strike.

"I know you think I was harsh with Talox. You're right. I was harsh. He's a great man. One of the best fighters. But he's not a great soldier. He's too big-hearted for it."

Light shone from the break in the ceiling, illuminating one wall. "Then why did you ..." Her words trailed off as she saw a relief carved into the stone.

The wraiths. The wraiths were carved into the ancient stone. Mulgars bled from their blades—mulgars with terrible markings, their faces dead. Not wanting to go on but unable to stop herself, Larkin shifted to the left, following the panel's progression.

The Forbidden Forest, filled with hometrees as beautiful as the ones in the Alamant. Below them, people died violently. Women. Children. Men. Old. Young. They all died or were turned—until there were none left on the ground.

"With the source of their magic broken or corrupted," Denan said, "Valynthia fell hard and fast."

Skeletal corpses hung from the trees.

"The people in the trees died from thirst or starvation," Denan said softly. "A few might have survived longer—a year or two at most."

Survivors fled into the forest.

"Like the arbor rings, the White Tree's magic is stronger in some places than others. Somehow, the barriers came into being. Only the strongest and luckiest managed to reach them."

This was the history of her people—Larkin's history—and it had been erased by the curse, by the wraiths. As if they had never existed at all.

The curse had always touched Larkin's life, even if she hadn't known it. But this made it personal. This made it real. Larkin's hands fisted at her sides, outrage buzzing through her sigils.

More forest. More dying and running. Fleeing into a city surrounded by a high wall. Ryttan. It was winter. Larkin could tell because of the bare-branched trees surrounding the city.

"The Alamantians still had magic. We could still fight, and the walls around the cities made them defensible. But cities aren't self-sustaining—especially cities overrun with refugees. People starved. Disease ran rampant."

The last panel wasn't finished. It was cruder, as if it had been carved with rudimentary tools. Mulgars and wraiths streamed over the wall and into the city. People ran, barricaded themselves in buildings—buildings like this one.

"There was a fresh water supply here. Drainage. Heat for the winter. The people lasted for months."

"How could they possibly last for months without something to eat?" Her voice felt rusty, old.

And then she saw it. People ... eating each other.

She staggered back in horror, bumping into Denan. He steadied her.

"Why are you showing me this?" she whispered.

"I'm a hard man, Larkin. I must be. I can't tolerate soldiers who don't follow orders. I won't risk you—not when you're the best hope we've had in centuries."

She wouldn't sleep for weeks after this. Angry that he'd sprung this on her and flushed with horror, she whirled on him.

Something crunched under her foot, the soft snap echoing stillness through her.

He crouched beside her, his eyes fixed on whatever she'd stepped on. Crushed bone. One piece of it stuck out. He gently dug away the dirt and worked it free. He held up a tiny, delicate human jaw. Brittle with age, the outer layer of the bone had thinned into porous gaps, revealing pockets of adult teeth embedded beneath the baby teeth. When she'd stepped back, she must have crushed the rest of the skull.

Fresh horror wrapped clammy hands around Larkin's throat. This was not some ancient ruin. It was a graveyard. She gasped and backed up, then froze in fear of crushing another skull.

He twisted the jaw in his hands. "Men's and children's bones litter the place. I think they locked themselves in here while the women died fighting off mulgars."

She could easily imagine it. They'd bolted the doors until the steam grew suffocating. The sounds of death and dying outside. Then the silence of morning.

She bolted for the exit, tripped, fell. Her ribs jarred, hurting worse than they had in days.

"Larkin!"

She didn't stop until she was outside again. Until the weak evening light touched her face. Until the fresh breeze cooled the sweat on her brow.

She would never be comfortable in the dark again.

Denan caught up a moment later, the jaw thankfully missing from his hands.

"I don't know if I can ever forgive you for that."

His head fell. "It will happen again, Larkin. The White Tree is centuries old. It's dying. And when the magic dies ..."

There would be no protection from the wraiths—nothing to stop them from repeating what they had done before.

"We have to stop it," she said, voice shaking.

He nodded. "Now you see."

Ancestors, she wanted to hit him. But he had been right. She'd thought she'd understood the curse, the stakes. She hadn't. "I'm keeping Talox as my personal guard."

Denan gave a curt nod. "He'll fit better there anyway."

Side by side, they strode back to the tree, Larkin's mind whirling with images of people dying. She remembered what he'd said, about the women fighting while the men had hidden with the children. "Wait, women fought off mulgars?"

Denan shrugged. "In the Alamant, women's magic was the warrior magic. In Valynthia, it was reversed, and men were the warriors. It would be the same now, if Valynthians could still manage magic."

Valynthians. "Idelmarchians," she corrected him. "The Valynthians are all dead and forgotten." She couldn't keep the bitterness from her voice. Women warriors. She couldn't wrap her brain around it. "Why were they reversed?"

"Our tree is female, and their tree is male."

"That doesn't make any sense."

He shrugged.

"So what did the men do?"

"Played their pipes, I suppose."

"You suppose?"

"We lost the records in a fire, remember?"

She remembered him telling her something about that when they'd been in the Alamant together. "Three hundred years isn't that long ago."

"The curse has a way of warping things—including our history."

She eyed his muscles and his weapons. "So the men put down their pipes and became warriors."

"Well, I mean, we still use our pipes."

"But not like you used to."

"No," he said. "Not like we used to."

The magic had fallen into ruin as surely as their two kingdoms had. She shivered despite the heat.

He rested a hand on her shoulder. "They're long dead, Larkin."

"What's to stop it from happening again?"

"Me. Talox. Tam. And you."

She looked into his eyes and saw only sincerity shining back at her. She flared her sigils, admiring the long, lovely lines of the sword in her hand.

Could she really do this? Become a warrior like the matriarchs of old? She'd already killed a mulgar. Something awoke within her—fear and determination and a terrible knowledge that she would kill and kill and kill again if it meant stopping the wraiths.

"Talox has already begun my training." Her voice trembled with emotion. "Want to continue it?"

"As long as you swear to do as I command until you've managed to break the curse."

The burden of that task forced the breath from her. She braced her head in her hands. "I've tried, Denan. My sigils don't do anything."

"You'll figure it out. I know you will."

His faith only made her burden heavier.

He tugged her into his embrace, holding her without a word. "Swear it."

"I swear."

He glanced toward the sun. "There isn't much time left." He pulled out his sword and shield. "Aside from the ardents, mulgars aren't that bright. What—"

"So if I face an ardent?"

"You're not ready for the ardents yet. Run." He adjusted his grip on his sword. "Mulgars don't feel pain or fear, so it has to be a mortal blow. Pierce their chest or bash them in the head. Behead them if you can. In a pinch, you can cut their hamstrings and finish them on the ground."

The battle for this city had been here, right where she stood. Women had fought to protect their husbands and children. They had lost. Fear coursed through Larkin, hot and cold in turns. She shuddered.

"You have the strength of your sword and your shield. You have your wits and friends to fight by your side. You cannot lose."

She met his gaze, some of the fear abating. "Do you feel no remorse for killing them?"

Denan looked away. "They are not people—not anymore."

Only that wasn't entirely true. Maisy was proof of that. Still, she was a warrior. She would not balk at this. "Show me?"

He crouched behind his shield. "Here, swing at me slowly."

She did so. Her blade tapped his shield. He flung his shield and her blade to the side and thrust at her with his sword. "Sweep. Stab. Reposition. Now you try."

He worked with her until she could manage at nearly full speed.

Denan demonstrated how to take a charge by shifting to the side and letting her opponent fly past her. "Mulgars can survive almost anything, a broken back or a missing limb. To be sure, you always have to cut their heads off."

She stilled. "Venna's head wasn't chopped off." Denan turned away. "Venna fell thousands of feet. No one—nothing could survive that." So why did it sound more like a question?

Denan sniffed. "That mulgar—it wasn't Venna anymore. It was the monster who killed your friend."

"And did that monster survive the fall?"

He wiped at the sweat on his temples. "I don't … I don't know."

Gripping her amulet, Larkin faced the darkening woods. Her friend, or what was left of her, could still be out there. The pain of that thought … She gripped the amulet tighter. The sharp-edged branch slipped into her skin. She gasped in pain.

The forest darkened around her as if it had been covered with rotted black cloth. And on the other side of that cloth, images flickered, burning through until they replaced Denan and the city of Ryttan.

Gaping, horrible faces in the shadows pressed against what appeared to be layers of enormous shields that protected dozens of peoples. The shadows' screams and chittering shuddered down Larkin's spine. She summoned her sword and shield, cowering behind the latter.

The shadows' claws shredded through the magic like wet paper. The barriers hadn't even finished fading to ash before the shadows darted forward. They forced themselves down the throats of enchanters and enchantresses, who staggered, gagging, gasping, clawing at their throats.

Then they stilled, paused, looked up. Each of their eyes were solid black, forked lines flaring from their sockets. They were mulgars. Mulgars who hadn't been turned by a wraith blade, but the shadows themselves. She was watching the birth of monsters.

They turned on each other. Old and young. Men and woman. They turned and rent each other with their bare hands.

The second barrier fell. More people writhed and stilled and killed. One of them lunged at Larkin. She screamed, her shield out. But the shadow passed through her.

Panting, she spun in place. The battle continued around her as if she didn't exist. Because she didn't—not really. This was a memory.

A woman caught Larkin's attention. In the centermost barrier, she stood on a platform around a font surrounded by wicked thorns. Warm, golden light shot through with color that danced beneath the surface. Larkin recognized the place.

The White Tree. She was in the Alamant on the day the curse had come into being. At the center of it all was a woman in a glittering black dress. Larkin stumbled toward her, through one layered barrier after another, panicked people passing through her like shadows. She reached the stairs before the platform.

The woman was young, no older than Larkin. Hair was a pale gold shot through with silver, her eyes a warm brown. The diamond-encrusted black dress she wore was a piece of art that flashed with a hundred sparks of fractured color. But it was the sigil revealed by the plunging neckline that held Larkin's attention—a sigil that mirrored the one on Denan's chest, only hers was silver instead of gold.

This was the queen of Valynthia.

Beside her stood a sharp-featured man with dark skin and hair. The tops of gold branches peeked out from his collar. The king of the Alamant. Working together. Hadn't they been at war?

Their attention fixed on the distance. Larkin followed their gazes to see shadows spread throughout the city like smoke, devouring light, twisting people's expressions into rictuses of hate.

The king and queen played different flutes, the music impenetrable and unmovable. The queen manipulated the magic with her bare hands, the gold and silver splitting off into different colors that she wove with quick fingers.

She threw the resulting orb into the air. A large, domed shield flared, expanding to include those in the next layer of defense. Enchantresses and enchanters desperately fed their magic into the gleaming sphere. Together, they pressed it outward, driving the shadows back from one layer of defense to another until the entire White Tree gleamed—a refuge in a sea of shadows.

They were doing it. They were defeating the shadows. But Larkin knew the ending of this story, knew this rally couldn't last. Ancestors, why couldn't it have lasted?

Inexplicably, the expansion halted. The vault trembled like a drop of water about to fall. The king collapsed. His magic wavered. The queen knelt at his side and gripped his shoulder. Face flushed, he panted, his eyes unfocused.

What was wrong with him? "Get up," *Larkin said through clenched teeth. Every part of her tensed for these two to win, though she knew they would not.*

"Dray," the queen begged. "You have to keep fighting. Together, we can defeat him. I know we can."

He looked up at her, resolve shining in his eyes and his sigils gleaming white and gold against his dark skin. "Help me up."

She braced under his arm and strained. He leaned against her until they reached the font. He pressed his palm onto the hollow thorn, blood swirling through it.

"Please. See what's happening. Help me. Let me fight." For a moment, his face was stark with determination. Then he relaxed. He turned to the queen, all his sigils alight—the apex of power and strength.

He dropped, the light going out like a spent candle. As the fledgling shield fell to starlight and ash around her, he gripped her hand. Between their palms, the light flared. Blood ran between their entwined fingers.

"Use my light," he gasped. "Drive out the wraiths." His eyes rolled up, and he went perfectly still. He was dead.

The queen panted, looked at the bloody thing in her hand in horror. She held an amulet that looked like an ahlea.

The colors faded, the moth-eaten cloth surrounding her. Between the gaps, she could make out her world—the forest and ruins in the faded light. The cloth burned away. Larkin gasped in a breath. Arms held her close—too close. She shoved.

"Larkin?"

Denan carried her.

Disoriented, she clutched the amulet in her fist, blood running from her fingertips. She released it, hand aching, the puncture stinging. A vision. She'd had a vision. The amulet had triggered it.

She clutched his shirt, breathing deep his scent. "Put me

down."

He gently set her on her feet, though he kept an arm around her waist. "You're all right?"

She staggered, her head spinning. She was in the ruins, not far from the baths. "How long was I out?"

"A minute or two."

She looked around the dead place, searching for mulgars and blood and death. Instead, there was the quiet of the coming dark.

"Larkin?" Denan sounded worried.

She pinched her eyes shut and forced a deep breath into her lungs. She blew out slowly. "There was a king and queen there when the curse formed. The Alamant's king was Dray. What was the Valynthian queen's name?"

"The Curse Queen?" Denan asked.

"Curse Queen?" Larkin asked in confusion.

"Her name was Eiryss." Denan's expression darkened. "It was her dabbling in dark magic that brought the wraiths into being."

"But she was fighting the curse," Larkin protested. "Trying to stop it."

"Yes, and she broke the Silver Tree trying to right her wrong. It was she who condemned Valynthia." Denan ground his teeth.

"That can't be." Larkin reeled. The girl she'd seen had been no more than seventeen. And she'd been as horrified by the events as Larkin had.

"How did you know Dray's name?"

"I saw them." At his incredulous look, she started at the beginning and told him everything.

When she was finished, Denan watched her, brows drawn. "The story goes that on the day Queen Eiryss and King Dray were to be married, the wraiths descended and laid a curse upon the land. The wraiths came about as a result of her dabbling with dark magic. Eiryss used up all Valynthia's magic as queen to create a countercurse to stave off the shadow."

Larkin's two weddings hadn't exactly been happy moments, but at least her entire kingdom hadn't crumpled. "I thought Valynthia and the Alamant were at war?"

"They were. The wedding was supposed to bring the two kingdoms together."

"You're sure about that?" Larkin sat heavily on a large stone. "Your records were burned."

"Some stories aren't forgotten."

She supposed not.

He passed a hand down his face. "He was one of my ancestors."

"Who?"

"Dray."

"But he died!" Larkin said in surprise.

"He had two children from a previous marriage. Both survived."

She looked at Denan anew. Dray had been darker skinned, but she supposed they had similar sharp features and large builds. The resemblance wasn't enough to look like family, but then, what she saw was generations ago.

"Why this vision?" she asked.

"I've only ever had one vision—the vision of a bird in my hand." She'd heard this story before, but she held silent, wanting to hear it again. "If I tried to hold it, it died. If I let it free, it flew away, but always came back."

He sat beside her. "When I received the ahlea sigil"—the ancient sigil for women's magic—"I knew I would find the person to break the curse. And I gradually figured out that I had to let her come to me."

Larkin gave a half grunt, half laugh. She *had* gone to him. Granted, she'd had no other choice, what with a murderous mob on her heels.

He bumped her shoulder with his. "I did find her, and she did come to me. There's a message the White Tree wants you to learn. You'll figure it out."

She wished he didn't believe in her quite so completely. It would make the possibility of failure a little easier to bear.

Oblivious to her burden, Denan cast a glance toward the setting sun. "Come on. The battle will begin soon."

CHAPTER

RYTTAN

Larkin and Denan reached the base of the tree, where Tam had finally fallen asleep along with Talox. Denan strapped on his boiled-leather armor studded with metal.

Larkin studied the amulet, the way the light sparked colors across the surface like early morning frost. The way the depths gleamed silver. Next to it, the dampener flashed with colors, gold seaming the edges.

Her gaze narrowed. "Denan, this amulet is not made of the White Tree."

Denan pulled the chain over her head, the amulet and dampener clicking against each other, and held them in his fingers. He jerked his hand back. "You're right. They're from different sacred trees."

She felt naked without her amulet.

"The Silver Tree is corrupted," Denan said, eyeing the amulet like he was considering breaking it. "So is its magic."

She snatched it from him and held it behind her back. "It

saved my life." Once when it showed her the way out of the flood and again when it had formed a shield between her and Garrot. "And it gave me the vision you said I needed."

He reached for it. "Larkin—"

She shifted out of his reach. "If it was corrupted, we would have known by now."

Denan's expression tightened.

"It's my decision," she said firmly.

Denan sighed. Before he could argue, Tam whimpered in his sleep. Tears streaked from his eyes. Denan crouched next to him and shook his shoulder. Tam struggled to open his eyes. His gaze finally fixed on Denan. He pressed the heels of his hands into his eyes. "I saw them. I always see them."

Saw who? Larkin couldn't ask. This moment belonged between Denan and his friend.

Tam sat up and dragged his hands down the sallow skin of his face. He huffed, "Why couldn't I dream about Alorica?" He trailed into muttering.

Denan murmured something in return. Urgent piper music worked through the forest, calling soldiers to arms, calling for the Alamant to defend her people.

"That would be for the archers," Tam said, his fingers twitching toward his bow.

Talox groaned and sat up. He took one look at Tam and frowned. Denan and Talox exchanged a weighted glance, and then both men moved.

Larkin's magic ached to respond to the call to arms. She flared her sigils, the familiar buzz vibrating just short of painful. She embraced the pain. It made her feel alive, ready.

"Larkin?" Denan strapped his ax and shield to his back.

"Take me with you."

He followed her gaze to the front line. "We've talked about this. You haven't the training." And she was too important to risk.

She ground her teeth. "Is this what it means to love you? Long nights of not knowing if you are alive or dead?"

He tugged her forward and kissed her forehead. "What do I always tell you?" he murmured against her skin.

She sighed. "That you'll always come for me."

"You two are disgusting," Tam grumbled.

Larkin pressed her hands to her hot cheeks.

"As if you and Alorica are any better," Talox said. "I've seen you take food from her mouth."

"Now there's a woman," Tam said. "Do you think she's pregnant yet? I've always wanted to be a father." No sign of the tears he'd shed or the nightmare that must still linger.

Talox rolled his eyes.

"Your turn to stay with the women, Tam." Denan's gaze shifted to her. "That is, if Larkin can spare Talox to guard me."

Tam frowned. "But I want to kill mulgars."

Denan's gaze was worried for his friend. "I suppose I'll manage with just Talox."

"I'm fine," Tam insisted.

Denan stepped closer. "Get some sleep tonight—real sleep—and I'll let you kill mulgars tomorrow."

Tam wouldn't meet his gaze. "It's not that easy."

Denan rested a hand on his shoulder. "Try."

Reluctantly, Tam nodded.

"Come on, Denan," Talox said. "We need to go."

Denan squeezed Larkin's fingers. "Get up to safety." His gaze sought Tam. "Guard them."

Tam saluted. "An arrow to the face of every mulgar or wraith who dares look her way."

All too soon, Larkin's arms were achingly empty. She stared after Denan until the ruins and forest obscured him. All around came the sound of the pipers calling their men to arms.

"Come on. We need to get up." Tam started climbing. He took up a position with his back to the trunk, his bow beside him.

Larkin sat in her pod across from Mama, who watched her over the edge of her pod. "You really love him."

"Yes," Larkin whispered.

"Are you still a maiden?"

Mortified, Larkin buried her face in her hands.

Mama sat up and shifted so her legs dangled over the side of the pod. "We have to talk about this."

"No, we don't."

"I was the village midwife for twenty years. So yes, we do."

The tips of Tam's ears turned red. He cleared his throat and stuttered, "I'm just … Better shot. Up." He pointed as if that made his jumbled words any clearer and started climbing.

"Do you want to make love to Denan?" Mama asked.

Larkin's cheeks flamed. "The forest take me."

"So, yes," Mama said. "Making love isn't something you're suddenly good at. It takes practice, selflessness, and a good idea of how your body works."

From up in the tree, Tam peered down at them.

"Do you mind?" Larkin shot at him.

"Well, I'm just … ," Tam began. "If you have any tips?"

Mama glanced up at him. "We can have this conversation too, if you like."

He started back down.

"Later," Mama said. "In private."

He stiffened. "Right. Yes." He climbed back up.

Mama shook her head in disbelief. "Are all pipers this … open?"

"They take classes on women from their mothers."

Mama considered. "That's a good idea." She refocused on Larkin. "Now is not a good time to become pregnant—not until we're all safe—but there are other things you can do. And it's good practice."

Larkin groaned and wished to disappear, but deep down, she was also grateful. As much as she wanted to touch and be touched by Denan, she'd never been further than kissing. And while she knew what came next—she'd grown up on a farm with a midwife mother after all—that didn't make it less overwhelming.

Mama huffed. "You're lucky you have me. My mother never spoke of such things." She launched into a thorough description of how Larkin's body worked. To Larkin's surprise, the more Mama spoke, the less embarrassed Larkin became. She even asked a few questions.

"You can always ask more questions," Mama said.

They faded to silence. The sounds of the battle—shouts and screams and clashing arms—filled up the spaces around them. *Ancestors, just let Denan come back to me.*

Once again, Larkin was helpless. *Not for much longer,* she promised herself as her sword filled out the hollow of her hand.

"What ... What are they?" Mama pointed toward the battle. Larkin followed the gesture, her body stilling like a nestling at the slithering vibrations of a snake across a branch.

Just visible in the dying light, a wraith glided unnaturally behind the mulgars, which moved in complete sync with each other. It was driving them—driving them to their deaths.

A shiver broke out across Larkin. She fought it, but her instinct to hide from the wraiths was so strong that it didn't matter that the wraith was so far away she wasn't sure which one it was. It didn't matter that she was safe.

"Wraiths," Larkin whispered, relieved to be able to say the word to her mother. "Wielders of the dark magic."

"The ones who drive the mulgars?"

Larkin was finally able to explain the curse and the reason why the pipers took girls. "For three centuries, they've been fighting, stealing girls in order to continue, but they're losing. The White Tree is dying. When the White Tree is gone ..."

"So is the Idelmarch." Mama's lips pursed in a tight line. "Ancestors save us."

Larkin huffed. "It was our ancestors who got us into this mess."

Mama nodded in agreement. "Queen Eiryss."

Larkin gaped at her. "How do know the Curse Queen's name?"

Mama shifted uncomfortably and looked to the west. "Tell me about this Alamant."

Larkin watched her mother.

"We all have our secrets," Mama said. "Tell me about the Alamant."

Larkin sighed and decided to let it go. She thought of Denan's home. Heart aching with longing, she described the turquoise lake, the kaleidoscope of lights dancing along the edges of the fish, the elegant hometrees with magical barriers instead of doors and walls, and finally, the White Tree, like sunlit-gilded opals.

"You miss it?" Mama asked incredulously.

"Yes," Larkin admitted. It was more than just the beauty and the magic. Somehow, the Alamant had become her home.

Sela whimpered in her sleep. Larkin climbed into the pod with her little sister, who twisted around and laid her head on Larkin's chest. The growing damp spot on Larkin's tunic made it clear her sister was crying.

"What is it?" Larkin asked.

Sela didn't answer. It was as if, by not speaking, her sister had absolute control over one thing, and that made her able to bear all the things she couldn't control.

Larkin hummed and stroked Sela's hair.

The battle sounded like a distant thunderstorm punctuated with shrill notes. Larkin couldn't distinguish mulgar from piper in the darkness, silhouetted as they were by distant firelight. Sela gradually fell back asleep. Judging by Mama's even breathing, so had she.

Tam climbed back to his original branch. "You should get

some sleep." His gaze never left the distant battle.

"So should you," she murmured.

"Arrows in the face, remember?"

"If the mulgars break through, wouldn't you hear them coming?"

He wouldn't meet her gaze. She suddenly realized. It wasn't just mulgars Tam was meant to defend them from. It was also wraiths.

"They can form behind the lines," she whispered so her mother wouldn't hear.

Tam looked guilty. "We have wards, relics like the dampeners that we placed around the perimeter of camp."

Something about the way he said it made her think the wards weren't foolproof.

rate pools shone in a vivid shade of mint.

Larkin scrambled up the hill, climbing over enormous, hot pipes that must have once pumped water to the entire city. At the top, the page from before was already there, shooing the men from the highest level to the lower ones.

Their grumbling instantly ceased when Larkin and Denan came into view. Larkin blushed as, bare backsides flashing, the last handful jumped off the waterfall. A beat later came an echoing splash and whoops. The page gathered the men's dripping armor and clothes. He bowed as he trudged back the way he'd come.

Denan tugged at his own armor buckles. He eased into the water as if it were a touch too hot and pulled his tunic off, dunked his armor, and scrubbed it with a handful of sand before setting it in a neat pile.

As he worked, Larkin stared at the raised White Tree sigil taking up his entire chest—the sigil that named him the future king. On his back, a knotted, three-headed snake shifted under his coiling muscles. On the inside of his right forearm was a geometric flower with angular petals—the ahlea flower, sigil of women's magic. The sigil that convinced him he would find the one to break the curse. Her.

He scrubbed his tunic, the muscles of his body like hard stones that slipped beneath his soft skin. "If you want me to wash yours, just toss them to me."

She caught her bottom lip between her teeth. Any man that beautiful *and* willing to do her laundry ...

"Go nearer the waterfall. I won't be able to see you through the mist," he said as he scrubbed.

She slipped into the almost-too-hot water, careful of the uneven footing, and made her way toward him. "What if I want you to see?"

He went very still. Something in her expression must have told him everything. "Larkin, just because we're married and we love each other doesn't mean you're ready. I won't push you."

She took the soap from him and lathered her hands. She washed the blood from his cheeks, then his chest. Her palm slipped across the impossible smoothness of his skin, her fingers pale against his ruddiness. She scooped up a handful of water and rinsed the soap from him.

Her own tunic grew damp and soapy, sticking to her skin and riding up so a sliver of her belly showed. The tips of his fingers rested against her bared stomach. She gasped at the bolt of heat zinging through her. He froze, clearly unsure.

Slowly, she removed her tunic, her skin pebbling as the breeze danced across it. She held it out to him. "You said you would wash it."

"Larkin?" he breathed, his gaze devouring her.

"Are you going back on your word?" She said it like a challenge.

He balled up both their tunics along with the soap and tossed them to shore. His heavy hands rested on her hips. "Never."

The kiss trembled with promise—a promise that wrapped around them both. It solidified, growing heavy and ripe. She traced the irony of his body—all hard softness interrupted with knotted scars and raised sigils.

He pulled her flush against him and deepened the kiss. "Your mother will be coming."

In answer, she hooked the front of his trousers and pulled them deeper into the mist, the rushing water pounding past them. Supposedly, the pipers had herbs to prevent pregnancy. Larkin didn't have them. But that didn't mean they couldn't do other things.

So they did. So many beautiful, awkward things.

Larkin wrung out her tunic as best she could. Denan leaned over and kissed her bare shoulder. She smiled at him.

"Denan?" Talox called from somewhere out of sight.

Larkin froze and then hurriedly tugged her sloppy tunic over her head.

"Denan," Talox called louder. "It can't wait."

"The forest take him." Her voice was rough. "Because if it doesn't, I will."

"What?" Denan growled loudly to Talox.

"It's the king," Talox said. "He's here."

Larkin tugged on her trousers. "What's the king doing here?" She shivered, though it wasn't cold.

Denan gave a sharp shake of his head. "I have no idea."

They gathered their things and headed down the path. At the second pool, Larkin tried very hard not to notice the abundance of naked men whooping and cavorting.

His own shirt damp, Talox waited for them, his expression sheepish. "He's in the pavilion."

Denan pushed past Talox without a word. Halfway down, they passed Mama with the little ones. One of the pages held the baby. Mama covered Sela's eyes against the soldiers' nakedness.

"Aren't you going to help me keep an eye on your sister?" Mama asked in exasperation as Larkin passed her. Her eyes were bloodshot and lined with dark circles. Had Brenna let her get any sleep?

"My page will tend the little ones while you bathe," Denan said with a pointed look at the boy, who looked uncomfortable but nodded anyway.

"Go far enough into the mist and no one can see you," Larkin said over her shoulder.

Mama called after Larkin, who ignored her. She would pay for this later. Nothing to do about that now.

At the pavilion, four guards stood at each corner. Inside, King Netrish paced back and forth. Middle-aged and portly, he looked more like a tavern keeper than the powerful king his embossed mantle declared him to be. This was the man who sentenced Bane to die—the only man in the Alamant more powerful than Denan. He was the reason she'd been forced to take Bane and flee. The sooner Denan's magic came into full power and he could ascend to the throne, the sooner this man would be a relic.

Denan bowed. "My king?"

Netrish's expression landed on Larkin, at her tunic dripping a fat circle around her feet, and his mouth tightening with disapproval.

"I've received word of Gendrin's company." Netrish handed Denan a missive. "His runners couldn't get through the mulgars to reach you, so they came to me in the city. I managed to slip away with half a dozen of my best pipers."

Denan opened the seal. "Where is he?"

Netrish leaned over a map pinned to a small table and pointed to a patch of trees south of Landra and Cordova, the two cities on the northwesternmost tip of the United Cities of the Idelmarch. Denan and Talox clustered around the king.

"Ancestors, what is Gendrin doing there?" Denan scanned the missive.

"A half dozen men slipped through where a single scout couldn't? That doesn't make any—" Talox began.

"Ancestors save us!" Denan handed the missive to Talox, who read quickly.

Larkin wished she could read more than the few letters and small words Denan had taught her.

Netrish stepped closer. "You must send your army at once. Demry's too."

"What's happening?" Larkin asked in a small voice.

Denan let out a long breath. "The mulgars—we didn't thin them. They doubled back to attack Gendrin's men."

She remembered the name. Bane's sister, Caelia, was married to Gendrin. Caelia, who didn't know that her brother was dead or that her husband was in grave danger.

Larkin held her hand over her mouth. "What is Gendrin's army doing so far from the Alamant?"

"The treaty is over," Netrish said.

She'd forgotten. The pipers were cursed to never have daughters. In order to fight against the wraiths, they had to have children. So in exchange for protection, the Black Druids secretly allowed women to be taken. But since the Idelmarch had declared war on the Alamant ...

Larkin covered her throat with her hand. "Gendrin and his army ... they're taking girls."

Netrish huffed. "A reaping is a natural consequence of breaking the treaty."

"Reaping?" Larkin asked.

Denan met her gaze. "Usually, only those chosen by the White Tree go in search of their heartsong. During a reaping, all men can."

The time her villagers had tried to burn the forest ... the perpetrators had been found dead without a mark on them, and two dozen girls had gone missing.

Larkin rocked forward, hand on her forehead. Ancestors. It had been a reaping. And now it was happening again, all over the Alamant. How many girls were being kidnapped by pipers, never to see their families again?

"This ... this violence has to end." Larkin's voice shook with emotion. For kidnapping and forcing girls was violence, whether done gently or not. "The Idelmarchians and the Alamantians—we're not enemies. The wraiths are our enemies." Somehow, she must make both sides see this.

Denan turned away from the accusation in her eyes. "Tomorrow. I'll send my armies to rescue Gendrin tomorrow."

Netrish stepped closer. "They won't last the night. You know they won't."

"As long as they maintain their perimeter—" Denan began.

"Their perimeter has already fallen once!"

"I have women and wounded to protect!"

"You have your woman!" Netrish roared. "There are over five hundred women with that company—terrified girls who are all going to die so you can protect your own wife!

"Send Larkin and the wounded on to the Alamant," the king went on. "I'll go on ahead and sally forth with a company to bring them in. My guess is that the wraiths won't bother a small company of wounded when they have an entire army they can obliterate."

"You don't understand," Denan said. "This is a trap."

"Trap?" Netrish said in disbelief. "What trap?"

Larkin had spent one terrifying night high in a tree while the wraiths circled. These girls would know ten times that fear. "Denan—"

Denan slapped the table, causing her to jump. "The Wraith King is trying to draw us in, make us fight on his terms. He knows he can't defeat us from our strongholds. He won't let Larkin slip away—not again."

Netrish rocked back on his heels and eyed her. "Ramass has fixated on her?"

Denan nodded, and his gaze asked Larkin to tell the king the truth. Her look begged him to let this slide. She didn't trust Netrish. Denan nodded again, more insistently this time.

Talox cleared his throat. "Too many have seen it for the secret to remain much longer, Larkin."

Reluctantly, she flared her sigils. The sword and shield formed in her hands.

Netrish gasped and staggered back. "Ancestors save us, she has magic!"

"Now you see." Denan rubbed his eyes, his exhaustion momentarily getting the better of him. "If Ramass senses Larkin, he and his fellows will form near her and take her. A small company wouldn't stand a chance fending them off."

"She can't flee to the Alamant," Netrish agreed. "Not without a sizeable army."

Denan braced himself against the table. He and Talox examined the map. "The gully Gendrin is surrounded in is a death trap for any army caught inside it. Ramass is forcing me to abandon Gendrin or meet his army in the time and place of his choosing. Even if we do manage to defeat the wraiths, that adds an extra two nights in the Forbidden Forest—two nights in which he attacks us."

The Wraith King had realized Denan's forces were too strong to overpower unless he gave himself an advantage.

Netrish cleared the emotion from his throat. "He's my son, Denan."

Larkin slipped over to Talox. "Who's his son?" she murmured.

"Gendrin," Talox said, his eyes never shifting from the map.

How had Larkin not known Caelia's husband was the king's son?

"I could command you," Netrish said without feeling.

Denan rose to his full height and faced the other man down. "You may be king, but I am commander of these armies. And now you know the stakes. We can't risk her."

Netrish didn't meet Denan's gaze. "You think your men will follow you in abandoning their fellows and those women?"

Denan gestured wildly. "You think they'll forgive me if I let the only woman in three hundred years to possess the magic fall into wraith hands? I don't fight battles unless I'm confident I can win."

"We do what we must," Larkin repeated his mantra. He flinched, clearly not liking the idiom thrown in his face any more than she did. "You're a prince. You put your people first."

He breathed out in frustration. "Larkin, you need to understand the risk in this. No matter how well prepared or how superior our forces, battles are unpredictable beasts."

"You'll keep me safe. As you always do."

He scrubbed his hand over his head. "I don't see how."

"I know this gully." Talox tapped the map for emphasis. "It's narrow and steep. Surround him as he surrounds Gendrin."

Denan folded his arms over his chest. "And what of Larkin and our wounded? They won't be able to keep up with us—not at the pace we'll be forced to set. And if Ramass has reserves hidden somewhere in the woods, a small group would be vulnerable."

"Place the women and wounded at the top of that outcropping of rocks on the southeast side." Talox touched the map near the gully.

"The promontory?" Denan asked.

Talox nodded. "There's only one way in—a narrow pass, easily guarded. The rest is sheer cliffs."

Denan leveled him with a look. "Going after Gendrin would add two nights to our journey. Two nights for the wraiths to attack."

Larkin studied the map, noting how close Gendrin's army was to the Idelmarch. "Not if we travel Cordova Road."

Denan looked between them, a betrayed expression on his face. "You want us to invade the Idelmarch?"

Larkin hadn't been able to save Bane—not yet anyway—but perhaps she could face Caelia if she saved her husband. "Just … borrow the road for a little while."

Talox nodded. "Cordova Road is an easy march from the gully."

She traced the road eastward to Cordova. "How far from Cordova to the Alamant?"

Denan pursed his lips. "A day's forced march."

After the battle was over, they could cross the remaining forest and camp on Idelmarchian land. "The people of Cordova won't have dampeners," she said.

Netrish nodded. "Free Gendrin's army and spend the next

night in the Idelmarch. March straight from there to the Alamant." He grasped Denan's forearm. "Bring my son back to
me."

Denan nodded. "I'll do my best."

Netrish clapped a hand on Denan's shoulder. "If I'm going
to make it back to the Alamant before nightfall, we need to
move." He bowed to them, his gaze lingering on Larkin before
he strode from the pavilion back into the rain.

Denan braced himself against the table. "Talox, a moment
alone."

Talox grunted and left.

Denan waited until both men were both out of earshot.
"Larkin ..." He shook his head, as if searching for the right
words. "I don't think you understand—this won't be like the
other battles. It will be bloody and chaotic, and I can't guarantee
we'll win."

He was the one who would be fighting, and yet he was trying to prepare her, comfort her. He was leaving, she realized, and
he wasn't sure he'd be coming back.

"I pushed you into this. If something happens to you—"

He reached out, his hand encircling the back of her head. He
cradled her against him. "It's the right decision with the
knowledge we have. But the Wraith King will be waiting with
everything he has, and Larkin ..." His voice trailed off, his grip
tightening until it was almost painful. "I'm afraid."

She clutched him. He was alive and strong and hers. But by
nightfall, all that could change. "I love you."

Denan pressed his forehead to hers, his eyes bright. "No
matter what happens, I will come for you," he said roughly.

She sobbed, tears spilling down her cheeks. "Always."

He pressed his lips to her forehead, turned on his heel, and
trotted down the steps. He paused beside Talox. "You will keep
her safe, soldier."

"I swear it." Talox came to stand beside her.

Denan strode away. Dripping wet, Tam came jogging from the direction of the springs. Denan called for his captains and pages and flung out orders for the army to march double time back to the west. Tam shot them a questioning glance before falling in beside Denan.

Larkin turned away. She refused to watch Denan go. It hurt too much.

CHAPTER

BETRAYAL

"N early there," Talox said with a glance at the sun dipping toward the horizon. Sela hung off his back. "Praise my ancestors," Mama panted.

Larkin worried for her mother. She'd hardly spoken at all that day. Every time they'd stopped to rest, she'd lain down and fallen asleep.

Sweating under the wrap holding Brenna to her, Larkin pressed on through pine and rocky soil. Half an hour later, the three of them passed beyond a narrow fissure of rocks to a flat expanse that rose up sharply into the sunset.

The promontory. Larkin breathed a sigh of relief. They'd made it.

Coming up beside them, Magalia set down her end of the stretcher. The man inside had lost his left hand, the bandage bloody. She knelt next to the man and checked his forehead. "Still no fever. I told you I was the best healer in the Alamant."

He gave her a weak smile. "And the prettiest."

As a widow, she was also one of the few single women he would ever meet. Pretty as she was, Magalia probably had a new proposal every week. She rolled her eyes, and he chuckled.

More pipers filed in. Magalia directed them to lay the wounded in neat rows. The healers immediately set about caring for their patients. Larkin, Sela, and Mama passed out water, food, and blankets.

Of the three hundred or so men who'd accompanied them, fifty men remained behind to guard the fissure. The rest departed at a fast clip to catch up to the main army.

Two soldiers passed Larkin carrying something made of sacred wood—symbols had been carved all along the surface.

"What are those?" she asked Talox.

Talox glanced at them. "The wards. They'll set them out along the periphery."

Magalia sidled up to Larkin. "What do we do about her?"

Larkin followed her gaze to find Maisy scampering up a tree. She instantly looked for Sela, who was too busy handing out food to have noticed, and let out a breath of relief.

"Leave her be if you can," Larkin murmured. She realized she didn't know much about Magalia. "Where are you from?"

"Landra," Magalia said. "My father was a merchant."

"Do you miss him?" Larkin asked.

Magalia's movements slowed. "There are many people I miss." At Larkin's pitying look, Magalia smiled sadly. "I wouldn't change it any more than you would."

They both fell silent, the camaraderie of a common trauma binding them together.

"Larkin, Pennice, Sela, let's go," Talox said from behind her. "I want you all in a tree before sunset."

The guards from their first night—Dayne, Ulrin, and Tyer—flanked him.

"The healers need help," Larkin said. "And besides, you have the wards to keep the wraiths off."

"You want to help the wounded? You do that by getting in a tree." Talox motioned for the guards to follow him ahead.

Mama wasn't far behind. "Larkin, bring Sela."

Sela trotted up to Larkin and gripped her hand.

Magalia took the rest of the blankets from Larkin. "We're nearly done anyway. Go on."

Larkin frowned. "It's not fair that we have the safety of a tree and you don't."

Magalia shrugged as if it didn't matter. "I suppose that's just the way it is. Some people have magic and some don't."

Frustration welled in Larkin. "It won't always be that way. The curse can be removed—I'm proof that it can. We just have to figure out how to do it."

Sela looked between the two. She let go of Larkin's hand and motioned for Magalia to bend down. Shooting Larkin a confused look, Magalia crouched. Sela rested both her palms on Magalia's shoulders and seemed to peer deep in her chest.

Magalia gasped and fell backward. Eyes wide, she gaped at Sela. "What— What did you do to me?"

Sela cowered, ran to Larkin, and jumped into her arms.

Larkin staggered under the onslaught. "What do you mean?"

Magalia pressed her hand to her chest and breathed out. "Something cold and dark was inside me. I didn't even know it was there until she took it away."

Eyes wide, Larkin looked down at her sister. The last of the sunlight lit her downy hair—just like it had the day Larkin had found Sela inside the forest everyone else was terrified of.

She'd been covered in mud and grinning, a fistful of flowers in her hair. *"The trees are our friends."* Sela had said those words then, and she'd said them again when Larkin found her in the arbor ring mere days ago.

It was Sela.

Sela who'd Denan found first.

Sela who'd tried to go into the forest again because the trees were singing to her.

Sela who'd rested her hands on Larkin's shoulders. Warmth and light had flooded her where before there had been darkness.

A thousand little clues. Larkin had missed or dismissed all of them. All the while, the truth had been right in front of her.

Sela had broken the curse.

Not Larkin.

Never Larkin.

Larkin couldn't catch her breath. A dark, ugly feeling took root inside her. For a while, she had thought she was special. She wasn't. It had always been Sela—her sweet, lisping little sister. She was breathing hard, and she thought she might be sick.

Magalia pushed to her feet, her hand out. "Larkin, what did she—"

Larkin's glare stopped her in her tracks. She became aware of Sela trembling and sweating in her arms. This was her sister, her little sister, whom Larkin loved with everything she had.

"Larkin!" Talox barked, gesturing from the top of the promontory.

"I don't know," Larkin answered Magalia's question. "But I'll figure it out. Just promise not to say a word to anyone until I have."

Mouth pursed in a thin line, Magalia nodded.

Larkin turned and started up the hill. Sela shifted in her arms. Larkin rubbed a shaking hand over her little back, the knobs of her spine bumping under her fingers. "Don't be scared, Sela," Larkin breathed, because she could not bear for the truth to be spoken any louder than a whisper. "You've done a wonderful thing. A truly wonderful thing."

Sela looked up at her doubtfully.

Larkin forced herself to smile. "I'm so proud of you." And she was, even as tears filled her eyes.

At the peak of the promontory, Talox waited beside the

largest trees. Larkin's pod had been set up in one, her mother and sister's in the other. Her mother was already in the one on the right. Thankfully, the trees were far enough away that they would have to shout to hear each other.

When she reached the top, Talox noted the tears streaking down her cheeks.

She didn't meet his gaze. "Can you take Sela to Mama?"

He nodded. Larkin pressed a quick kiss to Sela's temple and handed her over. Sela went willingly. She'd clearly grown attached to the big man along their journey. Larkin wiped her cheeks and climbed the tree. Tyer was in the lower branches, and she was relieved when he pretended not to notice her.

In the middle branches, she collapsed into her pod and sobbed hard and silent, one of the blankets stuffed in her mouth. Sometime later, the branches shifted as Talox climbed up. He had to notice her pod shaking with her sobs, but he didn't say anything.

When the tears passed, she sat up. Her nose and eyes felt swollen, and no doubt her face was a blotchy mess, but it wasn't like the two men didn't already know she'd been crying.

Gathering her courage, she emerged from the pod. Below, Tyer had rested his bow across his knees, his arrows within easy reach. Talox sat sideways in his own pod, telescope in hand. He didn't say anything as she climbed out of her pod and joined him in his, their sides pressed hard together.

Larkin peered down into the deep, narrow gully surrounded by rocky outcroppings and strangled trees. Less than a mile away, Gendrin's army had been surrounded and forced well behind their initial defenses, a burned-out ring of ash and broken pikes. Bodies littered the ground. She was grateful to be far enough away she couldn't make out their faces.

Shapes shifted along the distant ridges—Denan and Demry's armies moving into place. Worry spiked through her.

Talox pulled out a pouch of dried meat and held it out to

her. There would be no fires and no cooking—not tonight—but the smell of their supper made her stomach turn. She shook her head.

Denan was down there. As was Tam. And she'd been crying because she wasn't special anymore.

"You want to talk about it?" Talox asked around a mouthful.

She shook her head again.

"Fair enough." Talox handed her a telescope and peered down his own.

Larkin cut a glance to the sun, orange dissected in half by black. When the wraiths appeared, they'd instantly sense Denan's army and know that he meant to surround them.

"Will they be in place before sunset?" Her voice sounded rough, disused.

Talox hesitated before shaking his head.

Larkin surveyed the steep sides of the wide gully—easily three miles wide and a mile long. "Even so, they won't be able to escape."

Talox didn't answer.

Unable to sit, Larkin stood and wrapped one arm around the main trunk for balance. She peered down the telescope. It took her a moment to locate Gendrin's army. Then she found what she was looking for. High in the trees, girls huddled together.

She wasn't watching the sunset, but she knew when it happened. She was always aware of the position of the sun now, whether she consciously realized it or not.

"One, two, three, four," Talox counted.

Larkin didn't have to ask to know he counted wraiths. Her clothes were damp with perspiration—she'd grown chilled with immobility.

Larkin lowered the telescope. It was good for gauging details, but if she wanted a sense of the overall battle, it was too confining. Watching the battle with her bare eyes and using the telescope for details was the best way to go.

She counted as Talox had but became distracted by the battle, which had moved to the base of the trees. Wanting more detail, she lifted the telescope again.

Two mulgars boosted a third into the lower branches, who climbed, his gaze fixed on the girls who scrambled higher, the tree bending beneath their weight, their mouths opened in screams Larkin couldn't distinguish from the din.

A piper jumped into the tree and hauled himself up. When he was close enough, he hooked the mulgar's leg with the ax heel and jerked. The mulgar clawed at the girls as he fell. The soldier tied back his ax and released an arrow. Overrun, pipers scrambled into the trees to protect the girls.

"Hurry, Denan," she murmured.

In the dying light, shapes moved along the rim on the opposite side. She shifted the telescope for a better look. The mulgars and wraiths hadn't noticed them. Why hadn't the wraiths sensed them yet?

With a shout, the pipers rose up and charged down the decline. Larkin searched for Denan, but she couldn't distinguish him from any other solider.

Moving as one, the mulgars turned from their prey trapped inside the trees and charged toward Denan and Demry's men. The pipers' archers hung back. The moment the mulgars were within range, they loosed arrows. Mortally wounded, some mulgars fell. Bristling with arrows, the rest continued.

In the dying light, the four wraiths glided like shadows up the incline. Piper archers took aim with bows and sacred arrows, the wood refracting light in a dazzling array. The archers released. One wraith dropped immediately. One limped on. The third staggered one way and then the other. The fourth was uninjured.

"That's impossible," Larkin breathed.

Pulling himself up, Talox swore, confirming what Larkin already knew. Wraiths didn't limp. They didn't collapse. They faded. When dealt a mortal blow, they imploded into writhing shadows. But one was clearly on the ground. Two others were clearly injured.

They weren't wraiths at all. They were mulgars.

Before Larkin could make sense of it, the mulgars reached the fires meant to keep them out and grabbed burning branches with their bare hands. They threw those branches into nearby trees—trees that held girls and pipers. The rest carried burning branches up the incline toward Denan and Demry's men.

"No," Talox whispered, aghast. "Wraiths and mulgars never harm the trees."

Heedless of the pipers cutting them down, mulgars set fire to more trees. One mulgar, then two, then a dozen became torches themselves. They continued running, flames trailing. Trees caught fire, driving pipers higher, trapping Gendrin's men and those helpless girls.

"Why?" Larkin asked. The evil dark sliding up her spine answered her question. Her mouth filled with the dirt and rot of the grave and something else—something like pitch and smoke.

"Larkin," a wraith chittered from somewhere out of sight. The voice echoed strangely, making it impossible to tell how close it was.

Nostrils flared, Talox lifted a finger to his lips; the wraith couldn't sense them from the trees. All she had to do was remain still. Larkin prayed Mama and her sisters stayed utterly silent.

The wards are in place, she reminded herself. *We're safe.* Still, doubt wormed its way inside her. She looked back at the wounded men and healers. There were fifty pipers left to guard the pass. Surely they had sacred arrows. Surely they could keep everyone safe from a wraith weakened by the wards.

"Come," the wraith said. "And I will spare your pipers."

Something wrenched inside her. "Talox," she mouthed.

He shook his head, mouthing, "Lies."

He thought she meant to give herself up. "Fire," she mouthed back. "What if they set the tree on fire?"

She didn't know if he understood her. Talox searched the ground and smoothly withdrew a sacred arrow. She spared a glance back at the battle. The pipers were no longer fighting mulgars but the flames that could easily destroy them all.

Movement below. Tyer loosed an arrow at something climbing the cliff face—something climbing a rope. Before she could wonder how a rope got there, a mulgar appeared, a flickering torch in his mouth, half his face eaten by flames. The arrow had embedded in the mulgar's shoulder but didn't stop him. More mulgars appeared. From the other tree, Dayne and Ulrin loosed as well.

"Breech!" Talox cried.

Before the pipers guarding the fissure could take more than a dozen steps toward them, two wraiths slithered into being and began laying waste to the injured. The men guarding the entrance shouted in alarm.

"Talox!" She pointed.

Growling in frustration, Talox continued releasing on the dozen mulgars climbing over the cliffs and running toward their tree. Each bore a torch nearly extinguished by the speed of their passing.

"Bring them down," Talox cried. He and the other three guards sighted and loosed arrows. A dozen mulgars and their torches fell, flames skittering along the dead needles littering the ground. Some staggered forward, injured but still moving.

Only one remained uninjured—a woman. She was matted and filthy. Her gaze fixed on the tree with a single-minded determination. She darted through bushes, arrows embedded in the trees and dirt around her. One hit her arm. Another her side. Another her leg. She didn't even slow.

"Kill her!" Talox roared.

An arrow bloomed from her chest. Her expression didn't

change as her body faltered. She threw the torch as she collapsed. Time slowed as it spun end over end, the flames disap-
pearing. It struck the heart of the tree. Flames exploded unnaturally fast along the trunk.

Heat roared up at Larkin. She choked on smoke.

"They've doused it in pitch," Tyer shouted.

That explained the smoky, acrid smell of before.

"Move!" Talox gripped the back of Larkin's neck, forcing
her down through heat and smoke.

Coughing and unable to see, Larkin fumbled for hand and
foot holds. Flames licked at her feet.

"Jump!" Talox said. She had no idea how far the ground
was or whether she would break both her legs when she landed,
only that the wraith waited below.

She hesitated too long. Talox wrapped his arm around her
and jumped, dragging her with him. They slammed through
burning branches. The ground rushed toward them. She landed
hard on her belly, her lungs frozen. The pain in her bruised ribs
flared hot. Embers fell around her.

Tyer was already on his feet, fighting a wraith—the woman,
Hagath. She moved preternaturally fast, her swords trailing
shadows like dark flames. Tyer's back arched, his mouth open
and his eyes wide with shock. He dropped to his knees, his
sword slipping from his fingers, and collapsed.

Talox launched at Hagath, shifted to avoid her thrust, and
batted at her with his sword.

"You don't defeat a wraith—not alone." Talox's words
echoed through her. Heat bore down on her. She gasped in a
wisp of air, enough to fight back the encroaching darkness. Another strangled breath, and she managed to drag her hands under
her. Another breath. The smell of burning hair—her hair. Another.

She staggered to her feet and flared her sigils, her sword and
shield forming in her hands. As though Hagath could sense her

magic, the wraith's head whipped in her direction.

"Mine," another wraith hissed. Amid the carnage of the wounded, Ramass slid up the incline toward her. An involuntary whimper clawed up her throat.

"Run, Larkin!" Talox cried as he stabbed Hagath. Writhing shadows imploded. "Find a tree and hide!"

No sooner had he said the words than Ramass attacked him, every strike brutal and efficient. Talox countered a beat too slow. Ramass knocked his sword from his hands and kicked at Talox's chest, knocking him flat.

Talox—that immovable giant of a man—defeated. Ramass lifted his sword.

No. No. "No!" she screamed. She lunged, standing protectively over Talox, and jabbed. Ramass easily blocked it. The moment Larkin's magic blade connected with his, oily shadows skittered down her magic. She felt the wraith's hunger. Its need.

For her.

The wraith slashed. Larkin barely managed to block with her shield. He kicked her feet out from under her, and she fell onto her backside. He gathered himself for the next strike.

Why had Larkin ever thought she could fight against these monsters?

Talox attacked from the right, his shield slamming the wraith back, forcing him to turn. "Run!"

Below, the pipers fought wraiths and mulgars. Her mother and sisters were still safe in their tree. At least, until the fire spread. Larkin couldn't save her family, but she could draw the wraiths away.

Her feet skittered across loose needles as she scrambled away from heat and living shadows to the edge of the promontory. There, she found one of the ropes the mulgars had used to climb up half buried in dirt. They'd been here before they'd climbed the promontory.

The wraiths had known they were coming. How could they

have possibly known?

Her hands closed around the fibers as she dropped into the falling dark.

Alone.

CHAPTER 11

SHADOW

L arkin's foot touched solid ground at the base of the promontory. Her raw hands released the rope—a rope that never should have been there. She staggered back, her shoulders and arms on fire.

Ready for anything, she pivoted and flared her weapons so they barely shone. In the time it had taken her to climb down, full night had come on, the stars distant pinpricks of useless light beneath the dense canopy and thick smoke. A mulgar could be a mere handful of steps away, and she would never know.

And what about Mama and Sela and Brenna? Denan? All the people she'd left behind? All the pipers fighting the fires. She choked on a sob.

No.

She was not helpless, and she was not finished—not yet. If a mulgar or wraith had been lying in wait, it would have attacked already. Denan and his army were before her. If she kept moving, she'd run into them eventually, providing the fire hadn't driven them out yet. If the wraiths found her before then, she would take to the trees and pray they didn't burn it down. And if all that failed, she would fight.

Hands out, she felt her way through the pitch dark toward the distant glow of fire. Smoke irritated her throat. Wrapping her shirt around her mouth, she fought the urge to cough. The rough, uneven ground forced her to slide her foot forward one careful step at a time.

She had no idea how many steps she'd taken when she stepped wrong and turned her ankle. Gritting her teeth, she limped on, even as it swelled tight and hot in her boot.

The ground beneath her feet sloped downward. Rising smoke blocked out the stars, the fire beneath making its rolling underbelly glow. That meant she was moving closer to the fires and the pipers. She hoped.

Shapes became defined in the dark—the messy tangle of branches, leaves, and needles and the sharp demarcation of upright trunks. She must be getting closer to the fire.

Distant, indistinguishable voices sounded to her left. She choked on a sob that was instantly silenced by the smell of old rot upwind of her—between her and safety.

Her mouth opened in a silent gasp. So close. She'd come so agonizingly close.

Steps quiet, she found a tree with low-hanging branches. Her arms had more strength than her legs. She pulled herself up one branch and then another. She had no idea how high she was, but her arms were shaking so hard she feared they wouldn't hold her weight.

She draped herself over a branch and tried not to breathe. Her ankle throbbed with each beat of her heart, the skin stretched tight and hot. She only had to hide until morning. Surely she could make it that long.

She wasn't sure how long she lay motionless, even as a spider skittered across her face and into her hair. A voice called for her—a familiar voice.

"Larkin," Venna whispered in a high, terrified whisper. "Larkin, help me."

No. Venna was dead. She'd jumped off a cliff—the wide, churning river so far below it had only been a dark ribbon. She couldn't have survived.

But perhaps a mulgar could.

Their words are poison, Larkin reminded herself.

"The wraiths released me. As they released Maisy. Please, Larkin, I've been wandering for days, and I'm afraid."

There was only one way Venna could have found Larkin, and that's if the wraiths had sent her. The creatures must have lost Larkin, but they knew she hid somewhere nearby.

Morning. I just have to make it until morning.

"I have been to Valynthia, Larkin. I have seen the truth of the wraiths. I know how to defeat the curse."

Despite herself, Larkin found herself listening as Venna sang.

Blood of my heart, marrow my bone,
Come hear the saddest story e'er known.
A cursed queen, her lover lost,
A forbidden magic and dreadful cost.

Consumed by evil, agents of night,
Seek the nestling, barred from flight,
Midst vile queen's curse of thorny vine,
Fear not the shadow, for you are mine.

In my arms, the answer lie:
A light that endures so evil may die.

The same song Sela had sung.

Venna's lovely voice drifted to silence. Her shadowed silhouette appeared, weaving through the trees three dozen paces ahead.

"The answer is in the song." Venna sang again:

In my arms, the answer lie:
A light that endures so evil may die.

My arms. The Curse Queen's arms? But Eiryss had been dead for three centuries!

"I know you think I'm a mulgar, that I'm trying to trick you. I'm not. You must come with me, Larkin. You must break the curse."

In the silence, Larkin's breaths thundered in her ears. Surely the wraiths could hear her pulse drumming in the night. She ached for a glimpse of her friend, even if she was a mulgar. Just to see her face again—she'd forgotten it, Larkin realized. The features lost to time.

"You are wise to remain hidden, to suspect us." A new voice echoed through the dark, along with the twisting sense of wrongness and the smell of an opened grave. "I can sense your presence." He drew a thick breath. "I can smell your fear."

He stepped between two trees not a dozen paces to her right, moving toward her like a dog on the scent. He opened his hand, revealing a tiny lampent, the light unable to penetrate the weightless shadows that shifted around him against the wind. He reached out a mailed hand and beckoned to Venna.

She stepped into the light, the tined shadows etched in her face and the black nothingness of her eyes wrenching deep inside Larkin. He tucked the lampent behind her ear and shifted behind her. His hand wrapped around her fragile jaw.

The shadows seeped from her eyes and skin into his hand. Her eyes cleared, turning the gentle brown Larkin remembered. Venna blinked once, twice, then rapidly. "Talox," she whispered. She began to cry.

"I can give her back," the wraith murmured. "I will give them all back. If only you will come with me."

Larkin wanted to stuff her fist in her mouth and cover her ears. She dared not move. *Poison. Poison. Poison. Poison. His words are poison.*

"All of them in exchange for you, Larkin. Am I not generous?"

Larkin ached to block out his words, to keep the sob tucked tight in her throat. *Loyalty and self-preservation. Poisonous lies.* Even if he kept his word and gave all the mulgars back, they would be like Maisy, mad and unable to care for themselves.

"No?" He stepped closer to Venna. "Perhaps I shall remove her curse and take her home with me. She would make an excellent pet, would she not? The sound of her screams would be ... stimulating."

Venna whimpered. There came the sharp scent of urine.

The forest take him! Larkin pushed up. She would die or she would kill him. Either way, she wouldn't bear another moment of him torturing her friend. She dropped to the ground before him.

The wraith suddenly whipped around to look behind him. A sacred arrow stirred the shadows past his head, barely missing him. Tucked behind his shield, Talox slammed into the wraith, throwing him back. Venna fell to the ground with a scream. Talox grabbed his ax and bore down on the wraith, striking with a determination the wraith could only retreat from. Larkin rushed to Venna's side and turned her over.

"Kill her!" Talox cried. "Before it's too late."

It was already too late. Her eyes were black nothingness. She lunged at Larkin. The two rolled through the forest floor, something hard smacking into Larkin's ribs. She gasped, her arms losing their strength. Venna whipped behind Larkin. Her legs wrapped around Larkin's waist, her arm around Larkin's neck.

Stars exploded across Larkin's vision, light eaten away by dark bursts that grew.

No.

She would not fail Venna again. She flared her magic, the sword and shield giving off a faint light. She swung her shield above her head. It connected. Venna's grip loosened just enough for Larkin to twist. Her sword came up and in, pushing into Venna's soft middle.

Larkin swore she could taste Venna's fresh bread slathered with butter and strawberry jam. A strangled groan slipped from Venna's lips. Larkin gasped on a sob.

Venna crawled back, one hand gripping her stomach, black blood pouring between her fingers. Her friend was still in there somewhere. But she couldn't want to live like this. Larkin stepped forward and pulled back her arm to strike.

A rushing sound. Larkin turned as the wraith imploded, his shadows flailing in his death throes. The oppressive evil was gone, though the smell lingered. Talox gasped and stumbled a few steps before falling to his backside.

Larkin hurried to his side. "Are you all right?"

"Did you kill her?" he panted.

Larkin winced and looked back, to the place Venna had been. The girl was gone.

The light take her, she had her friend's black blood on her hands. She crouched down and scrubbed the back of her hands with dirt so hard they bled.

"I don't— I don't know. Maybe."

Talox hunched around his drawn knees and sobbed.

Larkin had thought nothing could be worse than stabbing Venna, but seeing Talox like this was just as bad. "Talox," she snapped. Her own eyes were dry, the pain distant. But if he kept it up, she would lose it too. And then they would both die.

She reached down, hauled him to his feet, and shook him. "How many wraiths are still out there?"

Choking down his sobs, he wiped his streaming eyes and grabbed the lampent, as it was now full night. "Just Vicil." He limped a couple of steps before his gait settled to normal.

Relieved he was moving, she fell in behind him. "The other wraiths?"

"Gone, I think."

"Shouldn't we hide?"

He headed toward the smoke lit up from below by fire. "Not if mulgars are burning trees."

Mulgars never harmed the trees was one of the proverbial laws of the Forbidden Forest, and it had been broken. Why?

They trekked through the forest, the lampent lighting their way. Talox set a grueling pace. Exhausted as she was, she struggled to keep up as they climbed a hill. "How much farther?"

"Just to the top of the ridge." Something was off with his voice. She looked closer. His ashen face shone with sweat. And he hunched to one side.

A wave of cold heat washed through her. "Talox," she breathed.

Ignoring her, he limped the last dozen steps to the ridge. Half a mile distant, the pipers fought mulgars and fire at the base of the gully. Talox's knees buckled, and he dropped with a muffled groan. "Running has made the poison spread faster. I can't— I can't go any farther."

By the distant light of the fire, she could see the wound through his torn trousers—a wound that dripped black, tined lines snaking up the back of his neck.

The wraith blade had cut him. And when the poisoned lines reached his eyes, he would become a mulgar. Just like Venna.

A sob tore through her. "Oh, Talox. No."

He bowed his head. "Tell Denan I kept my promise."

She knelt before him. "There has to be something I can do. My magic—"

He pushed the crushed lampent into her hands, though it

was bright enough with the fire not to need it. "If you ever find me as ... as one of them, promise me you won't hesitate."

The forest take her. "I-I promise."

He pushed her away from him and drew his bow, laying it across his legs and reaching for his arrows. "Run, Larkin. Don't look back. I'll cover your retreat as long as I can."

The tined lines were already at his cheeks. Within minutes, perhaps seconds, they would reach his eyes, and he would become a mulgar. He would kill her.

Larkin turned on her heel and sprinted away from Talox—from the fate that awaited him. She ran from shadow and curses and broken men. Toward fire and death and blood, she ran.

The sense of wrongness came upon her sharply. The last wraith—a dozen steps to her right. A screech. She risked a glance behind her.

Vicil—his mantle of wicked thorns distinguished him from the others. She tried to run faster, harder, but she'd already pushed her body far beyond its limits. She struggled on, breath sawing out of her throat, her legs trembling hard. Another screech, so close the sense of wrongness enveloped her like an embrace from the dead.

She screamed. Below, pipers turned, so close she could see their startled expressions. Two dozen more strides and she would reach them.

Too late. The wraith shoved her. She crumpled, breath heaving in and out of her throat. Vicil loomed over her. She flared her magic and batted her sword at the hand that reached for her. He deflected, his fingers brushing against her skin like ice and fire and death.

The snap of Talox's bowstring. Something rushed through the center of Vicil, his shadows swirling around the sudden hole that opened up in his middle. The wraith screamed, his head thrown back. He was injured, but not yet dead.

Larkin knew how to fix that.

Using what little strength she had left, she swung her sword through his chest. Cutting through him was like cutting through mist. Her sword didn't even catch. He imploded, leaving a shadowy outline. Then he was gone as if he'd never been.

On the ridge, Talox wavered, convulsed. He rose to his feet, swayed, and shambled toward her. The Talox she knew was gone. If he caught up to her, one of them would kill the other.

A sob choking her, she scrambled to her feet and ran. An envoy of pipers rushed up the hill toward her. At the flash of colors on the ground, she bent down to snatch up the arrow Talox must have loosed through Vicil.

To save her life, he'd allowed himself to turn into a mulgar.

The pipers parted, enveloping her. She was safe. Swaying on her feet, she held the arrow close, the pain in her chest overwhelming her.

A hand on her shoulder. "Princess? Are you hurt, Princess?"

She took a deep breath and braced herself. "No." She looked up into the face of the piper standing over her, his brow furrowed with concern. She wavered, leaning against him for support. He reached for the arrow.

She jerked back. "No!" It was the last thing Talox had touched.

He eased back a step. "Why are you here instead of at the promontory?"

"Wraiths got inside the wards—I don't know how. I tried to lead them off."

He barked orders to a few of his men and led her deeper into the gully. The fire raged to the west. Denan's army shifted to the east. The last of the mulgars had been slaughtered. The commander—his name was Idin—led her to where the taken were being kept, half a dozen pipers playing songs to keep them calm.

Larkin balked, one hand wrapped around her dampener, the other around her amulet. "I want to be with Denan."

"This is the safest place in the army right now, Princess," Idin said. "Denan will come for you when he can." Having delivered her, he left again with his men.

The takens' clothes and hair were singed. Ash ringed their noses from breathing smoke. Even with the music, their eyes were wary and haunted.

Larkin wanted to collapse. Sleep. Instead, she steeled herself and approached one of the guards with a request for medical supplies.

She might not be the woman meant to break the curse, but she wasn't useless. She could at least help with the healing. He directed her to a healer who was already moving among the women.

She limped to him and wrapped the raw rope burns on her hands. Tucking the arrow in her belt, she moved among the women, assisting as he treated the worst burns by peeling away the dead skin, rinsing it, patting it dry, and bandaging it. The women didn't protest or react to the pain.

Some were pale and shaking. Those he directed to sit near the fires.

Their silence and dead eyes ... they reminded her of mulgars. So much so that she found it harder and harder to touch them, to look at them.

The rising sun was a bloodred drop in the gray-brown sky, when Larkin realized someone called her name. Had been for a while. Coughing against the thick smoke, she staggered to her feet and caught sight of Denan searching among the taken for her.

Alive. He was alive. Relief speared through her. She called out to him. He ran toward her. Her strength spent, she collapsed onto the ground.

Women ignored Denan completely as he wove through them to kneel before her. He gathered her into his arms. He reeked of smoke. He squeezed her aching, bruised body as if he'd never let her go.

"Ancestors, when I heard you were here ... But you're all right. You're all right." He kept repeating it as if to reassure himself.

He had found her. He was alive. Talox was not. She wrapped her arms around him and held on—her anchor in the storm. "My mother, Sela, and Brenna?"

"I sent Tam and my best men to fetch them. I'm sure they're fine."

They were fine. They must be. Talox was not.

She couldn't tell him.

She must tell him.

"When I heard the report, I thought the worst." He pulled back to look her over. "You're not hurt?"

It didn't matter.

"Larkin? What is it?" She shook her head, the words she must say tangling in her mouth. By the dark foreboding in his eyes, he already knew. "Talox?" he whispered.

His name drew a gasping cry from her. She handed him the arrow. "He kept his promise." His life for hers. Deep, wrenching sobs overtook her. Denan stared at the arrow, then at her. He shook his head, fighting the truth.

"I'm sorry. Oh, Denan."

"Is he dead?"

No. Not dead. Worse. "He's a mulgar."

He reeled back from her and lay, stunned. Then they sobbed together as day broke over the distant hill.

CHAPTER 12

REAPING

At the edge of the circle of taken, Larkin watched as the smoke cut off, the thick column shifting to rising tendrils.

"Fire never lasts long in the Forbidden Forest," Denan said.

When Larkin was a child, her village had set fire to the forest; it had snuffed out in hours. By doing so, her people had unknowingly broken the treaty between the pipers and druids. In retaliation, many girls were taken over the next week.

She stared at her lumpy porridge, nausea turning her stomach. A piper staggered past, his eyes bloodshot from crying. He didn't bother to climb the tree—just lay down with his sword and shield in hand and closed his eyes.

Denan's army was in no condition for another forced march. They would rest for the day in the forest and the night behind the safety of the barrier that protected Cordova Road. There, the only danger came from the armies of the Idelmarchians, led by druids. Even if they managed to muster their army to attack the interlopers, they'd never march on them before morning.

"What happened to Gendrin's army? The taken?" Her throat was raw from running and smoke.

"We didn't lose a single taken," Denan said.

"And Demry's men?"

"We saved so many. Thanks in no small part to you."

"Me?"

"Had you not insisted, I wouldn't have come back for them, my curse breaker." He reached out and squeezed her hand.

Curse breaker. She should tell him the truth: she'd never been the one the Alamantians had been searching for, the one the wraiths mistakenly hunted. But then she wouldn't be his curse breaker. He wouldn't look at her with pride and total belief. The words congealed in her throat.

"We have to make over thirty-five miles tomorrow. Eat." Denan tipped the bowl to his mouth and swallowed. He wiped his mouth with the back of his hand.

She forced a spoonful into her mouth—one after another until it was all gone. She became aware of Denan calling her name.

He held out his hand. "Here, I'll wash it."

He hurt every bit as much as she did, thanks to a slice across his ribs and a horrible bruise on his thigh, yet he was still taking care of her. "I need to soak my ankle."

Mouth pursed, he nodded and helped her limp to a nearby stream. She unlaced her boot and eased it off her foot. Her ankle was black and fat, the outline of her boot impressed on her skin. She lowered it into the water with a hiss while he rinsed out their bowls.

She washed her face and hands as best she could and lay back. As the cold water numbed her foot, she sighed in relief. She fell asleep like that, exhaustion pulling her under. A cry woke her with a start.

"Larkin!"

She woke from a deep sleep to find Mama bearing down on her. She hugged Larkin tight, the baby squirming in protest between them. Behind her, Tam held Sela's hand. Looking hollow-eyed, Dayne and Ulrin trailed behind him.

Tyer was dead, Larkin remembered with a start. Killed by wraiths in those first few moments after they'd all fallen out of their burning tree. Another life spent to protect her, the curse breaker. Guilt and shame ate through her like acid.

Trembling, Larkin eased her numb foot out of the river. Her face felt hot—sunburned, probably. She pushed her mother back to arm's length. She looked no worse for wear than she had the night before.

Mama sobbed. "I can't do this anymore! I can't!"

Even when their father had abandoned them and Mama had been giving birth as their home flooded from the swollen river, she'd never faltered. Now she broke down like a child.

In a way, her mother's distress was also Larkin's fault. By taking her family from the Idelmarch and the druids, Larkin had meant to protect them. Instead, she'd brought them into the midst of a war.

Mama rounded on Denan. "You said we would be safe on that promontory!"

He rubbed the sleep from his face and shot Ulrin and Dayne a look.

Ulrin picked Sela up. "Come on, Sela. Let's wash you up downstream, eh?"

Sela didn't protest as he carried her away. She was only four, and yet she was somehow communicating with the White Tree—something the Arbors of old had done. What would this mean for her sister? A four-year-old child. Far too young to bear the burden that had crushed Larkin. She had to tell them. The forest take her, this was Larkin's burden to bear, not Sela's!

Denan waited until they were out of earshot. "The wards have never failed us before."

"Just like the mulgars never burned trees or attacked during the day," Mama's voice vibrated with anger.

Denan pushed up and walked a few steps away, his back to them.

"None of this is his fault." Larkin said angrily.

Mama sank down and held her head in her hands.

"That was our last night in the forest." Larkin rubbed her mother's back.

"I smelled the wraiths, Larkin. Oh, ancestors, I *felt* them." Mama covered her mouth with her hand to stifle her sobs.

"We'll be in the Alamant in two days. It's the safest place there is. What about the others?" Larkin asked. "Magalia? Maisy?"

"Both fine," Tam said. "The wraiths left as soon as you did. Most of the others survived."

"What about the ropes?" Denan asked.

Tam frowned. "As far as I can tell, the ropes were carefully concealed before we ever arrived."

"And our wards?"

"One was broken," Tam said.

Denan swore. "The other three wards are nearly useless without the fourth."

"They knew where we would go," Larkin surmised.

Tam shrugged. "It was the best tactical position. They must have guessed."

Denan had warned her the wraiths would lay a trap for her, and they'd walked right into it.

Denan rose to his feet, drew Tam a few steps away, and murmured something.

"What?" Tam cried.

Denan shook his head.

"Ancestors." Tam gasped in a sobbing breath. "I should have been the one to stay behind. I'm better with the bow." He roared in frustration and kicked at a log once, twice, three times.

As much as Talox's loss hurt Larkin, it had to be so much worse for Tam and Denan. The three of them had been friends since childhood. How many memories, how many scraps had they survived together? Larkin had to look away. She couldn't bear her own pain, let alone anyone else's.

Mama frowned at Larkin's ankle. "Where else?"

"Bruises is all." Larkin cleared the lump building in her throat. "What happened to the Curse Queen after Valynthia fell?" She directed the question to the pipers.

Denan wiped the tears trailing through the soot on his cheeks. "Eiryss saved those she could and brought them to the safety the White Tree had created for them. She signed the original treaty with our last queen—Illin. Why?"

"Venna said the Curse Queen had the answers we need," Larkin said. "The answers about how to kill the wraiths."

"Poison, remember?" Denan said. "You can't trust anything or anyone tainted by wraiths."

Tainted … And yet Larkin was sure Venna had been trying to reach through the taint to reveal the truth.

Tam sniffed and wiped his eyes. "If the Curse Queen had answers, she would have defeated the curse long ago."

"It means something. I know it does." Larkin had a feeling she had all the pieces; she just needed to figure out how they fit together. Needing comfort, she reached for Brenna. Mama gave her up easily. Larkin laid the baby against her shoulder, her sweet breaths tickling her collarbone. She breathed deep the sweet baby smell.

How many times had she caught Talox doing this exact thing? He would have been a wonderful father, as Venna would have been a wonderful mother. Now they were both lost to the wraiths.

"When you're older," she murmured, "I will tell you stories of the man who saved my life."

Even enchanted by hundreds of pipers, the taken flinched as they passed through what the Idelmarchians called the stirring. The first time Larkin had crossed it, she'd seen melting trees snatching at her—an illusion meant to keep the Idelmarchians inside. It also acted as a barrier to keep the wraiths and mulgars out.

Thanks to her sister, Larkin only felt a cool wash, like passing through glass. Sela didn't react at all. Neither did Mama or Brenna.

Sela had lifted their curse as well.

"The barrier," Larkin said. "It will keep us safe."

Sela didn't seem to hear. Worse than not speaking, Sela had shown no emotion the entire day. She went where she was led without protest, ate the food placed in her mouth. She had seen the attack last night, watched the wraiths kill Tyer and dozens of other men. What did that do to a child?

Thankfully, Brenna was too young to remember any of this. She slept peacefully strapped to Mama's chest. For her part, Mama trekked on without complaint. She seemed numb and exhausted. They all were.

Tam took it the worst. He only spoke when spoken to, and then only in monosyllabic answers. Larkin missed his teasing and jokes, his smile. She often lost sight of him as he ranged ahead, though he always kept them in sight. She didn't know how Denan fared—he'd gone ahead with the scouts.

Moments before the sun set, nearly three thousand pipers and their captives invaded the United Cities of Idelmarch simply by stepping onto Cordova Road.

CHAPTER 13

INVASION

The Forbidden Forest ended abruptly, as if the trees dared not venture another branch closer to Cordova Road. Breathing a sigh of relief, Larkin stepped over oxen manure that littered the rutted road. Grass struggled to grow between cart ruts.

An eighth of a mile wide, the road led to the capital city of Landra two days away. To her right, it widened and curved out of sight, but she could make out chimney smoke, which indicated a good-sized town on the other side, which had to be Cordova.

A little way down, a farmer driving a cartload of pigs started and gave a shout. Shields out, three pipers bore down on him. He backed away, his gaze whipping from side to side. He must have realized he was hopelessly outnumbered and dropped to his knees, hands in the air.

He was bound and tucked beneath his own cart with a blanket around his shoulders. He was an Idelmarchian, as Larkin was. Did that make her a traitor to her own people? Or were the Alamantians her people now?

The farmer looked about in bewilderment and caught sight of them. His gaze lingered on their clothing—Mama and Sela dressed in their traditional skirts and shirts, while Larkin wore a tunic and trouser that were obviously too big for her.

"Can you help me?" He must have realized they were Idelmarchian.

Larkin had wandered close without meaning to. The forest take her, she should have stayed away. "They won't hurt you if you don't give them any reason to."

"Please," he begged.

Tugging on Sela's hand, Larkin turned her back on him and returned to her mother. It would be night soon. They needed to eat supper and set up camp.

Never far from them, Tam arranged sticks for their fire. He'd managed to shoot a grouse. Mama laid out the herbs and roots she'd gathered.

"We'll let him go come morning," Tam said. "We'll be as safe as if we were in the Alamant tonight. I promise."

He'd clearly misunderstood Larkin's discomfort. "And if the people of Cordova attack?" Ancestors save her, she didn't think she could stand them killing each other.

"They'll be asleep," Tam said.

Because his pipers would be putting them to sleep. But there was something about the way he wouldn't meet her gaze … like he was hiding something and feeling guilty. "You're taking girls. After nearly losing the last ones?"

Molding shredded bark in his hand, Tam turned away from her. "They won't even have one night in the Forbidden Forest."

She was going to be sick. "Tam …"

"We are reaping every unmarried woman who can survive the trek into the forest—all of them. Cordova was Demry's last stop."

"What?" Mama choked out in a thick voice.

Tam breathed out. "We've been cursed never to have daughters, but to keep fighting, we must have children. So we take wives."

Larkin's fists clenched with anger. Those weeks when Denan had hunted her—when she'd been driven into the forest and thought she would never see her family again—were the worst of her life.

Mama unstrapped Brenna and set about plucking the grouse. "This is wrong."

Larkin wanted to scream and rage, but she would not upset Sela—not after everything she'd been through and everything that was coming. "It's kidnapping," she said through clenched teeth. "It has to stop."

He snatched his bow. "What would you have us do, Larkin? The druids are the ones who had the gall to break our treaty altogether and start a war with us. And after we've been fighting three centuries to protect them from the wraiths!"

The forest take the druids and drop them in a gilgad nest, she thought bitterly.

He huffed in a breath and scrubbed his free hand over his curls. "If you want to be angry, be angry with them." He stormed off, paced at the edge of the forest, and muttered to himself. Even angry, he never let them out of sight.

Sela watched Tam pace, let go of Larkin's hand, and sat with her back to all of them. Larkin tried so hard to shield her sister from this, but it just wasn't possible.

Just when Larkin thought she'd forgiven the pipers, accepted that kidnapping girls was a forced necessity, something happened to break open the wound inside her. The hurt of being kidnapped would never go away, she realized. It could never really heal—not when it kept happening to other girls.

Kneeling, she emptied her satchel of the watercress she'd gathered at the stream and struck flint to steel, sparks dancing across the shredded bark Tam had left for her.

"The wraiths are the real enemy," Mama said. "If we weren't so busy fighting each other, we'd see that."

One of the sparks caught. Larkin held it up and blew. She fed it pine needles and then sticks. Pipers gathered at a bend in the road, out of sight of the town—lying in wait for the town to sleep so they could kidnap its girls, as Denan had lain in wait for her.

The terror and dread that had consumed her when Denan had first enchanted her hit her in full force. For days, she'd managed to evade him. But in the end, she'd gone with him willingly—if only because her village had turned against her.

She couldn't stop it, but she had to see it. How it was done. How it had been done to her. The fire was going well enough now to leave it. "I'm going to find Denan."

"Larkin," Mama said, clearly worried.

"I'll be all right."

Mama looked at Sela, then back at Larkin. She wanted to argue, but she wouldn't do it in front of Sela—not when she was so fragile.

Larkin headed toward where the pipers clustered at the edge of the forest. Tam started toward her. She waved him off. "Stay with my mother."

"I'm supposed to keep an eye on you."

As if she needed a guard in the middle of an army of pipers. "I'll be fine."

Larkin caught sight of Dayne following a dozen paces back, his gaze fixed on her. So, Tam wasn't her only guard. She looked around, and sure enough, Ulrin wasn't far off either. Denan had set two guards on her without telling her. She ground her teeth.

Keeping her eyes on the uneven ground, she picked her way up the road in the falling light. Around her, pipers trickled in from all over the camp. All of them were single, as evidenced by their shaved heads, a single lock of long hair behind their ears.

Normally, only those few chosen by the White Tree would make their journey for their heartsong—and some of those would never find a wife at all. Now, all the men in the army would have a chance to try for a heartsong.

She climbed out of a wheel rut and avoided another pile of manure—the road was obviously well used. They'd been lucky to only come across one pig farmer—and then only because it had been nearing nightfall.

Maisy waited on the other side. She reached out and hauled Larkin up close. "A knife in the night for your husband. We could both be hours away by morning."

Larkin pushed away. "Touch him and I'll gut you myself."

Maisy looked hurt. "I couldn't kill my father either."

As if Larkin's refusal to kill Denan was because she was afraid. There was no use explaining that Larkin loved Denan—not when Maisy thought every man should be dead.

Denan had good reason for taking Larkin, and he'd never touched her against her will. Still, Maisy's words sat like a rock in Larkin's middle. The shadows settled in the curse marks on Maisy's cheek.

Larkin was certain Maisy knew more about the wraiths than she'd let on. Still, Larkin hesitated, not wanting to set Maisy off. "Why are the wraiths after me, Maisy?"

Maisy stiffened. "Break and make. In order to break, you must make."

Larkin wanted to shake her. "Give me something," she said through clenched teeth.

"They search for their Wraith Queen."

Larkin gasped. "I'm no wraith!"

Maisy's haunted eyes pierced her. "They will try to make you one."

They reached the edge of the crowd of silent, still pipers. Larkin was uncomfortable with so many men—so many *pip-*

ers—in such tight quarters. Hopefully, Maisy would be even more so and slink off.

Larkin set her teeth and plunged forward. She edged and murmured apologies to move through. The pipers took one look at her and Maisy and immediately moved. Some bowed. Some grumbled. Some did both.

Larkin was just starting to feel more confident when a man blocked her path. His dark eyes narrowed to a glare. "My brother died to free you from Hamel."

The memories assaulted her so fast that she gasped. *Piper music shifted around Larkin, dragging her steps despite the dampener she wore. Her sister was heavy in her arms, her body weak from drawing too much magic. Arrows clattered onto the cobblestones. Pipers fell from the rooftops, their bodies broken and dying.*

She shook her head, desperate to clear the memories. "I'm sorry."

He ground his teeth. "Sorry doesn't bring him back."

"Nor my son," an older man said.

"Nor my cousin," the other man said.

Maisy hissed, which made the other pipers shift uncomfortably.

"Stop it," Larkin muttered to her.

Before Larkin could comment one way or another, Dayne and Ulrin were there, both of them frowning.

"Chev," Ulrin said in a flat voice.

The man, Chev, nodded to the other two men. With a final look at her, the group slunk off into the crowd.

Larkin turned to her guards. "Am I safe here?" If she wasn't safe among the pipers, she wasn't safe anywhere.

"Of course you're not safe," Maisy scoffed.

Ulrin wiggled his mustache, his unibrow scrunched in unison. "There are grumblings, Princess. But no one would dare lay a finger on you."

Grumblings. She'd been aware of a few dark looks, but Denan had kept the extent from her and instead assigned her guards. Perhaps she should thank him. She had enough to worry about without angry pipers factoring in.

She nodded her thanks to the guards. "If you'll lead the way." She had no desire to be confronted by more irate pipers.

The younger of the two, Dayne, dipped a bow and took the lead ahead. Ulrin positioned himself behind her and Maisy. There were no more interruptions, no more dark looks. Whether because of the guards or the implied threat of Denan finding out, she wasn't sure. Dayne approached the Forbidden Forest and stepped beneath the trees without hesitation. Larkin paused at the edge, a cold sweat breaking out over her whole body.

The barrier is a quarter mile inside the woods, she reminded herself. *I'm safe.* Still, she had to make herself take that step.

The entire forest was packed with pipers all the way to the barrier. Every unmarried man in the entire army. It was dark enough now she had to watch her footing, so she didn't catch sight of Denan until they were nearly upon him.

Someone whispered to Denan. He looked back at her in surprise before striding toward her. "Larkin, what are you doing here?"

She crossed her arms. "I need to see how it works."

Denan grimaced. "It will only upset you. Let me take you back to the camp. I'll enchant you. You'll sleep soundly and—"

Maisy grunted from Larkin's other side. "So you can lure in another wife?"

He glared at her. "I already have a wife."

Larkin released a long breath. "What about their families? What about the generation of daughters who will never be born because you're taking their mothers?"

"It can't be helped, and I promise they will be well looked after."

"As if no one ever takes advantage of a taken," Maisy spat.

Larkin had to admit that she agreed. She'd seen the strong lord over the weak too many times.

He was silent a moment. "It has happened before."

"Ha!" Maisy crowed in triumph.

Denan ignored her. "With our magic, we always know the truth. The penalties are severe—as you already know."

Larkin shifted. "I can't— I can't reconcile this in my mind, Denan."

"We do what we must."

She hated when he said that.

"Whatever you have to tell yourself to blunt the guilt," Maisy hissed.

He pointed back to the encampment. "You. Over there."

She set her chin. "I go where I want."

"Go, or I will enchant you to go."

Hand on her own dampener, Maisy glared at the men around them. "I warned you, Larkin. Remember that." She slipped away into the crowd.

Larkin watched her go. She wished she could be what Maisy needed, but she was barely managing to take care of herself and her family.

"Worst bargain I've ever made." Denan cracked his neck. "You can stay, Larkin, but only if you promise not to interfere."

Interfering wouldn't change anything. She nodded.

He signaled to his men. A select few of the pipers lifted their pipes and began playing their heartsong. Even with the dampener Larkin wore, their songs niggled against her, offering the sweet release of sleep.

Denan took her hand and led her through the playing pipers toward the edge of the forest. "We don't want to put the whole village to sleep all at once," Denan explained. "Someone could fall asleep in their barn and be trampled to death or too near a fire and wake up burned. We work up to a full force, so the enchantment just makes them more and more sleepy until they find their beds."

She could make out the village spread out in the valley below. There was a lovely lake with a dock. Orchards and farmland dominated the land outside the village. Beyond the pipers' music, silence—not even the chirp of crickets or the croak of frogs.

One by one, lights went out in the village. The people below were being enchanted, and they didn't even know it. The pipers' magic controlled their feelings and moods, but only temporarily. It worked best when the subject was relaxed, hence why the girls were taken at night.

As night came on, more and more pipers played, the music trying to haul her under. When night completely blanketed the earth, unmarried pipers—some of their queues threaded through with gray—stepped into full view of the village.

From the village came the first sounds in many long moments: doors creaking open. Women in their nightclothes slipped into the dark, their faces gilded with moonlight.

At first, a dozen, and then twenty. And then hundreds of them. Gliding with steady purpose, they looked neither to the right nor the left as they climbed the rise, their feet falling in perfect time to the beat.

Gray threaded through one woman's hair, the first signs of lines fanning out from her lovely eyes. She paused before a man at least ten years her junior. Joy lit her face when she reached him, her fingers trailing down his cheek. She closed her eyes and swayed to the beat, her face tipped toward the breeze. That joy felt like a betrayal. For when these women woke, it would be to fear and anger at all they had lost.

Her piper frowned and dropped his head. Taking a deep breath, he played before the enchantment could fade, took the woman's hand, and led her toward one of the fires.

Larkin watched them, her mouth set in a tight line. "I lost everything, but at least you wanted me."

Denan followed her gaze. "They warn us not to build up our

wives too much in our heads. The women might be older or younger, beautiful or not, sweet or salty. The key is to love the good and let go of the bad."

"And what if *she* never wants *him*?" Larkin asked.

"She will," Denan said. "The heartsong is never wrong."

Larkin's skin felt brittle and dirty. "So I never had a choice?"

He gave a half shake of his head. "The magic knew who we would choose."

Larkin caught sight of another girl, face still round with baby fat. She couldn't have been more than twelve. She reached out, embracing a young man and laying her head on his chest.

Larkin rounded on Denan. "No," she said firmly. "Put her back." The young man led the girl toward a warm fire. "Denan," Larkin warned.

"She won't be married until she's old enough," Denan said.

The music turned hollow, aching. All the women had been claimed, but the men played on, begging for their song to be answered.

Larkin swallowed hard at their sorrow. "How old is old enough?"

"When they're that young, they get to choose. She'll live with his family, and he'll live somewhere else."

"And what of her family? What about their grief? And can she truly choose when she's been kidnapped by her supposed true love?"

Denan stepped closer, his voice low. "Would you rather the alternative?"

She tasted the vision—like copper and smoke. It came on sudden and hard.

Wraiths glided over the elegant wall of the Alamant. Their evil swords cut through the people like scythes through wheat. Darkness trailed after them—a dark stain that spread like smoky tendrils, reaching, grasping for the White Tree until it was no longer white at all, but black as a night forsaken by stars.

The vision, she'd seen it before. It was what the pipers had feared for generations. The reality carved into the walls of a ruined city.

She woke in Denan's arms as he carried her into camp.

"What did you see?"

"Wraiths in the Alamant." She closed her eyes against the memories.

The pipers' songs changed, shifting to one of slumber. The older woman and the girl both lay on blankets their pipers had arranged for them and instantly fell asleep.

She watched the young man and the girl. He'd settled a respectable distance away. When the girl woke in the morning, he'd play again until he'd lured her so deep into the Forbidden Forest she'd have nowhere to run.

"Please put me down. I don't want to see anymore."

He obeyed. She staggered away from him, pushing through pipers and newly taken.

"Larkin." He gripped her elbow.

She jerked free as if stung. "I thought I'd accepted this. But I can't. I just can't."

She ran.

CHAPTER

CURSE TREE

L arkin sought out her mother. She was not by the fire. Instead, Tam lay near her sisters. Not meeting his gaze, she
swiped her eyes. "Where is she?"

Wordlessly, he pointed toward the forest. She took off at a
trot.

"Let her go," Tam said softly from behind her, probably
talking to Denan, who had most likely followed her.

Larkin searched the borders of the forest and found her
mother standing before a thorn tree. Ribbons and scraps of fabric
shifted on the breeze.

Larkin hadn't seen a curse tree since she'd left Hamel.
"Nothing good comes from the Forbidden Forest," the old saying
went. So the people wrote curses for themselves on scraps of
cloths or ribbons while hoping for the opposite.

She walked through wicked curses that broke apart beneath
her feet like ashes. Face streaked with tears, Mama held a handful of curses. Some had faded to a tattered gray. Others reflected

the firelight, their colors bright. She held one out to Larkin, who took it in her hand. The ink had feathered through the weave, but she could still read the words: *May the beast take my daughters. All of them.*

Larkin's breath caught in her throat.

"When those mothers wake in the morning," Mama said, "they will know the sorrow I knew: the pain of losing a child forever, of not knowing if you should hope for them to be dead so they won't suffer—rent by the claws and teeth of a beast that doesn't even exist." She sobbed quietly.

A curse tore free, cavorting until it landed at Larkin's feet. She bent and picked it up. A blue print with white and yellow flowers, so faded it was more gray than blue. She imagined it on the skirt of the girl taken just tonight, a girl not even out of childhood. The letters were faded, but Larkin could still read them: *May my daughter have a horrible death.*

Larkin closed her eyes, imagining the girl spinning in the sunshine, her blue dress twisting about her legs. Her family would wake in the morning and grieve for the child they would never see again. More faces flashed in Larkin's mind—girls covered in soot and burns sitting placidly under the pipers' enchantment.

"This has to stop." Mama looked at Larkin. "You must stop it."

"Me? How?"

Mama waved over Denan, who watched them solemnly from beside the fire. Denan motioned for Tam to come with him. Coward. Mama moved away from the curse tree, away from the forest, and settled herself on a rounded rock to wait for them.

They paused before her warily.

"You know taking girls is wrong," Mama said, "but you feel justified because it prevents a greater evil. Yes?"

Denan nodded.

Mama hmphed. "Well, you're wrong. The greatest evil is

the unwillingness of the Alamantians and Idelmarchians to work together. That is the only way to defeat the wraiths."

Denan folded his arms. "The curse and the druids have kept it that way."

Larkin shot him a death glare, and he withered. "The curse is broken."

"One small piece of it is broken," Tam corrected her.

"Larkin has broken the Idelmarch's curse of lost magic and memory," Denan said. "We Alamantians still face barrenness and shadow."

"It's at least enough to stop the reaping," Mama said.

Denan looked toward Cordova as he rubbed his jaw. "The last messenger I sent to the Black Druids was returned to me in pieces."

Larkin flinched. "The messenger ransoming Bane?"

"That one hasn't come in yet," Denan admitted.

Because he would be returning with Bane. Larkin refused to believe any differently.

Tam started pacing.

Mama paled. "The Black Druids aren't the only ones in power."

Denan raised an eyebrow. "You mean the old nobility?"

"Iniya Rothsberd is a force to be reckoned with," Mama said.

"The Mad Queen?" Larkin asked. The woman had never actually been a queen. Her royal family had been murdered when she was seventeen, and she'd lost her mind. The druids had saved her life and taken over. What good could she do?

"She's not mad—at least not anymore," Mama said. "Bitter and angry, but not mad."

"How do you know anything about her?" Larkin asked.

Denan blinked at Mama in surprise. "Iniya Rothsberd hates us nearly as much as she hates the druids."

Ignoring her, Mama leaned forward. "She hates the Black

Druids more. The old nobility is loyal to her—their support is one of the only reasons she's still alive. Back her claim to regain the throne, and she will help you overthrow them."

Denan rocked back on his heels.

"A coup would be much easier to manage than an outright war," Tam said.

Denan considered. "Whatever force Iniya Rothsberd might have mustered has long since lost their outrage."

Mama huffed. "The Idelmarchians endure the druids because they believe they protect them from the beast. Tell them the truth—that the druids have been lying to them for decades—and the people will rise up against them. Iniya could spread that message."

Larkin stared at her mother. "How do you know all of this?"

Mama flinched. "It was too dangerous to tell you."

"Tell me what?" Larkin asked.

Mama took a deep breath and met Larkin's gaze. "Your father is Iniya Rothsberd's only son."

Larkin's mouth fell open. Her father, the town drunk and wife beater, was a prince?

"What is a prince doing in a squat little town like Hamel?" Tam asked.

"He was disowned."

Larkin reeled. She was the granddaughter of the Mad Queen? A born princess. "And you never told me?"

Mama shook her head. "It was too dangerous. The druids were looking for us. My father would have taken me from you. He hates your father nearly as much as Iniya hates me."

Larkin's mind spun. "Your father? Who is your father?"

Mama rubbed her palms on her knees nervously. "Master Fenwick."

"The leader of the Black Druids?" And therefore the leader of the Idelmarch. "And neither of you bothered to tell me?" Betrayal filled Larkin's head with a rushing sound. Unable to sit still, she began pacing.

Mama watched her, guilt playing out behind her eyes. "You don't understand. We grew up with our parents' mutual hatred. It's what initially brought us together—forbidden friendship is a powerful draw for two teenagers who resent their parents' heavy-handedness."

"Obviously, you were more than just friends," Larkin huffed.

"You don't defy my father and walk away unscathed." Mama's eyes slipped closed. "When he found out I was carrying a child, he demanded I tell him who the father was. When I refused, he called for a midwife to get rid of Nesha." She choked. "Your father and I fled. You have to understand. My father would have taken me from all of you and locked me away. He may very well have killed you simply for existing."

Larkin sat on the damp ground. "And Iniya?"

Mama wrapped her arms around herself. "She disowned your father, said to never darken her doorway again. Harben took what he could. We used it to buy that plot of land in Hamel, not realizing it was such a bargain because it regularly flooded."

"And I thought my family had a lot of drama," Tam muttered.

"Well, you are married to Alorica," Denan muttered back.

Larkin knew they were trying to lighten the mood, but now was not the time. She gave them a stern look, and they straightened, chagrined.

"Why tell us this now?" Denan asked.

Mama sighed. "Because Iniya doesn't care about family or wealth or riches. She cares about power and revenge. Give her that, and she will do whatever you want."

Denan nodded. "I'll arrange for one of my spies to make contact." He turned to go.

"Nesha," Mama said. "What do your spies tell you of my daughter?"

Denan cut an uneasy glance at Larkin. "She's still in Hamel with Garrot. They show no signs of departing."

Larkin never wanted to hear anything about her sister again—not after Nesha had betrayed Larkin to the druids, twice. She stood to leave.

Mama grabbed her arm. "She's still your sister."

How long had it been since they'd left Hamel? Days? A week? Larkin's anger hadn't faded. "Have you forgotten, Mama? Nesha gave me up to the mob." She touched the knife scar on her throat. "If not for Denan, I'd be dead now."

Mama released her, head dropping with shame, though she'd done nothing wrong. "Just tell me, is she well? And the baby?"

Bane's baby. Such a storm of emotions. Ancestors, how could Larkin love and hate them both at the same time?

Denan reached out and took Larkin's fist in his hand. Gently, he pried open her fingers and held her hand. He looked at her as he said, "Nesha and her baby are both fine, Pennice, but I'll ask you not to bring them up again in front of Larkin."

Without a backward glance, he tugged Larkin toward the campfire. "Let me enchant you?" Denan asked. "You're exhausted."

Grateful, she rolled the tension from her shoulders. "Yes."

Not caring what her mother thought, she curled up against Denan's side as he played a melody.

CHAPTER 15

VISION

*L*arkin was in a high tower. It was the hour between night and morning—shades of charcoal giving way to dove gray. Tasteful furniture graced the room, including a bed, the mussed sheets covered with what looked like bits of colored, broken glass.

Had violence been done here? But there was no blood.

Larkin followed the trail of jagged glass to a wide balcony. She recognized the woman by her gold and silver hair—more silver than there had been before. Glass littered the floor at her feet. The woman rested the fingertips of her right hand on an amulet at her throat.

Larkin instantly recognized the bare branches, one sharp enough to puncture the skin—the same amulet Larkin now wore.

Eiryss stared into the distant forest, her gaze filled with longing so deep it made Larkin's own heart ache. She could hear it then, the faint strains of music so full of hollow loss and longing that tears filled her eyes. The woman stood there as the mu-

sic faded away with the light of morning, the sun washing the horizon in crimson and gold.

Larkin studied the city. Men were already hard at work in a long trench. Some swung pickaxes, others shoveled the loose dirt into wheelbarrows, while yet others carted that dirt away. They were building some sort of channel between the houses.

This must be the capital of the Idelmarch, Landra, when it was still new.

"My queen?" an older woman asked from the doorway. "You did not come down to breakfast. Malia wants you."

When Eiryss didn't answer, the woman stepped farther into the room, her eyes lighting on the sheets full of glass. She rushed inside. She breathed out in relief at the sight of Eiryss on the balcony. "Eiryss, what's all this glass about?" she demanded. She started at the sight of her bare feet. "Are you hurt?"

Larkin was relieved someone was asking the questions she couldn't.

"Have you forgotten, Tria?" Eiryss said, her voice as distant as the far-off forest. "I am no longer your student to scold."

Tria reached toward a piece of glass, then seemed to think better of it. "Eiryss," her voice gentled. "What happened?"

Eiryss wiped the tears from her cheeks. She stared at the liquid on her fingertips, the tears coming faster. Tears that were gold instead of clear. "It's not glass. It's sap."

Sap? Tree sap? That didn't make any sense.

"What?" Tria placed the inside of her wrist on Eiryss's forehead.

Eiryss closed her eyes. "I'm dying, Tria."

"Nonsense. It's just the stress of building a new kingdom from the ground up."

Sniffing, Eiryss pulled up the sleeves of her nightdress to reveal thick black vines growing over her skin like a strangler fig growing over a tree.

Breathing hard, Tria took a pair of scissors from the table.

Eiryss screwed her eyes shut and turned away. Tria wrenched back one of the vines and used the scissor's edge to cut it from her skin. Eiryss cried out. Larkin gaped at the meat and sinew beneath. The rivulets of running blood were thick and orange.

Tria staggered back. "Is it the curse?"

Squeezing her wounded arm, Eiryss nodded. "'You, Eiryss, shall watch as shadow devours land and people, starting with your beloved Valynthia and ending here.'"

"He's dead," Tria said, fear obvious in her voice. "He can't hurt us anymore."

Eiryss chuckled bitterly. "He'll never stop hurting us."

They had to be speaking of the Wraith King.

Eiryss turned back to the forest. "He's calling for me, Tria. And every night, it gets harder and harder to resist." She shuddered. "You must keep me under constant guard. Make sure I never set foot inside the Forbidden Forest."

Tria heaved a sigh. "I swear it."

Eiryss went to her writing desk and shifted through the papers. She held out a loosely bound book to Tria. "It's my journal. See the songs set to music and have the minstrels sing it in every village."

"Why the songs, Eiryss? The people can't even remember Valynthia anymore. They've forgotten everything."

Eiryss took another amulet—this one shaped like an ahlea flower—out from inside her shirt and held it in her hands. "Because someday one of my line will break the curse, and she will need all our help."

Larkin gasped awake. It was deep night. She'd had another vision. Why? Why now? Her hand throbbed, harder with each beat of her heart. She released her amulet clutched in her fist, a thin line of blood trickling from her palm to drip onto her blankets. She picked it up, the dampener clinking against it.

Her tree amulet had given her the visions.

The first, of the day the curse had begun. And now, she'd

seen Eiryss in Landra. Ramass was haunting her, and the curse changing her, killing her. But it was the last bit that snagged in Larkin's memory. Eiryss had held up a journal, with songs to be sung at every village. Why would she do that?

Suddenly, Larkin understood. "The lullabies—they're messages."

"What lullabies?" Mama asked wearily.

In the firelight, sentinels patrolled the edge of the encampment. Larkin rolled over and shook Denan. "I had a vision."

He peered blearily up at her. Knowing he must go through his routine to wake up, she waited as he stretched, his back cracking and his bare chest peeking out from beneath his blankets. He yawned and shook himself. He pushed up, grabbed his tunic, and pulled it on. "I'm ready."

Larkin grasped the edge of the dream to keep it from fraying apart. "Eiryss was in Landra. She was dying—vines kept growing over her. The curse was making people forget Valynthia and the wraiths. Denan, I think she hid messages in the lullabies for us to find!"

He rubbed his head, clearly still half asleep. "Lullabies? What messages?"

"'Blood of my heart, marrow my bone.'" She froze, realizing something else. "If Eiryss was the first queen, does that mean she's my ancestor?"

Mama nodded. "Oh, yes. Iniya was always proud of that fact."

Larkin's head filled with a rushing sound. She looked at Denan. "Then both our ancestors were there when the curse began—on their wedding day."

That Larkin and Denan would meet and marry now, when the curse was falling apart—it couldn't be a coincidence.

And the lullaby ... Blood and marrow of Eiryss's bones. "She said one of her line would break the curse," Larkin said. Sela already had, in part.

Denan and Mama exchanged uneasy glances.

Larkin closed her eyes and tried to remember what came next. "'Come hear the saddest story e'er known. A cursed queen, her lover lost.'"

"Dray and Eiryss?" Denan asked.

"Has to be," Larkin said. "'A forbidden magic and dreadful cost.'"

"Clearly the curse," Mama said before launching into the next line. "'Consumed by evil agents of night, seek the nestling, barred from flight.'"

Larkin shuddered. Because the evil agents of night were seeking her like a snake eyeing a clutch of nestlings.

Mama rested her hand on Larkin's knee. "'Midst the vile queen's curse of thorny vine, fear not the shadow, for you are mine.'"

Eiryss hadn't seemed vile. She'd seemed desperate and determined and cursed. Someone to be pitied instead of hated.

"'In my arms,'" Larkin recited the last, "'the answer lie. A light that endures so evil may die.'"

The three of them sat in silence as morning eased away the shadow. A light. What light? Her eyes widened with understanding. When Dray had lay dying, he'd given Eiryss an ahlea amulet and told her to take his light.

"Light! Denan, the other amulet!" she cried. "What happened to her ahlea amulet?'

He only lifted his hands. "We don't know that. And even if we did, if Eiryss couldn't use an ahlea amulet to break the curse, what makes you think you can?"

"I heard her say it in the vision. She wrote it in the lullaby."

"An amulet? Like the one you're wearing?" Mama gestured to the one hanging from Larkin's neck.

"No." Larkin nodded to Denan, who lifted his sleeve to reveal a geometric flower with angular petals on his forearm. "It's shaped like that," Larkin said.

Mama stared at the sigil without blinking. "I always wondered about that flower—it never looked like anything I'd ever seen before."

"Mama?" Larkin asked.

Mama shook her head as if coming out of a dream. "It's carved on her tomb."

Larkin gaped at her. "Where?"

Mama hesitated. "In the crypts beneath the druids' palace."

Larkin looked west, toward Landra. As the sun broke over the horizon, a vision superimposed over the encampment. A little bird with a copperbill flew toward the capital city.

Larkin's mind spun. What if she wasn't useless after all? Perhaps she hadn't been the one to break the curse, to become the Arbor. But she could still do something. Still make a difference. "I'm meant to go to Landra."

"What?" Denan burst out.

"Go to Landra, get the ahlea amulet, break the curse," Larkin said in a rush, excitement making her giddy.

Tam snorted awake, sat up, and fumbled for his bow. "Where are the—" He looked at them and blinked. "Did I miss something?"

"Larkin is going to Landra," Mama said.

Denan looked at Mama, aghast. "You can't want her to do this."

"She's the one with the visions of Eiryss," Mama said. "And after seeing all those girls taken … I think she's meant to do this."

"Larkin isn't that foolish," Tam said.

"I am," Larkin said.

Tam blinked at her.

"What if Garrot recognizes her?" Denan said.

Mama nodded to herself. "You said yourself that Nesha is still in Hamel, that Garrot is overseeing the trial."

Bane's trial. Larkin's breath whooshed out of her. Bane had

saved her life twice. He'd been an idiot, but he was also her best friend. And Nesha ... Larkin couldn't think about her sister. It was too painful.

"Send her to Iniya in the guise of Nesha," Mama said. "Tam will accompany her. The Master Druid invites the entire city into the keep for the spring equinox. Druids and their wives will come from all over. It will be easy for Larkin to blend in. Iniya can get her into the keep."

"It's too dangerous," Denan said.

"There's one way to know for sure." Larkin squeezed her amulet. The sharp branch bit into her palm. The vision swept her up.

Eiryss was clearly dead, her skin so pale it gleamed white beneath the full moon. She'd been laid out beneath an archway, a blanket crusted in pearls and diamonds tucked under her hands. A thin film rested over her, like spun glass. And at her throat was the amulet Larkin had seen before—the one Dray had made with his dying breath.

With the vision came the undeniable sense that Larkin must go to the queen, to the Black Druids' crypts. "Yes. This is what I'm meant to do."

Denan crossed his arms. "Your amulet is from the Black Tree. We can't trust it."

Larkin shook her head. "You're wrong. This was Eiryss's amulet—I saw her wearing it. It has its own magic that I used against the druids and you. Somehow, it contains her memories."

Denan stood and moved to the edge of their fire, his back to her. "I'll consider it."

"It isn't your decision to make," Larkin said.

He turned to her, his expression fierce. "As commander of the Alamant, it is."

She was aware of Tam slinking into the shadows. "I'm not Alamantian."

Denan stormed toward camp. She caught up with him and

grabbed his arm. But he spoke first, not meeting her eye. "You know what will happen if the druids catch you."

The shouts and accusations of her neighbors calling for her death overwhelmed her.

"Look at me, Denan." He stiffened but did as she asked. She flared her weapons. "I am meant to fight. My magic is made for fighting."

"You know I can't risk you," Denan said. "We're almost there. By tonight, I'll know you're safe and well and I can finally rest easy."

But he *could* risk her—because she wasn't his curse breaker. Choking on a sob, she turned away.

"Larkin?"

She kept her back turned—she couldn't say this while looking at him. "I am not the prize you think I am." She cleared the emotion from her throat. "I'm only a girl with red hair and freckles."

"What?"

Part of her wanted to deny the truth. Lie. Give him some other version. But she'd promised him after she'd told him that he was her choice: no more secrets. "I never removed the curse on the magic. Sela did."

Silence from behind her.

She shivered. "You were meant to find the one with magic, and you did. It just wasn't me."

"How can you be sure?"

"That day in the forest, the day we met, she did something to me. I didn't understand. Not until I saw her do it to Magalia on the promontory. She's removed the curse on my mother and sisters too—it's why they didn't react to the barrier."

"Is that what you think you are to me—some sort of prize?"

Remembering the pipers who'd confronted her earlier, she sniffed and wiped her nose on her sleeve. "I've made so many mistakes. How many men have died because I escaped, Denan?"

He stepped up behind her and turned her to face him. He tipped her chin up and held it there until she finally met his gaze.

"You are brave. How many would risk the dangers of the Forbidden Forest, not once but twice, to save three girls—one of whom was her enemy? You are loyal. How many women would leave the majesty of the Alamant and the man she'd fallen in love with to save her childhood friend? You are resilient. How many women would face a horde of Black Druids to rescue me?" He brushed his fingertips down her cheek. "And yes, you need to learn a balance between loyalty and self-preservation, but Larkin, your heart has always been the thing I've admired most."

She hesitated, not sure she believed him.

"Would you love me any less were I not a prince?" he asked.

"I think"—she swallowed—"I think it would be easier." Less pressure and scrutiny, certainly.

"Just a girl with red hair and freckles." He shook his head and took a step toward her. "I love your hair. It makes it easier to spot you in a crowd. And your freckles—I can see every place the light has touched you."

She practically leaped into his arms. Chuckling, he stroked her back. She gloried in being loved just as she was.

All too quickly, the feeling faded, leaving her with a heavy stone of dread in her belly. "For the first time in three centuries, women have magic again. I thought I'd brought it back." She shook her head, fighting back tears. "But I didn't. My sister did. It took me a day to tell you, because I was afraid it would make me less in your eyes—as it did in my own."

He opened his mouth to argue. She held out her hand. "Now I have a chance to retrieve the ahlea amulet. To put an end to the wraiths. To bring our people together as one, as they are meant to be."

"You can't ask me to stand by while you walk into a death trap."

"I've watched you walk into battle plenty."

"You've not been trained."

"This isn't the kind of thing you can train for." He had no more reason to keep her from fighting in her own way than she did him. "Am I nothing more than a vessel for your sons?"

His expression hardened. "I never said you were!"

She swallowed hard. "You told me the White Tree gave you a vision once of a bird held captive in your hands. It died over and over and over again—until you opened your fingers and set it free." She stepped closer to him. "You have to set me free."

He wouldn't look at her. "I'm not sure I can."

"Talox told me to own my destiny. That's what I intend to do."

"Larkin?" a small voice said. Sela stood between them and the fire, her hair plastered to one side of her head.

Larkin gave her a trembling smile. "Sela, you're talking again?"

"She told me I have to," Sela said. "Talking will make me strong again."

Denan crouched before Sela. "She? The White Tree?"

Sela bobbed her head and choked on a sob. Finally, finally, Larkin would understand her part in all this.

"Larkin has to go." Sela's bottom lip trembled and her eyes filled with tears. "But I don't want her to either."

Larkin knelt, arms wide open.

Sela darted into them and cried, "The light. You have to get the light."

Eiryss's amulet. Larkin looked at Denan, who held his hand over his mouth. "How is this possible? She doesn't have a sigil."

Larkin had had visions before her sigil. Magic too. Because of a sliver. Larkin's eyes widened. The bloody elbow Sela had received at the arbor ring. Larkin pulled up her sister's sleeve, revealing a nearly healed scrape and a dark sliver embedded and swollen.

"Hurts," Sela sniffed.

Larkin couldn't stop Sela from being the Arbor, but she could put it off for a few days. She pinned her sister's arm and slid her thumbnail toward the sliver's opening. It shot out in a burst of pus.

Sela flinched and wailed, "I can't feel her anymore. Where did she go?"

Denan crouched beside Larkin. "You shouldn't have done that."

"It had to come out." Which was true, even if it wasn't her primary reason.

Mama hustled over and gathered Sela into her arms. "What happened?"

Larkin embraced her mother and sister. "I have to go."

"You're not going anywhere," Denan said.

She faced him. "I won't forgive you if you force me again, Denan. I can't."

He pulled his hands through his short hair, paced toward her and then away again. "I can't go with you, Larkin. I can't risk being captured by the druids."

But she could, and they both knew it. "Come first light," Larkin said, "I'm going."

Denan turned on his heel and stormed away.

Larkin changed into the clothes Tam had pilfered from Cordova on Denan's orders—a fine dress and corset in dour black. Her mother and sisters were still asleep. She'd said goodbye to them last night, so she simply bent down, pressing a kiss to Brenna's downy head.

They would be safe in the Alamant by tonight. "Love you," she mouthed.

Larkin and Tam started through the slumbering camp. She

glanced around for Denan. "Will he really not say goodbye?"

"If he doesn't, he's an idiot." Tam straightened his robes. "You're sure I look druidy enough?"

She glanced over his long robes, the intricately tooled belt cinched at his waist. All in deepest black instead of the rich browns and greens the pipers wore to blend in with the forest. Last night, Tam had stolen it from Cordova's resident druid along with a fine dress and cloak for Larkin. "You look positively evil."

Tam grinned. "Perfect."

Larkin could feel Denan watching her. But it wasn't until she reached the edge of the encampment that she saw him standing on a hill. He lifted his pipes to his lips and played their heartsong.

It tugged a cord deep inside her. The dampener muted it enough that she could resist. She didn't want to resist. She ran to him and wrapped her arms around him.

His eyes slipped closed, and he pulled her into his grasp, his body trembling. "I will always come for you, little bird."

"And I will always come back."

They held each other a long time—long enough for the shape of his body to imprint on hers. When he finally released her, he pressed a tender kiss against her mouth before pulling back. He licked his lips as if tasting her.

"Tam?" he said. She looked over her shoulder to see Tam watching them from a dozen paces away.

"With my life," Tam whispered.

Larkin winced—Talox had said the same. He'd kept that promise. She couldn't bear to think of Tam dying for her.

The pipers weren't the only ones capable of protection. *And with my life,* Larkin thought, *I will protect you.*

His fingers slipping from hers, Denan turned and strode back to camp, calling out orders to his pages and captains to get the army up and moving. Dawn was coming.

CHAPTER 16

LANDRA

Safely tucked out of sight, Larkin and Tam spent two days traveling in the forest between the barrier and the road. Now, they secreted themselves beneath the dense, dripping canopy.

Through the steady drizzle, Larkin studied Landra in the distance. Bane had told her stories of the capital, but he'd focused on the people and food. He'd never adequately expressed how beautiful it was. The city had changed so much from Eiryss's time as to be completely new.

The druids' white palace gleamed beneath its turquoise copper roof. The river passed through cleverly built channels in ever-widening concentric circles. A long land bridge cut through the center of it.

Such a beautiful place seemed so at odds with the darkness of the druids who ruled it.

She and Tam waited for a break in the steady streams of refugees coming from Cordova. Though the pipers had melted into the forest right after dawn, apparently the Cordovans thought an attack imminent from an army that didn't fear the forest—an army whose arrival and departure had coincided with the reaping of their daughters.

Hundreds of them had fled for the safety of the capital city. When they'd come close enough to listen at the edge of their campfires at night, Larkin and Tam had heard a dozen rumors. All had a single thread in common. Starting with the attack on Hamel, men were coming from the forest to attack the Idelmarch. Since the beast ruled the forest, he also ruled this mysterious army.

Finally, a break in the carts and foot traffic. Larkin and Tam hurried from the forest and waded through dripping grasses to reach the road. Mud caked her boots and splashed onto her hem. Doing her best to avoid the puddles, Larkin kept her hood low and her head down to hide her striking hair.

Mindful of the rain, she slid out the map Mama had drawn for them. Her grandmother's house was far too near the druids' palace for Larkin's liking. For the hundredth time, she marked each turn they needed to make.

"Easy." Tam smiled and waved at a field worker. "We belong here, remember?"

She jerked his hand down. "Druids don't wave!"

"Not all druids are dour."

"Yes, they are. Glare. Be condescending."

Tam grumbled under his breath and arranged his impish features into his best imitation of severity. Clearly an imitation. But perhaps someone who didn't know him would buy it.

"The forest take me," she muttered. "We're both dead."

They slipped in with the Cordovans as they approached the newly constructed wall, the stones stained black by rain. Workmen used a lever to heave heavy stones up to the top, where they were rotated and laid across mortar. It slipped, slamming off-kilter with a deafening boom that made Larkin jump and cover her ears.

Tam yelped.

The foreman screamed and cursed at his workers.

A pair of soldiers moved toward them. A drop of rain soaked through her hood and drew a chill line down her scalp. She shivered.

She stopped walking, her whole body tensed to run. *They aren't looking for me,* she reminded herself. *No one is looking for me.*

"It's all a game, Larkin," Tam said.

"It's not a game when we could die."

He huffed. "We're not going to die."

They crossed a bridge over a wide river. The stench of rot washed over her. She followed the smell to corpses swinging from their necks from scaffolding. This was how the druids dealt with criminals, which included traitors.

He paled. "Life is a game. In the end, we all lose."

She shot him a sardonic look. "So helpful. Thank you."

The refugees bottlenecked at the partially closed gates, the space beyond dark as a night without stars. A clutch of soldiers stood guard, halberds gripped in both hands.

"Like I said," the foremost soldier shouted, "unless you have direct family members to stay with, you will not be allowed to enter the city."

Larkin took a tiny step closer to Tam, glad he'd stolen robes. All druids would be welcome into the city to celebrate the equinox.

"We woke to an army on our doorstep," one women cried. "All the unmarried women were taken. You can't leave us out here undefended."

The soldier held out his hands. "We are calling up soldiers as we speak. They should be arriving in Cordova shortly. In the meantime, we suggest you begin construction on your own perimeter wall."

"At least allow us to camp outside the city," a man said.

"We can't have you trampling our crops," the soldier said. "Now turn back and see to your own defenses. An army should be arriving from Hamel in a few days."

Hamel. Larkin stiffened. She'd been under those soldiers' watchful eyes for days. If someone from her village recognized her, the game was over.

Tam touched the outside of her hand, his face a serene mask. "You're making panicky faces. Stop making panicky faces."

"What if one of the soldiers recognize us?"

"Why would foot soldiers be at the palace?" Tam said.

"And the druids?"

"Still seeing to the trial."

She forced herself to take a calming breath.

Tam shot her a cocky grin, grabbed her elbow, and pushed through the people. He eyed the soldier, who took one look at Tam's robes and let them pass.

"Told you these clothes were a good idea," Tam said.

Larkin paused at the edge of the shadows. She sensed that once she stepped beyond, she'd never come out alive. She glanced back at the forest, memories of her departure pulsing hot. She stepped into a dark like the night. She searched the shadows for wraiths. Her heart thundered in her ears. She grabbed for Tam's arm, holding on for dear life. Water dripped from the murder hole above and slid down her neck.

They emerged into the city, and she gasped for breath. Tam watched her, eyes wide. She was gripping him hard enough to leave bruises. She quickly let go.

He rubbed his arm. "What was that?"

"I think—" She swallowed hard. "I think I'm scared of the dark."

He grunted. "As are we all."

She was relieved he seemed to understand.

Head high and shoulders back, Tam strode into the city as if he owned it. Taking a breath to steel herself, she followed him. With each step she took, she shed a little of the mud from her boots. They crossed the first row of neatly kept houses, a canal filled with boats passing beneath them. Plots of vegetables grew along the sides of each house.

People kept their gazes pinned to the cobblestones as they bowed in Tam's direction. Murmurs of "druid" followed them in a wave.

Larkin and Tam passed a curving side street when Tam's head came up. "Do you smell that?"

"What?"

He filled his lungs. "Meat puffs." He abruptly changed course.

"We're not here for meat puffs," she hissed.

"Do you have any idea how long it's been since I had something besides gilgad stew and dried meat?"

"We had grouse a couple of nights ago."

He stopped before a stall. "Don't worry. I'll buy you some too."

"You are not spending what little coin we have on—"

"Ten for myself and my lovely sister," Tam told the man who eyed them from the other side of the flour-covered table.

The man handed them a steaming hot bag of pastries the size of a small egg. They were filled with meat, cheese, and vegetables fried in bacon grease. Tam popped one in his mouth and moaned in pleasure. He looked down at Larkin and winced. "Again with the glaring."

The baker eyed their travel-worn clothes with interest. "Where have you come from, Druid?"

"Hamel," Tam said.

The man's eyes widened. "Is it true what they say? Are the beasts who steal our daughters really men?"

Tam choked on his second puff and coughed, his eyes watering.

Larkin pounded his back with relish. "What have you heard?"

The man stared at the ground and shuffled awkwardly. "Surely you know, Druid?"

"Of course I do," Tam snapped. "Answer the question."

A woman stepped out of the darkened building behind the man's stall. "Rumors of men from the forest with some strange, dark magic who attacked Hamel. In all the towns and cities of the Alamant, hundreds of unmarried woman have disappeared. And last night, those same men were seen around Cordova—surely you've seen the refugees, Druid."

"The rivers are choked with candles for missing girls," the baker said.

"Some of the men have taken to marrying off their daughters as young as twelve," his wife said.

Larkin paled. "Ancestors."

Without a word, Tam took her arm and hauled her away.

"Their mothers," Larkin said softly. "Oh, their poor mothers."

"We've been over this."

She jerked free. "How can you stand it?"

Tam whirled on her, all traces of humor gone. "I'm sick of being blamed for it."

She was a little afraid of him. He reached into the bag of meat puffs and pushed one against her lips. She breathed it in, her mouth watering.

"Eat it."

She opened her mouth obediently.

"Chew."

She did. It was delicious. Hot and flavorful and greasy. Despite herself, she groaned in pleasure.

Tam nodded in satisfaction. "Better than gilgad soup?"

"So much better," she agreed.

"Now, what are we here to do?"

She took a deep breath. "Find the mansion my mother described. Convince Iniya to help us into the druids' keep during the chaos of the festival. Retrieve the ahlea amulet and Eiryss's journal. Get out."

He linked arms with her, and they strode onto a bridge. Before she knew it, the bag of meat puffs was gone. She was warm and full, her anger held back at arm's length.

Tam grunted in satisfaction and pushed the bag into her hands. "Now, be a good little druid's sister and throw away my rubbish."

She made to argue when she saw druids riding toward them. Long coats covered their legs, and wide-brimmed hats kept the rain off. Head down, she took the bag to one of the wheeled barrels meant for refuse.

"Brother," they murmured to Tam, who repeated the greeting in kind as they passed.

Larkin held her breath until they rode beyond her. She glanced around the edge of her hood to see if they looked back.

Tam stepped up beside her and gripped her arm again. "Keep moving."

The citadel walls loomed before them, the high, arched gates painted a lurid crimson. Two guards in full armor and halberds stood on either side, their helmets obscuring their faces. The symbol on their armor was two descending crescents bisected by a sword.

Larkin's ancestors had lived here. She found herself searching the towers for the one Eiryss might have looked out of in the vision. A drop of rain splashed in her eye, making her blink hard. Tam tugged her forward, as far away from the palace as he could manage.

"I had no idea my grandmother's home was this close," she murmured.

The red doors swung open, and men in black robes with

tooled belts streamed out. Half a dozen headed their way. Larkin gasped, memories swarming her.

Above her, Hunter slid out his knife from his sheath and held it against her exposed throat. She knew she was going to die. Knew she drew her last breath and saw her last sky.

She would never again fly across the fields while her mother and sisters chattered and laughed. Never know the joy of a warm fire after bitter cold or the taste of spring water when she was thirsty. Never stand on the ridgetop on a windy day and imagine she could fly.

"I am sorry," he said as he pressed the blade into her delicate skin.

No! She wasn't going to die! Not today! She twisted and bucked.

The knife slipped across the surface of her throat—but Hunter rocked back, his gaze going wide. They both looked down at the spreading red stain at his chest. Larkin marveled at an arrow haft buried in his ribs up to the fletching. He gave a single gasp and coughed. Warm, wet blood splattered her face and dripped into her hair.

Larkin came to with her face mashed against Tam's damp shirt, her body seizing up. She had to run, hide. But the world spun so fast. She smelled the damp wool, sweat, forest, and campfires. The blackness faded and the spinning eased. She pushed back to stand on her own feet, wobbling.

"Are you well?"

A young man stood behind her, a druid. Hands clasped behind his back, he raised a perfectly arched eyebrow. He was handsome, with pretty blue eyes and waving hair to his shoulders. She stared dumbly at him. She realized she needed to say something, but no words would come.

"We've come a long way, brother," Tam said easily, though she noted his hand slipping to the ax hidden beneath his robes. "Her sister was taken by the beast only days ago."

The man's mouth tightened in sympathy. "I swear to you, lady, we will end the reign of the beast before the snow comes."

She shuddered, but not for the reason the man supposed. "Thank you, sir."

He bowed and slipped away.

Tam watched him go. "If it was easy, it wouldn't be fun."

She breathed out. "So fun."

He grinned. "Now you're getting it."

Larkin shot Tam an exasperated look and hurried down the nearest side street. Finally, she came to the mansion her mother described. A hulking, two-story building with a wide, wraparound porch and grand windows. She couldn't picture her father growing up in such luxury. And certainly not him ever willingly leaving it behind.

Inside was Larkin's grandmother. Larkin looked down at her dress in despair. It was fine, but they'd been traveling for two days, and the mud didn't help.

She sighed. There was nothing to be done. Taking a fortifying breath, Larkin pushed against the gate, which opened on silent hinges. Squaring her shoulders, Larkin marched up to the door and knocked.

Smoothing her gray smock, a serving girl with black hair, brown eyes, and enormous teeth answered the door. She inclined her head at Tam. "How may I serve you, Druid?"

Tam stood stiff and straight. "We are here to see Iniya Rothsberd."

The maid eyed their muddy boots and tsked disapprovingly. "I'm afraid Lady Iniya is not well."

Larkin blinked, unable to believe a druid would be denied entrance anywhere.

"I'm afraid I must insist," Tam said.

"My lady is not well, Druid." The maid wasn't budging. "I must insist you come back at—"

Tam pushed open the door. "Then take us to her bedside."

The girl's mouth tightened, but she didn't argue. She led them to a sitting room, the walls covered with taxidermied heads of leopards, deer, and mountain goats. There was a full-sized gilgad and a bear as well. A man rose as they entered. "Tinsy, who—"

He cut off, staring at Larkin as she stared back. He had her same unruly red hair. Her same smattering of freckles. Eyes wide, he came toward her.

Larkin cocked back her arm and punched her father full in the face.

CHAPTER 17

FAMILY

Harben staggered back from the blow, his hand going to his jaw. Tam stepped between them, his hand on his ax handle. "Larkin?"

Larkin pretended like she hadn't just broken her wrist, letting it hang limp from her side. "Tam, this is my lying, cheating, adulterous father."

To her surprise, Harben made no move to strike back, only stared at her in amazement. He was dressed in a fine shirt and trousers, his normally unruly hair cut short and his scraggly beard neatly trimmed. Only his bloodshot eyes and trembling hands betrayed him for the useless drunkard he was.

"You're alive," he breathed. "You're here. How?"

Furious tears filled her eyes. The forest take her, her wrist hurt. "You don't get to ask questions."

Harben, she'd vowed never to call him Papa again, nodded to the maid. "Tinsy, go to the cellar and fetch a few cold slabs of raw meat."

"But, sir," Tinsy said.

He held out his hand. "Tinsy, please."

She turned on her heel and left the room.

Eyeing Tam, Harben wisely put a couch between them. "Who is this?" When Larkin didn't answer, Harben paled. "Not a piper—your husband? Surely you're not fool enough to bring one of them here."

While Larkin and her family had been fighting and running for their lives from the wraiths, her father had been lounging in this mansion. Ancestors, she didn't think it was possible to hate him more.

"He's not my husband, and how do you know anything about the pipers?"

"Oh, good," Harben breathed. "And I know because I figured out enough for my mother to explain it to me."

"He is a piper," Larkin said with more than a little satisfaction.

Harben groaned. "It's not safe for you. Go back to the forest."

The forest wasn't safe either. "The forest take you and your mistress and your son." The son he'd always wanted. Ancestors, she hated him. "I came to see my grandmother, not you. Where is she?"

The maid, Tinsy, came back with two raw chunks of roast. Harben pressed one to his cheek. The other he held out to her. She crossed her arms, hiding the wince that came from the pressure on her wrist. "I don't need it."

Tam took it from Harben and shoved it at Larkin. "You're going to want to keep on top of the swelling," he murmured.

Larkin threw the steak on the floor and blocked the retreating maid. "I will speak with Iniya. Now."

Tinsy shot Harben a look. He nodded reluctantly, which saved him from another punch to the face.

"I'll fetch her, miss," the maid said. She bowed and left.

Tam picked the steak off the floor. None too gently, he took Larkin's wrist and rested the steak on the back of her hand. She flinched at the bolt of pain and shifted the meat to her wrist. She ignored Harben, though she could feel his stare. Instead, she studied the room. With its forest-green paint and taxidermy, it seemed a mockery of the real forest.

The click of a cane and hard heels preceded Iniya's entrance. She wore her white hair piled in an elaborate updo atop her head. Fine-boned, with a thin, graceful neck and severe wrinkles, she wore a spotless, perfectly pleated dress in solid black.

Her pale blue eyes looked Larkin up and down, from her muddy boots to her soaked clothes. Her gaze lingered on her wild mane and freckles. "The lost son has returned, and he's brought more mutts with him." Her voice was high and warbling.

Larkin huffed. "I've come to bargain with you on behalf of the pipers."

"The pipers have nothing I want." Iniya's gaze narrowed on the slab of meat her son held against his swelling cheek. "What happened to your face? You look as though you've wrestled with the beasts of the game room and lost."

Harben grunted.

The old woman noted Larkin's meat-wrapped wrist. "Savages." She turned her back on them and went to a sideboard, which she unlocked with an iron key hanging from a ribbon around her neck. She pulled out a tumbler and glass, poured herself a finger width, locked the cabinet back up, and took a swallow.

"My son is no longer allowed to imbibe," Iniya said.

Larkin scoffed in disbelief—her father never stopped drinking for longer than it took to sleep off his hangover or discover Mama's stash of money.

Iniya glared at her. "We can only assume the weakness in his blood—from his father's side, of course—is inherited by his children, so you'll excuse me for not offering—"

Harben tossed his steak onto the coffee table. "Mother, that's enough."

Iniya gaped at the bloody, dripping meat in horror. "Tinsy!" her voice turned shrill. The girl immediately hustled into the room. Had she been lurking behind the door, listening?

"My late husband's decorating taste aside," Iniya said, "I do not allow carcasses inside the game room. Kindly remove them before I remove you from my staff!"

Pursing her lips, which didn't quite close over her teeth, Tinsy took the meat from the table and from Larkin.

Iniya started toward a chair and then noted a bloody imprint on her rug. "Oh, the forest take me and all mine. Girl, get a bucket of soapy water!"

Iniya finished her drink, unlocked the cabinet, and poured herself some more. After locking it, she sat in one of the chairs, her feet flat on the floor and her back ramrod straight. "Now, what must I do to be rid of you?"

Larkin set her jaw. She didn't know what to expect from the woman who'd turned her back on her own son, but perhaps remorse. "I come with an offer from the pipers to help you regain your throne."

Iniya waved her hand. "As if the pipers could do anything except get me hanged for sedition." She sipped and tipped her glass toward her son. "Are there any other banished relatives you'd like to yank from the mud and set on my door. Perhaps another barmaid turned mistress? I'm not running an orphanage or a brothel!"

The barmaid—that would be Harben's mistress, who had given birth shortly after Brenna was born.

"She's my wife," Harben ground out.

So he had married the woman, then. Larkin could almost feel sorry for her, if she didn't hate her so much.

"I'm not an orphan," Larkin said through gritted teeth. "I'm your granddaughter."

Iniya leaned back in her chair. "You have your mother's eyes—traitorous and conniving wretch that she was. She tricked my son into marrying her—the Master Druid's daughter! Of course I disowned Harben. Told him never to step foot inside my door until he was rid of her."

Harben dropped into the chair opposite hers. "Or until I gave you a grandson."

That's why Harben had been so eager for a son, why he had finally abandoned them?

"Queens can't rule in the Idelmarch." Iniya took another sip. "A convenient little law the druids enacted before I came of age. I needed an heir if the nobility was to support me."

Harben mumbled something. Iniya glared at him. "Don't mutter, boy. And sit up straight. You have to command presence if you are ever to inspire an army to put you upon the throne!"

Her father on a throne? She'd once found him sleeping in a pigsty for warmth because he'd been too drunk to find his way home.

Harben sank deeper into his chair, a mulish expression on his face.

Iniya rounded on Larkin. "I'd offer to have Tinsy pack you a lunch to see you on your way, but I'm afraid it might attract more strays." She made a shooing motion.

Larkin came around the other side of the couch. Iniya stiffened, her grip tightening on her cane. Larkin simply fluffed out her fine cloak—which was soaked and filthy from two days of travel—and sat on the felt couch. From the corner where he'd taken residence beside a lunging gilgad, Tam grinned.

Iniya's mouth fell open in horror. "How dare you!"

Staring right in the older woman's eyes, Larkin folded her muddy boots under her. Harben nodded in approval. As if she would ever need or want anything from him. Tam's grin widened to show his teeth.

Iniya stamped her cane in outrage. "Tinsy! Fetch Oben from the stables. Tell him to bring the whip!"

Running steps and a slamming door announced the maid's obedience. Larkin wasn't afraid. With her magic, a man with a whip couldn't even touch her.

Harben leaned toward Larkin. "How did you escape the pipers?"

Iniya turned toward her son. "You will have nothing to do with this wild whelp of yours."

Harben folded his arms across his chest. "I have my monthly allowance—more than enough to provide for my daughter."

Now he wanted to provide? Where was his providing when her belly had cramped with hunger? Where was it when she wore her shirt through so badly it had gone transparent? When Nesha had gotten so sick that her mother had been forced to beg Lord Daydon for the money to pay for her medicine?

Larkin's sigils vibrated with anger. "I do not need you providing for me."

It was as if Iniya and Harben hadn't heard her. Iniya's face went white with rage. "I will not allow my money to be—"

"My money," Harben interrupted. "It's in the contract you signed in exchange for my cooperation."

"There are stipulations!"

"None of which disallow donations for charities!" Harben turned back to Larkin. "If you don't need money, what do you need?"

Larkin looked at this man—the father who had beaten his family and stolen their money meant for food and wasted it on cheap beer, the man who had thrown her in the river and nearly drowned her. How could she let that man help her?

Harben must have seen some of this in her gaze. He leaned back. "Just because you use me doesn't mean you forgive me."

Use him. She could use him. "I need to get into the palace."

"My palace," Iniya said with a stamp of her cane. She did

that a lot.

Surprise crossed Harben's face. "Why?"

"There's a book of lullabies in the library," Tam said.

"And I need to see Queen Eiryss's tomb," Larkin said.

"Eiryss's tomb?" Iniya's voice turned speculative.

Harben cocked an eyebrow. "Why?"

Somewhere a door shut, and heavy footsteps thundered toward them. The servant with the whip was coming.

Larkin half shook her head. "I won't tell you that."

An enormous man came in, whip in hand. His forehead loomed over deep-set eyes. "Mistress?" Despite his monstrous appearance, his voice was as high as a girl's.

Iniya jabbed her cane in Larkin's direction. "See that this fiend is removed from my property."

The man unwound his whip as he stalked toward her. Tam moved to intercept. Larkin motioned for him to stay put. When Oben reached for her, she formed her shield and sword and let out a carefully controlled pulse, knocking the man on his backside and blowing over a vase with fresh flowers. Feathers from a grouse fluttered down from where they'd been blown up to the ceiling. The entire right side of the bird was bald, the eye glaring indignantly at Larkin.

Glorying in their shocked expressions, Larkin assumed a fighting stance. "Want to try that again?"

Oben scrambled to stand between her and Iniya. He might be shocked, but Larkin could admire that he was also well trained and loyal.

"She has magic," Iniya breathed. She glared at her son. "You never told me she had magic!"

Harben gaped at Larkin in shock. Outside the pipers, only her mother, sisters, and a handful of druids knew.

"I need a way into the palace," Larkin repeated to Harben.

Iniya set the rest of her drink on a side table. "It's well known that my granddaughter is a traitor to the Idelmarch. The druids would know who you were."

"Not if you make me look like Nesha," Larkin said. "Dye my hair. Cover my freckles." Larkin couldn't do much to imitate Nesha's eyes—a startling shade of violet—but only someone who had seen her sister would know that.

"Unlike you, Nesha would be welcome in the palace." Iniya considered her. "What could you possibly want from Eiryss's tomb?"

Larkin ignored her. "Can you get me in or not?" she asked Harben.

"He can't," Iniya said. "But I can." The woman nodded to her servants. "I pay well for your discretion. Neither of you breathes a word of this to anyone." The old woman gestured with her cane. "Out."

They backed from the room.

Tam watched them go, his hand on his sword. "Money is a poor motivator, especially when the druids likely have more."

Iniya leveled him with a flat look. "I took them from the streets as children, and I've tested their loyalty many times. They've always passed."

Iniya motioned her son to the door. "You too."

"I—" he began.

"Now!" Iniya commanded. "Make sure that barmaid of yours stays out of my jewelry."

Harben ground his teeth and left.

Iniya sat back, a speculative look in her eyes. "You mentioned a bargain."

Larkin let her weapons fade back inside her sigils. "You weren't interested before."

"That was before I knew the pipers had anything I wanted."

Larkin fought the urge to run from the woman's hungry look. "Prince Denan has pledged soldiers to support your bid for the throne. After you become queen, the Idelmarch will join with the pipers to defeat the wraiths."

Iniya rose to her feet and trembled with eagerness. "Give me magic—the magic of the ancients—and I will give you whatever you want."

Sela could remove the curse. Denan could find a way to take the woman to the White Tree. But Iniya's eagerness made her uneasy.

"You won't have magic," Tam said. "But soldiers."

Iniya turned her back on them. "Then we have no bargain."

Larkin bit her lip. "Why magic?"

Iniya studied Larkin. "The people would never stand for a queen who used the thieves of their daughters to put her on the throne."

Larkin hadn't considered that, but the old woman was right.

Iniya stared into the cold hearth. "If I have magic, I won't need to be gifted my kingdom by those who will hold it in trust depending on my obedience. I will win it and bear it with my own power."

Tam pulled Larkin aside and whispered, "It's not a good idea to have women's magic in the Idelmarch."

"Even if the woman wielding that magic is our ally?" Larkin asked.

Tam pursed his lips. "People like her only have one ally. If we give her an advantage, she may end up a problem we'll have to deal with later."

"What do you suggest?" Larkin asked.

He faced Iniya. "We can pledge troops. Nothing more."

Iniya's eyes glittered. "You mean to keep the magic for yourself."

"We—"

"The very reason the war began all those years ago," Iniya interrupted. "Over who could and could not have magic."

Tam stilled.

Had it? Larkin didn't actually know. How had Iniya learned so much about the history the curse was intent on erasing?

"What do you know of it?" Larkin asked.

"Enough," Iniya said bitterly.

Larkin knew loss when she saw it. What had the curse cost Iniya? "How can we trust you?" Larkin asked.

"Or know that you can deliver what you promise?" Tam said.

Iniya huffed. "Trust? This had nothing to do with trust. It's a business arrangement. I need your magic. You need me to get you into the palace." At Tam's doubtful look, she went on, "My influence may not be what it should, but I hold the loyalty of the nobility. We are still a force to be reckoned with."

"And what's to hold you to your bargain?" Tam asked. "To form an alliance with the Alamant after the Idelmarch is yours."

She eyed the piper with distaste. "What other options do you have, piper?"

Tam shot Larkin an uneasy look. "We don't have to agree to anything."

They could still run away, slip into the forest. She shook her head. "We can't." They needed the ahlea amulet and the journal. But there was another reason Larkin had come. "If we give you this, you must agree to have the Idelmarchians' curses lifted." They could figure out the logistics of bringing people to Sela later. "The practice of keeping the people in ignorance must cease."

"Done," Iniya said.

"Even if we take you to the White Tree and give you a thorn," Larkin said, surprised that the curse let her say as much. How had Iniya gained so much knowledge? "There's no guarantee it will work."

"Then our agreement is for one sigil," Iniya said. "If not for me, then for someone of my choosing."

Reluctantly, Larkin nodded.

Iniya turned on her heel and clicked from the room. "Tinsy!" she shrilled. "Find a lice comb."

CHAPTER 18

PREPARE

A lice comb? Why did they need a— "Lice comb!" Larkin stormed after her. "I do not have lice!"

"I'll not take any chances with the linens." Iniya opened the door to a wide back porch hemmed in by ivy. Beyond was a courtyard vegetable garden and pots of herbs. "Tinsy!"

The maid opened a door under the porch and hurried up, a tray of tea in hand.

"Never mind that," Iniya said. "Send one of the linen girls to scrub out the game room from top to bottom." The maid took off. "Oben!"

A beat later, the huge servant stepped from a long house on the other side of the yard. "Start a fire under the tub." She looked over Larkin's clothes. "We've some things to burn."

"What gives you the right—" Larkin began.

Iniya stepped nose to nose with Larkin. "If you want my help, you will not spend one more moment in my house in those filthy rags."

197

Larkin looked down at the stolen dress in disbelief. "This is a fine dress!"

Iniya snorted. "For a country wife, perhaps."

Larkin gripped the full skirt in her fists. "I'm not going another step until you tell me what you're planning."

Iniya opened her mouth to argue before seeming to decide against it. "The equinox celebrations begin tonight with Black Rites. I will be expected to make an appearance with my family. It will give everyone a chance to see you and speculate on who you are—better that they come to their own conclusions than be told outright. They'll have less reason to question me. Plus, there's someone I need to speak with, and I need to do it in person.

"Tomorrow is the festival in the city—it's more for the peasants, so we needn't attend. And the final day ..." She paused and drew a deep breath. "The final day is the feast in the keep. You will either find the things you need or you won't—there won't be another opportunity until the next equinox." Iniya eyed Larkin. "If you want to pass as Nesha, you'll need your ridiculous hair and freckles tamed."

"How do you know what Nesha looks like?" Had the old woman kept an eye on them all these years?

Iniya turned on her heel and started down the stairs.

Tam shot Larkin a frustrated look before trotting after her. "You're a political adversary," Tam said. "I don't understand why the druids let you live, let alone participate."

Iniya's gaze was sharp enough to cut. "You seem a strapping boy. You can help Oben."

Tam lifted an eyebrow. "I'll stick with Larkin."

"That will be awkward," Iniya said. "As she's about to be naked, and you are not her husband."

Tam turned a brilliant shade of red.

Iniya's eyes narrowed. "What exactly are you to her?"

"I'm her guard," Tam said.

Iniya hummed low in her throat. She scrutinized Larkin before rounding back on him. "Well, if you're going to stay here, you'll have to endure the lice comb as well. In the meantime, stay out of my house." She brushed past him to the yard. "Errand boy!"

"Mistress?" a voice called from above. A boy of no more than twelve peered down at them from the roof. His hands were filthy.

"Whatever are you—oh, never mind," Iniya said. "Fetch me a basket full of walnut shells. Quickly now!"

He scampered down the side of the house like a squirrel, bounded over the low wall, and took off.

Iniya reached the garden and turned to a heavy door behind the stairs. Beyond was a huge space divided into five crude rooms, two along each side and the fifth, center room taken up by the enormous cistern. To the right were the kitchens and the laundry rooms. To the left was a long room filled with pallets and some sort of bathing room with a long copper tub partially in a fireplace. A couple of spigots protruded from one wall.

As this was all mostly underground, it should have been cool, but the fires in the kitchen and laundry made everything humid and hot. Oben built a third fire beneath the tub filled with water from the cistern.

Iniya circled the cistern, peering in at the women kneading bread and tending the stove. Two more women stirred what looked like sheets in a huge tub. Iniya hmphed in approval.

"Not one nit left," she said to Tinsy before clicking back outside and shutting the door behind her.

"This way, miss," Tinsy said. She motioned to a battered wooden chair before a vanity. Above it lorded a fancy silver mirror corroded black around the edges. Her own hair covered with a tight rag, Tinsy retrieved a comb and started on Larkin's scalp, parting and combing, parting and combing.

"I'm not finding anything," the maid said.

"I already told you that," Larkin huffed.

"I had to check, miss." Tinsy attacked Larkin's ends with a comb.

After only a few strokes, Larkin's scalp stung, and her hair had exploded into a wild bush. Tinsy jerked and tugged and grumbled until the comb snapped in half. Tinsy blew a tendril of her own hair out of her face and glared at Larkin's hair, which stuck out like a head full of dandelion seeds—or a pissed-off tabby cat.

"When was the last time you combed this?" Tinsy asked.

Larkin frowned at the maid's silky-smooth locks. "I don't."

The cook brought in a pot filled with a paste made from boiled walnut husks. They made Larkin soak her hair, eyelashes, and eyebrows in it for nearly an hour before rinsing it out over the drain in the floor. Her hair had shifted from vibrant red to a rich auburn. Larkin had always hated her hair, but it was as much a part of her as her fingers and toes. Seeing it in a different color felt like a lie.

Huffing, Tinsy motioned for Larkin to undress.

"I can bathe without you here," Larkin said.

"Mistress insists I make sure it's done properly. Besides, I can massage your scalp."

Grudgingly, Larkin slipped out of the stolen dress. Tinsy immediately threw it in the fire. Larkin snatched it out of the coals. Thankfully, it was still damp, so it wasn't singed.

"You don't waste a perfectly good dress like this!" It was finer than anything she'd ever had in Hamel. She glared at Tinsy, daring the girl to try something like that again.

Rolling her eyes, Tinsy gathered a collection of soaps and oils onto a tray and turned around. Her gaze landed on Larkin, and she gasped.

Larkin looked down at herself, at the bruises that bloomed up her side and had turned the toes of her right foot black and green. Thankfully, her wrist didn't appear swollen, and it didn't hurt as much as it had—probably just sprained.

But it wasn't her bruises the girl's eyes lingered on, but Larkin's pale, raised sigils. Her wedding sigils formed cuffs of twinning vines. Her right hand and left forearm bore geometric sigils for her sword and shield.

The sigil on her upper arm formed a vine filled with ahlea flowers that trailed down until it mingled with her wedding vines, blossoms peeking out here and there. The one on her neck formed diamond facets that surrounded her spine from the base of her skull to below her shoulder blades.

They were beautiful.

"Wh-What are they?" Tinsy asked.

Larkin opened her mouth, but the word *sigil* wouldn't leave her lips. Neither would *magic* or *pipers*. The curse's dark work. No wonder Idelmarchians thought the taken enchanted. Instead, Larkin flared her sigils, colors flashing beneath her skin. Her sword and shield were a comforting pressure in her hands. "This is what they are."

Tinsy took a step back. "How?"

Larkin let her weapons fade. "The beast is not what you think it is." It explained nothing, but it was all the curse would allow her to say.

Tinsy recoiled. "Your water is getting cold."

Steam curled across the top. Clearly not, but Larkin didn't push the girl. She stepped gingerly onto the wooden platform that spanned the bottom of the tub, eased gingerly down, and scrubbed herself with the bar of vetiver soap Tinsy provided.

She sighed in relief. She hadn't been truly clean since Denan had taken her to the waterfall. Delightful memories made her cheeks flush with embarrassment.

Thankfully, Tinsy didn't seem to notice as she poured water over Larkin's head. As she'd promised, she lathered it and massaged her scalp. When she was finished, she poured more water. Rivulets of brown suds slipped down Larkin's skin, staining the water. Larkin closed her eyes and allowed herself to relax.

By then, the water was practically boiling her alive, even though Tinsy had raked the coals. Larkin rinsed and oiled her hair. Stepping out, she wrapped linen around herself and gently scrunched her hair. Someone knocked on the door. Tinsy opened it to three girls. Larkin tightened her hold on her linen. The trio ignored her as they brought in a table, chest, and a horrible black dress with pearl buttons before leaving as quickly as they'd come.

"Put the dress on," Tinsy said without looking at her.

Larkin pulled it down from where the girl had hung it on a spigot and stepped into it. It turned out to be skirts divided for riding and a shirt with pearl buttons rather than a traditional dress. The material felt stiff and uncomfortable.

Tinsy loosely tied the corset, did up the tiny row of buttons, and motioned to the chair. Larkin sat. The woman tugged Larkin's hair into an elegant twist, curls framing her face. Then she rummaged through the trunk and pulled out an assortment of jars.

She eyed Larkin, then the contents of the jars, then Larkin, then the contents. She mixed some of the powders into an empty jar, dabbed it with her finger, and ran a streak of powder on Larkin's cheek. She made a sound low in her throat and mixed in another powder. After shaking it, she put another streak on Larkin's other cheek.

"That's it," she said in satisfaction. She dipped a brush in the powder and dusted every inch of Larkin's exposed skin. One stroke at a time, Larkin's freckles disappeared behind a thick layer of makeup.

Finally, Tinsy stood back and frowned at Larkin. "You'll have to be careful in the palace. Dour as the druids pretend to be, all men like beautiful girls."

Larkin looked down at herself. "I don't understand."

Tinsy motioned to the mirror before stepping aside.

Bracing herself, Larkin stood before it. She blinked at the image of her sister, Nesha, peering back at her.

No. Not Nesha, but Larkin's own face.

Her hair had gone from frizzy copper to curling auburn. Her skin from mottled with freckles to smooth as cream. Even her plain brown eyes gleamed, though they were still the wrong color.

Larkin shifted uncomfortably. She'd always disliked her hair and her freckles. Until Denan had traced them with his thumb like he was drawing constellations, had spun her curls around his finger. She'd begun to realize that maybe what made her different also made her beautiful.

"Will it wash out?" Larkin tried to pretend the answer didn't matter.

"Eventually." Tinsy pulled the drain on the tub, the water splashing into a channel in the floor that led toward the yard.

The heavy door pushed open. Oben stepped aside; Iniya clicked into the room behind him. She looked Larkin up and down. "Well, you're no great beauty, but covering those ridiculous freckles and taming that hair has helped."

Larkin understood why her father had been so willing to leave all this wealth behind. "What does what I look like matter?"

Iniya hmphed. "Even here we have heard stories of the traitor girl allied with the beasts of the forest and her beautiful sister who drove her from the village, not once, but three times."

Larkin winced. "Nesha is pregnant."

Iniya held out a dome-shaped pillow.

The only way the old woman could know that … "You've been keeping track of us."

Iniya stiffened, clearly affronted. "Can I help it if your father talks?" She turned on her heel, the click of her boot heels and cane forming a cadence.

Not quite believing her, Larkin hurried to catch up to the old woman as she stepped outside. "Where's Tam?"

Iniya pointed to a black lump under one of the trees and started up the stairs. "It's his turn to be thoroughly inspected for nits."

"Tam," Larkin called.

The black lump shifted. Rubbing sleep from his eyes, Tam took one look at her and bolted to his feet, his hand on his ax hilt. He stared at her hair, then her skin, then back at her hair.

Hating that she'd woken him from sleep, she raised an eyebrow. "What?"

He settled and brushed detritus from his stolen clothes. "You look just like that evil sister of yours."

Larkin's first instinct was to argue—defending Nesha was as ingrained in her as never wasting a single scrap of food. She rubbed at the headache starting at her temples.

"You'll frizz your hair!" Iniya called from the doorway.

Larkin jerked her hand down and muttered something not very nice under her breath.

Tam strode to her. His eyes were puffy, as if he'd cried himself to sleep. "I can see why your father ran away."

As much as Larkin hated her father, she couldn't disagree. She rested a hand on his arm. "Tam …"

"Come," Iniya demanded from the house. "Dinner is ready."

Tam pulled away from her touch, his face transforming to an impish one. "Do you think they have more meat puffs?"

Larkin swore she could feel the weight of Talox's hand on her shoulder, his voice in her ear. *"Humor is how Tam deals with the fear and pain."*

Ancestors, how could Talox be gone?

She wished Tam would talk to her—she missed Talox too. Instead, she rolled her eyes as she followed him inside.

"I don't think meat puffs are fancy enough for—" She stopped at the sight of her father's new wife seated at the table.

Raeneth's gaze fixed on the tablecloth. Everything about the woman was round, from her breasts to her arched shoulders and her belly to the bottom of her buttocks. Even her face was round. She didn't look like a willing accomplice in tearing Larkin's family apart and nearly destroying her mother.

Larkin turned on her heel. "I'll eat outside."

Iniya banged her cane on the ground.

Oben instantly blocked the doorway. He glared at her from under his craggy brows. Where had he come from?

Larkin glared over her shoulder at her grandmother. "Do you honestly think he can stop me?"

Iniya calmly spooned soup into her bowl. "Are you in the habit of murdering servants simply because they're in your way?"

Larkin rounded on her. "He spent the money meant to buy our food on cheap beer and her." She jabbed a finger at Raeneth. "You want to negotiate with me? I want her gone."

Raeneth winced. Harben rose to his feet, his face the furious mask Larkin knew so well. His hands balled into fists at his side; he took a menacing step toward her. Relief surged through Larkin. This was the moment she'd been waiting for. The fight—the release—she'd needed ever since she left Denan. She took a defensive stance, all the lessons Denan, Talox, and Tam had drilled into her filling her head.

Raeneth's hand shot out, gripping Harben's forearm. "Don't." She looked up at him, brown eyes pleading. "You promised." She pushed back from the table. "I'll go." She left without a backward glance.

The fight sloughed off Harben like a snake shedding his skin. "This fight is between us, Larkin. Leave her out of it."

Larkin shook her head in disgust. "You have them all fooled, but not me. You won't stop drinking. You'll never stop."

Harben held out hands that trembled. "Look at me, Larkin. Really look."

He wanted her to see his clear gaze. His face was pale, lacking the flush of drink. His actions and words were crisp. She wasn't fooled.

"He hasn't had a drop since he came to this house," Iniya said. "Nor will he."

"As if you could stop him," Larkin said.

His hands fell to his sides. "I—" He shook his head. "I'm trying, Larkin. That's all I can do."

Larkin trembled with pent-up rage that had nowhere to go. "The fact that you're trying now is more of a betrayal than anything."

Head down, he left the room.

Tam eased a step closer. "Larkin, you don't have to like them to make a deal with them."

"Raeneth is part of the plan," Iniya said.

"How?" Larkin demanded.

"Sit down and find out." When Larkin hesitated, Iniya buttered her scone. "I don't like her either—a barmaid may well be a step down from your trollop of a mother—but she gave me a grandson, so I tolerate her presence."

Like she wouldn't tolerate Larkin's or her sisters' presence. That baby held more weight to the old woman than any of them, just because he was a boy. She was wrong. So wrong. Sela was the most important person in all the Alamant—and the Idelmarch, for that matter.

And I am a warrior. As well as a princess, though Larkin didn't feel she'd done anything to earn that title, aside from being kidnapped by a prince. She considered rubbing all of that in her grandmother's face, then decided the old woman didn't deserve to know the details of her family's life.

Let her believe her lies.

Larkin folded her arms, wincing at the soreness in her wrist from punching her father. "You don't need a grandson anymore."

Iniya's gaze sharpened. "Someone has to rule after I am gone." Her voice was as smooth as the butter she spread.

Larkin didn't believe her for a second. She let out a long breath and released the tension from her muscles. She plopped down at the table. "Fine. Let's hear this plan of yours, *Grandmother*."

CHAPTER 19

UNWANTED

Tam settled in the chair Raeneth had vacated and started loading both his and Larkin's plates. "Yeah, let's hear it, Granny."

She stared at him, eyes popping out of her head. "Did I not make it perfectly clear you would not be allowed in my house until you've been thoroughly inspected—"

Tam flattened her with a look. "My house in the Alamant is twice as grand as this. When I'm not serving as the prince's personal guard—or Larkin's—I command my own unit of a hundred soldiers. Your own granddaughter is a princess." He dunked his scone in his soup and bit into it. He winced, probably realizing it was a sweet bread, and shook the remains in Iniya's direction. "So from now on, you're going to pretend to be respectful."

Iniya blinked, opened her mouth, and shut it again. "A princess?"

Tam rolled his eyes. "And unlike in the Idelmarch, Larkin has power."

Not yet. Still, Larkin wasn't about to argue.

Iniya's gaze turned inward. "Very well, Tam, Commander of a Hundred Men and Defender of the Prince. You may remain." She took a delicate bite of her own scone. "The feast begins in two days. While I'm not technically allowed to bring more than two guests, the druids won't turn away Nesha and her guard"—she looked pointedly at Tam—"sent by their very own prize Black Druid, Garrot."

Tam huffed. "Appears I've been demoted." He leaned into Larkin. "I might actually miss terrorizing Idelmarchians as a druid. It's more fun when you can see their reactions."

Rolling her eyes, Larkin tore apart her own scone and slathered it with butter and jam. "Garrot is important to the druids?"

Iniya stirred her soup, ran the edge of her spoon over the bowl's rim, and set it delicately on her plate. "If all goes according to his plans, Garrot will be the next Master Druid."

The forest take him and my sister both, Larkin thought darkly.

"And the current Master Druid would be all right with his disowned granddaughter at his celebrations?" Tam asked.

"The hero of Hamel?" Iniya scoffed. "He could not very well turn her away."

Nesha, a hero—for betraying her family and nearly getting Larkin killed, twice. She hid her clenched fists under the table. "And after?"

"Leave that to me," Iniya said. "But first, we attend the Black Rites."

Larkin didn't like the sound of that.

Tam looked up. "Black Rites?"

Iniya lifted her bowl to her lips. "Any regular druid who wishes to become a Black Druid must enter the Forbidden Forest and discover its secret."

This was why the Black Druids were feared and admired—they had survived what no one else had.

Tam's eyes widened. "Without knowing what's inside?"

"A few make it back intact," Iniya said.

Tam sat back with a huff. "That's not far off from murder."

"What's a few less druids? While there, I must speak with a man, Humbent."

Larkin looked between Tam and Iniya. "Just like that? We attend the equinox celebrations and try to get inside the crypts and library?"

"Just?" Iniya huffed. "If the druids realize who you are, we'll all be part of the equinox's culminating activity: the public hangings."

Tinsy led Larkin upstairs to a darkened room. She opened the first set of three drapes, revealing pale blue everything—from the walls to the tufted furniture, drapes, and bed frothing with lace.

Against one wall, a dusty row of dolls sat in size from largest to smallest. They wore elegant gowns. Their wooden faces were beautifully painted, though that paint had faded and chipped.

Larkin touched the gorgeous embroidery on one dress, the jewels on the bodice of another, the dusty hair of a third—real and as riotous a red as Larkin's own. "Whose bedroom was this?" Her father had been an only child.

Tinsy opened the last set of drapes. "These are Madame Iniya's things from her days at the palace."

Fitting that the Mad Queen would have a room full of dolls. There were other dolls with different color hair—blondes and reds. Hair from those long since dead.

They were her family too, she realized. Her great-grandparents and the rest of their children killed at the palace. Larkin recoiled and brushed the dust off her fingers. She wandered to the glass doors, released the catch, and stepped out onto the round balcony. The castle spires loomed high and to the right above the curtain wall. No guards surrounded Iniya's house. Why was Iniya allowed to live autonomously outside the walls of the palace that should have been hers?

"Do you know Iniya's story?" Larkin asked.

Tinsy stiffened. "She never speaks of it." She left the room without another word.

"Is this what I'm meant to do?" Settling on the couch, Larkin took her amulet out and pushed the sharp branch into the skin of her forearm. She hissed at the pain.

The vision came with the taste of ashes and copper—the same vision she'd had before, of the day the curse began. Larkin wandered among the dead and dying, the shadows devouring. At the dais, she watched Eiryss and Dray fight and lose.

When the vision released her, she lay panting, tears welling in her eyes. What did it mean?

"How am I supposed to guard anyone with this?" Tam said from the doorway. He crossed the room, holding a dull metal sword. He pushed the tip into the rug. "It doesn't bend! One good hit, and it will shatter like ice. And they didn't even bother giving me a shield!"

Sitting up, Larkin pressed against the puncture mark to stop the bleeding. "You can't very well show up with your sacred sword, can you?"

He harrumphed. "What is it you always say: 'the forest take you'? More like the Idelmarchians take you. I don't know how you stand these dark, dank houses."

She stiffened. Her home in Hamel had been a beehive hut made of staggered stones and a dirt floor. There had been no window, and when the wood of their door had swelled, it wouldn't open at all.

"Sorry," Tam said.

She shrugged as if it didn't matter. It did. Poverty wasn't

something one shook off. It haunted her. It would always haunt her.

Tam looked about the room and made a face at the dolls. "I guess you can take the bed and I'll sleep on the couch." He started pushing the furniture to the edge of the room.

"What are you doing?" she asked.

"Well, we can't exactly practice in the yard where anyone from the street might see." He produced two sticks, the branches freshly trimmed. He grabbed two pillows off the bed, tossing her one and holding the other like a shield. "In a line, you stand shoulder to shoulder. Mulgars only come at you from the front. They're all wild animal and no finesse. So when they crash into you, sweep your shield, stab from below. Reposition."

Sweep. Stab. Reposition. "Denan showed me this before."

"Not in working with a line, he didn't."

He stood shoulder to shoulder with her, and they repelled a dozen imaginary mulgars.

"Shouldn't you be teaching me to fight druids?" The mulgars couldn't reach them here.

Tam took a deep breath. "If we're caught, we're dead. Unless we can convince them to ransom us."

She swallowed. "It might make a difference."

He considered her. "Your sword and shield are a last resort. If anyone sees you using a magic blade, it's over. Here, wrap me up from behind." She wrapped her arms around him. "Slice your foot down my shin, stomp on my foot, and throw the back of your head into my nose." He demonstrated slowly. "Now you try."

She worked on the move until he was satisfied.

"You can throw an elbow into my guts too. Always remember—hard to soft. So elbow to guts, fist to throat, fingers to eyes, knee to groin, that kind of thing."

Her lip curled in distaste. "One more time."

He wrapped his arms around her. She slid, stomped, elbowed, and headbutted. "Good."

"Now for the front." He turned her so she faced him. "In this pos—"

"What is going on?" Iniya stared at them from the doorway, her jaw tight.

Larkin and Tam jumped back, though they'd done nothing wrong. "He's teaching me to fight."

Iniya jabbed her cane at them. "The only fighting you'll be doing is with your wits." She tossed something at Larkin. A dome-shaped pillow and a rag belt used for monthlies. "We've the Black Rites to attend. Tie that around your middle. The horses are waiting."

The pillow stuffed under her shirt to imitate Nesha's pregnancy, Larkin settled into the saddle atop a placid gelding. It had been a long time since Bane had taught her to ride on his own horse, but her body remembered what to do.

Ancestors, Bane. I wish you were here with me. Was Denan having any luck with ransoming him? Surely the Black Druids would value money more than hanging a lord's son.

Feet planted firmly on the ground, Tam stared at his horse. "Could we not take the carriage?"

"The roads outside the city will be a swamp from all the rain." Harben swung effortlessly into the saddle. He reached down and patted his mare's neck. He seemed happy, content even. It wasn't fair after what he'd put them through. Thankfully, Raeneth stayed home with her baby.

Oben pushed Iniya's rump into the saddle. She winced, rubbing her hip as if it pained her. "Surely the Captain of a Hundred Men can master a dumb beast."

Tam glared at her. "We don't have them where I come from."

"Why?" Harben asked.

"Horses can't climb trees," Tam said darkly.

Larkin winced to think of an innocent horse faced with mindless mulgars, gilgads, and evil wraiths.

"Stay behind if you like." Iniya kicked her own horse into a smooth trot.

"It's all in your legs," Larkin told him.

Tam pulled himself awkwardly into the saddle, his expression set like when he faced down mulgars.

After the first few blocks, he settled. "This isn't so bad."

They passed beneath the gates they'd crossed only that morning, workers still constructing the wall and dead men still hung by their necks. Shortly after, the sun set. Larkin found herself sweating, her hands shaking. She itched for the nearest tree—she suspected the impulse to hide at sunset would never fully leave her.

"We're late." Iniya kicked her horse into a lope.

Tam's eyes widened. "There's nothing natural about this."

Larkin held back her horse, which fought to keep from being left behind. "Roll your hips and brace your legs when the horse hits the ground."

One hand on each rein, Tam tried to hold his horse back, but it took the bit between its teeth and took off. Larkin released her own gelding and leaned forward. Tam's arms flapped and his backside bounced, but he managed to hold on. Larkin caught up with him. The look of fear on his face … She tipped back her head and laughed. He glared at her.

She swallowed the rest of her laughter. "I'm sorry. It's just nice to be better at *something* for once."

They slowed the horses when they reached a muddy road between green fields of all different types of grains, vegetables, and orchards. In the distance, before the dark smear of trees, bonfires roared, throwing long shadows on the hundreds of people gathered.

Their voices rose like rushing water punctuated with a woman's wailing. At the back of the crowd, the rich rode horses like Larkin and her companions, offering a better view and keeping them out of the mud.

In the center of the crowd of hundreds stood a huge curse tree. Lanterns had been tied to the upper boughs so that it gleamed like starlight reflected on water. They drew closer, the fresh, bright colors dancing on garlands through the boughs as the druids tied up the last of them. Closer still, and Larkin could make out thorns the size of her smallest finger.

Even wearing leather chaps, jackets, and gloves, some of the druids sported bloody bandages from the worst of them. Larkin's group shifted to the left, keeping back far enough that they could speak softly without being overheard.

Beneath the tree, twenty or so men stood side by side in a long line. They wore druid black, weapons bristling from their backs and hips. Before one of those men was the wailing woman—his mother, clearly—and behind them, a platform had been built. Upon it stood a bald man with shoulder-length silver hair, his jowls scruffy. The flames on his elaborately tooled belt marked him as the Master Druid.

"Your grandfather, Fenwick," Harben said tightly from beside her.

Larkin tried to find something of her mother in this man. Perhaps she was too far away, perhaps it was the living shadows in the hollows of his face, but all she saw was her own hatred reflected at her.

Fenwick held up his fist. The crowd fell silent. He turned to the druids. "Tonight, you face the Forbidden Forest of your own free will. You have studied and prepared and trained. Throw that training away."

The druids looked uneasily among themselves. The crowd murmured.

"I take it this isn't his usual speech," Larkin said to Iniya.

"Fenwick is a soldier turned politician," Iniya said. "The older he gets, the more the politician dies."

"Nothing is what it seems," Master Fenwick went on. "Knowledge waits inside the forest. But that knowledge comes with a price. Some of you—perhaps all of you—will pay with your lives. Those who wish may proceed. Those who do not will remain behind, ignorant but alive. Make your decision."

Larkin searched the shadows beneath the trees. Two dozen paces in lay the barrier. Then they would face gilgads and mulgars and wraiths. If they didn't figure out to hide in the trees after sundown, they wouldn't survive a single night.

"Someone should warn them," Larkin said.

"The curse binds our tongues," Iniya said. "This is the only sure way they can learn the truth of the forest."

"And how did you learn?" Larkin asked.

"My father took me inside the forest to meet with the pipers when I was six years old," Iniya said, her voice heavy with grief.

Six? What kind of father took his daughter into the forest at six?

The first man stepped beneath the shadows. Two more followed a few steps behind. Then three. Then a dozen. Until two men remained. One looked at the other and stepped out of sight into the Forbidden Forest. The last ducked his head and marched back into the crowd toward one of the horses. He mounted up and galloped through the crowd and past them without looking to the right or left.

"Well," Fenwick said. "Bast, if you will make the offering to the forest." The man nodded to someone in the crowd. A pair of druids brought out a bleating goat.

Larkin looked away. As a child, she'd always hated this part. As she grew older, she lamented the waste of a healthy animal. And now ... knowing this was all just theater made it that much worse.

Motioning for them to follow, Iniya reined her horse toward

a cluster of men and women. "Humbent. Manervin."

A man and woman around Iniya's own age turned to them. The woman was slight, willowy even. The man had a large paunch and a solid build.

The man frowned at Harben. "Iniya. It is good to see you out of the city."

"Do you remember when we were children?" Iniya said. "The year none of the druids came out of the forest alive."

The man exchanged a look with the woman, then stared at Larkin and Tam. "Who are they?"

"My granddaughter and her trusted guard."

Humbent glanced around nervously, but they were far enough back from the crowd, and his group was all around him.

"Two old friends chatting after a ceremony is nothing suspicious," Iniya said. "It's the clandestine meetings they watch for."

"It's been over fifty years, Iniya." His voice pitched low.

"Your father and mine were the best of friends, Humbent," Iniya hissed. "You swore when the time came you would support us."

His mouth tightened. "And what chance do you think we stand? The druids have an army."

"An army made up of our own people," Iniya said. "People who are tired of the druids failing to keep them safe."

Humbent shook his head. Iniya gripped his arm. "Come to my house. Tomorrow. I swear you'll understand."

He considered her before nodding. Iniya released him and turned her horse away from the gathering.

Larkin started after her. "What if Humbent doesn't agree to help us?"

Iniya didn't even glance at Larkin. "He will." She kicked her horse into another lope, Harben following.

Larkin's mouth thinned. Behind her, the crowd stilled. She turned, wondering how so many people could be so utterly quiet.

She quickly found out. From far away came the sound of a man's terrified screams.

CHAPTER 20

NIGHTMARES

*I*n the early morning light, Larkin pushed through the willows to the spot she and Bane always went swimming. But when she arrived, the river was gone, and instead she found herself pushing into his barn. She blinked in confusion and glanced around.

"Bane?"

No answer.

The barn was empty of even the animals. Not even his dog came out barking with her puppies in tow. Larkin checked his house. It, too, was empty.

She stood on the front step. "Venna? Bane? Daydon?"

From the village came the sounds of shouts. Had another girl been taken? Larkin started running and instantly found herself amid a crowd. She spun, seeing all the people she'd known her entire life. "What's going on? What is it?"

No one would speak to her. No one would answer. They wouldn't look at her. It was like she was a ghost. But they were

219

shouting at something. She pushed through them, trying to see what they were looking at.

Over their heads, she could make out the top of an enormous tree; through the press of bodies, neatly arranged sticks fanned out. She stumbled through and fell onto the sticks. She looked up to find Bane chained to the tree.

Not sticks. Kindling.

Someone threw a torch, fire racing toward his feet. He sobbed and yelled while the crowd chanted, "Traitor, traitor, traitor."

Larkin flared her magic, but nothing happened. She lunged for him. But for every step she took, he only seemed to get farther and farther away.

"He's not a traitor," Larkin cried. "Please."

Swallowed by the crowd, she screamed as the tree lit up like a torch.

Larkin bolted upright, the smell of burning strong in her nostrils. Somewhere a baby wailed. She took a gasping breath and caught sight of a figure hunched on the end of her bed. She gave a startled cry before remembering her weapons. Her sword flared in her hand as she jumped to her feet atop the bed.

The figure didn't move. Larkin eased her sword forward, so it illuminated the upturned face of Maisy, her arms wrapped around her legs.

"Maisy?" Larkin gasped. "What are you doing here?"

Her feet were bare, her entire body streaked with soot. She reeked of cinders. Why did she reek of cinders?

"How did you find me? How did you get in the room?" Larkin caught sight of the open window. One question answered.

"You left me," the girl accused in a small voice.

All the fight drained out of Larkin, her knees unsteady. She sat, her sword fading away. She rubbed at the dull headache forming at her crown. "Maisy ..."

"First, you tell me to stay away, then you leave without so

much as saying goodbye."

How had Maisy found them? "Maisy, you were safe with the pipers."

"You're not safe."

"Some risks are worth taking."

"You need to leave this place, Larkin. Leave before it's too late."

Larkin reached for Maisy, but the girl pulled away. "Can you hear him? The beast is coming for you."

This was not the first time Maisy had referred to the wraiths as the beast. A chill crept up Larkin's spine and into the hair at the nape of her neck.

"Go to Cordova and head straight east at first light," Larkin said. "Follow the river to the lake. Can you do that?"

"Listen, Larkin. Listen." Maisy rocked back and forth.

The beast comes. The beast takes.
That which he takes, he breaks.
That which he breaks, he remakes,
And then a beast like him awakes.

A beast like him. The wraiths wanted to make Larkin into one of them. Fear broke out in a sick sweat over her whole body.

Shuffled steps and the tap of a cane sounded down the hall. Maisy's head whipped toward the sound. She vaulted off the bed and bolted for the balcony beyond the open glass doors.

"Maisy, wait!"

Larkin's door banged open. Barefoot, hair disheveled, Iniya appeared in the doorway with an oil lamp in hand. Maisy climbed over the balustrade.

"Harben!" She set the lamp down and pressed a catch on her cane, releasing a short sword. She advanced on Maisy.

"Wait," Larkin cried as Maisy dropped out of sight. Larkin reached the edge of the balcony just as Maisy disappeared over the garden wall. Larkin swung out to go after her.

Arms gripped her, hauling her back. "What's going on?" Harben asked.

"Are you hurt?" Iniya said.

Larkin jerked free of her father's grasp. "Don't touch me!"

Limping heavily, Iniya bent down to retrieve the cane that had hidden her sword. She pushed it firmly into place. "Explain."

"She's a girl from my village," Larkin said. "Taken by the wraiths years ago. When she came back, she was mad. She's attached to me, that's all."

"That was Maisy?" Harben said.

"How did she find you?" Iniya said.

"I don't know."

The baby's wails finally settled. Her half brother, she realized.

Motion at the door. Tam appeared, his bow and arrow out. He scanned the room before lowering it. "What happened?"

Iniya collapsed.

Harben rushed to her side. "Mother?"

"Oh." The weak sound slipped from her lips.

The sight of indomitable Iniya on the floor stunned Larkin to stillness.

Tam hurried over with the lantern, which revealed her pale skin shining with sweat. "Is she sick?"

"All of them. How can it be all of them?" Iniya cried. She rolled over and vomited onto the floor.

Larkin jumped back to keep from being splashed. Them? Who was them?

"Tinsy!" Harben scooped her into his arms and started toward the door.

Larkin followed, but Tam stopped her with a hand on her arm. "What happened?"

"Maisy."

"Maisy?" he cried.

Tinsy appeared in the hallway, her hair covered by a kerchief.

"She was sick in the blue room," Harben said as he edged past the maid.

"Yes, sir." Tinsy hurried downstairs.

Larkin followed Harben to the opposite end of the hall. He shouldered open a door to a severely bare room. Iniya trembled so hard she nearly vibrated out of his arms before he managed to lay her in the bed. She was pale, her skin coated in freckles that had been all but invisible the day before.

"Leave me," Iniya said.

"Mother—" Harben began.

"I said go!" Iniya pulled the blankets beneath her chattering teeth.

Harben pursed his lips before herding Larkin out. She started to protest. "It will only make it worse," Harben said.

He shut the door on Iniya's muffled sobs. They stood in silence, listening to the older woman cry. Larkin hadn't thought the woman capable of something so base as tears.

"Will she be all right?"

"She's never been all right, Larkin—not since *they* died."

The *them* she had called for. Her entire family. Dead. "How did it happen?"

He led her away from the door. "When she was seventeen, armed men stole into the castle. She was yanked out of her bed, bound and gagged, and hauled into the courtyard where she watched the mob behead her entire family, including all her siblings."

Larkin knew what it was like to wake to a mob screaming for her blood. She still had nightmares about it. She couldn't imagine watching while that mob killed her family. "But not her?"

"The druids came at the end and saved her. They rounded up the men who'd done it and hanged them."

"Then why isn't she queen?" Seventeen was old enough to rule.

"She wasn't ... well for a long time afterward. The druids took over. And when she was finally ready to take her place, they had decided not to give the kingdom back."

"She never fought for it?"

Harben dropped his head. "No one would support a woman on the throne."

And Harben had abandoned it to be with Mama. No wonder Iniya had disowned him. He'd been her only hope for taking back what was hers.

"Who were the men they hanged?"

He sighed. "The druids claim it was a coup led by the king's top advisor. Iniya claims the druids hired criminals and blamed the whole thing on an innocent man."

Ancestors, that's why Iniya hated the druids. Perhaps Larkin was better off growing up in the mud, far away from the machinations of the druids and the royals. And Iniya planned to take them all on.

She stepped back from him. "You gave me a life of hunger and bruises. You'll give your son a short drop at the end of a rope."

He winced as if she'd struck him. "Kyden will have a chance to change things, to stop the druids from lying and manipulating our people."

Kyden. Her brother's name was Kyden. She turned on her heel and marched back to the blue room, shutting the door firmly behind her. Her rug was gone.

Tam waited on the couch. "What did Maisy want?"

"Can you hear him? The beast is coming for you."

Larkin scraped her hands over her face. "She wanted me to leave." She started pacing while Tam watched her, dark circles under his bleary eyes. "Why do you have trouble sleeping?" she asked.

Tam was silent a long time. "Talox wasn't the first I've lost."

She rubbed her sweaty palms on her knees. "Do you have nightmares?"

He sighed and pushed the blanket off. "Might as well get some training in."

She looked down at her floor-length nightgown. What she wouldn't give for a pair of piper trousers and a tunic. She pulled the divided skirts from yesterday under her nightgown. It would have to do.

Tam opened the drapes to let in the early morning light. He pinned her to his chest. "Knee to the groin. When I hunch, grab my ears, and shove my nose into your thrusting knee."

Two hours later, Iniya found them sweating and panting. She looked hollowed out and fragile, her freckles hidden again under a thick layer of makeup. Larkin felt a sudden kinship with the woman. She knew what it was to be hunted. Hated. Powerless.

"I chased you out yesterday," Iniya said.

Tam wiped sweat from his forehead. "The sword in your cane is a good idea. So is this."

Iniya considered him. Tinsy appeared behind Iniya. She stepped into the room, her gaze fixed on the ground. She set plates and a pot of tea on the table.

"Fetch another setting, Tinsy. The Commander of a Hundred Men will be staying."

It seemed some sort of truce had been worked out between Iniya and Tam. Larkin wondered if that truce extended to her and if she would accept it if it was.

As if sensing the tension, Tinsy left the room as quickly as she'd come. Forgoing a plate, Tam bit into a sweet roll, this time with butter and jam, as it was meant to be eaten. Crumbs scattered down the front of his shirt. He'd never had such bad manners before, which meant he was baiting Iniya.

"You are a heathen and a slob," Iniya said.

"Yes," Tam agreed.

Iniya sighed and sat at the table, but she made no move to eat. "Humbent will be here this afternoon. The other lords follow where he goes. I need you to garner his support."

"How?" Larkin asked.

Iniya poured herself a cup of tea. "Show him your magic. Leave the rest up to me."

Larkin frowned. "Men have all the power in the Idelmarch. What's to stop Humbent from taking the throne for himself?"

Iniya stamped her cane. "Men are a sword in the daylight and a knife in the dark. Women, of necessity, must be subtler."

"Subtler than a knife in the dark?" Larkin asked.

Iniya leaned forward. "We must be the one to convince the wielder to strike."

Humbent was her wielder. But the weapon could still turn on her. Unless Iniya had magic.

"Magic won't protect your son or his," Larkin said. "Not after you're gone."

Iniya's gaze narrowed. "You let me worry about that."

Larkin flared her weapons. "I don't need to be subtle about any of it anymore."

Iniya huffed. "And when faced with a bigger, stronger, faster, more experienced opponent who wields equally deadly weapons?"

Ramass. In a contest with the Wraith King, Larkin would lose. Feeling his oily shadows on her, she moved to stand in the midafternoon light streaming through the window.

Iniya hummed. "So you do know."

"Know what?" Tam asked.

"What it is to be made to suffer at the hands of those more powerful than you," Iniya said.

Tam shifted.

"You know it too," Iniya said in surprise.

His fists opened and closed, his expression dark. "Who doesn't?"

It seemed all three of them were haunted by their pasts.

Iniya glanced out the window. "Larkin needs to prepare for Humbent's arrival. Tinsy!" She stood and smoothed her skirts. "Tam, you will stay out of sight."

"Ladies." He gave a mocking bow and left Larkin alone with Iniya.

An awkward silence descended that Larkin itched to fill. She motioned to the dolls. "Your hair?" The moment the words left her lips, she wanted to reel them back.

Iniya froze and then sagged. "Mine, my sisters, and my mother."

So Larkin had inherited her hair from her grandmother.

Tinsy entered the room.

"Ah, good," Iniya said. "Tinsy will prepare you for our trip to the tailor."

"The tailor?" Larkin asked. "I'm only going to be here for a few more days."

Iniya started for the door. "And during those days, I need you to look like the granddaughter of a queen."

"What about you, madame?" Tinsy said.

"I will lie down for a moment. Wake me when she's ready."

CHOOSE

A covered carriage was already waiting for them in front of the house. Oben helped his mistress inside. Larkin had never seen a covered carriage let alone ridden in one. Ignoring the servant's meaty palm, she lifted her fake pregnant belly out of the way and climbed in after the old woman. The carriage swayed as Tam stepped onto the back and Oben climbed into the front.

It lurched and shuddered over the cobblestones through the misty city. Larkin leaned forward to peer out the window.

"Stop goggling. Someone might think you're a tourist." Iniya handed her kid gloves.

Clearly, Tinsy had reported on Larkin's sigils. Larkin pulled the gloves on all the way up to her upper arms and used them to clean the fog off the glass. People trudged through the rain, heads down, collars up. Everywhere Larkin looked, she caught sight of candles in the windows for the coming equinox—one for each girl taken.

One window had three candles.

Not wanting to see anymore, Larkin sat back.

"What is it like?" Iniya asked, as if she had guessed Larkin's thoughts. "Being taken."

Larkin closed her eyes to try to shut out the fear. The loss. And not just hers, but the hundreds of soot-darkened, wide-eyed girls from the hollow. The older woman and the young one from Cordova. Her friends from the Alamant: Magalia and Caelia and Aaryn. "Were you not forced from your bed as a girl? And you've never really been allowed to go home."

Iniya clenched her fists until the sinew stood out. "You didn't watch them die."

"No," Larkin said gently. "But I would have never seen them again either. Nor they me."

Iniya panted, one hand braced against the carriage. Pity welled in Larkin, but not enough to wish she could take the words back. Iniya needed to know how wrong the druids were.

"If you were to bring handsome, well-off men to the towns," Larkin said, "and inform the girls that the men will take them to a place so beautiful it will bring tears to their eyes, a place with magic and eternal summer, then the pipers won't have to steal girls. They'll go willingly."

The forest take her, Larkin would have fought her way to the front of the line. "When you are queen, the Idelmarch and Alamant will see it happen."

Iniya watched Larkin. "I swear it."

Larkin nodded, a weight lifting from her shoulders.

The carriage stopped at one of the shops. It was three stories high, with windows as tall as she, filled with dresses and hats.

Iniya led the way, the door opening with a merry jingle of a trio of bells. Larkin adjusted her gait to the waddle her mother always reverted to toward the end of her pregnancies. Three girls sat sewing in the corner. They took one look at Iniya, and the youngest rushed to the back of the room.

Half a moment later, a man pushed through the curtains, his hands out at his sides. His mustache shone with oil, and he wore a tailored cream shirt and brown trousers with a lovely vest in teal and gold.

"My lady Iniya, you should have told me you were coming. I would have had all your favorites laid out." He placed a kiss to her cheek.

"Not for me, dear man, but my granddaughter. She's an autumn."

His eyes dissected her. "And what a beauty she is. Just like her grandmother at that age."

"Don't flatter me, Gus." Judging by the tiny smile at the corners of Iniya's mouth, she didn't really mean that. And judging by Gus's self-satisfied smirk, he knew it.

Larkin was surprised at this vain side of her grandmother. And that her grandmother seemed to have friends? The forest take her, the woman had even sort of smiled.

Gus kissed Larkin's cheek. His mustache poked her, and he smelled of too much pomade. He whisked Larkin to a platform and stretched her arms out to her sides, examining her this way and that.

"You were right; she's an autumn. I have a moss, mustard, and eggplant already made up that will complement her coloring nicely. They can easily be taken in after the baby."

Baby. Nesha and Bane's baby. Suddenly, Larkin was drowning in emotions. Loss that she would never meet the child created by two people she loved … and hated. Loathing that she was weak enough to feel loss at all. Guilt that she'd ever kissed Bane when he had been with her sister, even if she hadn't known.

"I've always detested autumns," Iniya said. "No sense of propriety in the whole lot."

The man chuckled. "Summers are the classiest of the seasons." They exchanged knowing looks.

Larkin fisted her hands on her hips. "I can hear you."

"Yes, child," Iniya said matter-of-factly. "But you can't understand a word we're saying, which makes it all the more fun."

Before this was over, Larkin was going to strangle her grandmother. "I thought druids' wives always wore black." She was supposed to be Nesha, after all.

"Which is why you will be in color," Iniya said. "You'll stand out like a flower in winter."

Seemed like a colossal waste of money to Larkin.

"Oh, don't look so put out." Iniya headed toward the back of the shop.

Gus folded his arms, offended. "Any girl in the city would rob her own mother to trade places with you."

"Gus is the best, you see." Iniya patted his arm. "Forgive her, darling, she's from the country."

He harrumphed.

Iniya examined a bit of lace. "Her arms, hands, and the back of her neck must be completely covered," she said.

The tailor shot her an incredulous look. "She'll be overheated."

"Do it," Iniya said.

He harrumphed and herded Larkin into the back, behind the curtain. "Down to your shift. One of my girls will help you dress."

The girl cinched Larkin up until her small breasts were forced up as far as they would go. The girl laid out a simple dress of shiny, moss-green fabric, the hems lined in the softest brown fur, the skirts full. Next, she chose a long leather vest that had been tooled and cut until it resembled lace. It had been overlaid with gold and jewels until she shone like a star. The girl laid it over Larkin's shoulders and buckled the decorative straps at her chest and waist to hold it in place. Larkin stared at herself in the mirror. She was beautiful in the way she'd always wanted, and yet it felt fake. This wasn't the real her.

When she came out, Iniya and Gus stared at her a moment. "You see? The right clothes and any girl can be beautiful."

Larkin wasn't sure whether she should be insulted or not.

"Yes, but curls are so out of style," Iniya grumbled. "The bane of the daughters of my line."

Larkin straightened her shoulders. "I like my hair."

The tailor gave her an approving look. "We'll bring it back in style." He lifted one of her curls. "Pile these curls over one shoulder with a hat and some peacock feathers."

"More makeup to cover her blotchy collar," Iniya added.

"They're not blotches—they're freckles," Larkin said. "And I like them."

"Child, you don't know what you like." Iniya found a copper brooch inset with purple and green stones. "We'll take the moss and purple."

"Don't you want to try the purple on?"

Iniya waved her hand. "I trust your work, Gus."

The tailor preened under her words. He selected a moss velvet hat with peacock feathers sticking out of the band, settled it on her head, and pinned it in place.

Iniya pressed the brooch into Larkin's hand, the stones gleaming. "Pin that to your cleavage. Ancestors know they need all the help they can get." She left the shop.

Denan seems to like them just fine, Larkin thought tartly. She hurried after her. "I can't accept all this." She tried to hand the brooch back.

Iniya waited for Oben to open the carriage door. "The stones are only paste."

"I'm only here for another few days."

Iniya took Oben's hand, climbed into the carriage, and sat with a sigh of relief. "And how many kingdoms have toppled or risen because of the right dress?"

Larkin climbed in after her. "None that I know of."

"Then you do not know men. Your father, for instance, toppled mine for the right dress."

Larkin settled into her seat; the carriage turned. "It wasn't the dress. It was the woman."

Iniya stared unseeing out the window. "He was so in love with her that he turned his back on everything. Twenty years later, and he wants nothing to do with her."

Larkin wouldn't have believed her grandmother—except she'd seen her parents in love. The first half of Larkin's childhood had been filled with hard work and laughter. "Everything changed when he started drinking."

"When was that?" Iniya asked.

Larkin considered. "Years ago. Our crop failed, and we didn't have anything to eat. Mother was pregnant with Sela. Father overheard her saying she was certain she would have another daughter." Larkin had nearly died that day.

Iniya's eyes slipped closed. "I see."

Nothing more was said between them for the rest of the ride.

When they arrived back at the mansion, Tinsy waited for them. "Humbent is here, madame."

"Early?" Iniya took the purple dress from Oben and pushed it into Tinsy's arms. "Put them in the blue room for tonight." She smoothed her hair. "Humbent is never early."

"He's taking tea in the parlor," Tinsy said. "I've tried to delay him."

Iniya made an unhappy sound low in her throat.

Dress in hand, Tinsy scurried up the stairs. Iniya looked Larkin over and straightened her fake belly. "I cannot stress enough how much we need Humbent's support. Nor how much I need you to keep your coarse tongue between your teeth."

And yet Larkin was the princess and Iniya was not. "I'm the

one with a sword, remember?" Iniya needed the man's support to make a bid for queen. Larkin needed Iniya's support to overthrow the druids. So she would play along nicely, but if the woman insulted her one more time …

With a huff, Iniya pushed open the parlor doors. Sitting beside a side table holding an empty teacup, Humbent stood—surprisingly spry for a man of his size.

"You're early," Iniya said.

"My business in the city concluded ahead of schedule," Humbent said.

Iniya shut the parlor doors behind Larkin. "And how are things in Hothsfelt?"

"The dealings in Hamel, and now in Cordova, have left us all uneasy. Men coming from the forest to attack our cities and towns—as if the beast wasn't bad enough."

Clearly, Humbent didn't know the truth of the forest.

Iniya sat on the chair across from Humbent and rubbed her hip. Larkin vacillated between assisting an exhausted elder and letting the wretched old woman suffer. In the end, she fetched Iniya a cup of tea. Humbent took this as his cue to refill his cup and sit, though his rough features and largeness looked decidedly out of place in the delicate mauve couch.

"And the druids?" Iniya said. "How are the people dealing with druid-led armies in their cities?"

How long was this small talk going to go on? Why didn't they just get to the point already?

Humbent sat back on the couch. "The druids have no business running the armies. That has always been our job."

Iniya folded her hands. "Then you'll be pleased to have the job back."

"The people won't revolt against the druids, Iniya, even if I were to back you. They're too afraid of the forest."

"They won't be for long," Larkin said.

Iniya shot her a pointed look. Right. Larkin was supposed to remain silent.

Iniya raised an eyebrow. "And if they realize the truth of the forest: that the druids have been lying to them for centuries?"

Humbent raised an eyebrow. "I'm listening."

Iniya nodded to Larkin. "Demonstrate."

Feeling like a show horse, Larkin flared her weapons.

Humbent shot to his feet and took a defensive stance. So, he knew how to fight. Good. The Idelmarch would need warriors.

He stared at Larkin, his breath coming fast. "What is this?"

"What does it look like?" Iniya asked.

He wiped his face. "It looks like magic." He ground his teeth. "Magic comes from the forest, and we all know nothing good comes from the Forbidden Forest."

"That's what the druids would have you believe," Larkin said. "There are many different kinds of magic."

He glanced from Larkin to her sword. "This isn't Nesha. It's Larkin."

He'd heard of her. Lovely. Now she couldn't let him leave—not unless he was on their side. She stood and moved between him and the door.

He watched her suspiciously. "You were in league with the men who came from the forest."

Larkin let her weapons fade, ready to be called back at a moment's notice. "I was taken by them in the middle of the night into the forest. It was there I learned the truth."

Humbent's gaze shifted from Iniya to Larkin. He sat back down. "You're saying the men from the forest are the ones taking our daughters?"

"Yes," Iniya said.

"But I've seen the carcass of the beast that takes the girls," Humbent protested. "You have one in this very house."

"And who is our intermediary with the forest?" Iniya asked.

Humbent's head came up in understanding. "The druids are in league with the men from the forest—these pipers."

"They were," Larkin said.

His face darkened to a terrifying fury. "So the druids have known the truth about the disappearances all along."

Oh yes. They needed this man on their side.

He considered her. "Why are these men taking girls? Why attack us now?"

"They aren't attacking us," Iniya said. "They're attacking the druids for breaking the treaty."

Larkin huffed. "If the pipers were attacking the Idelmarch, you would have already fallen."

Humbent ground his teeth. "My niece was taken by the forest. If the pipers are the ones who took her, I'll kill them myself." He shot Larkin a look of disgust. "And you've allied yourself with them."

"The pipers do what they must to protect us all from the true beast," Larkin said.

He sat silent and still before rising to his feet. "I will go into the Forbidden Forest and see the truth of this for myself, just as the druids do."

Larkin shot a panicked look at Iniya. They couldn't let him leave. One word in the ear of a Black Druid, and he could be the undoing of them all.

"The same arrangement as before is in place." Iniya pushed from her chair, her limp more pronounced.

"My daughter married long ago."

What did his daughter's marriage have to do with anything?

"You have a granddaughter," Iniya said.

Humbent's mouth thinned. "She's only thirteen."

"She'll be a queen," Iniya said. "What does her age matter?"

Larkin stiffened. They wanted Harben to marry a girl younger than Larkin? "He's already married." He'd abandoned Larkin and her family for the woman. Their child was supposed to be the next king.

Iniya waved the comment away. "Easily enough remedied."

"Harben didn't cooperate last time," Humbent said.

"He signed a contract," Iniya said. "And he's older now. He knows what it is to live in the dirt."

Humbent pushed to his feet. "I'll consider it."

Larkin didn't budge from the doorway. "He could expose us all," she said to Iniya.

"Humbent is one of the few people in the world I actually trust," Iniya said.

He looked at Larkin. "I may not join you, but I will not betray you."

"And if you don't make it out of the forest alive?" Larkin asked.

"My son has his orders not to betray you either," Humbent said.

Larkin's gaze flicked to Iniya. "Sons don't always obey their parents."

Iniya rose to her feet. "Humbent is my cousin, Larkin."

Larkin's mouth fell open. "How many family members do I have?"

"More than you want," Iniya said.

Humbent considered her. "Most lords can claim some relation to the royal family. It's why they were given lordships."

"Does that include Lord Daydon of Hamel?" Was she related to Bane?

He turned back to Iniya. "A cousin somewhere along the line, I think?"

She nodded. "His father did something to earn the ire of my great-grandmother and was sent as far away as possible."

Larkin didn't just have a grandmother she didn't know about. She had an entire family complete with aunts, uncles, and cousins—all descended from Eiryss. Of all of them, Sela had been the one to break the curse. Why?

"You must be high in the boughs of the trees before sunset."

Larkin moved aside to let the older man pass.

His brow furrowed, but he nodded. The door shut behind him.

Larkin turned back to Iniya. "What if he wants the throne for himself?"

Iniya hmphed. "He's a cousin on my mother's side, and so has no claim to the throne. Eiryss's line comes from my father."

Larkin still didn't like the risk. "Will Harben really agree to this?"

"The barmaid signed a contract as well. They both knew this was a possibility."

"And Raeneth won't mind losing her husband and her son's claim to the throne?"

Iniya rose ponderously to her feet. "I don't really care what she's fine with. She will do as she's told. After you're long gone, of course. Can't have her running to the druids in a huff."

A knock at the door. "Dinner is ready, madame," Tinsy said.

Iniya left the room without a backward glance. Larkin hung back. This whole operation was spinning out of her control. She'd only meant to find a way into the palace, not become embroiled in family politics.

Tinsy appeared at the doorway. "Madame Iniya would like you to know everyone is waiting."

Withholding a sigh, Larkin followed. The moment she crossed the dining room threshold, she froze. Raeneth sat beside Harben. And between them was a white bassinet, a tuft of red hair visible.

"She didn't betray you," Iniya said before Larkin could protest. "Your father did. Your quarrel with him can wait until after dinner. Now sit."

Hiding the glow of her sigil with the opposite hand, Larkin steeled herself and sat down. She served herself ham and potatoes while Tinsy poured her a cup of tea.

"Well," Iniya said in her warbling voice. "It's a relief that someone can come to their senses in this family without pouting for a fortnight." She sipped her own tea and made a face. "Tinsy, there is far too much honey in this cup."

Tinsy hurried around the table. "Sorry, mistress. I'll fetch you another."

"Larkin," Raeneth began. "I want you to know—"

"Don't," Larkin cut her off. "Just don't."

Raeneth fell silent. From the other side of her, the baby squawked. His mother bent down and scooped him up, patting his back and holding him close as if she drew comfort from him instead of the other way around.

His hair was the same bright copper as their father's. Would he have freckles too? Not her brown eyes—those she got from her mother. Larkin forced her gaze away. Kyden was of no concern to her. She'd be gone in a few days and never see him again.

Everyone ate in silence, save for Iniya's occasional complaints about the potatoes being too cold or the ham too salty or the tea too hot. Afterward, she drew her cane to her and rose to her feet. "My constitution has been tried enough these past few days. I need all my strength for the morrow, so if you will please leave me in peace until the morning."

She left the room, cane tapping. Raeneth ate quickly, then shot Harben a sideways look that Larkin couldn't interpret before leaving the room.

Harben cleared his throat. "We need to talk."

Larkin figured it was better to remain silent than call him a horse's arse.

He sighed and turned fully to her. "Larkin, how did you escape? What about your sisters? Your mother?"

The hairs on the back of her head lifted with anger. She turned to face him. "Why do you care?"

His head fell. "Larkin, I'm sorry. I was in a bad place when

I left you—"

"When you left us? You threw me in a river and nearly drowned me when I was a child! You beat us and left us to starve for years!"

He cradled his head in his hands and spoke to his empty plate. "Your grandmother told me when I left that my marriage with your mother would be cursed. Not a year later, Nesha was born with a twisted foot. I tried to deny it. But then your mother lost a son. I went to your grandmother after our crop failed. I begged her for just enough money so my children wouldn't starve over the winter." Harben wiped his eyes and turned away. "She told me to come back when I had a son to give to the throne. When I returned and overheard your mother saying she would have another girl ..."

He'd been furious and cruel, mocking Nesha for her twisted foot. So Larkin had hit him. For that, he'd thrown her in the river. She'd almost drowned, until Bane had pulled her to safety. Harben had served his time in the stocks for that. Instead of coming out contrite, he'd been bitter.

"After I hurt you, I realized the truth. I had failed my mother. I failed Pennice and you children. I couldn't even sire a son to save us all. I wasn't any good. I never would be.

"When they released me from the stocks, I got roaring drunk—so drunk I no longer cared about anything. It was ... blissful." He closed his eyes, as if even now he craved that bliss. "And before any of that, I did something, Larkin." He buried his head in his hands. "I did something awful."

What could be worse than what he'd already done? She didn't want to know. She had to know. "What did you do?" Larkin breathed.

He shook his head. "I couldn't live with myself if it was my fault. I buried the guilt. I blamed you. My family. Never myself. And I drank."

He sobbed, sounding so heartbroken Larkin was tempted to

pity him. But then she remembered the feel of his fist in her belly. His kicks on her thighs. The humiliation of having the town drunk as a father. He deserved to feel awful.

When he was finished, he wiped his face. "It was my fault. I never should have pursued your mother, never should have left home, but you've seen how your grandmother is." He spread his hands. "I had to get away."

"And now you've come crawling back," Larkin hissed.

His jaw tightened, some of the old anger crawling back, but he reined it in. "You were better off without me."

Larkin threw down her napkin. "You couldn't try to be sober for us? But for her, you will. For your new son." Iniya had already traded the boy's future away; they just didn't know it yet. "And for what? To bring your family back to that harpy? In the end, you're still the same selfish, cruel man."

"We couldn't stay in Hamel. The people turned against us as surely as they did you. Our son will have a better life here. An education."

Larkin pushed up from her chair. Harben grabbed her arm and looked up at her. "Have you never made a mistake, Larkin?"

"Nearly killing your daughter wasn't a mistake. Hitting your wife and children wasn't a mistake. Abandoning us wasn't a mistake. They were choices. And you made them over and over again. I won't let you hurt me anymore. I won't let you hurt me ever again."

She tried to pull away from him, but he didn't let go. "Let me say what I need to say. Then I won't bother you again. I swear I won't."

She gave a jerky nod. Unable to bear looking at him, she crossed the room to put some distance between them and looked at a painting of a pair of red-haired children. They wore dark clothing, and their hair was short. She didn't know whether they were boys or girls or one of each.

"My mother was not always as she was now. She was never

241

very affectionate, but she tried—until my sister and father died of the putrid throat, not long after this painting." He pointed to the child on the left. "That's her. Nesha."

Larkin started. She'd never imagined her sister being named after someone. She tried to imagine her father growing up alone in this stuffy house, buried under mounds of rules and regulations and expectations that could kill him if the druids ever found out that Iniya meant him for the throne.

Harben wiped the tears from his cheeks with fingers coated in freckles. Threads of white wove through his hair. Without his beard and with eyes not muddled by drink, he looked ten years younger. He was handsome, Larkin realized.

"Pennice was the first real friend I had. And she hated my mother as much as I did."

"So you ran away."

"I don't remember a lot of what happened—or maybe I don't want to remember. But I woke up."

"And it took an affair to wake you up?"

"No!" He shook his head and breathed out through his nose. "It took me realizing I had become as bitter about life as my mother had. She swore as a girl she would take back her throne someday. So far, she's failed. She lost so much—again and again. She was too much of a coward to risk love, to risk losing it again, so she wrapped herself in resentment like a warm blanket. I understand if you can't let me back in your life. But let hardship make you better, not bitter." He stepped closer to Larkin, his voice dropped low. "Choose love. Again and again and again."

Larkin watched him walk away until tears welled up in her eyes, blurring her vision. She blinked hard and turned away.

CHAPTER

PALACE

Larkin woke to the sounds of a baby crying. She lay in bed, orienting herself to the foaming blue lace, the dolls staring at her with unblinking eyes. She waited for Harben and Raeneth to shush their baby, but his wails continued unabated.

She hadn't slept much. Between the nightmares and her racing thoughts, she never did anymore. Unable to bear it another second, she hauled herself out of the bed. She followed the cries to the last door on the right at the end of the hallway. Inside was a small room, comparatively. It was perfectly round—the circular room above the parlor, then. The walls had been painted with animals.

In the center of the room was a crib. Kyden pumped his fists and his legs and screamed. Larkin backed into the hallway and opened the door across from the nursery. A mussed bed, but Harben and Raeneth were nowhere to be seen.

Sighing in exasperation, Larkin marched back to him, picked him up, and bounced him. He would only be a week or two younger than Brenna. His swaddling was dirty. She laid him out on a table, unwrapped him, set the dirty swaddling in a bucket, and washed him. He calmed as she wrapped him back up and laid him against her shoulder.

She patted his little bottom while he stuck his fist in his mouth and sucked. Despite having different mothers, he looked like Brenna—the same chubby cheeks and round face. The same pouting lips—a white callous on the top from nursing.

Her half brother. She stroked the back of her finger down his smooth cheek. "I'm sorry, baby." Sorry she had ever hated him. Sorry she wouldn't be there to make sure he was cared for the way she had for her sisters.

Footsteps sounded in the corridor behind her. Her father's laughter. Larkin started to set Kyden down. He wailed in protest. She didn't want to make him cry, but she didn't want to be caught with him either.

Before she could decide, Raeneth pushed open the door, her hair damp and long down her back. Her round eyes in her round face widened as she took in Larkin holding her baby.

Larkin crossed the room and settled Kyden into his mother's arms. "He was fussing. I changed him. He's hungry." Larkin pushed past her to see Harben peering at her from within the room across the hall, his damp hair curling around his ears. She ducked her head and hurried toward her own room.

"I— Thank you," Raeneth called after her.

Larkin shut the door and leaned against it. She looked up at the ceiling. For her mother's sake, it felt disloyal not to hate her father, Raeneth, and Kyden. They had wronged her and her family so thoroughly … The pain of it still throbbed in Larkin's chest.

A knock at her door startled her.

"Miss, the water is heated in the basement if you'd like a turn showering," Tinsy said.

So that's what Harben and Raeneth had been doing. Show-

ering. Together. Larkin could see them suddenly—wet and naked and in each other's arms. Gah! She shook her head violently.
If only she could scrub it from her brain forever.

"Miss?" Tinsy called.

Right. The feast was tonight. After Iniya got them into the
castle to look for the journal and ahlea amulet. "Yes," Larkin
blurted. "I'm coming."

"I'll be waiting with towels, and we'll do your hair," Tinsy
said. "Would you prefer to bring down the purple dress, or shall
I?"

"I'll bring it."

An hour later, her oiled hair was smoothed back in an elegant updo. Layers and layers of makeup covered every one of
her freckles. The high-backed dress and gloves hid her sigils.
The pillow had been stuffed under the dress to mimic Nesha's
pregnancy. She was already sweltering.

Larkin didn't recognize the woman staring back at her,
wasn't even sure she liked her. But the dress … She very much
liked the dress. Floral-embossed leather crisscrossed the bust and
the waist, the buckles gold and beautifully cast. Other buckles
went around her arms. Tinsy fussed with the sleeves so they
draped just so, and then she belted the overskirt around her
waist. Leather and gold panels fell just so.

Tinsy placed a velvet hat with a brown feather on her head
and picked up the breakfast tray. "Iniya will be waiting, miss."

Larkin stood and smoothed her hands down the soft velvet.

Tinsy rested a hand on her wrists. "Good luck, miss."

Surprised by the sudden show of emotion, Larkin couldn't
think of a proper response before the girl fled. She made her way
into the mansion and crossed the hallway. Harben and Iniya were
indeed waiting beside the front door. As was Raeneth, the baby
in a basket at her feet.

Larkin still didn't know why the woman was coming. "Isn't
this a little dangerous for an infant?"

Raeneth picked up the basket, her expression determined.

"You think either of them will be safe if we're caught?" Iniya said. "No, we succeed or fail together." She eyed Larkin critically. "Let me see the limp."

Larkin turned her foot inward and stepped on the outer blade, drawing her steps short to mimic the way Nesha walked with her club foot.

Iniya nodded in approval. "A trollop and a cripple besides."

Larkin gritted her teeth as she came to stand beside them. "Perhaps if you hadn't turned your back on us, we wouldn't have been forced to make such choices."

Iniya raised a perfectly arched, painted-on eyebrow. "Are you defending the girl now? She nearly had you killed."

Larkin turned away as shame, humiliation, and hurt caught fire inside her.

Harben glowered at her. "Be civil or be silent, Mother," he snapped.

Iniya harrumphed.

"Have you any word of Humbent?" Larkin asked.

"We won't for a few days." Iniya turned—the click, click, click announcing her retreat. "Oben is waiting."

Larkin squared herself. If someone realized their deceit, they would pay with their lives. She flared her magic and muttered to herself, "But I'll take down as many of them as I can before I go."

Harben turned back to her. "What was that?"

She shook her head. "Nothing." She limped past him. At the landing, she paused. For once, it was a lovely day. Brilliant sunlight filtered through the spring-green leaves. The bark was black, the moss growing on the north side even brighter than the leaves.

Larkin could have grown up here. Grown up in the beautiful house with the trees and the servants. Instead, she'd been born and raised in the mud of her family's fields and her father's steadily increasing drunken rages.

Dressed in a brown jerkin and wearing a guard's sword at his hip, Tam leaned against a tree. He nodded to Larkin and hopped on the back of the carriage. Larkin felt the tiniest bit of tension drain away. She vacillated a moment before sitting beside her grandmother. Her father sat opposite, Raeneth coming in last. Oben handed the basket up to them.

Raeneth held it in her lap. Kyden sucked his tongue in his sleep, his mouth puckering adorably. Larkin looked away. There was no sense in becoming attached to the child. She never should have held him.

Oben shut the door, and the carriage lurched into motion. Larkin leaned out the window to keep from looking at any of them.

Iniya huffed in disgust. "Stop gawking."

Larkin ignored her.

"Remember what we're here for," Iniya said. "The book and the tomb. As soon as we've accomplished those goals, we leave."

Larkin ignored her as the carriage retraced the steps that she and Tam had made only two days before. This time, the palace's red doors were thrown open wide. Dozens of people streamed in. One little girl skipped ahead of the rest, her hair a blonde halo around her head. She reminded Larkin so much of Sela—the old Sela—that tears formed in her eyes.

She missed her mother and her little sisters. A part of her missed Nesha too—or at least the friend she used to be. And Kyden. What kind of life would he have? Groomed by their cruel grandmother to become an even crueler king or cast aside like offal. But short of kidnapping him, Larkin wasn't sure what could be done about it.

The crowd bottlenecked just beyond the door. Oben shouted, and people scattered, casting curious looks their way—probably trying to catch sight of the Mad Queen.

After everything Iniya had been through, could anyone blame her for going a little mad?

Gritting her teeth, Larkin studied the wide courtyard. Food vendors lined three sides of the curtain wall. Games had been set up all around, with men competing at log tossing. Children played horseshoes. Acrobats flipped across a stage, hangman's nooses shifting in the wind behind them. The scent of roasted nuts and maple sugar filled the air.

Lording over it all was the magnificent palace, with its whitewashed walls and copper turrets. Wide stone steps angled toward the door, which were inlaid with copper crescents bisected by a thick line. These doors—red like the outer ones—were also thrown open.

Carriages lined the white gravel. The mass of people in the courtyard did not come within a dozen paces of the gravel, did not so much as look toward the palace. It was as if that white-gravel line demarcated two worlds, and one could never touch the other.

Despite the warmth, Larkin shivered. "You lived here?" she asked Iniya. The woman's house had been overwhelming enough. This … this was so far beyond anything Larkin could imagine living in.

"My father's palace." Iniya's voice trembled, betraying her.

The carriage lurched to a stop. Oben opened the door. Larkin followed Iniya out. Harben, Raeneth, and Kyden came last. Tam jumped down from the back of the coach and stepped up beside Larkin. "Ready to break the curse?"

"And if we don't, at least we can take some druids down with us."

He grinned. "I have taught you well."

As one, they climbed the narrowing stairs. Two druids waited for them at the top. The one with pretty blue eyes bowed. The other had a sour expression and examined his list. "Lady Iniya, I'm afraid I only have you down for one guest."

Iniya shot them a haughty expression. "Surely you can find a few more chairs for the Hero of Hamel, my very own grand-daughter."

Both druids' gazes whipped to Larkin.

Larkin lowered her eyes, exactly as Nesha would have done.

"The Hero of Hamel," Blue Eyes said in awe.

"Garrot didn't send word of his ..." Sour Face trailed off awkwardly. Because Nesha was not Garrot's wife. Cripples couldn't marry. "Nesha," he finished lamely.

"And her guard, of course," Iniya said.

Sour Face looked Tam over. "Guard?"

Tam rested his fist over his heart and bowed. "I escorted Nesha to the safety of her grandmother's tender care"—Blue Eyes choked on a laugh and Sour Face glared at him—"and will continue my duties until Garrot returns to her side."

Iniya looked Blue Eyes over as if memorizing his features for future retribution. He stiffened, clearly worried. He should be more than worried. He should be terrified.

"I'm sure we can find a place for Nesha. Your guard will have to wait along the wall with the servants." The druid waved down a boy and whispered something to him. The boy turned wide eyes to Larkin before scampering back inside the palace. Sour Face waved them on.

They stepped into a grand foyer with copper inlaid in the floor. From the high, lead-glass windows, brilliant shafts of sun-light speared across the room, sending dazzling rainbow sparks across the milling people. But for all the grandeur, the space was surprisingly bare. The faintest dark squares hinted at paintings or tapestries that had once graced the walls. Family heirlooms, surely. What had the druids done with them?

A servant showed them into an enormous dining room, one wall all floor-to-ceiling windows. Fireplaces graced each end, the interior wall as bare as the one before. On one end, a single table had been laid out upon a platform. Long tables had been set with plain tin dishes. Tin. As if the druids wanted to prove they were humble.

Ridiculous. Taking down the paintings and eating off tin didn't change the fact that they were in a palace—or that the Idelmarch served the druids, not the other way around.

The room was already filled to overflowing with druids in their black robes and their equally dour wives. Servants rushed about to seat everyone—it appeared Larkin's group had nearly been late.

Iniya clearly planned it that way, as a hush fell across the room at their entrance. The druids' gazes lingered the longest on Larkin, whether because her purple dress, with its embossed leather, stood out in a room full of black or because of the false pregnancy, Larkin wasn't sure. All at once, Larkin remembered that this was not the first time she'd faked a pregnancy. She had to suppress the sudden urge to laugh.

Everyone stared, but no one approached—Nesha was a hero, but also a fallen woman. No one seemed to know how to react.

Resounding footsteps. The crowd shifted, Master Fenwick pushing through. Up close, her grandfather bore the look of a man bowed by an immense strain that had not broken him. His murderous gaze fixed on Harben even as he paused before Iniya.

Iniya gripped her cane in both hands. "Lay a hand on him, and you'll live to regret it."

"I regret everything to do with you, Iniya Rothsberd." Fenwick's eyes shifted to Larkin. She swore regret flashed in their depths.

An older woman, her eyes white and blind, appeared behind him, a servant flapping at her side. "I'm sorry, master. She would not be persuaded."

The old woman took a step past Fenwick before he caught her arm and pulled her back.

She bowed her head. "Please, husband. Send them away."

Larkin stiffened.

Harben leaned toward Larkin and said in a whisper, "Fawna, your other grandmother. She has as much backbone as soggy bread."

Larkin searched for something of her mother in Fawna, something of herself. All she saw was clouds of defeat and hopelessness behind rheumy eyes.

Fenwick softened and took her under his arm. He whispered something to her and motioned for the servant to lead her away. The woman went willingly this time.

Fenwick watched her go before rounding on them. "Nesha, is it?"

Larkin inclined her head. "Master Druid."

He looked pointedly at her foot. "Enjoy the dancing." He turned on his heel and caught up to Fawna.

No matter what Nesha had done, Larkin would always loathe anyone who mocked her twisted foot. "Is everyone in my family so hateful?"

"If you want compassion," Iniya said as she pushed past Larkin, "look among the peasants."

CHAPTER

CRYPTS

A servant led them to a table near the front on the far right. Tureens were laden with dishes of early spring vegetables—fresh peas and asparagus, garlic potatoes, lettuce, spinach, and cabbage. Larkin sat with Tam on one side and Iniya on the other, Harben and Raeneth across from them.

Servants brought in fat, juicy pigs roasted with apples and onions; lambs roasted with fresh garlic and garnished with sprigs of mint. There were breads too—round loaves with a crunchy exterior and soft rolls with perfect golden tops.

One woman served Fenwick at the high table first before the rest of the servants shifted through the rest of the room. Larkin took one of the rolls in her hands. Curling wisps of steam rose when she broke it open. She could already taste it. Fresh churned butter and strawberry preserves. Just like Venna used to make. Tears welled in her eyes.

"Ancestors save us, girl," Iniya whispered. "Are you weeping over bread?"

No. She wept over a sweet girl who'd been turned into a monster—a monster Larkin had slipped a sword inside.

Larkin sniffed and put the roll back. "How much longer do we have to stay here?"

"Long enough to belie suspicion," Iniya said between her teeth.

Across from them, Raeneth bounced her baby nervously while Harben loaded her plate with far too many spring peas.

At the end of the room, a Black Druid stood before Fenwick's table. "We have survived another winter with the beast clawing at our door and stealing away our weakest, our most vulnerable like the wolves thinning the flock. The forest takes her tithe, and we are left with the strongest, the best."

Only the Black Druids knew the truth of the forest. The rest were kept beneath the shadows of the curse just like the rest of them. At least, that was how it used to be. But now even the baker had heard of the pipers. The rest of the Idelmarch must be questioning the druids now.

"How can Fenwick keep repeating that lie?" Larkin murmured to Iniya.

"If word gets out the Black Druids have been lying for centuries," Iniya said, "the people will turn on them. He sticks by the lie or he goes down with them."

Fenwick lifted his cup. "To those strong enough to resist the call of the beast."

Up and down the tables, druids lifted their cups. "To the strongest," a few said half-heartedly. Others grumbled.

Fenwick was losing the support of his druids. Perhaps Iniya would have an easier time seizing control than they'd thought.

Not wanting to appear nervous, Larkin forced herself to eat a few bites. The pork was delicious, but it turned her stomach the moment she swallowed. She forced a few bites of each dish, the meal sitting heavier and heavier in her stomach.

"The hero of Hamel," someone shouted. Larkin looked up

to see a man standing three tables over and lifting his glass to her. "Tell us what really happened in Hamel. Tell us the story of how you resisted the beast and escaped its dark enchantment."

She swallowed, her stomach revolting.

"Is it true that the beast is not a beast at all, but men?" a young druid asked. "That men have been taking our sisters?"

Larkin glanced around the room, druids sliding knowing expressions to each other. At some point, they had figured out the truth. They knew the Black Druid's secret: the beast wasn't a beast at all.

Fenwick stood, his chair screeching. He leaned over the table and looked over the druids with a thunderous expression. "The Forbidden Forest has always been good at keeping her secrets—secrets an individual could only learn after the Black Rites. Because the forest has suddenly decided to spill some of her secrets changes nothing."

"We deserve the truth!" a druid shouted.

Fenwick eyed the man. "Then you should have followed your fellows into the forest."

The men grumbled.

"Not one of the candidates has returned yet—not one!" one man shouted in outrage.

Fenwick slapped the table. "It has always been this way. Must always be this way. You don't believe me, ask my fellow Black Druids. Now be still or be expelled."

Most of the shouting died to grumbling. Three men continued. Black Druids bound all three in irons and escorted them out. Fenwick sat with a huff, his face red with fury.

Servants brought around thick slices of apple pie—probably made with the last of the winter apples—a thick dollop of clotted cream sliding across the top. They didn't notice Iniya replacing her slice with one that had been hidden in Raeneth's basket.

Iniya gave a shriek of outrage and pulled out a mouse from inside her pie. Soaked in juices, a chunk of apple falling off its leg, it looked as though it had been baked inside.

Men and women gasped in horror and pushed their pie away.

Iniya's face went pale, her lip trembling with outrage. She shook the mouse in Fenwick's direction. "I'd think the druids were trying to kill me a second time, were they not eating the same slop themselves."

Fenwick rolled his eyes. "None of us tried to kill you the first time, Mad Queen."

Iniya threw the mouse onto the table and gagged, a lacy handkerchief over her mouth. She tried to stand and plopped down on her chair. She glared up at Larkin. "Don't stand there staring, girl. Can't you see I'm in need of assistance?" She gagged again for good measure.

Larkin gripped her bony elbow and helped her to her feet. They hadn't made it two steps before a servant intercepted them, his hands wringing. "Lady Iniya, I must ask that you take your seat. The feast—"

"That mouse—" She gagged and vomited on his shoes. He jumped back, his face twisting with disgust. Chairs scooted away. Some pushed to their feet to get away from them.

Larkin felt a presence behind her.

Tam scooped the old woman up. "Find us somewhere to go, man!"

The servant glanced at Fenwick. Face twisted with disgust, the Master Druid waved him on. Behind them came a high-pitched squawk. Kyden's face reddened, his arms and legs flailing as he screamed. The front of Raeneth's white dress went damp and transparent with milk.

She launched to her feet and hurried after them while Harben calmly took another bite of pie. The servant led them down a wide corridor to the nearest door, into what looked like a sitting room.

"I need somewhere to lie down, you incompetent nitwit. Do

you suppose your master's wooden chairs would suffice?" She gagged again.

The servant jumped back in alarm.

Iniya waved her handkerchief toward a door four rooms down. "That one has a lavatory and a bed, if I remember correctly."

Without waiting for the man's permission, Tam strode toward it and shouldered open the door. It was a bedroom, with a cheery fire spaced neatly between two large windows. The walls were lined with thick paneling.

Tam set Iniya gently on the rich, velvet coverlet on the bed.

Her back to the servant at the door, Raeneth pulled out a blanket soiled with baby poop, laid it over Kyden, and turned toward the servant. "Oh! I didn't bring a spare."

He blanched as he backed out the door, his hand fumbling for the knob. "I'll fetch you a few buckets of water. I'll just leave them outside." He shut the door firmly behind him.

They all held their breath, waiting for something to go wrong. Then everyone moved at once. Iniya jumped from the bed. Raeneth took pillows from the chairs and stuffed them under the blankets in the basic shape of Iniya's thin form. Larkin drew the heavy curtains, plunging the room into shadow.

Raeneth unloaded the basket of blankets Kyden had been lying on and handed Larkin a bag of torches as well as a smock. Raeneth plunged a torch into the fireplace and watched as it caught fire.

"What's this for?" Larkin held out the smock.

"Put it on." Iniya paused at the corner of the room and pressed a catch on the wood paneling. The bottom panel swung outward, revealing a narrow opening barely wide enough for a trim person. A damp breeze that smelled of mineral and abandonment wafted up from below.

Iniya looked Tam up and down. "The library is on the top floor, northwest tower. It should be unmanned, but if anyone asks, tell them Garrot sent you to fetch him a book. If they don't believe you, die without giving us up."

What if they went through all of this and never found Eiryss's journal or her ahlea amulet? Or worse still, what if they found them and they revealed nothing? Larkin couldn't bear to be wrong—not after everything she'd risked.

"Don't get caught," Larkin said breathlessly as she adjusted the smock, pulled out the stuffing around her belly, and hauled the bag of torches over her shoulder. "And don't die."

Tam saluted and left.

Iniya handed Larkin her cane. "You go first. Catch me if I fall."

More likely they'd both tumble to their deaths. "Are you sure you can manage it?"

Iniya gave a hard shake of her head. "You'll never find it without me." She dropped the torch, the fire nearly going out before it landed about a story down.

Larkin shot a dubious look at the ladder—how many decades had this sat in the damp dark? At least it appeared sturdily made. Steeling herself, she swung out and started down.

"Stay in the lavatory," Iniya said to Raeneth. "Make plenty of unsavory noises if someone comes in."

Iniya swung out over Larkin and shut the panel door, plunging them into shadow. Down, down, down Larkin went. She kept her gaze on the smoldering torch until she stepped into the center of a room about the size of her hut in Hamel. Dust-caked shelves filled with rotted food and casks of wine dominated one side. A sunken, moldering bed the other. In the ceiling were a dozen other openings, though the one they'd come down was the only one with a ladder. The air was heavy, sitting deep in Larkin's lungs. Aside from the greasy scent of the torch, the room smelled of rotting wood and mold.

"What is this place?" Larkin asked.

"Father made me practice reaching his bolt hole a dozen

times a week," she panted. "Many rooms in the palace had secret doors that lead here."

"And Fenwick doesn't know?"

Iniya took her cane from Larkin. "That's what comes of stealing a palace that isn't yours—you don't know where the secret passages are."

So why hadn't Iniya and her family hid themselves here? Larkin wanted to ask, but the worlds felt sticky and impossible in her mouth.

Iniya gestured to one of the side walls made of gray brick. "Put your shoulder into it."

It looked like a solid wall to Larkin. But then, so had the paneling. Bracing her feet, she pushed. Nothing happened.

"Push harder, girl!"

Bracing her feet, Larkin pushed with all her strength. The wall gave with an unholy shriek. She admired the central pivot and the masonry on the sides that cleverly disguised the opening. She took the torch and eased into a cavern filled with rows upon rows of sarcophagi, each with the likeness of the inhabitant at the peak of youth carved across the top. Three centuries of Eiryss's offspring. Larkin's ancestors.

Larkin brushed cobwebs out of the way. A thick layer of dust coated the tombs, easily as thick as her finger. Behind her was a solid wooden door, the hinges rusted.

No one had been down here in a very, very long time.

"No one to care for our ancestors." Iniya's voice trembled. She wiped the dirt off the face of a man and woman. "When my time comes, I should have a place beside my parents, my siblings." Three child-sized sarcophagi and three adult-sized ones lay beside their parents. Seven children. Only one had survived.

Iniya sniffed. "Fenwick won't let me. He won't risk elevating my family by burying me here." The old woman shifted among the tombs, dusty cobwebs coating her smock—so that's why they'd brought them. "At each equinox, our people would bring candles, until the whole cavern shone like stars."

Iniya paused before the tomb farthest back. Larkin wiped through decades of dust, exposing white marble. Carved into the lid was the likeness of the woman Larkin had seen in her vision, right down to her flowing hair and weak chin.

"This is her," she breathed.

"Eiryss," Iniya agreed. "The first queen of the United Cities of the Idelmarch."

Larkin scraped away the dust at the woman's neck. Sure enough, she wore an amulet carved in the shape the ahlea flower. At some point, Pennice had found her way to this chamber, had seen these tombs.

Larkin flared her sword, which had cut through vines without so much as shifting them. Two-handed, she lifted it over her head.

"What are you doing?" Iniya cried.

Larkin swung down at the top of the tomb, just above the carving's head. Her eyes slipped shut at the last moment. The sword sliced through the marble as though it were a thick loaf of bread. The top of the tomb was cut nearly all the way through.

Iniya grabbed her arm—she was stronger than she looked. "This place is sacred!"

Larkin gripped the front of the woman's smock in her filthy hands. "You want the pipers' support? This is the price. I didn't come here to pay respects to the dead. I came to take something."

Betrayal shone in the older woman's eyes. "Don't ever love anyone, Larkin. Don't ever trust them. They will only ever hurt you."

As Larkin had just hurt her. Larkin released her as if the old woman's touch had burned her. "Eiryss left it for me to find. I don't dishonor her by taking it."

"Left what?" Iniya asked.

Instead of answering, Larkin swung again. The top teetered.

She shoved it, shattered stone grinding as it fell with a crash and an explosion of dust.

Larkin knelt and peered inside. It was so dark. She carefully edged in her gleaming sword. No rotted cloth. No grinning skeleton. And certainly no ahlea amulet.

"Empty," Larkin gasped. It couldn't be. She jerked the torch out of Iniya's grasp and thrust it into the echoing space. "How can it be empty?"

The only answer was Iniya's click, click, clicking steps.

Larkin hurried to catch up to her. "There has to be some mistake. That can't be Eiryss's tomb." But Larkin had seen Eiryss's carved face with her own eyes. "If Eiryss isn't here, where is she?"

Iniya slipped into the chamber. "Close the door."

Larkin froze in place. "No. No, I cannot fail. I cannot return empty-handed—not after everything."

"Whatever it is you were after, you don't need it." Iniya finally deigned to look at her. "All my life, I have lived for only one purpose: to destroy the druids. And I will do it, I swear upon my life and the lives of all my posterity."

Larkin huffed. "You don't have the right to swear anything on my life, old woman."

"Larkin, Iniya, hurry," Raeneth hissed from above.

Iniya struggled up the rungs. The sound of knocking echoed down the tunnel. "I must insist you let us in," came a muffled voice.

"Just a moment, sir," Raeneth said calmly. "The lady is not quite dressed."

"You've been saying that for five minutes," someone grumbled. "I've brought the healer. Now let us in."

Five rungs down from the top, Larkin shoved her shoulder into Iniya's rump and pushed. Raeneth reached down and hooked her arms under Iniya's. Between the two of them, they managed to heave her out of the passageway. Larkin slithered out and pushed the panel door shut with her foot.

Raeneth hauled off Iniya's smock and tossed it into the fire. Larkin couldn't believe they were wasting valuable cloth, but better to waste it than get caught and have to explain what they were doing with it. She tossed hers in on top of Iniya's, washed her face and hands in a bucket, and ran her damp hands over her dusty hair.

"How is it?" Larkin asked Raeneth.

She looked up from where she ran a damp cloth over Iniya's hair. "You missed some cobwebs in the back."

"Open the door," someone demanded from outside.

"Leave me in peace," Iniya panted loudly. Her face was pale and shiny with sweat.

Raeneth gathered the cobwebs from Larkin's hair. Together, they dumped the water down the lavatory hole. They hurried back to the room, and Raeneth gasped, "Larkin, your belly!"

Larkin swore and shoved the pillow up the front of her dress. No sooner was it in place than the key turned in the lock and Fenwick burst in with two druids and a man in healer robes.

The healer went to Iniya's side and knelt before her as she moaned. Raeneth immediately picked up her baby and backed into a corner.

Larkin squared off before Fenwick, her magic an itch she dared not scratch. "Since we are clearly not welcome to rest in the palace, I insist you help us take Iniya home."

"She does indeed appear unwell," the healer said.

"Pick her up," Fenwick said. "And see she's taken home." One of the druids lifted her.

"Take your filthy hands off me," Iniya panted.

Harben stepped into the room. "I'll take her."

Fenwick's narrowed gaze shifted to Larkin. "Where's your other friend?

So they hadn't found Tam. "He went to fetch our carriage."

Fenwick watched her, clearly not believing a word she said.

"Have you ever seen the druids dispense justice?"

Was he inviting her to the executions or threatening her? Probably both.

Iniya gripped Larkin's arm, her nails digging in. "I need my granddaughter with me."

Fenwick followed them into the corridor and watched as they left, a heavy foreboding in his dark gaze.

CHAPTER 24

HANGING

Larkin couldn't shake the feeling something was wrong. That feeling was reinforced when she stepped out of the palace a step behind Harben holding Iniya and Raeneth holding Kyden.

The square was packed to overflowing. Older children packed the trees; younger ones sat atop someone's shoulders. The air smelled of roasted nuts—druids handed it out in greasy bags. Crushed white shells littered the ground beneath their feet. The crowd jeered and elbowed and jostled. And along the wall to Larkin's right stood a long line of men and even a pair of women in chains—all waiting to die before a crowd that chanted for their blood.

Larkin had experienced this frenzied excitement before— the day her own town had turned against her and called for her death by hanging or drowning or fire. Cold sweat broke out on her brow, and she found she could not move, could barely breath.

The world swayed, details lost to the nothingness rushing at her from below. A hand closed on her arm. Tam's face appeared before her. The others waited at the bottom of the steps. Raeneth held her baby tight—maybe she wasn't such a bad mother after all. Iniya lay in Harben's arms, glaring at Larkin.

Tam shook her. "The carriage can't get through. Stay right behind me."

Gone was the trickster, the jolliness. His elfin face had shifted to all hard angles and a severe expression. He felt it too.

Something was wrong.

"Do you hear me, Larkin? Stay right behind me."

She nodded faintly. He placed her hand on his back. "Hold on to my shirt. Don't let go."

Fisting the fabric in her hand, she followed as he hustled down the steps, the others falling into step behind them. They plunged into the crowd, which had managed to break the invisible barrier between druid and Idelmarchian, spilling onto the white gravel. Tam elbowed and shoved and glared. Out of nowhere, a fist connected with his face. Tam's head popped back.

The Idelmarchians did not love the druids. They feared them. But right now, they feared nothing. This was why the druids handed out roasted nuts to appease the crowd and stood atop the battlements for safety. They knew this crowd was one step away from becoming a mob.

"Keep moving." Tam's teeth were bloody, a stream dribbled from his chin. He barely seemed to notice.

Larkin glanced back to make sure Raeneth and Harben were behind her. They weren't. She was suddenly shoved hard from the side, losing her grip on Tam. She staggered and would have fallen had the press of bodies not kept her upright. That same press formed a current that left her unable to get her feet under her.

She fought to keep upright, to regain her balance, to find Tam, when she fetched up against a hard chest. The handsome guard from the front door—Blue Eyes—wrapped her up in a tight embrace.

He smiled, showing too many teeth. "The Hero of Hamel and the whore of Garrot."

She shoved, but he only tightened his grip. One hand reached around, cupping her bottom and pulling her up and into him so the fake belly pressed hard against him.

"Not even his child, as he's been gone less than a couple of months." He backed up, dragging her with him toward the stables. "Come on now, what's one more tumble in the hay when you've already—"

Larkin's magic flared. But she could not use it—not here. She gripped his shoulders to steady herself and thrust her knee into his crotch. He grunted and hunched forward. She grabbed his ears, jerked down, and drove her knee into his nose.

She felt a wet crunch, blood sliding down her shin. But she was already gone, instinctively shifting to a less crowded area. The crowd spat her out. She landed in rotten potatoes, the smell and slime making her gag. For a moment, she lay, breathing in the rot and the horror because she could not make herself move.

"Larkin?" said a male voice.

Not Nesha. Someone had called her by her real name. Her head jerked up. Before her was the long wall where the prisoners were chained. They were covered in rot, the filth and bleakness they wore making them nearly indistinguishable from one another. People clustered around the condemned, weeping and pleading.

One prisoner staggered toward her and collapsed. She recoiled. Until his eyes locked with hers—a dark brown ring surrounding amber. His face was even paler than normal, his black hair greasy and lank. He was thinner too, the hollows of his cheeks carved against his proud face.

"Bane?" she gasped.

His hands came down on her shoulder. "I knew you would

come for me. I knew it."

Come for him? All at once she understood. The chains at his wrists and feet—Bane would hang ... today. Hang for killing druids to save her life. He thought she was here to save him.

Guilt was a burning ember in her chest. A thousand memories roared through her, but two floated to the surface and mingled into one. She was in the river again. Cold water slid through her clothes and hair, down past her throat and into her lungs. A druid stood over her. His ax swung toward her head.

Bane was suddenly there, killing the druid and pulling her from the river and shoving her toward Denan. "I'll hold them off as long as I can." Alone, he'd faced the druids bearing down on them as Denan had hauled her into his arms and run.

Bane's hands tightened on her shoulders. The hope in his eyes nearly killed her. He expected an army—or at least a plan. She hadn't even known he was here.

She hadn't known.

"You can't, Larkin." Bane shuttered his hope away, killed it with one hard blink. "It's a trap. You have to run."

Her mind clawed its way out of despair long enough to register his words. "A trap?"

"They're waiting for you to try to free me. You have to go."

She reached for his cuffs, her sigils buzzing beneath her gloves. She could easily cut him free. Just a tiny bit of magic. A sliver instead of a sword. No one would see. She could melt into the crowd one way, he another.

Bane gripped her hand above her sigil, which prevented it from forming. "Don't."

"Bane—"

"The druids are watching, waiting for someone to try to rescue me. We're surrounded. There's nowhere for me to go."

"But—"

"Garrot will find you."

She froze. Garrot was here? Then the trap wasn't meant for

just anyone. It was meant for her. And Garrot wouldn't be fooled by dyed hair and a fancy dress.

Denan had told her she would have to learn a balance between loyalty and self-preservation. Even with an army, she couldn't save Bane—not in time. She could only die with him, and she could not do that to Denan.

Bane must have seen this in her eyes, for what little remnants of his hope snuffed out like a light guttered. He closed his eyes, jaw clenched as if he couldn't bear it. "Don't watch me die."

She pressed a kiss salted with her tears to his cheek. "I love you." Not in the way she loved Denan. But she loved him still.

She backed away from him. His hands held the shape of hers before slowly falling away. Ancestors, she was leaving him to die. Choking on a sob, she turned back to the crowd, pushing and shoving her way toward the gate.

She hadn't gone half a dozen steps before two men blocked her path, their gazes fixed on her like a hunter sighting its prey. She turned to the right. Two more blocked her. She turned to the left. Two more—Blue Eyes and Sour Face.

The push in the crowd, Blue Eyes grabbing her—none of it had been an accident. They had been separating her from the others, herding her. They had wanted her to find Bane.

Not *they. He.* Garrot.

Her magic burned hot, but she did not draw it. Not until she had to. "What do you want?"

Six of them converged on her. From behind her, Bane swore. The crowd scattered from the druids as if repelled. A few at a safe distance called for her death.

She tensed, waiting. And then Garrot pushed between a pair of druids. "Hello, Larkin."

He didn't look surprised. Almost like he'd known she was here all along. Of course he had. The druids had known her identity from the start. Bane was right; it was a trap. And she'd walked right into it, just not for the reason the druids had suspected.

Fear burst inside her, coating her tongue so thick she couldn't swallow. She flared her sigils and dropped into a fighting stance behind her shield. The crowd gasped at the sight of her magical weapons. People murmured—some in confusion, some in fear, some in awe. This was not the spectacle they'd come for, and they clearly hadn't decided which side to land on—hers or the druids.

Garrot and his men advanced on her. Wanting the wall at her back, she retreated, past the line of rotten potatoes, until she stood shoulder to shoulder with Bane. She spread her shield in front of him as well. Desperate for escape, she risked a glance up, up, up the high curtain wall. Druids silhouetted black against the bright blue of the sky, all of them watching her.

"Oh, Larkin," Bane whispered. "I'm so sorry." Sorry because he thought she would die with him.

An arrow clattered onto the packed earth at Bane's feet. He hissed and jerked, his hand over his ear, blood welling between his fingers. She hadn't thought to shield them from above. She widened her shield until it encircled them.

Garrot shouted at the druids on the wall, "Stand down!"

A dozen more Black Druids pushed through the crowd to line up in a semicircle around Garrot. Sixteen druids, all of them armed with staffs, paused just beyond her shield.

"You cannot hold your shield forever, Larkin. Surrender."

Larkin hoped wherever Tam was—wherever her hateful family was—they were far away from here and would not try to come back for her. She licked her lips. "Grant Bane his freedom, and I will."

"Larkin, this isn't why I sacrificed my life," Bane whispered.

"You're in no position to bargain," Garrot said.

"Aren't I?" She glanced pointedly at the druids around him.

"You said yourself you want me alive. How many are you willing to lose to take me?"

Garrot grunted. "Alive? Not for long."

If she was going to die today … She spared a glance at Bane and grinned. "We'll take as many with us as we can." Hadn't Tam taught her that?

He grinned back. "Better to go down fighting."

She cut through the center of Bane's chains. He gripped the links and tried an experimental swing, the chains shuddering against her shield, making it ripple. She ignored the faint echo of pain.

"I'm going to pulse my magic," she murmured. "It will throw them. Take out as many as you can, then retreat back to the wall."

He gave a curt nod.

She pulsed and threw the druids back a dozen feet. She charged, aiming for Blue Eyes. Flat on his back, he managed to lift his shield. Her sword easily cut through hardwood and then flesh. She tensed for a pulse of regret—she'd never killed a man before.

All she felt was satisfaction.

The man next to him died just as quickly. Then the druids were up. Three charged her—one at her front and two at her flanks. She managed to block one's swing, her sword slipping easily through the shield of the other.

Too late to duck the swing of the third, she braced for impact. Bane's chains slammed across the druid's chest. The man's staff hit her back with half the original force. Still, her lungs froze, refusing to draw breath. She staggered. Half a dozen druids swarmed her. Her hands were wrenched behind her back.

Out of options, she pulsed, the shock wave throwing them all. She landed hard, the edges of her vision going dark. Bane lay stunned beside her. A druid stood over them, blade aimed for Bane.

Sucking air into her spasming lungs, she stabbed and spread her shield around them. She gasped and heaved in a breath, the darkness giving way to color and light.

Bane rolled to his knees beside her. He bled from numerous wounds, the worst sheeting blood from his middle. "You all right?"

She managed a nod.

Relief touching his face, he hunched over, his face ashen. The druids regrouped as well, more of them pushing through the crowd.

Bane had managed to grab a sword and shield. He held out his chains. She cut them off at the first link.

"How many more times can you do the pulse?" he asked.

Her magic already felt thready. "That was it."

Bane winced. "All right, then." He kissed her full on the mouth. She froze, too shocked to react one way or another. He pulled back just as quickly. "Before I lose too much blood."

She stared at him. This brave, cocky man. They never would have lasted—not with his womanizing ways—but she loved him still. And if they were going to die ... Well, there were worse ways.

She squared off beside him and released her shield. Two dozen druids swarmed them. She managed to take down three in one swing before they tackled her. Her arms were bent cruelly behind her back, her wrists tied so she couldn't use her sigils. Her sword and shield sputtered out. A druid hauled her up.

Bane had been tied just as tightly. Garrot wrapped his arm around Bane's neck and backpedaled, dragging a weakened Bane up the steps to the stage. Larkin surged after them, only to be wrenched back, her shoulders screaming with pain.

Garrot wrapped the noose around Bane's neck. She didn't want to beg for Bane's life—not when she knew Garrot would not give it to her. She didn't want to give him that satisfaction. Still, a word ripped from her throat. "No!"

Heaving, Garrot stared at her, hatred screaming from his expression. And she was back to that awful day—the day the druids had hauled her up the stairs to the gallows. She'd stumbled. Garrot had pushed her, and she'd fallen to her knees. The crowd had screamed for her death.

Bane had saved her. He'd shoved her away from a frenzied mob and into a second-story window while screaming for her to run. And she had. She'd run as fast as she could into the Forbidden Forest, where she'd fallen in love with another man. When Bane had come for her, she'd only gone with him to save his life.

Despite all that, Bane had once again risked his life to save hers. Now he was dying for that choice, dying for her. And despite the power coursing through her, she couldn't save him— not like he'd saved her.

"Don't watch," Bane said.

Garrot was breathing hard. "Make her watch."

The druid holding her pinned the back of her head against his chest.

Bane shook his head and mouthed, "Don't watch."

He was still trying to protect her. He didn't want her to have this memory of him to carry for the rest of her life. But she would gladly carry it, so he wasn't alone in these last moments.

"Please," he mouthed, and the pleading on his face … She closed her eyes. It was the best she could give him. She would not watch his death, but she would not let him face it alone either.

She waited, dreading the moment when the trapdoor snapped. When it came, even the crowd's shouts couldn't drown out the crack of Bane's neck. And then she had to see. Had to know if it had really happened. She opened her eyes—only for a moment. It was enough to sear the image into her memory for the rest of her life.

Larkin dropped as if her knees had been cut out from under her. The druid's arms around her kept her from falling. *I couldn't save you,* she screamed in her head, for she would never give Garrot the satisfaction of knowing how deeply he'd wounded her. *I'm so sorry I couldn't save you.*

CHAPTER 25

DRUIDS

L arkin was hauled into an echoing two-story room packed with druids all the way up the second-story gallery. At the opposite end, Fenwick sat upon a throne on a raised dais. *My family's throne,* she realized. On simple chairs on each side of him sat three Black Druids, all of them staring at her in disgust. Kneeling in chains before the dais, Harben, Raeneth, and Iniya watched as she was dragged into the room and shoved to the hard marble floor. Her knees barked with pain, but it didn't really touch her, didn't really register.

"Where is Kyden? Tam?" Larkin asked.

Iniya shook her head as Raeneth wailed, "They took him from me! They took my baby."

"The child is fine," Fenwick said in disgust.

He said nothing about Tam.

Ancestors, Larkin had sworn Tam would not die for her.

No. He was not dead. He couldn't be.

Fenwick sighed as if he were tired of the whole affair. "Iniya Rothsberd, you have conspired with the pipers to free the prisoner Bane of Hamel and made an alliance with the pipers that would see you restored to power. The former having been witnessed under the watchful eye of dozens of high-ranking druids. The latter was confessed by your own son, Harben Rothsberd, in the hopes it would spare your lives. It will not. I sentence Iniya, Harben, and Raeneth to death by hanging. To be enacted immediately."

Why were they sparing Larkin's life? It was not mercy. No. The druids had another plan for her. Dread curdled in her gut.

Raeneth cried out and collapsed, shivering and whimpering. Harben stared off into nothing.

Iniya glared up at Fenwick. "I charge you, Fenwick, with the murder of my parents and siblings."

"You have no authority here," Fenwick said.

"I have the authority of a queen!" Iniya cried with righteous indignation. "An authority usurped by the druids."

The crowd murmured.

Fenwick eyed the people. "Do not listen to the Mad Queen."

"Mad Queen, ha!" Iniya shook her head. "A slur created to undermine my authority. I was not mad. I was grieving the murder of my family—a murder that you contrived!"

"I saved your life," Fenwick cried.

"Only so you could marry into the royal family," Iniya spat.

Larkin reeled, too numb and horrified to process what she heard.

Fenwick motioned to the guards, who hauled Iniya, Raeneth, and Harben to their feet.

"I was only seventeen years old!" Iniya screamed. "I demand that you hang. I demand my throne returned to me. I demand—" She continued listing demands that would never be met. They were all going to die.

Larkin hated her father. And yet she loved him too. Raeneth had done horrible things. And yet she was her brother's mother.

She had helped them at great risk to herself. And Iniya ... Ancestors, what had the woman been through? Why was Larkin not hanging with them?

"Please, Grandfather," she begged.

Fenwick flinched and refused to glance her way. The guards dragged the three of them toward the door.

"I am the rightful queen of the Idelmarch," Iniya cried. "I have allies still, Fenwick. They will rise up and—"

Fenwick shook his head. "Your aging lords are too content with their wealth and their heirs to risk a coup simply to go back to the old ways."

Larkin struggled against the druids holding her down. "Have you forgotten who I am, Master Fenwick? I am the princess of the Alamant. An assault against my family is an assault against me."

His gaze slowly, reluctantly turned to her. "Take her to the dungeons."

"No!" she cried.

"Please, Master Druid," came a new voice. "I would ask for mercy."

Larkin knew that voice—a voice that chimed like bells. A voice that caused Iniya to pause in her shouting. The guards stared as Nesha limped into the room. Her large pregnant belly did nothing to detract from the beauty of her auburn hair or her violet eyes. The black of her gown only made her rich coloring flare. Even her limp was dignified as she stepped up to the throne and bowed before it.

Larkin was aware of her own torn and soiled gown—her fake belly had fallen out sometime in the scuffle. Now that the druids had seen the real Hero of Hamel, they would never again mistake Larkin for her gorgeous sister.

"My father isn't much of a man," Nesha said into the silent crowd. "He is a drunk and a coward and a traitor. But I ask that you spare him. And my grandmother, though she disowned me before she ever knew me." She looked at Raeneth, who was sobbing uncontrollably. "And I ask that you spare his mistress, if only so my half brother doesn't lose his mother."

Raeneth looked up at Nesha, gratitude shining in her eyes.

Fenwick's gaze softened as it never had for Larkin. "I cannot spare them, for they will only rise up against the druids again and again."

She looked up at him through her lashes. "Banish them to the forest, then, Master Druid, and let fate decide."

Fenwick stared at her a long time. His gaze rose to Iniya, an ancient guilt fleeting across his face before vanishing. "Very well, Nesha. For your unwavering loyalty and service to the druids, I will grant your request." His gaze fell on Iniya. "But if you ever step foot inside the Idelmarch again, I will tighten the noose myself."

He waved his hands, and Iniya, Raeneth, and Harben were dragged away. Iniya was still cursing, Raeneth still cried, but her father met Larkin's gaze.

"Take to the trees at night!" she shouted after him. "If you want to survive, you must be in the trees by sundown! Find the river. Follow it upstream."

He gave one hard nod, then they were out of sight. Surely Denan's spies would hear of this. Surely he would find them and see them safe. Relief gutted her. She would not lose anyone else—not today.

Of their own volition, her eyes sought out her sister. Nesha locked gazes with her. Her sister's betrayal stung all over again. What had Larkin ever done to Nesha to make her hate her so?

"And what would you have us do with your sister?" Fenwick directed the question to Nesha.

Nesha's gaze landed on Garrot. He gave a slight nod. "Do with her as you will," her sister said.

Larkin locked her jaw to keep from sobbing. "Bane is dead." The father of Nesha's baby.

Nesha froze, her breath sucking in a startled gasp. So she hadn't known. Larkin shouldn't have felt satisfied at the obvious pain on her sister's face, but she did. The forest take her, she did.

"And whose fault is that?" Nesha ground out.

"Yours," Larkin spat.

Nesha rounded on her, but Garrot stepped between them and brushed his hand tenderly up and down her arm. He whispered something in her ear. She shot a poisonous look over his shoulder at Larkin before turning on her heel and quitting the room.

Garrot glared at Larkin. "And what will happen to the Piper Princess?" He directed the question at Fenwick.

The old man sat heavily in his chair. "Take her to the pit."

Larkin sat for unending hours in the complete dark of the open pit. She feared the dark. She'd thought she'd understood that fear. She had understood nothing.

To keep the terror at bay, she sat with her back against the wall and held her sigils open, the light illuminating the pit for a step in every direction. Her magic had grown strong enough that she was able to keep them up for hours on end without fail.

She wasn't sure how long she sat with her memories playing over and over again, the dark held at bay by nothing but her magic. How many times she watched Bane die. Felt her sword sink into Venna's middle. The satisfaction she'd felt when she'd ended Blue Eyes.

She'd come to believe the dark would never end when light appeared around the edges of a door that opened near the ceiling. The light grew brighter. Muffled steps scuffed on an uneven path. Someone was coming.

There was nothing Larkin could do about her red, swollen eyes or the puncture marks on her arms from where she'd pierced herself with her amulet, only to see the same vision of the curse's origins over and over again.

Unwilling to be caught huddled in a corner, she pushed her stiff, aching body upright. The steps came closer, the light brighter. Alone and carrying a wooden chair, Garrot stepped through the doorway and looked down at her. Unfortunately, he was too high to reach with her sword. She let it fill her hand anyway. Let the threat slide over him.

Unperturbed, he settled his chair on the side of the pit and sat in it.

"I will kill you for what you did to Bane." Her voice sounded abused.

"Bane was tried and convicted as a traitor. He paid for his crimes with his life."

"He died for getting Nesha pregnant!"

Garrot clenched his fists—she'd hit her mark.

"You can't stand that it's not your baby she's carrying, can you?"

"If not for me, she would be an outcast, starving on the streets or whoring in some brothel to feed herself. If not for me—"

"You think yourself a savior," Larkin spat. "But you're nothing more than a petty murderer."

He took a calming breath. "I do what I have to, Larkin."

Ironic how like the pipers he sounded. "You spared my family. You spared me. But not Bane. You wanted him to die. And you wanted him to die in front of me." She choked on a sob. "You're the true monster."

"I, the monster?"

"Where's Tam?"

He leaned back in his chair and watched her.

"Why am I still alive?"

"Let me tell you a story," Garrot said. "Long ago, two boys were born to a prostitute in the hovels of Landra. When the boys were six and five, their mother died of pox. The boys stole and begged to survive, but it wasn't enough. It was never enough.

"Until one winter day the oldest boy was caught and beaten so severely that he knew he wouldn't survive until morning—not unless he found somewhere warm. With the help of his younger brother, they broke into an empty house, ate everything they could out of the larder, and curled up on a soft bed.

"The boy awoke only a few hours later to a scream. Too weak to run, he stared up at a girl about his own age, with dark skin, tight curls, and eyes the color of cinnamon. Her father came running, a knife in hand. The boy managed to stand on his broken leg before his little brother. The man wrenched the boys up to throw him out, but the pain was so great, the older boy screamed and wept.

"The girl begged her father not to throw them out. And as the father loved his only daughter very much, he finally agreed. The boy's wounds were dressed. The brothers were fed and clothed. The younger was given a job as an errand boy for the wealthy merchant. The older apprenticed to a guard in the man's caravans.

"The girl made it her goal to teach both boys to read and figure their sums. And over the years, the three of them became fast friends. Until the oldest boy fell in love with her—a girl so far above his station in life he knew it could never be.

"So you can imagine his surprise when this girl demanded that her father apprentice the boy in his merchant business so that someday she could marry him. You can imagine his even greater surprise when the father agreed.

"The boy worked hard—harder than he ever had before to prove himself worthy of her, of all that he had been given."

Garrot paused, his shoulders rounded under the weight of his story—for it was his story. And Larkin knew what came next—she'd always known Garrot had lost someone he loved to the pipers.

"So when this boy who was now a man woke to the father's deepest grief, he knew what had happened. And he vowed he'd do anything to bring her back or die trying."

A girl from Landra, her father a merchant. Magalia. It must be. The boy Magalia had loved, twisted into this hateful, duplicitous man. Larkin would never tell him the truth. He didn't deserve to know.

"You went into the forest after her," Larkin breathed.

Garrot met her gaze. "I found her. And the pipers with her. They killed my brother and left me for dead."

She hated this man. She would always hate this man. But she pitied him too.

Garrot lifted a necklace out of his shirt and stroked the tooth. "This is all I have left of my brother. I keep it as a reminder of what I lost and the vow I made—to stop the pipers. So that no man would ever have to endure what I have."

"You're trying to save my sister the way that little girl saved you." She shook her head. "Nesha isn't her, Garrot. Nor is she your mother."

His mouth tightened. "Will you help me defeat the pipers, Larkin?"

"The pipers aren't our enemy, Garrot. The wraiths are."

"You're not entirely to blame for what has happened to you. The pipers' enchantment never really leaves a girl once taken."

"A lie." The forest take him.

He reached into his coat and pulled out a slim, worn book. The gold foil letters had long since worn down to the corners of the embossing. Eiryss's journal—it must be. Tam was supposed to fetch it. Now Garrot had it.

Tam hadn't escaped as she'd hoped. The druids had him. "What did you do to Tam?"

"Tell me, what do you want with this?" Garrot asked.

Larkin folded her arms to keep from reaching for it. Garrot obviously knew it was important, but not why. She couldn't see the harm in telling him. "I will tell you, if you tell me what happened to my family and my friend."

"Your family has been released into the Forbidden Forest. As for you piper friend, he is alive—for now."

It took everything Larkin had not to gasp in relief. Alorica would never forgive Larkin if she didn't bring the girl's husband home alive. "You harm him at the risk of the Piper Prince's wrath."

"Tell me." He held the journal up.

The druids must want the curse broken as much as the pipers did. If they understood that, perhaps they would help her. "We think Queen Eiryss might have left clues to breaking the curse inside."

"In lullabies?"

"The curse doesn't allow for outright truths."

Eyebrow raised, Garrot flipped through the pages. Some of them crumbled in his fingers, brittle paper spinning like falling leaves into the pit. "What good does a book do for a girl who can't read?"

She refused to be humiliated about that. "Others can read it for me."

Garrot leaned back in his chair. "Shall I tell you the short version? There are lullabies and a few ramblings from our first queen. The important bit is this: the wraiths didn't start the curse."

He seemed to be waiting for her shock. Larkin had seen the day the curse had taken shape. Whether or not Eiryss had begun the curse, she'd done everything in her power to stop it.

Garrot perched a pair of spectacles on his nose, flipped through the book, and read, "'In the five years since we fled the forest, no woman of the Alamant has borne a daughter nor successfully taken a thorn. The men's magic is greatly reduced.

"'And we of Valynthia—the magic is lost to us. To me. Already, the people forget from whence we came—our past lost to the shadow. Even for me, it becomes … difficult to write these words. As if my own hand will not obey me. Light, it's my fault. If only I had realized the cost of the dark magic we wielded …

"'But it cannot be undone—not by a man or woman living. So we must endure. Illin has ratified a treaty in which we will offer up our daughters so the Alamant may continue to protect us.

"'As for me … the shadows lie in wait. The trap has been set. Soon, I will fall into it, and my people will be ignorant to the danger that hunts them. So I took what was left of the council and charged them with acting as liaisons between the pipers and my people—to protect our people as best they can.'"

Garrot looked down at her. "The council eventually became the druids, so you have Eiryss to thank for that too."

"So the druids didn't start off an evil organization bent on suppressing and controlling their people?"

"'Even with what we have done,'" Garrot read on as if she hadn't interrupted him, "'we will never defeat the wraiths. All our valiant efforts, all our sacrifices won't matter. The magic will fail. In trying to protect our people, I have cursed us to ruin.'"

He looked up at her, waiting.

"You misunderstand her."

"It's simple, Larkin. Your own ancestor used dark magic to win the war between Valynthia and the Alamant. That dark magic created the curse. She tried to reverse it and only managed an ineffective countercurse—one that banished us from our rightful inheritance, from our magic—then she created a treaty that left us beholden to our conquerors."

"Conquerors? The pipers only take what they must to fight the curse."

"Is that what has happened over the last few days? To the seven hundred-odd women the pipers have kidnapped?"

"You broke the treaty."

Garrot shut the book with a snap. "Over the years, the curse seems to have morphed, to have pushed back the countercurse that keeps it in check. All because the pipers refused to end it."

She shook her head in disbelief. "The pipers have lost so much more to this curse than you. How can you believe they would choose this?"

He leaned forward, his elbows braced against his knees. "No, Larkin. They could have ended the curse before it ever began, but they refused."

"The wraiths kill pipers and turn them into mulgars. The pipers would do anything they could to stop that."

"Even give up their precious White Tree?"

She stilled. Their sacred tree, opalescent and lined in gold. The source of their magic.

He nodded. "You see it now, don't you? The pipers would have to use up every scrap of their magic, all of it. It would kill the tree, but it could be done. But the pipers refuse to do it."

The White Tree was all magic and power and beauty. Destroy it? The last of its kind. No. The pipers wouldn't do it. Neither would she. "And if you're wrong, killing the White Tree will destroy any hope we have of survival."

He rose to his feet. "I'll take that risk."

"You don't understand. You can't—not unless you see it for yourself. There is something majestic and holy about the White Tree."

"I will do what I must to put an end to this, Larkin, even if I must profane something holy."

"There is another way," she said. "Join with the pipers. Our curse has already crumbled—I've seen it myself. All that remains is to defeat the wraiths and barrenness."

Garrot tossed the book at her. She caught it. "Here. Keep it. It's yours anyway, I suppose. And there are other copies. I'll leave the lantern for you. See for yourself if the Curse Queen left us any hints to breaking the curse. As for me, I mean to do it."

He picked up his chair and turned to go.

She laid her hand on the cover and looked back up at him. "And what do you mean to do with me?"

He looked back at her. "I will do what I must to break this curse. Always remember that, Larkin."

Why did his words feel like a threat?

CHAPTER 26

COUP

Larkin woke with a scream echoing in her ears. She bolted up from the hard rocks, her magic buzzing beneath her skin as she called up her sword. The light illuminated a small circle in the darkness. She clutched her sword and panted.

"Just a dream." Her voice sounded strange after so many days of silence. She'd lost count of how many. Instead, she judged the passing of time by the fading of her bruises. The black bruising from her ankle had shifted to her toes, which had turned a sickly green.

She dared not close her eyes for fear she might see their faces again—the faces of the families of the men she'd killed. The remorse that had been so absent when she's sliced through them had seeped in slowly as she wallowed in the pit. Every time she closed her eyes, she saw a child crying for her father. A mother for a son. A wife for her husband.

She dragged her nails through her greasy scalp. She itched. Everywhere. The reek of her unwashed body made her own stomach turn. She was weary, body and soul. She longed for sunlight and water and, most of all, the comfort of Denan's arms around her.

How much sleep had she managed? Surely no more than three hours. Even if she tried, she wouldn't go back to sleep—not with the taste of the nightmare still fresh on her tongue.

She dragged herself to the book—Eiryss's book. For however long she'd been down here, it had been her only companion. She squinted at the words in the half light. Careful of the brittle pages, she sounded out the letters, painfully blending the individual sounds like Denan had taught her.

After Eiryss's initial entry came stories of her life with her young daughter, fights with the council, and the building of their new kingdom. Interspersed throughout were the lullabies. They were similar enough to the ones she knew, so after the first two or three words, she could usually guess what came next, though sometimes whole lines were different.

For instance, in the book, one poem read:

Snatching his daughters from their dreams,
Never a chance to voice their screams,
Back to the forest, he doth go.
Find the light and fight shadow.

In the version Larkin had been taught, "his daughters" had been replaced with "virgins," and the last line had been replaced with "to nibble and dribble their bones just so." The lullaby as she knew it was about the beast. This was clearly about Ramass. But who were his daughters, and why was he snatching them?

There was another lullaby Larkin had never heard before.

Bound by shadow dark as night,
A curse queen, four ravens white,
Failed to drive the shadow into light,

Heal the darkness, cure the blight.

Wielder of light? Eiryss had mentioned light before. Larkin eased back a few pages. The queen had almost used it as an expletive. And why did Larkin get the feeling the wraiths thought that Larkin was the nestling they'd been searching for? They clearly thought she'd broken the curse. But that was Sela. What exactly did they want her little sister for?

There was one last poem, just two lines.

Light through dark and shadow pass,
Then tighten and trap the poison fast.

The sound of footsteps announced the guard's arrival. His hair and thick mustache were always slicked down tight in contrast to his bushy sideburns, so she'd taken to calling him Sideburns.

"Please, do you know anything about my family or the man who was with me?"

Instead of answering, he tossed her a bag of food and a cask of water.

She sighed. "Can I have some water for washing?" This, too, she always asked.

To her astonishment, he returned shortly with a bucket of water, which he lowered to her along with soap, a simple, full skirt, and a shirt before locking the door behind him. She washed twice and used the remaining water to launder her awful dress in case she was desperate for clean clothes later. She reveled in the feeling of clean hair and the smell of her skin.

Sideburns came back before long with half a dozen other men. Between them was Tam, bound and gagged, but looking healthy.

"Tam," she gasped. She'd begun to doubt she would ever see him again. "Are you all right?"

He winked.

She breathed out in relief. "Maybe Alorica won't kill me."

He grinned through his gag.

"You will submit to being bound," Sideburns said, his first words to her. "Any wounds you give us will be meted out to your guard. Understood?"

She nodded.

"Take him back to his cell," Sideburns said.

They took Tam away again, and men lowered a ladder. After she'd climbed to the high platform, she allowed them to bind her hands and climbed the long set of stairs. She was relieved to leave the damp, dark cave with its resounding silence behind. The light from the windows made her blink, eyes stinging.

She was taken to the throne room. The gallery was packed with druids, as was the main floor. Judging by the tooling on their belts, they were all Black Druids—either their ranks had swelled or every Black Druid in existence was present.

Fenwick sat on the dais with his council on either side. All of them watched her in utter silence. Would they hang her, as they had Bane? She wished for one friendly gaze in the room—just one person who didn't want her dead.

Instead, she caught sight of Garrot in the front row. He looked at her eagerly, as if he'd been waiting for her appearance. Uncontrollable, her sigils gleamed hot beneath her skin, the angry buzzing setting her teeth on edge. If not for the threat to Tam's life, they would have formed in her hands, and she would have used them.

Sideburns nudged Larkin, his hand on his sword. She'd stopped at the doorway without realizing it. She swallowed hard. Whatever came, lingering or fighting wouldn't change it. She forced herself to take one step and then another. Heads swiveled, watching her. She passed Garrot on her left and resisted the urge to spit on him.

Sideburns escorted her all the way to the foot of the dais and then took a step back.

Fenwick stared down at her. "Larkin of Hamel, you, as well as your guard, have been ransomed by the Piper Prince. You will be escorted into the forest and released."

All the breath left her lungs in a whoosh. Released. To Denan. Color came back into her world. She wanted to drop to her knees and weep, to cry out in relief. Instead, she forced herself to remain calm.

Denan had come for her, just as he promised.

Fenwick waved his hand toward his guards. "Take her to the appointed place in the forest."

Sideburns stepped up beside her and took her arm.

"I must protest this," Garrot said softly from behind her.

A shiver of horror cut through her relief.

Fenwick turned to one of his councilors, either not hearing or ignoring Garrot. "Now, about that dispensation."

"I must protest this," Garrot shouted.

Dread curdled in Larkin's stomach until she thought she might be sick.

Fenwick rose to his feet. "You have forgotten your place, Garrot. We all saw how easily they sacked Cordova, how easily he could sack us all if he truly wanted."

Denan had sacked Cordova?

"We cannot defeat their magic," Fenwick continued. "Nor should we try—not with the wraiths bent on destroying us both." Echoing silence answered him. Fenwick gestured vaguely to Larkin. "The Piper Prince has agreed to return Cordova in exchange for his wife and an increase in the tithe. We will be grateful that's all he demanded. The army will be disbursed, and things will go back to how they were."

"I told you," Garrot said into the echoing silence. "I told you he would try to save her—his own granddaughter, the traitor of Hamel."

"I am not a traitor," Larkin said.

"That has nothing—" Fenwick began.

"It has everything to do with it." Garrot eyed the druids in the gallery. "Brothers, can you not see that for the last three centuries, we have been sacrificing our daughters in the fight against the wraiths when all along, we should have been fighting the pipers?"

"What folly is this?" Fenwick cried. "The wraiths crave the death of all humanity."

"They do not," Garrot said darkly. "They only want to end the curse. As do we all."

Fenwick's eyes widened. "You've spoken with them?"

Garrot's silence was answer enough.

"You've allied yourself with them?" Fenwick gestured to a pair of guards standing on either side of the dais. "Garrot of Landra, you have grown mad in your grief and your thirst for revenge. I hereby strip you of your rank. You are banned from ever setting foot in the druid palace again."

Iniya's palace, Larkin thought bitterly.

Fenwick waved. "Throw him out."

Their hands on their weapons, the guards advanced on Garrot. He wore no weapons and made no move to defend himself. Until they were half a dozen steps away. Then he gave a shout. Over a dozen men around him slid into defensive stances, swords and shields suddenly appearing in their hands. In Garrot's hands.

Larkin gaped at Garrot's blade and the shadows swirling off it. A wraith blade. It had appeared in his hand as if by magic. But not the magic of the pipers. This was the magic of the Black Tree.

The guards stumbled back in shock. The councilors bolted to their feet. Fenwick shouted for more guards. They hustled from the four corners of the room to form a wall between Garrot and Fenwick.

"What madness is this?" Fenwick asked.

"Surrender, and you will live," Garrot said.

Fenwick sized up Garrot's men with their magic blades—blades that would easily cut through the weapons of his guards. "Only a fool aligns himself with the wraiths and think they would not turn on him."

"Surrender or die!" Garrot cried.

Fenwick's gaze swept across those in the gallery, the main room, and finally his councilors. He took his blade from his belt. "Black Druids of Idelmarch, stand with me. Cut out this rot before it spreads. Kill them!"

His councilors and guards pulled their own swords and cheered with him. With a shout, Fenwick charged, his council rushing with him.

A hand snaked around Larkin's waist. Sideburns hauled her away from the battle. No. She must stay with Fenwick. He meant to return her to Denan. She fought and kicked. He only wrapped her up tighter as he dragged her away from the churning, fighting mess interspersed with sprays of red. So much blood that the floor ran slick with it, fighters slipping and falling in the sloppy mess.

And then it was over. Larkin wasn't even sure who'd won—not until Garrot stepped onto the dais. He paced the length of it, looking at the druids, his gaze wild, his body soaked in blood. Larkin was once again at his mercy.

Fenwick had gambled on the rest of the Black Druids rushing to his defense, on the sheer number of them overpowering the wraith blades. His gamble had failed. She looked for Fenwick but couldn't find him among the scores of dead and dying.

He was a monster, but he was also the master. Someone must remain loyal to him, someone who could help her.

She rammed her shoulder into Sideburns. "Let me go to Fenwick. Please."

Sideburns studied her. His gaze swung to the locked doors. He must have decided she had nowhere to run and no one who would help her. He released her, staying a step behind as she rushed through the bodies.

"Years ago"—Garrot's voice carried through the room—"my brother and I went into the forest after my own betrothed. Imagine my disbelief when I tracked not some beast, but a man. I found that man. He killed my brother and left me for dead. And when night came, so came the wraiths. But they did not try to harm me. No. The Wraith King took me to his home—a place of magic twisted to darkness. His servants bound my wounds, brought me food and water.

"It was there I learned the truth. Ramass was a man cursed long ago by the pipers, as was his home and all his people. If he could just reach the source of the pipers' magic, he could use the last of that magic to break the curse."

Larkin found Fenwick, his black robes soaked through, blood streaming from his mouth, which opened and closed soundlessly. She knelt beside him. "Is there anyone I can trust?"

His gaze fixed on her. "Fawna. Run. Her brother."

Larkin instantly understood. Fawna must run to her brother for safety. She nodded, though she was in no position to help him or his wife. "Can you help me?"

He shook his head, tears streaming from his eyes—whether from pain or fear or regret she couldn't guess. He would die the same way he'd condemned Iniya's family to die—by treachery and blood. She had no pity for the man before her, save for the man he could have been had he made better choices. Now it was too late.

Still, she didn't let go of his hand until his eyes slipped closed. He stopped breathing, gasped, and didn't breathe again.

"Brothers," Garrot said. "Can you not see? With the gifts bestowed by the wraiths, we are more than a match for the pipers. No more weeping parents. No more hollow-eyed children. No more lovers stolen in the night. With the weapons of the wraiths, we are our own masters. We will defeat the pipers and the curse at once!"

The druids murmured. A few cheered.

"You are a fool and worse," Larkin said, her voice trembling. She felt the attention of the room swivel to her as she pushed to her feet. Fenwick's blood ran down her shins. "The wraiths will turn on you and kill you all! They—"

Sideburns took hold of her arm and shook her. "Stop talking."

"Take her back to the pit," Garrot said in disgust.

Sideburns shoved her toward the door, through Black Druids who murmured uneasily. The word *wraiths* sliding through dozens of lips like a curse.

"When they are finished with you," she shouted, "you will all become mulgars—as will anyone else touched by the wraiths' dark magic."

A druid stepped before her. Sour Face. He backhanded her. She staggered, fell to a knee, and spat blood, her teeth throbbing and her ears ringing.

"You killed my friend," Sour Face said.

Her eye rapidly swelling shut, she looked up at the man. "You're all going to wish you were dead."

"You first." He drew back his foot to kick her.

Sideburns drew his sword and stood over her, his gaze deadly.

"She is still useful to us, Met." Garrot's voice drew closer with each word until he stood beside her.

Met pointed at her. "She deserves to die for what she's done."

"Hold her, West."

Warily watching Met, Sideburns—whom Garrot called West—held her by the arm. Garrot hauled out his knife. This could not be how she died—in a room full of death and hatred. She struggled against West.

"Easy," he murmured in her ear.

Instead of plunging the knife into her chest, Garrot nicked her shirt at both shoulders and ripped the sleeves off, baring her sigils for all to see. He gripped her arm, pulling her tight against him, and said in her ear, "You're part of my plan, Larkin. I need you alive, but I don't need you healthy. I don't need your piper friend at all. So keep your mouth shut, or I'll make you wish you had."

Plan? Oh, ancestors, what plan?

He hauled her up the steps and pushed her to the center of the stage. "A child of Idelmarch, bearing the magic of the pipers—the magic they could have freely given us but refused to share."

Larkin wanted to scream the truth, but she'd sworn to defend Tam's life with her own. Right now, she thought that might be easier than keeping her mouth shut.

Garrot tore open his own shirt, baring his chest, which was covered in black markings in the shape of twisted thorns—the antithesis of her sigils. The longer she stared at them … they seemed to move. Writhe. She wanted to look away, ached to look away, but they sucked her in, much like the wraiths' poisoned gaze.

"Yes, brothers. The Black Tree has endowed me with magic. As well as my men. It will endow you as well."

He turned from her, breaking the spell. She staggered back, blinking and gasping—she hadn't realized she'd been holding her breath. To her astonishment, no one else seemed mesmerized by Garrot's sigils. She didn't know what that meant, but it made her afraid.

As if on command, another druid approached the dais with a tray covered in glittering black thorns. "Come, brothers, take what is ours by birthright—the ancient magic of our own people. The power to defeat the pipers, to defeat the curse."

No. Even the druids understood evil. Surely they wouldn't embrace it.

A man came forward. Sour Face, or Met. Garrot slid a thorn into his skin. Larkin stared at the bulge as blood painted a garish line down his arm.

More and more men lined up, their gazes eager. More and more received their thorns.

The pipers were stretched to the limit defending against mulgars and wraiths. Would their sacred blades stand up to magical ones? If the Idelmarchians joined the wraiths' side … She bit her fist to keep from screaming.

"Make note of the ones who come last," Garrot said under his breath to Met, who nodded. "End any who refuse."

"You are all going to die for this," Larkin said.

Garrot started as if he'd forgotten she was there. "Lock her back in the pit and make sure she stays there until the army is ready to march."

CHAPTER 27

WEST

L arkin stumbled to the edge of the dark nothingness of the pit, her cheek hot and throbbing from where Met had hit her. "How long do I have?"

The guards shifted.

"We depart in four days," West said.

Her eyes slipped closed. "Have you ever seen a"—her mouth refused to form the word *wraith*—"shadow, West?"

"You need to go down the ladder."

"I have," she whispered. "I have smelled their foulness—the mineral rot of the grave. I have felt their touch—all screaming shadows. Heard their inhuman voices." She turned to face him. His eyes reflected the lantern light. The three men with him had their hands on their clubs. "I would die before I let the shadows defile me."

She charged him. He'd clearly been anticipating it. But instead of drawing his club, he wrestled her to the ground and held her tight. "Prick her."

The druids had gilgad venom. The wraiths' doing, surely. The dart's sting was familiar, as was the pepper-tasting antidote that halted the poison from spreading to her lungs and killing her.

"My name is Larkin. I am the daughter of Pennice and the wife of Denan. I will not be taken by the shadow."

As the gilgad venom robbed her ability to move, her eyes grew heavy.

"My name is Larkin," she slurred. "I am the daughter of Pennice and the wife of Denan. I will not be taken by the shadow. I will not …"

She woke in the pit. Her head throbbed nearly as hard as her teeth. West sat on a boulder beside her, one hand holding his opposite wrist. He pointed to the rim of the pit, where a man stood with a blow gun and dart.

"Say my name, West," she murmured.

He pointed to a tureen of soup and some soft bread. "Any more trouble and we'll dart and drug you. Do you understand?"

"Did you dart and drug Tam?"

"I didn't."

She heard what he wasn't saying—someone else did. Ancestors. Why did she think she could ever make the pipers and Idelmarchians work together? She never should have left Denan's side.

"Say my name." She didn't know why it was so important. Then she did. She wanted him to see her as a person. Not a traitor. A person. With a name.

He pushed to his feet and left without a word. She waited until he and the other man were gone, until only the lantern kept her company. Then she wept.

Four days passed slower and faster than she could have ever imagined. Four days in which the ghosts of the dead and her dread for the future haunted her.

Garrot's words echoed through her. *"You're part of my plan, Larkin. I need you alive, but I don't need you healthy."*

Ancestors, he was aligned with the wraiths. Eiryss's words from the journal came to her mind.

Consumed by evil, agents of night,
Seek the nestling, barred from flight.

Wraith Queen. Maisy had said they were searching for their Wraith Queen.

Garrot was taking her to the wraiths. They were going to make her one of them. She felt Ramass's burning cold, evil embrace, the oily corruption seeping into her soul.

Larkin would die first.

She pierced herself over and over again with her amulet until her arm grew infected and she made herself stop. And all she had to show for it was the same vision over and over again, until she had memorized Eiryss's and Dray's every movement. She read the lullabies until she knew them word for word. She became so wrapped up in Eiryss's and Dray's past that it began to feel more real than her own.

All that kept her sane was Denan's promise. He would come for her.

Or she would escape and go to him.

She practiced the moves Tam, Talox, and Denan had taught her until her muscles screamed for her to halt. West brought her another bucket of water and change of clothes. She barely recognized her reflection in the bucket's still water. Her cheek was swollen and black, a dark wedge of bruising had settled in a line along her jaw. Blood splattered her skin. She probed her teeth, which didn't feel as loose as they had before.

She washed blood from the creases of her skin, throwing the ruined dress into the shadowed recesses of the pit, and dressed in another simple skirt and shirt. She wished for the soft trousers of the pipers—it would be much easier to fight her way free in pants.

Every day, West brought her soup and some tea for the pain. Knowing she needed her strength, she ate hungrily, careful to chew with only the left side of her mouth—her teeth were still sore—and downed all her water. When she saw the light coming for her, she paced, shook out her limbs to loosen them, and practiced a few kicks and lunges.

Her body was not responding as she liked, sluggish from so many days spent underground with such monotonous food. Plus, she was still healing from her injuries. Her braid was still damp from her bath when West appeared with two other men, a stretcher between them.

He looked at her in disappointment.

She didn't understand his expression but didn't care. She flared her shield and sword. "I'm afraid you're going to have to come get me this time."

He leaned against the wall. "We'll wait."

She huffed. "You're going to have to wait a long time, Druid. I know where you're taking me. And I will not go willingly."

"I'm not a druid," West said. "I'm a soldier of the Idelmarch."

She eyed his companions, who wavered. She blinked to clear her eyes. They didn't look like soldiers, but servants. Insulting. "I'm not going to the shadows."

West only watched her. She shrugged her shoulders to loosen them. Losing her balance, she stumbled to the side and struggled to remain upright. She froze and looked at him in horror. The soup. "You drugged me."

Whatever they'd given her worked faster and faster. She sat down hard, her magic snuffing out. She would be at their mercy in moments. And afterward ... "Everything the shadows say is poison. As soon as they no longer need you, they will betray you."

"I'm just a soldier," West said. "I have no more say in the matter than you."

"Is that what you tell yourself?" Her body tipped forward. She caught herself, pushed herself back upright. "Help me. Free me. I swear, my husband will reward you."

West didn't answer.

She tipped forward again. This time, her hands didn't have the strength to hold her up. She collapsed, her face mashed against the rocks, her bruises throbbing.

She came around to pain on her arm. West scratched her with a dart—like what had happened to Maisy. She'd retain some of her ability to move and speak. They bound her hands and rolled her onto the stretcher. Pinching herself, she fought a wave of exhaustion as they carried her to the side of the pit. West tied her legs to the poles while the servants tied two dangling ropes. So that was how they meant to haul her up.

West straightened and pointed to one of the servants, a handsome boy about her own age. "Keep her steady."

They climbed the ladder out of the pit and disappeared over the edge. The servant knelt beside her. His hand cupped between her legs. "You know what we do with traitorous whores, little princess?"

She managed a terrified groan as his hand slipped up her skirt. He covered her mouth. "Oh, shh. None of that. Might interrupt our fun."

She moaned again.

"What are you doing?" West shouted from above.

The servant jumped back. "Nothing, sir. Just arranging the ropes."

West dropped down the ladder so fast he nearly fell. "Were you manhandling the prisoner?"

The servant backed away. "Of course not, sir."

West eyed her mussed skirts. She managed a trembling nod. He lunged, his fist flying into the servant's face.

The man hunched over, his hands cupping his shattered nose. "You broke it! The forest take you, you filthy—"

West's foot jammed between the servant's legs. The man's face went white, and he fell to his knees. West knelt next to her and rearranged her dress.

"That won't happen again. I swear it."

She gripped the sleeve of his shirt. "Not the first time," she stumbled slowly through the words, "one of you has groped me." She closed her eyes as Blue Eye's face flashed in her mind, his hands gripping her bottom.

West's mouth hardened. "It won't happen again, Larkin."

Her name. He'd said her name.

She collapsed, her mind wandering and her body boneless as they hauled her up. *Like that first night with Denan.* She'd been drugged against the pain and carried over his shoulder into the boughs. The wraiths had come that night, their oily evil coating her one stroke at a time.

Days of preparation in the pit, of planning and determination—all undone. She was helpless. The druids would make sure she stayed that way. She had to face the fact that she might not have a chance to escape. If that were the case, she still had her weapons. She could turn them on herself.

She gasped on a hard sob. She did not want to die. Did not want to leave the people she loved. Did not want them to suffer because of her. But better safely dead than twisted into something evil that would hunger for their destruction.

She dozed then, unable to fight anymore, and woke in fits and starts as they wedged her onto the bed of straw in a wagon already packed with crates of food. West perched on one of the crates beside her and glared at the druids who leered at her over the edge of the wagon. One hocked through his nose and made to spit on her.

West stood, his sword scraping free of its scabbard. "I've been charged with making sure no one molests her. And I mean to do my job."

The man turned and spat onto the ground. He glared at West, motioned to his friends, and moved off.

West watched them for a while, then he crouched down beside her. "Would you rather be completely covered so they can't stare at you? It might be hot."

West wasn't a bad man. Just a soldier doing his job, and he had enough kindness in him to let her keep her dignity. A kind, honest man wouldn't agree to work with the wraiths—not if he really understood them. She could use that to her advantage. Plant the seeds of truth and wait for them to take root. And maybe, just maybe, West would help her escape.

She managed to nod. He dug around in a bag and produced a large blanket. He laid it over her, mused for a bit, pulled it off again, and arranged the blanket to create a sort of canopy over her. He nodded in approval and hopped down. From the direction of her feet came a pair of clopping hooves.

"How is the mandala root working in conjunction with the gilgad venom?" Garrot asked.

Mandala. That made sense. Her mother gave it to sleepless mothers who suffered from melancholy after the births of their babies. It was dangerous though. Too much led to death.

"She's groggy and limp, but aware," West said.

"Good." The saddle creaked, and the horses made a few steps as if it was leaving.

"Master Druid," West said.

Master Druid. Of course they'd made Garrot the master. Of course they had. At least she needn't worry about seeking revenge. There wouldn't be much of the druids left to pay for what they'd done to her—not after the wraiths were finished with them. But then again, there wouldn't be much left of her either.

"What do you mean, *manhandled* her?" Garrot's shout startled her out of her thoughts.

Hushed murmurs.

"Where is this man?" Garrot grunted.

"I left him in the pit," West said. "He might be able to walk by now."

Garrot huffed. "Leave him there. You were right to hide her. I should have commissioned a box for her."

A pause. The threads of a whisper.

"Well," Garrot said, "there's nothing else for it, and West will see to her."

More whispers, more insistent this time.

"That won't be necessary," Garrot said.

"I will not let a bunch of uncouth men around her when she's vulnerable like this," Nesha's voice ground out. She must have been the one whispering earlier. She obviously hadn't wanted Larkin to know she was here and now no longer cared. Why did she care about what was done to Larkin? They hated each other.

"Really, my dear," Garrot said. "West apprenticed to healers long before becoming a soldier. He's more than capable of caring for her."

"He hasn't done a great job so far," Nesha huffed.

An awkward silence. "It won't happen again, miss," West said.

Nesha hmphed.

"We will check on her tonight, and you may ask her how she fares," Garrot said. "Will that satisfy you?"

Tonight? But surely Nesha had just come to say goodbye to Garrot. Surely Garrot wasn't such a fool as to bring his pregnant wife to a meeting with the wraiths.

"At midday," Nesha said. "I will help her with her needs."

A sigh through the nose—probably from Garrot.

"I understand your familial connection, Nesha," he said. "But you must remember that Larkin is still under the pipers' enchantment. She is not to be trusted."

"Of course I remember," Nesha said.

Garrot hummed low in his throat. "Very well."

The wagon swayed as someone stepped into the seat. The harnesses jangled, and the wagon lurched into motion. It wasn't long before Larkin was sick to her stomach. Deciding sleep was better than this, she allowed herself to drift away.

Larkin woke at midday when West pulled away the blanket covering her and dropped the tailgate. He climbed in with her and propped her against a bag of beans, high enough she could see out between some of the crates. They were on one of the roads that connected the cities—either Cordova Road or Landra Road.

Not in the forest, thank her ancestors.

West settled a tray of cooked beans, some buttered bread, and a waterskin on her lap. He tucked a napkin into her shirt. "Can you manage the spoon?"

She glared at it. "Don't want it."

West took a spoonful and swallowed. "There. See?"

She stirred the watery beans as he hopped down. Still not trusting it, she took the bowl in her bound hands and threw it out.

Hands on his hips, he stared at the mess, some of it on his pants.

I need him on my side, she reminded herself. "Sorry," she mumbled.

He gave her a flat look. "So you're just not going to eat at all?"

"How long do I have?" she asked.

He seemed to understand what she meant. "The pipers are meeting us for your ransom at a bend in the river in three days."

"Ransom?" There was no ransom. They were turning her over to the wraiths.

His guilty eyes met hers, and she suddenly understood. Denan thought he was ransoming her. He marched into a trap. She must warn him. But first, she must wake up. She must get out of these ropes and escape the encampment.

Her seat bones hurt. She tried to shift, only to flop around like a stranded fish. The movement made her bladder hurt. "I need to pee."

West blushed scarlet.

"I thought you apprenticed to a healer?" she asked in exasperation.

"None of my patients were pretty," he muttered.

She rolled her eyes. West scooted her forward. When she reached the edge, he carried her a dozen steps toward the forest.

"Where are you going with her?"

West turned, allowing her to see Nesha riding toward them on a beautiful bay, Garrot loping behind her. "To see to her needs."

Nesha stared at Larkin, her mouth a thin line. She turned to Garrot. "This isn't something a man should help her with."

"Nesha," Garrot said gently. "She's not safe to be around."

"She would never hurt me. And besides, her hands are bound." He didn't seem convinced. She smiled sweetly at him. "You'll be right there if anything happens."

Garrot nodded. Nesha rode to the edge of the woods, clambered down from the saddle, and handed the reins to Garrot. She pointed into the wood. "There, that log will do nicely."

Nesha maneuvered Larkin's skirts so she wasn't sitting on them as West got her into position with her backside hanging over the opposite side of the trunk. Nesha took West's place, propping Larkin against her. West backed away. Nesha gathered

Larkin's skirts, exposing her backside. Larkin finally released her bladder.

She sighed in relief. Beneath her cheek, Larkin could feel the baby squirming. She rested her fingertips against the shifting—an elbow maybe? Bane's baby. A piece of him in the world lived on even after his father had perished.

"The mandala is in the water, not the food." Nesha slipped a waterskin from a loop at her belt and held it to Larkin's mouth. "Drink all of it. Now."

Larkin pushed back, not trusting her sister. "What? Why would you help me?"

"Because even after all you've done, you're still my sister."

"All I've done? I didn't turn a mob loose on you."

"Drink," Nesha hissed.

Larkin drained Nesha's waterskin. Her sister eased it back onto the loop around her waist. "In ten minutes, act groggy and sloppy, like you were this morning. When they give you water, pretend to drink it but pour it out instead."

Larkin opened her mouth to ask one of a dozen questions piling up in her head.

"West," Nesha called before she could. "She's ready." Nesha held her skirts so Larkin's backside was covered, but the hem wasn't hanging in the urine.

West picked Larkin up. Confused, she watched her sister limp back to her horse and smile brightly at Garrot before riding away.

CHAPTER 28

NESHA

L arkin stared gratefully at the blanket West had placed over
her as the sleep draft and gilgad venom leeched from her
system. Little by little, she felt more awake, and her body
regained its strength. It was almost painful not to shift against the
bruising wagon. To pretend to sleep whenever West looked in on
her. She was bored and hot and starving.

They paused around supper time. This time, they offered
her applesauce and dry, crumbly biscuits. She wasn't sure what
of any of it she could trust. Perhaps Nesha would tell her. "I need
to relieve myself first."

West got her out of the wagon. Nesha waited to help her,
Garrot at her side. They found another log for her, then left her
with Nesha to hold up her skirts.

Nesha instantly pushed the waterskin to Larkin, who drank
hidden in the fold of her sister's divided skirts. "They're giving
you a stronger dose tonight. Pretend to be sound asleep, no matter what."

"Is the food safe?"

"Eat a little and wait to be sure." She leaned in. "Mama, Sela, Brenna?"

Larkin's mouth compressed in a thin line. "They were fine when I left them with Denan."

Nesha shuddered. "Fine until one of those pipers marries my four-year-old sister."

Larkin's first impulse was to spout back something hurtful. Her second impulse was to defend the pipers. Neither would do any good. She needed Nesha on her side. "That won't happen."

Nesha made a noncommittal noise in her throat.

"Do you know anything about Iniya, Harben, and Raeneth?" Larkin asked.

"Why do you care about any of them?"

"Just answer the question."

"I saw them released into the forest. That's all I know." At least Garrot hadn't lied about that.

Nesha took a damp rag and cleaned Larkin up, which was humiliating.

"Why, Nesha? You were my best friend. The person I trusted the most in the world. Why did you betray me?"

Nesha huffed. "You were always everyone's favorite. Mama and Papa. Even Sela. But you couldn't see it. You wanted your freedom. It's all you ever wanted. You never saw that you already had it. You could run and dance and marry and escape while I ... I could have none of those things. I was the one trapped."

Larkin had never known this—never known how deep her sister's jealousy went.

Nesha sniffed. "All I ever wanted was to marry Bane and be a mother to his children." A sob hitched in her throat. "But you had to take that too. You took everything I ever wanted."

"So you wanted me dead?"

Nesha's hands shifted to fists. "I wanted to hurt you. I

wanted you to suffer as I had." She shook her head. "But I never wanted you dead."

Larkin pulled down the collar of her shirt, revealing the horizontal scar across her neck. "Hunter tried to slit my throat. He would have succeeded if Denan hadn't killed him, hadn't saved me from that mob."

Nesha shook her head as if trying to deny the proof right in front of her. "Garrot swore to me—he swore on his life—he wouldn't let any harm come to you. Hunter must have been acting on his own."

"I'm sure Garrot was very sorry the mob got out of control. And very sorry weeks later when he locked me in a room and tried to force me to marry Bane."

"It was for your own good! You were enchanted!"

"I was never enchanted!"

"Then why keep the pipers' secrets? For decades, the pipers have terrorized us, and you did nothing but defend them. At least Garrot is trying to stop them!"

"Nesha," Garrot said from behind her, his brow drawn. He motioned for West.

Nesha hurried to make Larkin decent. West picked her up. Nesha brushed the front of her dress as if rubbing off Larkin's touch. Garrot saw her wounded expression and pulled her into his arms.

She sank into him, her head tucked in the crook of his neck. "I can't make her see, Garrot. No matter how hard I try. I can't get through the enchantment."

Garrot's hands stroked up and down her back—the same hands that had wrestled Bane to the gallows and forced the noose around his neck. Bile rose in Larkin's throat. Bile and hatred strong enough to choke on. *Plant the seeds of truth. Wait for them to take root.*

"Ask him who killed Bane, Nesha."

She started and looked at Larkin. "Bane killed seven druids,

Larkin. He was sentenced by the courts. Garrot spoke for him, tried to defend him."

Larkin barked a laugh. "Ask him who put the noose around Bane's neck and shoved him into the abyss." Garrot glared at her. She glared right back. Let his own actions condemn him. "And when you're done with that, ask him who killed our grandfather and all his councilors. Ask him how much blood stains his hands."

Garrot wrapped his arm around Nesha's waist and led her back to the horses. "Washerwomen follow the company. I'll hire one of them to see to your sister's needs."

Larkin wanted to fight free of West's arms, but she forced herself to move slowly, sloppily. "Ask him why he's turning me over to the wraiths to be tortured, Nesha. Ask him what he plans to do with Bane's baby once it's born!"

Nesha's head came up, and she looked back at Larkin, one arm wrapped protectively around her belly. The first seeds of doubt clouded her expression.

Garrot motioned to West. "Gag her."

"Garrot," Nesha protested.

"No," Garrot said firmly. "I won't let that woman fill your head with lies."

West set her down and tried to shove a cloth into Larkin's mouth, but she bit his hand and spat it out. "The marks on his skin, Nesha. They're from the shadows! He's made an alliance with them."

Cursing, West covered her mouth with his hand. "Stop talking."

She couldn't stop talking—not until Nesha knew the truth. "I'm not the one enchanted, Nesha. You are. And Garrot didn't have to use a bit of magic to do it!"

Another soldier came to help West. He pinned her head while West shoved a rag in her mouth so deep that she gagged. The man tied it down. All of West's weight was on her. She couldn't breathe, couldn't stop gagging.

Garrot lifted Nesha into the saddle. "I will not allow your sister's lies to ever harm you again. I swear it." He took the reins in his hand, mounted his own horse, and led her away.

Larkin screamed through the gag. For she finally understood. Garrot's touch was every bit as poisonous as the wraiths he served.

Straddling her, West waited until Garrot was far out of sight and cut the gag. Larkin rolled to the side and gasped for breath.

"You shouldn't—" the soldier protested.

"Let her holler if she wants." West smoothed his mustache. "As long as Garrot and his pretty mistress aren't anywhere to hear."

Larkin looked up at him. He watched her, his expression unreadable. "Time for lunch, Larkin. And you're going to eat all of it."

He watched as she ate and handed her the water skin. She filled her mouth, then pretended to wipe her mouth while instead spitting it down her sleeves, which dripped onto her skirt. She must have managed to swallow some of it, for she slept sound and deep, waking stiff and sore in the morning. A morning in which they abandoned Cordova Road for the wilds of the Forbidden Forest.

Tucked away in a large tent, Larkin swore she could feel the sun sinking into the horizon. Night was coming. And darkness. Her heart kicked in her chest, and her stomach tightened into a fist. She should be high in the trees. She should have sacred weapons to protect her. Instead, she had West. All he could do was die—or worse.

And for Larkin … Worse waited for her.

Sweat dripped from Larkin's temple into her eyes, making them sting and burn. Unable to bear it a moment more, she pushed to her feet.

West started. "You're supposed to be drugged."

She backed toward the tent flap. "Just let me sleep in the boughs. Please. I swear I'll come down in the morning."

West gripped her arm. "Larkin, what are you so afraid of? You're in the midst of an army. You're going to drink your draft and wake up perfectly safe in the morning."

She laughed—a laugh full of sharp, jangled edges. "You don't have any sacred weapons. You're as helpless against the shadows as I."

Not letting go of her, West bent down to a waterskin and held it out to her. "Now. Drink all of it."

"When they come, don't try to fight them. You'll only get yourself killed. Or worse."

"Larkin, I—"

Wrongness and death swept over Larkin. She shoved West and lunged for the tent flap. Shadows like writhing snakes condensed right in front of her. Ramass had come. As he'd promised.

She staggered back into West and held her bound hands up to him. "Cut me free! It's your only chance."

Instead, West drew his sword and shoved her behind him. "Breech! Guards! Breech!"

Ramass solidified, his crown as sharp as the shadow-wreathed blade he carried. Sickly yellow eyes glared down at her, trapped her.

"It is time, Larkin," came his dry rasp.

"No," she whimpered.

West stayed firmly between her and the wraith. "My orders are that she doesn't leave this tent."

The wraith drew his sword.

"What are you?" West asked.

"Don't," Larkin said. "You're no match for him."

"I am a wraith. You should have listened to her." The wraith charged. West tried to counter. The wraith's sword flicked out unnaturally fast, cutting through West's sword at the hilt like a twig. West collapsed around his bleeding hand, screaming.

The wraith moved toward her, the wrongness growing so thick she choked on it. She couldn't move away as his hand wrapped around her throat. She fell into that nothingness, dissipating into shadow and chaos. A moth-eaten veil filmed her vision, revealing a tree of solid black, glittering against a turquoise lake.

All her plans, all her efforts had failed.

"No!" a voice shouted.

Ramass released her. She came back from somewhere far away. Crumpled into a boneless heap on the ground. Remembered how to draw breath into her starving lungs.

"She is mine!" the wraith hissed.

Garrot stared at the wraith without freezing, his dark sigils seeming to suck in all light. "Not until Denan sees her, she's not."

Denan was being lured into a trap. She coughed. "He won't risk his men." Her voice sounded ruined. "Not even for me."

Garrot's gaze narrowed at her. "You'd be surprised what a man would do to keep the woman he loves."

"She's mine," the wraith chittered.

"After the battle," Garrot said firmly.

The wraith made an inhuman, hissing wail. "If she is not in my hands then, Garrot of the Black Druids ..."

"She will be." Garrot gestured back the way they'd come. "Come to my tent. I have maps I want you to look at."

Ramass stared at her before following Garrot beyond the

tent. The sense of evil slowly faded. A strange, metallic taste spread across her tongue—she'd bit her tongue and hadn't realized it—but she was not taken. Relief speared through her, so sharp she curved her body around it and took a breath. Two.

On the other side of the tent, West moaned. Larkin crawled to his side. He held his bloody hand to his belly.

She pried away the fingers of the opposite hand. "Let me see."

He finally released his left hand. The tips of the three outer fingers were gone. Already, the wound was black, the poison spreading. Larkin had seen this before—the poison slowly crawling up the victim's skin. Seen the mutilated pipers who were only alive because their limbs had been removed.

Really, a few fingers didn't seem so bad.

She grabbed his sword with her bound hands and gestured to the ground. "Lay your hand flat."

West recoiled.

"If I don't cut out the poison, you'll be—" Her voice choked, unable to say "mulgar." "Dead by morning."

West watched her, his face bloodless. "The forest take me, they're giving you to that thing?"

The poison passed his second finger joint. There wasn't time for this. "Do it!" Larkin barked.

Sweating, West laid his hand flat on the ground, his index and thumb curled in tight. He closed his eyes and turned away. She lined up the sword and chopped. West's eyes rolled up, and he collapsed in a jumbled heap.

A pair of guards burst into the tent, took one look at her standing over West with a bloody sword, and charged.

Larkin dropped the sword. "No. You don't—"

The first one bowled into her, knocking the wind from her. Garrot stepped back into the tent. "You are not drugged."

"West needs a healer." Had she cut away all the poison?"

Garrot didn't even glance the man's way. "Force her to

drink all of it." He turned to leave.

"Send Nesha back to the Idelmarch."

He turned toward her, outrage sparking in his eyes. "Don't dare tell me what to do."

"She doesn't understand the monsters you've made an alliance with. I do. Send her to safety."

"She is perfectly safe."

"Now you're lying to yourself."

He stepped closer. "The only reason you're still alive at all is because I know what the wraiths will do to you."

She bared her teeth at him. "Make me a wraith, and I'll come for you."

He smiled a wicked smile. "Become a wraith, and you'll do exactly as I say."

He turned on his heel and left. The two guards shoved the tip of the waterskin into her mouth and plugged her nose. She could swallow or she could drown. She considered it. But there was still time, still hope. She chose to swallow.

CHAPTER 29

NEGOTIATIONS

Larkin came to on the back of a horse. She groaned, her head pounding in rhythm with her heartbeat. Her torso had been rubbed raw from the saddle. *Wonderful,* she thought. *They'll match my wrists.*

Steeling herself, she lifted her head, her amulet dangling and the wind blowing her loose hair over her face. She peered through the strands. Two guards had replaced West—if he was lucky, he was headed back to Landra. If not, he was holed up in a wagon somewhere. Either way, he couldn't help her now.

Nesha was her last hope.

One guard led the horse, the other trotted to catch up from behind.

"Where are we?" she croaked.

Both guards jumped at her voice. Casting terrified looks into the woods, the guard from behind, the bald one, lifted her head by her hair and peered into her eyes, which cranked her neck painfully. "Can you sit in the saddle?"

A fair question. She wriggled her legs. "I think so."

He untied her knots. The other guard, the one with the small nose, held her waist as she slithered down. Her legs buckled at her weight. The man held her until she could straighten them, then the two men helped her onto the saddle.

"Who are you two?"

"Bins," the bald one said.

"I'm Nedrid," the one with the small nose said.

She pulled her shirt away to look at her sore torso, which was thankfully just red. She looked around at the army snaking in all directions around her. Horses and donkeys wore bulging packsaddles. The soldiers watched the forest like it was a snake about to bite them. She snorted a laugh. They had no idea the horrors the night would bring. Still fighting the sleeping draft, she dozed, coming awake with a jerk whenever she tipped or the wind blew dust into her face.

At midday, they stopped for a meal. The forest shook and trembled above her. Bins and Nedrid huddled in the hollows of the tree, jumping at every sound. Maybe it was time to plant some seeds of fear—terrified soldiers were more likely to run than fight.

"There are worse things than beasts in these woods," she said.

Shifting nervously, they eyed her. "Like what?"

She met their gazes, hers unwavering. "Wait until nightfall and find out." She eyed the beans and water that had been set beside her. "I'd rather be hungry than drugged."

"He said you might say that," Bins said. He took a bite of her beans and bread, and a hearty swallow of her water. "All safe."

She waited a good ten minutes, just to be sure. The food was cold by then, but she was too hungry to care. She napped the rest of the grogginess off until the men were ready to move out. After two days of sitting, she was glad to walk, glad for every step that brought her closer to Denan. That's what she focused on. Not the wraiths. Not the coming trickery. Denan.

He would come for her. He'd promised. If anyone could find a way to free her, it would be him.

Larkin sat placidly in the center of the large tent the two guards had erected around her. She heard footsteps and murmured voices outside. The tent flap pushed open. At the sight of Garrot, she closed her eyes.

She had the strength of her sword and her shield. She had her wits and friends to fight by her side. She could not lose. And if she did, well, no one lived forever.

She opened her eyes and smiled at Garrot, a smile that was all teeth. "Did you ever stop to think why the wraiths want me so badly?"

He grabbed the back of her collar and hauled her out of the tent. Bound and gagged, Tam waited for her. She let out a breath in relief. He was still alive. And if he was still alive, there had to be a way out of this. Garrot pushed her through his army, who turned to watch her, their eyes wide. Time to plant more seeds. She might not be able to fight Garrot with her sword and shield, but she could rot his army from the inside out.

"When the wraiths turn on you," she said loudly, "I want you to remember this moment. Remember I warned you and you did not listen."

"And when you're a filthy mulgar," Garrot said, "I'll happily never listen to you again."

She spat in his face.

He slapped her, sending her sprawling. She smiled up at him through the blood and the dizziness. "I'm used to men hitting me, Garrot. You don't frighten me."

He huffed in disgust and pointed to Nedrid. "Gag her."

Tam shouted muffled threats through his gag. His meaning was clear, even if his words weren't.

Not if I kill him first, Larkin thought.

Her guards hauled her up.

"My name is Larkin. I am the daughter of Pennice and the wife of Denan. I will not be taken by the shadow." Then the gag was in her mouth, and she could say no more.

To punish her, Garrot slapped Tam twice.

Oh yes, she would kill Garrot. Wraith or no.

Nedrid and Bins half marched, half dragged her between them through the army of onlookers who cheered and jeered and cursed her. She gripped the amulet, the branch sliding into her skin. She relived the vision for the hundredth time—every motion, every word, seared in her memory. She came to in Nedrid's arms. He noticed her awake and set her down.

Why doesn't the tree tell me what I need to do? Why isn't she helping me?

They had left the Idelmarchians behind to enter the eerily quiet forest. They stepped past a ring of trees, their branches arching and tangling above them. An arbor ring, and not just any arbor ring, but the one Larkin had found her sister in all those weeks ago. The wind didn't touch inside the ring. The sudden lack of wind left her noting her chapped cheeks.

At their head, Garrot stopped before the massive center tree. He paced back and forth, searching the high branches. "Well, piper, I have brought her, as I promised."

Head still spinning, Larkin struggled to understand.

A flash of movement. Three men dropped from the tree. They hit the ground, stood, and pulled back their hoods. Demry and Gendrin. And in their center, Denan, his gaze locked on hers. His eyes traveled up and down, pausing on the blood soaking the gag and the bruises, faded and new, on her swollen face.

He drew his ax and shield. Instantly, Nedrid had a knife at her throat. Tam's guards had a knife at his. Gendrin wrapped a hand around Denan's arm, holding him back.

"Another step and they both die," Garrot said.

"I will kill you for this," Denan said.

"What do you want?" Gendrin asked.

"Tomorrow night," Garrot said. "You choose the battlefield. Defeat me, and she's yours. Fail ..." Garrot shrugged. "Well, you'll be dead, so I suppose it doesn't much matter what happens to her."

She was just one woman. Not a curse breaker. Just his wife. She would not have more men die for her—men with wives of their own, men needed in the battle against the wraiths.

Denan's gaze met hers. She mouthed, "No."

Around him, his generals conversed. He didn't seem to hear them. Larkin knew Denan, knew how he thought. She could practically see his mind running through different scenarios. Risks versus rewards. Expected casualties. Expected gains. *"Never start a battle unless you know you can win,"* he had told her. *"And always, always choose your terrain."*

Garrot had the numbers. Denan had knowledge of the terrain, more battle-hardened soldiers, and a chance to rid himself forever of the druids. He thought he had enough advantages.

He'd already decided, his expression hardening with his decision as the generals finished their whispering.

She loved him. So much. She couldn't let him do this. She had to find a way to warn him. Because what none of them could ever guess was that Garrot had an army of wraiths and mulgars on his side. The blade divoted her neck, a threat not to move.

She shook her head anyway. "It's a trap!" she cried through her gag, but it came out garbled and meaningless. The blade parted her skin, blood slipping down her neck. Nedrid wrapped his hand over her mouth.

The pain was a distant, meaningless thing. She was so tired of being threatened, so tired of being cowed. She threw her elbow. The knife dipped deeper, Nedrid's hold tightening.

"Larkin!" Denan snapped.

His voice stilled her. She met his gaze across the distance—so short and yet so vast. "Stop," he begged, his throat bobbing.

She stopped.

Denan's gaze shifted to Garrot. "I swear that every injury she suffers, you will suffer tenfold."

"Is that a yes?" Garrot asked.

"What assurance do I have that you won't harm her further?"

"None," Garrot said. "But take comfort in the fact that I haven't yet."

"Tomorrow," Denan said. "Ten miles to the east, along the banks of the river Weiss."

"Tomorrow." Garrot motioned to his men, who dragged her and Tam back the way they'd come. Denan didn't move, simply watched as she was pulled back into the Forbidden Forest and out of sight.

The army marched through the next day, setting up her tent on a rise overlooking the piper encampment that evening. Denan had chosen his battlefield well. His army was entrenched on the high ground beside the river that curved around his back and flank. Down the hill from him, Idelmarchian tents formed vast rows.

By all appearances, the pipers had every advantage. What Denan didn't know—what he couldn't know—was that while the druids came from the north, the wraiths and their mulgar horde would attack from the south. If the mulgars managed to cross the river—and Larkin had no doubt they would find a way—they would trap the pipers in a vise.

Her throat freshly stitched, Larkin slept little that night. Every time she closed her eyes, she was assaulted by nightmares of shadows and death. The tent shuddered and shook , the snapping of the canvas driving her mad.

The next morning, the army marched out to attack before dawn. Not long after, the tent flap shifted aside, and Nesha stepped in with a pale West beside her, his right hand heavily bandaged. His normally tidy mustache was in bad need of combing, and his sideburns were bushier than usual.

Nesha wore a heavy cloak, her hair tied back in a tight braid.

"Miss, you aren't allowed to be here," Bins said.

Nesha looked him and Nedrid up and down. "I have questions for my sister."

Bins pursed his lips in disapproval.

"Garrot is gone," Nesha said. "As are the rest of the druids. No one knows I'm here."

"Ah, come on," Nedrid said softly. "Don't you have questions too?"

"Why are you here?" Bins asked West.

"I've been left behind to guard Nesha," West said.

West should be in bed, not guarding anyone.

Bins considered Nesha. "I suppose a few questions wouldn't hurt."

Nesha turned back to Larkin. "Nearly a week ago, Garrot came to our rooms covered in blood. He wouldn't tell me why."

Larkin had been covered in blood too—only she hadn't been allowed to wash it off for days. "He slaughtered our grandfather—Fenwick—and the councilors so that he could become Master Druid."

"Why would the other druids accept this?" Nesha asked.

Larkin had seen their eyes—full of lust and fear. "He used wraith blades to do it. He promised them the same power."

She wasn't surprised that her mouth didn't trip over the word *wraith*. Nesha was obviously in Garrot's inner circle. She had to have figured much of this out.

"The marks? On his skin?" Larkin nodded. "What are they?"

The wind howled, causing the canvas to snap. "Sigils from the Black Tree." Larkin hesitated before asking her next question. "How long have those markings been there?"

"As long as I've known him." Nesha shivered.

Ancestors, Garrot had been allied with the wraiths from the start.

"What will happen?" Nesha asked.

In the distance came the war cries of the druids over the rushing of the wind.

"Garrot will attack from the north, the wraiths from the south." Denan was surrounded, and he didn't even know it. "The pipers have the advantage and experience. They also have the high ground. But Garrot and his druids have dark magic. And a numerous army of mulgars." Now it was Larkin's turn to clench her fists.

"Who will win?" Nesha asked.

Larkin huffed. "Win? There is no winning. If the druids overcome the pipers, they'll lay siege to the Alamant." She'd had visions of this—of the wraiths sweeping into the city of trees, their dark stain destroying all they touched. "If the pipers win, the Idelmarch will be lost. Either way, humankind will be weaker than we've ever been."

"And will the Alamant hold against a siege?" Nesha asked.

The wraiths couldn't cross the water. But Garrot could. And with his dark magic … "I don't know."

"Why is this city so important to the wraiths?"

"If the Alamant falls, the last of the sacred trees will turn dark. The wraiths will be so powerful that nothing left on earth could stop them. Nothing will stand between mankind and the end."

Nesha was silent a long time. She blinked hard, twin tears plunging down her cheeks. "I'm sorry, Larkin. I'm so sorry. But

I mean to make it right." Her robes parted, and she lifted a cross-bow, aiming it at Bins and Nedrid.

CHAPTER

TRAITORS

"I can't kill both of you before you take me down," Nesha said. "But the first to move will die."

Bins and Nedrid gaped at her. Keeping clear of Nesha's line of sight, West advanced on the guards with ropes. He was helping them now?

"Nesha," Larkin whispered in despair. Her sister was now in every bit as much danger as Larkin. Perhaps more, for she had no magic and was cumbersome with child.

"Toss Larkin your knife and set your weapons down slowly," Nesha said.

"If she escapes, Garrot will kill us both," Nedrid murmured.

Bins's mouth tightened. As if on cue, both men lunged. Nesha shot Bins through the center of his chest. He dropped wordlessly. West ran Nedrid through. The man gasped and started to yell. West whipped around him, one hand going over the man's mouth, the second drawing his sword across his neck. West held his hand over Nedrid's mouth as he kicked and struggled before going limp.

Larkin gaped at the bodies, shocked at how quickly men could go from living, breathing, thinking beings to lumps of cooling meat. Aside from threatening her life the one time, both men had been respectful toward her. They didn't deserve to die. Larkin turned away.

West's fingers were bleeding, and a fine sheet of sweat covered his brow. "Hold out your hands."

She did as he asked. He sawed though her bonds.

"You're helping me now?" she asked.

"You were right—about the wraiths," West said without looking at her. "Anyone who thinks they can make an alliance with something that evil is delusional. And besides, instead of trying to run, you saved my life when Garrot couldn't so much as bother with me. I figure I owe you."

She'd been surrounded by an army. If running would have done her any good, she would have done it. No point in telling West that.

She turned to Nesha. "What changed your mind?"

Nesha stared at the bodies on the ground, her expression lost. "I followed him two nights ago. And again this evening. I saw the wraith. I saw … I saw Garrot hit you. I interrogated West. His story matched what you told me." A sob escaped. "Larkin, I'm sorry."

Pity welled in Larkin. Nesha's entire world was built on a foundation of lies, and those lies were crumbling around her.

West peered out the tent flap. His gaze went to Nesha. "The tent is watched. You can't both leave."

She sighed. "I know."

Larkin gaped at her. "What do you mean, you know?"

Nesha set down the crossbow and removed her dark green velvet cloak. "You have to go, before night falls and the wraiths find you."

Larkin's mouth fell open. "I'm not leaving you behind. Garrot will kill you."

"No," Nesha said. "West has fallen for your lies, you see. He lured me here under the pretense that you were sick. I came to find the guards already dead. He bound, gagged, and hid me in your place, where I will be found in the morning."

"What if Garrot doesn't believe you?"

Nesha wrapped the cloak around Larkin's shoulders. "I have wronged you so deeply, sister. Will you not allow me to make it up to you?"

Larkin looked at this woman, the best friend of her youth. She wished they could go back to that—to the joy and innocence of their childhood. But even with all the risks Nesha was taking … it didn't erase the damage she'd already done.

"If you don't go," Nesha said, "there will be no one to warn your prince or his people."

Larkin's mouth hardened into a thin line. Nesha nodded once and glanced down at the cut, filthy ropes lying at Larkin's feet. "Do you have any fresh ones?"

West produced some from a trunk and bound her hands. She winced as he pulled them tight. "Sorry, miss, but they have to be tight enough to be believable. Wouldn't hurt if you took some of the tonic too, to make it look like I drugged you first."

She shook her head. "It might hurt the baby."

He grunted and tied her to the stake that had been pounded into the ground.

Larkin stared down at her sister, helpless and alone. "How can I leave you?"

"Despite all he has done, Garrot has never harmed me," Nesha said. "Has never shown me the slightest unkindness. He loves me." She turned away, shame coloring her cheeks.

"You still love him," Larkin whispered.

"Love doesn't just go away because someone has done wrong, Larkin. You of all people should know that."

West gagged her.

"I hope you're right," Larkin whispered.

West peeked out the tent. "Stay behind me. Keep your head down."

Larkin pulled up the cowl. "Where are we going?"

"To free your friend."

West slipped out. Larkin shot one look back at her sister, who gave a solemn nod, before slipping into the dark after him. She was grateful for the cowl to hide her face and the cloak that hid her smooth belly.

"How do you intend to free Tam?"

"He has two guards. We'll have to kill them both, quickly and quietly."

Larkin had killed before, but it had always been in a fair fight, never an ambush. And even then, she'd been haunted by nightmares. Her steps faltered.

As if sensing her hesitation, West reached back and tugged her forward. "If you can't do this, we'll have to leave him behind."

Which meant Tam would face Garrot's wrath alone. She had a feeling he would not survive, no matter what the druid had promised Denan. She took a deep breath and nodded.

West hurried on. "Keep your head down and your cowl up. I'll get us in the tent and the men to turn to the prisoner. When I say 'filthy pipers,' we strike as one. Go for an instant kill so he doesn't make any noise. I'll pass any noise off as the prisoner protesting."

Filthy pipers. Strike. Kill. She sent up a prayer to the ancestors that she wouldn't mess it up. The tent was about half a mile from her own. West paused before the flap and shot her a look over his shoulder. She nodded.

"Miss Nesha to see the prisoner on behalf of Garrot."

"West? Is that you?" An older man with white hair pulled back the tent flap. Larkin felt the man's gaze slide over her. She kept her gaze fixed on her hands. He clapped West on the shoulder. "Boy, I haven't seen you since I boarded with your family last winter. How is your mother? Still making that apple pie?"

"Hanover?" West slid a look to her, his expression defeated. This man meant something to West. But she wasn't leaving without Tam.

"Sir," she murmured. "I would like to see the prisoner now."

Hanover bowed. "Of course, miss." He backed into the tent.

West grabbed her shoulder and whispered, "Hanover is my friend, Larkin. I can't—"

"Get him in a choke hold. Something. We'll tie him up."

"It's too risky."

"I'll flare my shield." She pushed into the tent and instantly locked eyes with Tam.

There were two guards, Hanover included. The second stood, his brow furrowed. It was the man who'd tried to spit on her the other day. He looked her over. "That's not—"

She stepped in front of West. "Down," she commanded.

Tam flattened himself as she flared her shield, throwing the guards back a step—she dared not use more lest she shake the tent. Then she was running toward Spitter.

She held her sword inches above his throat. "Don't move."

To her right, Tam locked his arms around Hanover's neck as he bucked and fought.

"Don't hurt him." West drew his own sword and glared at Tam.

Larkin's sword jerked as Spitter grabbed it with his bare hands and wrenched it to the side. It cut straight through his fingers, which rained to the floor. He stared at his ruined hands and opened his mouth to scream. She shoved her sword into his throat. His lips opened and closed, gaping like a fish. She wrenched her gaze from him.

"Tam, don't kill that one!" she hissed.

"Just putting him to bed, gentle as his mama," Tam said.

329

West shifted on his feet. "Garrot will kill him for failing. Larkin, he's my friend."

Larkin felt the man struggling on the other end of her sword like a fish on a line. Her skin crawled, and her gorge rose. She forced herself to face him, to shove her sword deeper, into his spine. He dropped, and his legs flailed against hers even though he was dead.

She let her magic fade as she turned to face Hanover. "I am Princess Larkin of the Alamant. I give you a choice, Hanover. Come with us or die."

Hanover pulled at Tam's arm, but his hold was unbreakable.

"Hanover, if the druids have their way, all of the Idelmarch will be lost," West said. "How many times have you told me the druids shouldn't run the kingdom and the army? Can you trust me, old friend?"

Hanover stared at West, his eyes bugging. He gave a slight nod.

Tam hesitated. "If you betray us, you'll die for it. As will many hundreds more."

Hanover nodded again, which she took to mean he wouldn't betray them.

Tam eased his hold. The man gasped in a breath. Then another. When he didn't scream, Tam released him. Hanover backed away and stared at West. "What would make you betray your own, boy?"

Larkin flared her sword and touched the edge carefully to Tam's bonds. They frayed, loosening so he could shake them off. Color immediately returned to his nails.

"Garrot has made an alliance with—" West's voice choked off. He looked at Larkin in confusion.

"You can't say it," Larkin said. "He has to see it for himself."

"What?" Hanover asked.

"Evil incarnate," Larkin answered. "Garrot has made a deal

with evil incarnate."

"Why—" Hanover began.

"Power," she said. "Do you swear to assist us, to not give us away?"

He cut a glance at West, who nodded. "Very well," Hanover said.

Larkin turned to West. "Is this tent watched?"

Hanover rubbed his throat. "Yes."

West bent down to the dead man and began stripping his armor. Mouth in a grim line, Tam helped. He splashed water from a nearby bowl onto the breastplate.

Trying to help, Larkin grabbed one of the straps and jerked back from the sticky blood—the blood of another man she'd killed. She could still feel him wriggling at the end of her sword, his legs thrashing against hers as his body had fought death.

She ran her fingertips down her skirt repeatedly. *Get it off get it off get it off.*

Tam splashed the corner of a blanket and held it out to her. "It was him or us, Larkin."

She scrubbed every trace from her skin and made no move to help with the straps again. "If we want to reach Denan before Garrot, we need horses."

"I hate horses," Tam muttered as he hauled the man's armor on.

"The druids keep the herd not far from here," West said.

"You'll never make it past the sentinels," Hanover said.

"We will if we tell them we're escorting Miss Nesha to the safety of Landra," Tam said.

"They'd never believe such a small group would risk the forest," Hanover said.

"They would if she was in need of a midwife," West said. He and Nesha must have already figured this out. "Besides," he continued, "the druids are aligned with the—" His mouth worked, coming up empty.

"You can't say it," Larkin said. "Not in front of Hanover."

"Say what?" Hanover asked.

"The curse binds our tongues," Tam said.

"The druids are aligned with the shadow," West said.

The four of them studied each other. One by one, the men all turned to her.

"It's the best plan we have," she said.

Hanover bent down and began shoving blankets in a satchel. "They'll never believe you're going anywhere without supplies."

West handed one of the blankets to Larkin with a meaningful look at her stomach. She stuffed the blanket under her shirt, praying it stayed put, praying West and Hanover wouldn't betray her. West's bandaged hand dripped blood.

"How's your hand?" Larkin asked West.

"Ask me again when the healer's medicine wears off," West answered.

Tam tied the dead man's sword around his waist. "Let's go."

They spread out around Larkin, Tam on one side, Hanover the other, West in the lead. She kept her cowl up, grateful that the dye in her hair hadn't completely washed out. They left the tent and crossed the mostly abandoned encampment, though a few men glanced at them as they passed.

A soldier approached as they reached the rope corral. "What's your business?"

"We're to escort Miss Nesha back to Landra," West answered.

"Papers?"

Papers? What papers? Larkin wondered.

"Anyone who could sign any papers has gone on to the battle," Hanover said.

Larkin could feel the soldier's gaze on her. "Without papers, I'm afraid—"

"Miss Nesha has need of a midwife." Tam gave her a pointed look. "Her time has come. Early."

Growing up with a midwife for a mother, she knew how squeamish men became about such things. She hunched over and moaned. "My waters have broken."

The man frowned. "Surely the healers—"

"They tried," Larkin panted. "The baby needs turned. They don't know how to do it."

"A ride through the forest at night is no—"

Hoping beyond hope the man had never seen her sister up close, Larkin marched to him. "I may not live through this night, soldier, but my babe still might. If I can get to a midwife who can save him." She let her voice waver. "Please."

He looked from her to the men with her. Finally, he growled. "I knew it was a bad idea to let women march with us. Especially pregnant women." He lowered one side of the rope.

"Your fastest mounts," Tam said, already pushing the bridle into the mouth of a muscled gelding.

"That one's lame," the man said. He pointed out four horses. "Those are the best I have left."

Larkin leaned against a tree to "rest" while the men saddled the horses and the soldier cleared their departure with the sentries. Holding the blanket firmly to keep it from slipping, Larkin mounted a black gelding. The four of them rode from the encampment. Larkin looked back once, toward the tent where she'd left her sister bound hand to foot.

She sent up a silent prayer to their ancestors, specifically to Eiryss, to watch over her and protect her from Garrot.

ALAMANT

E ast of the encampment, Larkin's group paused to look
over the two armies maneuvering into position. There
were no signs of the mulgars on the other side of the river.
Yet.

"How will they cross the river?" Larkin asked.

"I don't know," Tam replied. "But they mean to do it."

"The battle is scheduled to begin at dawn tomorrow," West
said.

Larkin was certain it would really begin tonight. She stood
in the stirrups. "We have to warn our friends."

Tam grabbed her hand. "They're already surrounded."

"We have to do something."

Hanover surveyed the battlefield. "Their only hope is reinforcements. If another army could come down the river and hit
the mulgars' eastern flank, they could circle around their rear
and trap them."

"King Netrish's men?" Larkin asked Tam.

Tam shook his head. "He can't risk leaving the city defenseless."

"If Denan's army falls," Larkin said, "it won't matter if the Alamant is defenseless. The druids won't be deterred by the lake. And when the Alamant is in the druids' hands ..." The wraiths wouldn't be far behind.

"How far is the Alamant?" Larkin asked.

"About a day's ride," Tam said.

"Let's go," Larkin said.

"Go where?" Hanover asked.

"We have to muster what's left of the Alamant's forces," Larkin said.

"Stay close," Tam said. "We'll take the old road."

Larkin nudged the horse into a trot, her throat choked with memories of Bane teaching her to ride in the fields behind his house. She ducked branches and circumvented brush and boulders until they reached the broken old road.

They pushed the horses hard, each stride bringing them closer to the Alamant. The animals were near spent, their ears drooping, their mouths hanging open, when they reached the edge of the lake just before nightfall.

A quarter mile distant, trees had grown in sheets that fused to create one continuous wall. The lower boughs formed arches that wove into a parapet shaded by smaller branches, all of which were covered in thorns and bright yellow leaves.

"What is it made of?" West pointed to the wall.

"Trees. The whole city is made of trees growing out of the lake."

"Ancestors," Hanover gasped.

"What kind of tree grows out of a lake?" West asked.

"Sacred trees," Larkin answered.

Tam lifted his pipes to his lips and let out a shrill, piercing note that instantly silenced all sounds of the forest. Atop the massive barrier wall, soldiers moved. Lights flashed, telescope lenses reflecting the dying light. Within moments, a few boats were swung out over the water and lowered slowly.

When the boats were halfway to them, Tam cupped his hands over his mouth. "I must speak with the king!"

One of the men in the closest boat stood and hollered back, "Why?"

"He's about to be overrun by shadows!" Tam called back.

The man relayed the message to the wall, and a couple of men scrambled to action.

"Will the king help us?" Larkin asked.

"He has to," Tam murmured. He motioned them all off the horses and started removing their tack.

"What are you doing?" Hanover asked.

"We've no use for them," Tam said. "The wraiths would just kill them come nightfall."

The pipers rowed toward them until their boats reached the docks where Larkin's group stood. The dark-featured man who had called out to them climbed out and clasped hands with Tam. "Good to see you, Tam."

"You too, Wott."

Wott bowed to her. "Princess Larkin, glad to see you've returned to us." He eyed Hanover and West. "Idelmarchians?" His sigils flared.

"They helped Princess Larkin and me escape in exchange for sanctuary," Tam said.

"Can they be trusted?" Wott asked.

"We're not fools," Hanover said. West hung back, his gaze split between the boats filled with pipers and the wall beyond them.

"Let's hope not." Wott turned to Tam. "Come. The king will have been sent for."

Wott helped Larkin into his boat. The rest of the men piled in after her and pushed the boat from the dock. They moved back across the lake. Beneath them, fish glimmered with flashing lights. Larkin could see the scarred place where she'd taken her sword to the wall when she'd escaped with Bane. She found herself gripping the edge of the boat, her knuckles turning white.

Wine-red tentacles bloomed beneath her, revealing a razor-sharp beak aimed right for her. She screamed as the tentacles snapped toward her and wrapped around her legs. Her scream cut off as it yanked her under. More tentacles wrapped her up in a too-tight embrace. She writhed, trying to pull her arms free. The tentacles twisted her around. She came face-to-beak with a creature that glowed red, its flesh textured like velvet, its shining eyes fixed on her as it shifted her toward its open serrated maw.

"Larkin?"

She started and found West's hand on her shoulder, his expression concerned.

"Are you all right?"

"She's probably just remembering the time she learned never to go into the water at night," Tam said, his voice light.

She punched his arm as he chuckled. She looked up as they passed beneath the barrier, waiting for the shimmer of magic. There wasn't one. She waited until they were on the other side, then peered back in shock.

"The barrier," Tam asked. "What happened?"

Wott glanced sidelong at her. "It's failing."

Larkin had used her magical sword to stab into the barrier, had seen the gleaming threads part. Her stomach tightened to lead.

"Larkin?" Tam leaned close, his expression concerned.

"Tam, I did this."

He glanced to the wall, then back at her. "If your sword could break the barrier, then so could Garrot's."

But Garrot hadn't broken the barrier. She had. Did everyone know? Did they blame her?

At the first tree, they docked, climbed the winding stairs to the canopy, and crossed the bridges linking one tree to the next.

A quarter of the way to the king's tree, Netrish came into view. Denan's father, Arbor Mytin, hustled beside him. And behind the Arbor was Larkin's mother and Sela.

"Mama!" Larkin cried. They pushed past the men and ran to each other. They embraced, tears welling in Larkin's eyes, their words a flurry around them.

"How are you?" Larkin asked. "How are Sela and the baby?"

"Fine," Mama said. "Brenna is with Wyn." Denan's twelve-year-old brother. "Sela is … different, but she's fine."

"Nesha believes me now," Larkin said. "She freed me from the druids."

"Is she with you?" Mama asked, pulling back to look behind Larkin.

Lips pursed, Larkin shook her head. She hesitated to ask her next questions, but she must know. "Did Harben make it with Iniya, Raeneth, and the baby?"

Mama winced but nodded. "A patrol brought them in a week ago."

Larkin wanted to know more, but she wouldn't push her mother—not about this. It was enough to know they were safe.

Movement smooth as water, Sela slipped her hand in Larkin's and asked in a clear voice, "What happened to your hair?"

Larkin gaped at her sister. She was talking … but it wasn't just that. "What happened to your lisp?"

Sela shrugged. "I don't have it anymore."

Larkin shot a concerned glance at her mother, who frowned, clearly unhappy. Is this what she'd meant by "different"?

"She can read," Mama said helplessly. "One day, she just picked up a book as big as her head and started reading it."

Was Sela's childhood the price for becoming the Arbor?

Sela tugged on Larkin's hand until she took a knee before her sister. She stroked her fingers along Larkin's auburn hair.

"I dyed it to look like Nesha's," Larkin said softly.

Sela's brow furrowed in confusion. "I made a flock for you."

Now it was Larkin's turn to be confused. Before she could ask, the king reached them.

"What is it?" King Netrish panted, his ruddy cheeks nearly scarlet. "What's wrong? And why are there Idelmarchians in my city?"

Mytin embraced Larkin. Ancestors, Denan was built so like his father. She almost broke down then and there. But there would be time for that later. She pushed back as Tam explained how Denan was trapped and about to be ambushed in the rear.

Denan's father paled. "Light save us. You're saying we could lose our entire army?"

Tam nodded. "You have to send reinforcements."

"And leave the entire city unprotected?" the king cried.

"We won't recover from this," Tam said. "Not the loss of three thousand men."

"Women's magic has returned to us," Netrish said. "The curse is breaking. We are safe in the Alamant. The druids can do nothing against us."

"You begged Denan to go after your son," Larkin said, voice trembling with restrained emotion. "Now you're just going to abandon them both?"

Netrish's head dropped, tears shining in his eyes. "Then, we had hope of bringing them all back. But now ..."

Tam shook his head. "The Black Druids have the magic. And with the barriers around the Alamant down, our people will be unprotected."

They would all be dead within a week.

Tears spilled down Netrish's cheeks. "We can't help them."

Larkin heaved in a breath. Her husband, his men—they would all be slaughtered come nightfall. A cry sounded overhead. A bird of prey crossed the sky. Two small copperbills swooped down, taking turns attacking the much larger bird. She remembered reading something in Eiryss's journals—she'd dismissed it until now. Something about the ancient women warriors being called copperbills.

"A flock," Sela had said.

Eyes wide, Larkin met her little sister's gaze.

Sela stood with her arms crossed, as if she'd been waiting for Larkin to acknowledge her. "Aaryn has been training them."

Her baby sister had made her an army? "How many?"

"Five hundred," Mama answered proudly.

Larkin flared her sigils, feeling the reassuring weight of her magical blade in her hand. She leveled a look at the king. "We don't need your army. We have our own."

Sela motioned for Larkin to follow her. "Come. I'll show you where they are."

Netrish blocked their path. "I cannot allow this."

Larkin leveled him with a look. "You think we will allow our husbands, the fathers of our children, to be slaughtered when we have the means to stop it?"

"Sire," Mytin said. "In ancient times, the women commanded their own army. You don't have the jurisdiction to stop them."

"We cannot risk our most precious commodity!" Netrish said.

"Netrish," Mytin began.

The king silenced the man with a gesture and rounded on Larkin. "I will not have you meddling in the affairs of my kingdom!"

Mama pushed between them, flaring her own weapons. "You will not speak to my daughter that way."

Larkin gaped at the sword in Mama's hand. A slow smile spread across her face. The two of them would never be weaker again.

Shaking herself, she stood shoulder to shoulder with her mother. "It is not just our husbands. Our fathers and brothers fight beside the druids. They don't understand they will be betrayed."

"I will imprison every last one of you in the cells on the islands if I have to," Netrish said.

The same underground cells they'd imprisoned Larkin in after she'd tried to escape the Alamant the first time.

Larkin advanced on the piper king, who grudgingly gave ground before her. "Women's magic is back. We're armed. We're pissed. And we're done being told what to do."

Sela held up her hands to both groups. "Stop this."

The king flinched. "Sela—"

Sela stared at him. "Do you think you can stop me?"

This was not Larkin's four-year-old sister.

The king pulled out his pipes. "If we have to."

Sela pointed her finger at him. "Both sacred trees have been working for centuries to set the right people and powers into place. Now is the time to see who will win. And if you think I'm going to leave off one of the most powerful wielders of magic, you are sore mistaken."

Larkin's mouth fell open. Sela should be weaving crowns made of flowers, not bossing around kings, but she stepped past the king without looking back. Larkin, Mama, Mytin, West, Tam, and Hanover hurried to follow.

"Stop them," the king ordered.

Larkin turned. The forest take her, she didn't want to fight, but she would if she had to. The sentinels who'd accompanied Larkin glanced between them and the king. They were clearly torn.

"Don't," Tam warned.

"Sire—" Wott began.

The king rounded on him. "You will do as you're ordered."

Wott stared at the king before shaking his head. "I don't think I will." He nodded to Larkin. "Go, Princess. I will see supplies gathered for your journey."

"Sedition," the king hissed.

Wott bowed. "Sire, my men will accompany you to your home, where you will remain until this is over."

"Come with me." Sela led them across bridges.

CHAPTER

SELA

"What happened to Sela?" Larkin whispered to her mother.

Mama's eyes were sad. "She's not a little girl anymore. She's ... old. Inside."

Ancestors, the price Larkin's family had already paid for this curse. "Sela," Larkin asked. "How do you know things?"

Sela eyed her. "The tree gives me visions, same as you."

Larkin struggled to keep her frustration in check. "How could you know that anyway?"

Having reached the last bridge, they wound down the spiraling stairs to the dock.

"Most people receive thorns," Sela said. "Saplings grow beneath their skin—new and untrained. But Arbors and monarchs receive a graft from the White Tree itself. Mostly, the Arbor receives visions. The monarch has the power."

"But I'm not a monarch or Arbor," Larkin said.

"No," Sela agreed. "When I see visions of your role, I see a woman diving into a lake. I don't know what that means, but I know it has something to do with your ahlea sigil."

Larkin had had the same vision. She covered her left arm. "I haven't used it yet."

"You will. When the time is right."

"Why have I only received two visions?" Larkin asked, hurt that the tree hadn't given her the answers she'd desperately needed.

"The tree doesn't know the future, Larkin. Only the past. She endowed us with power to forge our own path—our own destiny."

Embrace your destiny. Talox had told her that once. Larkin studied her little sister. "What have you seen?"

"The lives of my ancestors given to the White Tree."

There was something about the way she said it. "What does that mean?"

"The tree absorbs our dead," Mytin said.

Larkin shuddered. "But Eiryss died in the Idelmarch."

"Did she?" Sela whispered.

Larkin eyed her sister. "What do you mean by that?"

"We must hurry," Sela said.

"Sela—" Larkin began.

"No, Larkin," Sela said firmly. "Some things are better left unknown."

Larkin nodded at the gravity in her little sister's eyes. Sela led the way to a small boat, which they took to an island. Women, hundreds of them, wore armor that was too big for them. Pipers strode among them, correcting form and demonstrating maneuvers. Mytin jumped out of the boat first and hurried up the incline. Larkin helped Sela out.

"Thank you." Sela sighed and held out her arms. "These small legs are tiring. Will you carry me?"

Ancestors, this wasn't Larkin's little sister. Biting her lip, Larkin lifted her onto her back. Halfway up the rise, she looked back to see Tam motion West and Hanover to wait on the dock. Tam scanned the trees.

"Are you coming?" she asked him.

He waved her on. "We'll make sure no trouble reaches you."

She gave him a grateful nod and reached the top. Women sparred in practice rings with practice weapons. Sela slid down Larkin's back.

"Larkin?" Motion to her right. Denan's mother, Aaryn, strode through women who parted for her, Mytin a step behind. Her long, silky black hair was braided tightly back. She'd put on muscle since Larkin had last seen her, and a wicked bruise marred her right arm. But it was the sigils on her arm that gave Larkin pause.

Aaryn stopped before Larkin. "My army has been waiting for you."

Her army. A woman who loved weaving and cooking, who had two sons. But then Larkin remembered Wyn bragging that his mother had been trained by her father to fight the pipers. Ironic that she now used that knowledge to protect them.

"Denan—what kind of trouble is he in?" Aaryn asked.

"The kind where he needs an army on his flank," Sela said.

How did her sister know what a *flank* was? She was four years old! "It's not just Denan," Larkin said. "The druids have formed an alliance with the wraiths."

Aaryn nodded. "Sela said something like this would happen." She whistled, long and sharp. "Copperbills!" The women instantly stopped training.

"Copperbills?" Larkin murmured.

"It was what the women warriors were called long ago," Sela said. "I thought it needed to be redeemed."

Redeemed from what?

"Tam!" A voice cried. Alorica shoved through the crowd, her dark skin shining with sweat.

Tam left the dock, sprinting up the hill as Alorica sprinted down. They collided, wrapped up in each other, kissing and murmuring endearments. They were opposites of each other—Tam spry, with bright blue eyes and curling hair, and Alorica curvy, with black curls and dark features—but so in love. Larkin's upper lip curled in distaste and more than a little jealousy.

"Why do men and women do that?" Sela asked, her head cocked to one side.

Larkin chose not to answer.

"Alorica," Aaryn barked.

Alorica extracted herself from Tam's arms, though she didn't let go of his hand.

Kicking aside armor from a table, Aaryn climbed and stared at the gathering women. "The day we've trained for is here. Our husbands fight against our fathers, who have made an unholy alliance with the wraiths. And we will save them both."

Murmurs and shouts of alarm coursed through them.

"Idelmarchians would never ally themselves with the wraiths!" one woman cried.

"The Black Druids slaughtered the Master Druid and his council," Tam said. "He bears markings—sigils from the Black Tree. I've seen their shadow swords myself."

"Our husbands are trapped." Larkin's voice wavered. "When night falls, they will be slaughtered. And you know as well as I the wraiths will then turn on the victors. We will lose all of them."

"What are we to do?" one woman cried.

"What we have been preparing these last weeks for," Aaryn said.

"You want us to fight our fathers and brothers to save our husbands?" Alorica asked. She always was a troublemaker. Not to mention that her husband was already back safe.

Larkin shook her head. "I want you to fight mulgars."

"I only started learning a few weeks ago," a girl cried.

"Ah, come now," Tam said. "They're just mulgars. No smarter than a bird flying into a barrier!" Tam swung his sword in a fancy show. "Come on, ladies, who wants to save your men's arses?"

Alorica grabbed said arse. "I will!"

Aaryn jabbed her magical sword skyward. "For our fathers, our brothers, and our husbands! For our freedom and our lives!"

Soon after, five hundred women loaded into boats. Larkin was just about to step into one when a hand grabbed her arm. "Larkin."

She turned to find Caelia behind her, tears running down her cheeks and an infant in her arms. Larkin's chest ached. "You know?"

Caelia nodded. "Your father told me."

Did Caelia blame Larkin for not rescuing Bane, for turning her back on him? As if sensing her pain, Sela took Larkin's hand in her own.

"He was like a brother to me," Sela said to Caelia.

Caelia tucked her baby under her chin. "Did he say anything? At the end?"

He told me not to look. Larkin couldn't tell Caelia that. "He was brave. He fought for my life even when he knew his was over."

Eyes closed, Caelia embraced Larkin. "Thank you for saving my husband."

Larkin had forgotten about that. Caelia released her. Mama stepped up next. "I have to get back to Brenna. She'll be hungry. They're bringing the children here. Those of us who can't fight will look after them."

Larkin was glad her mother couldn't come, glad she and the little ones remained behind the relative safety of the Alamant's walls. She hugged her mother hard.

Mama stepped back, wiping her eyes. She held out her hand to Sela. "Come along. You can help with the little ones."

Sela took her hand and walked away without so much as a hug for Larkin.

"Sela?" Larkin called.

She turned back.

"Where is Eiryss's body? And why can I see visions of her? She was a Valynthian."

Sela's eyes went unfocused, as if she were seeing something far away. "The amulet you wear. It was hers." Her gaze sharpened on Larkin. "Did you find the other one?"

Larkin sagged in relief. She'd been right about the importance of the ahlea amulet, even if she hadn't found it. "No."

Sela frowned. "We must have it to defeat the wraiths, Larkin."

"Why?"

Her eyes went unfocused again. "I can't see what hasn't come to pass yet. Only how the amulet was made."

"You've seen that?" The shadows and death. Dray forming the amulet in his hand with the last of his magic. The birth of the wraiths.

Sela's gaze clouded over. "I've seen many things. I have lived so many lives." She contemplated the bustle at the docks. "You need to hurry if you want to save Denan."

Unable to resist, Larkin hugged Sela.

"It's all right," Sela said. "I'm never alone. I'm not helpless anymore."

"But you're a child."

Sela patted Larkin's back. "I don't know what I am anymore."

Larkin pulled back and said fiercely, "You're my little sister."

Sela gripped Larkin's cheeks in her little hands. Her eyes were heavy with sorrow so deep Larkin couldn't fathom it. "We're all going to die. It's how we live that counts."

What did that mean? Larkin exchanged a helpless glance

with Mama.

"Larkin!" Tam called. "Come on, we're nearly loaded."

Larkin split her gaze between her mother and her sister. "Look out for each other."

"Come back to us, Larkin," Mama said. "Please, come back."

Knowing she couldn't make a promise she might not be able to keep, Larkin left without a word. She stepped into a boat and sat down with Aaryn and Alorica on one side and Tam on the other—West and Hanover were staying behind. They rowed for the city gates, where a few dozen boats waited for them, pipers inside.

Larkin swore. "We can't fight our way through all of them."

Tam pointed out a man standing in the center boat. "We won't have to."

"I brought supplies," Wott called. "And a hundred men—it's all I dare spare."

Tam grinned. "Pipers can't let their wives have all the fun."

Would it be enough? It would have to be. The city couldn't function with less. Wott motioned, and the gates opened. The boats flowed out.

They took to the river as dark came on. Wott lashed their boats together and mixed the women in with more seasoned fighters—five or so women under the direction of one of the pipers. He and Aaryn stood in the center boat, having agreed to a joint command, with him taking the lead until she found her footing.

"We'll sneak in on the mulgars' left flank," Wott said. "When the charge is called, stay in line with the warrior next to you. Trust them to guard your side and your back. Remember, swipe the mulgar's weapons to the side and stab." He demonstrated with his own weapons. "Reposition. Repeat."

"I'm going to die, aren't I?" a young woman said from behind them.

"Of course not," Tam chided her. "Mulgars are scary looking and don't like to die, but they're not too bright. Sort of like killing angry geese."

Larkin gave him a look.

"Have you ever been charged by an angry goose?" Tam said. "They rush you with their wings spread, hissing. All you want to do is run. But all you have to do is shove them with your shield. Swipe, stab." He motioned. "And it's over. You win."

"Like killing a goose," she echoed.

"But they're people!" the girl cried.

Tam shook his head. "You can't kill what's already dead."

Only that wasn't true. Maisy was proof of that. Larkin didn't say anything though. Better for the girls to think they were killing mindless monsters.

A simple lunch of dried fish and nuts was passed out. Larkin ate hungrily. The food eased the tension until Wott called for quiet. Larkin lay down in the boat's bottom and slept hard and dreamless.

CHAPTER 33

ARDENTS

J ust before dusk, the boats bumped into the embankment on the south side of the river. Scouts were sent out to clear the way and determine the best path. Over six hundred men and women disembarked and made their way silently into the forest.

Tam had been assigned as the lead piper for Larkin's group, which included Alorica and three other women. He was still acting as Larkin's personal guard, so he positioned himself between Larkin and his wife.

Larkin opened and closed her hand around her hilt, eager for the moment she would spy the battlefield.

"I bet I down twenty to your measly five," Tam murmured to her.

"Twenty?" Larkin snorted. "Only if you can pick them off from the safety of a tree."

He held out his hands. "Why face them head-on when you can do it from the comfort of your own pod?"

"You two have certainly grown close," Alorica grumbled.

Tam kept his eyes straight ahead. "She's doing the glaring thing, isn't she?" he asked Larkin.

"I can see why you hate it," Larkin admitted.

Tam wiped his brow. "Right? It's like she's melting your face off with her eyes. Give me a slathering mulgar any day."

Alorica opened her mouth.

Larkin held up her hand. "Don't worry. He's a pain in the arse. I have my own to rescue."

"If you two don't shut it," Alorica ground out, "every mulgar within five miles will know we're here. And I call twenty-five."

Tam grinned. "That's my wife."

Larkin rolled her eyes. All up and down the line, men and women began murmuring the number of mulgars they thought they could kill. Talox had been right about Tam—his humor did ease the tension.

Larkin knew the moment the sun set. The sounds of battle rose up before them—mulgar screeches and men's shouts, the screams of the injured, and the thud and chime of axes and shields and swords.

How had the mulgars managed to cross the river? Had Denan anticipated Garrot's treachery? *Please don't let them be slaughtered. Please.*

With every step, those sounds grew louder. The blustering wind shifted, bringing with it the mineral stink of battle—the scent of muddy blood like on butchering day.

Larkin's insides twisted.

"Stay in formation," Tam said. "Let the mulgars break against us like surf against the shore."

Not a dozen steps later, the command hand-signaled up and down the line.

"Ready yourselves," Tam translated as he, too, signaled.

Larkin flared her sword and shield, the light as dim as she could make it.

"Just before they reach us, pulse your shields," Tam said.

The commanders signaled, and they tightened formation until they stood shoulder to shoulder, which they had to break to go around trees and brush. Then they were in a clearing lit by torches and bonfires.

The river lazed past on their left. Mulgars bottlenecked before floating bridges made of lashed-together barrels with a walkway lashed to the top. Evenly spaced, mulgars were sent across by ardents with crude mantles.

Two dozen running strides, and the mulgars were across, though many bristled with arrows. A few fell screaming into the river, where they flailed and sank. Half made it to the other side and charged up the embankment to the piper line waiting for them. Already, that line buckled in places.

An unearthly screech caterwauled above the din. His mantle of twisted thorns distinguishing him from the others, Vicil screeched again. Obeying their master's command, the mulgars entire eastern flank turned and charged Larkin and their copperbills. Was Talox among them? Venna? Would they recognize each other?

"Wait for the command to pulse," Tam said.

As the mulgars came closer, Larkin could see the details of their makeshift armor and stolen weapons. Their rotting teeth and sallow skin marked by forked black lines. The urge to run rose up within her, so strong she quavered with denying it.

"Just a charging goose," Tam said. "Keep steady, and they'll break against us like a wave."

The girl from Larkin's boat, the one who'd been so afraid before, turned and ran. Some of the women watched her go. Others shifted in place, clearly debating about running themselves.

"For our fathers!" Aaryn shouted from somewhere behind them. "For our brothers and our husbands!"

Larkin planted her feet and opened her sigils wider, magic pouring into her. Her blade brightened and turned razor sharp.

The mulgars came closer—close enough that she could see the individual hairs on their heads.

"Wait," Tam called.

The outrunners reached the front line, slamming into shields. Larkin chanted in her head. *Sweep up and to the left. Stab. Reposition.*

One of the outliers headed straight for her. He'd been a piper once, the tatters of his mottled cloak hung around his shoulders. His armor fit, though it was filthy.

He would be one of her kills. He swung down on her. She braced, shoved, stabbed, repositioned. Tam brought his ax down on the joint between shoulder and head. Larkin panted, not sure if she would throw up or soil herself or both.

"One," Tam crowed.

"That one was mine!" she cried in protest.

He grinned without looking at her. "Wounding doesn't count. Kills do."

"That's not fair!" she said.

The first wave of mulgars were nearly upon them. "Steady," Tam said. "Steady."

They slammed into their shields. No time for thoughts. *Sweep up. Stab. Reposition.* Her sword met resistance. She didn't know where she'd hit her foe, only that she had.

The mulgar collapsed. Larkin wasn't sure if it was a man or woman. It was hard to tell through the grime. The mulgar's sneer shifted to one of relief, as if she'd released it from torment.

She wasn't killing pipers. She was saving them.

"Pulse!" the piper leaders screamed up and down the line.

As one, the copperbills pulsed—a convex burst of golden light slammed into the entire line of mulgars. They were flung backward, arms and legs cartwheeling, weapons jarred from their hands as they slammed into the earth.

"Charge!" came the command.

Larkin swept down the hill, bashing at dazed mulgars'

heads, which was about the only sure way to end them. All around her, pipers and copperbills called out their kills.

"Fifteen," Tam cried.

"Ten," Alorica said.

Blast. "Five," Larkin admitted.

Double blast. She was not coming in last in this. One of the mulgars managed to stagger to its feet. She ran at it. The mulgar cowered. She bashed it with the edge of her shield. The mulgar screamed, his throat exposed to the edge of her blade. Her sword barely slowed as it parted his head from his shoulders.

A frenzied glee washed over her. "Six!"

"Form up!" came the command.

One of the ardents fixed her gaze on Larkin. She had long white hair, her skin wrinkled as a winter apple, but she moved like a girl.

Number seven. Larkin charged. The woman braced behind her shield of rotted wood held together by rusted bands of metal. She chopped for Larkin's legs. Larkin shoved her shield down just in time to deflect the blow, which brought the woman in closer. Larkin jerked her shield up, catching the mulgar in the jaw.

She staggered back, her jaw dangling. Larkin positioned her shield at her chin and charged. The woman spun at the last minute and whipped behind Larkin, kicking her backside and sending her sprawling.

Larkin rolled over, her shield coming up as the woman aimed for Larkin's exposed legs. She pulsed, the woman suddenly gone. Exhausted, Larkin gasped in a breath and pushed to her feet. All the other warriors had formed a line a few dozen paces up the incline. She was alone. More mulgars circled her, snarling.

Ancestors. She was trapped. She opened her sigils wide, but she didn't have enough left for another pulse unless she wanted to lose her sword and shield entirely.

Tam swore and charged after her. Alorica called after him, swore herself, and followed.

"Behind you!" Tam called.

Larkin ducked reflexively, feeling something sail over her head. The mulgar woman was behind her again, charging. Larkin deflected the swing too late, the ax skimming across Larkin's leg armor. The woman kicked the back of Larkin's knee, dropping her. Larkin managed to raise her shield, but the woman bashed it to the side and chopped down at Larkin.

Tam was suddenly there, his ax bursting through the woman's face. Black blood sprayed across Larkin. Arrows rained down on the mulgars around them.

"Back in line, Princess!" Tam growled.

"That one counts as mine," Larkin called as Tam hauled her up.

Alorica bashed the edge of her shield across the face of a charging mulgar, then swung around and sliced halfway through the torso of another. "Eleven! Twelve!" Alorica cried.

"I can see why you were scared of her," Tam said as he charged back into formation.

"I was never—" But Tam was already halfway up the incline. Growling in frustration, she charged after him. Just when she was sure she couldn't lift her arms for another swing, the reserves crowded them from behind.

"Fall back," Tam said.

She staggered back, the woman behind her taking her place.

Hands braced on his knees, Tam panted. "Seventeen."

"Twelve," Alorica said.

"Light, that's my wife." He gazed at her like she was the most beautiful woman he'd ever seen. She looked back, her expression softening.

"Bleck. If you two start kissing, I'm going to throw up." Larkin glanced around at the panting men and women.

"How many did you get?" Alorica asked with a raised brow.

Larkin opened her mouth to say *seven*, but the word wouldn't come. She was aware of blood running down her face, of how close she had come to dying. She couldn't catch her breath.

Tam stepped toward her. "Breathe. You're all right. Have some water."

She took it from him, but her hands were shaking too hard to hold it. What kind of monster enjoyed killing? Guilt slammed against her.

"What is it? Are you hurt?"

She shoved him. "They're *not* geese, Tam! They were people like us once, like Venna and Talox!"

He winced as if she'd hit him. "Keep thinking like that and you won't be able to kill them."

Tears smarted in her dry eyes. "I enjoyed it, Tam."

His expression softened. "Sometimes you do, in the heat of things."

"What does that make me?"

"Human. You don't have to worry ... unless the guilt doesn't come afterward."

"What happens then?"

His jaw bulged. "Then the violence won't stop on the battlefield."

Alorica settled next to Larkin. "Stop being so morose. You're just trying to cover up your shame at coming in last."

Tam clapped his wife on the shoulder. "Seven is pretty good for your first battle, Larkin."

"And you only nearly died once," Alorica said cheerfully.

Tam tipped back his head and laughed. "Drink and eat something. It'll be our turn again soon enough."

"That mulgar," Alorica said. "She was different."

Tam cleared his throat. "We call them ardents. They're cunning, leaders."

Larkin sipped water and ate bread. The pipers and copperbills fought on—an impenetrable line that curved around the mulgars' rear, driving them back until they were escaping across their bridges instead of charging across them.

On the other side of the river, the pipers were still faltering. Larkin had no way of knowing how their other front fared. "We need to get over there."

"Push ourselves too hard, and we'll crumble. Steady on." Tam took another drink.

She tried to find Denan in the firelight, but every piper looked like another. Even the mulgars were hard to pick out.

"Where are the wraiths?" Alorica asked.

"Far back enough to avoid being picked off by archers," Tam said. "Without them, the mulgars lose their drive pretty quickly."

Far too soon, their break was over. They eased up behind the line of fighters. "How many this time?" Tam asked.

"Fifteen," Alorica said.

Larkin felt his gaze on her, but she didn't want to answer, didn't want this stain on her soul.

"This is how it has to be, Larkin," Tam said. "If you can't manage your mind, you won't survive."

Alorica gripped her arm, nails digging in deep. "For your husband!"

Tam nodded and glanced up and down the line at tired, black-blood-splattered women who had watched friends die this night, who had killed. Tam's jaw tightened. He broke ranks to march up and down the line.

"Your husbands and fathers and sons and brothers are on the other side of that river, right now, dying. You will not falter. Not now. Not when the mulgars are on the brink of falling. Not when your men need you." He paused before a girl and pointed at her. "How many mulgars will you kill?"

She flinched. "I …"

"Five? Seven? Ten? How many?"

She blinked up at him. "Five."

He gave a curt nod and marched down the line. "And how many will you kill to save the ones you love?"

This woman lifted her chin. "Eight." He nodded and kept moving. "Call it out. How many mulgars will you kill?"

Women called out numbers—some lower, some astronomically high.

Tam paused before Larkin. "How many?" he whispered.

She met his gaze. "Eight." One more than last time.

He looked to the right, then the left. "Repeat it after me: For our fathers!" The women echoed him. "For our brothers!" Another echo, this one louder. "For our husbands!" Another. "For our freedom and our lives!"

Tam squared off in front of them. "March!"

They crowded the fighters, who retreated. Larkin took a girl's place—the skin on her cheek hanging where it had been cut—and found her rhythm. She didn't think it was possible, but she did. And she didn't stop at eight. Or ten. Or fifteen. By the time the last of the mulgars perished on the banks of the river, she had killed twenty-two.

Twenty-nine in one night.

CHAPTER 34

DARK BATTLE

In the light from the distant bonfires, Larkin looked uneasily at the bridges tied to posts driven into the ground. They bucked and shifted with the currents of the black water. Were they even anchored to the river bottom?

"Well, you can swim, can't you?" Alorica asked.

Water closing over her head in the dark. No sense of up or down. Only the cold wet and the burning in her lungs as the lethan wrapped its tentacles tighter and dragged her deeper. Larkin wiped her sweating palms against her trousers. "Yes."

"Is this about that time your father tried to drown you as a child?" Alorica asked.

"Alorica," Tam chided.

She shrugged. "What? The whole village knew. It's not like it's a secret."

No, this time came after. This time, Denan had been the one to fish her out.

Copperbills crowded them from behind. It was Alorica's

turn.

"Best do it at a run," Tam told her.

She flared her weapons for light and hustled across the bridge.

Tam boosted Larkin up. "Don't think about it."

She flared her own sigils, the light just enough to see where to place her next step. All that existed was that one step. And the one after that and the one after that. Denan waited for her on the other side. She must save him.

With every step, she moved farther from the light of the bonfires along the embankment and deeper into the shadows. The shush of the river and the sway of the bridge left her disoriented and dizzy, hands spread, searching for something to hold on to. Something to anchor her. But there was only the breeze against her open palms.

The bridge shuddered beneath her, as if something from the river had slammed into it. Larkin dropped to her knees and held the sides, water splashing over her knuckles.

"You're not that far," Alorica called to her. "I can see you. Come on."

With a shaky breath, Larkin pushed to her feet and flared her weapons again. An outline of trees far atop the hill was bathed in an orange glow, men fighting beneath them.

Sooner than she expected and yet far too late, she hopped down to the embankment. Almost instantly, she stepped on something squishy and round. Alorica braced her.

Larkin flared her sword and held it toward the ground. A silent, screaming, dead face burst into view, making her jump back, only to step on another body.

"Mulgars," Alorica panted. "The ground is littered with them."

Larkin shifted her sword. Mostly mulgars bristling with arrows. But some pipers too. Larkin searched for Denan's face and then stopped. If he … If he lay among the dead, she didn't want to see it.

Please, she prayed. *Not Denan.* Yet wasn't every other woman in their company praying the same? Not all those prayers would be answered.

Alorica still hadn't let go of her arm, and her fingernails were digging into Larkin's flesh enough to draw blood. "Alorica?"

She let out a shaky laugh. "You're afraid of fast-moving rivers. I have a problem with bodies. Especially bodies in the dark."

"Do you have to squeeze so hard?" Larkin asked.

Tam hopped down and nearly fell. He looked about grimly, then helped the other three girls down. "Come on. Our men will be in desperate need of reserves."

Larkin was relieved when Alorica shifted her grip to Tam. Pointing their swords at the ground for added light, Larkin and Alorica climbed over bodies, broken branches, and weapons. The ground was muddy with blood. The smoke from so many fires blew back at them, further obscuring the path and making Larkin's throat tingle with the need to cough.

Other copperbills climbed with them, ghosts in the night. They crossed beneath the trees where pipers loosed arrows into the druids from above. Finally, they reached the top of the rise. Fighting beneath torches and before bonfires, pipers formed a solid wall of men against mulgars and Idelmarchians, driven forward by druids. Tam hauled himself into one of the trees.

Larkin shifted from one foot to the other. "Do you see him?"

He stiffened and pointed. "There!"

Near the base of the hill, beside the river, the line bulged inward, mulgars forcing the pipers to retreat. Larkin didn't wait. She ran, stumbling over bodies and dodging trees. She scanned for Denan's face but couldn't make him out in the shadows, smoke, and chaos. She found a gap and threw herself into it.

The pipers on either side of her glanced at her in surprise, relief sliding over their faces before they went back to the fighting. More copperbills came, and slowly, slowly, the mulgars fell dead or fell back until the entire Idelmarchian line retreated.

Larkin let her watery arms fall, then heard splashing to her right. Denan was fighting an ardent, another sneaking up behind. She abandoned the line and ran toward him. "Denan, duck!" she cried.

He dropped, his ax and shield spinning around him. The mulgars' blades swung through empty air. Denan's weapons slammed into both ardents' legs and dropped them. He rose, ax raised high before coming down on one creature's head.

The other thrust up from the water, sword aimed between his shoulder blades. Larkin pulsed, shoving Denan and the remaining ardent forward. Her magic felt weak, thin, and brittle, but she managed a sword. The ardent looked up in surprise as Larkin beheaded her.

Larkin spun, looking for Denan just as he came sputtering up. Bloody, half his face covered in bruises, he wiped water from his eyes and gaped at her. "Larkin?"

She flew into him, embracing him with her wobbly arms and holding him up as much as he held her. She would have stayed that way forever and never let go.

"There's my warrior wife."

She had so badly wanted to be something more—the curse breaker, an Arbor like Sela. But as a warrior, she'd just saved her husband's life. It was enough.

"They're retreating," she cried in relief.

"No. Just regrouping. Come on."

He didn't release her hand as they splashed behind the piper line. Tam and Alorica were waiting for them. Tam and Denan embraced. Still, Denan didn't let go of her.

"I leave for a few days," Tam laughed, "and you nearly lose a three-centuries-long war."

Denan stepped back. "I wish you hadn't come. How many have you brought?"

"We started with around six hundred."

"Who's leading?" Denan asked.

"Wott and Aaryn," Tam said.

Denan started at the mention of his mother's name but recovered quickly. He scanned the line of men and turned to his five pages. "Find Aaryn, Wott, Demry, and Gendrin. Have them meet me at the top of the hill." They took off at a run. He started after them, Larkin, Alorica, and Tam trailing. "The west flank?"

"It was holding," Tam responded.

"Have you seen the wraiths?" Larkin asked.

"Glimpses." Denan passed a hand down his face. "No more."

In the distance, mulgar units led by ardents and Idelmarchian units led by druids shifted and reformed.

"They've never behaved so cohesively," Tam said in disbelief.

"They've been using tactics and maneuvers so far above anything we ever believed them capable of," Denan said. "I can only conclude the wraiths have been holding back for centuries."

Alorica swore.

They reached the top of the hill to find Wott, Gendrin, and Demry waiting.

"Where's my mother?" Denan asked.

"Took a sword to the thigh," Wott said. "She's with the healers."

Ancestors, not Aaryn.

Denan's mouth tightened. "Report."

"My men are holding but exhausted," Demry said.

"The left flank is stable," Gendrin said. "But even with reinforcements, we can't keep going like this."

"My copperbills are filling the gaps," Wott said.

"Can your men repel another charge?" Denan asked.

Gendrin and Demry exchanged a look.

"Maybe," Gendrin said. "But the charge after that ..."

Denan looked over the enemy line. "My army would have buckled under that last charge if not for the copperbills."

"We could escape over the bridges," Wott said. "Those remaining behind could cut the lines and take the boats we brought for the copperbills."

"You mean retreat?" Tam said.

"That would leave us scattered and running all over the Forbidden Forest," Denan said.

"And we need nearly all the men we have just to hold the line," Demry added.

"We have no more reinforcements," Wott said. "Men can't battle for hours on end."

"We'd be helpless in boats," Demry said.

"There's another way." All eyes turned to Larkin. "The druids and mulgars want us dead. The Idelmarchians only want their daughters back."

Denan started to reply, stumbled, and started again. "Larkin, you can't mean to surrender yourselves."

She flared her weapons. "Do you think you or the druids or *anyone* can make us do anything we don't want to?" The men stared at her. "Call for an armistice."

Denan hauled off his helmet, slicked back his sweat-soaked hair, and mashed it back on his head. "The druids—Garrot—refuses to meet with me."

Larkin and Alorica shared a glance.

"They'll meet with us," Alorica said.

Larkin nodded. "Bring me Magalia."

"Magalia?" Tam asked.

"The healer?" Gendrin asked.

"She was Garrot's fiancée," Larkin said. "If anyone can talk some sense into him, maybe she can."

Denan's eyes widened with disbelief, and he hollered at his

pages to find her. All five of them took off in different directions.

Denan looked at Larkin. "You need to take control of the copperbills."

"Me?" she cried. "Why?"

"Because you're the princess," Denan said. "Because you restored the magic and escaped the Alamant when no one else could. The women look up to you. They trust you. And because the Idelmarchians need to see a woman leading an army of women, not a piper enchanting his captives."

She didn't want to do this. "I don't have any experience leading warriors into battle, and the Idelmarchians will not react well to the Traitor of Hamel."

"Traitor of—" Denan began.

"It's what they're calling her," Tam said.

Denan rubbed his mouth. "All right. Magalia will help you."

Larkin rolled her shoulders to loosen the tension building there. "What do you need me to do?"

"Inform your copperbills what's going on," Denan said.

She nodded grimly. "Gather them together. Tell them we're going to pulse our kindred until they listen to us."

Denan's pages were gone, so he gave the command to Wott and his generals, who jogged off to spread the word for all the copperbills to gather at the top of the hill.

"I have patients," a voice barked. Magalia marched up the incline. Her arms were soaked in blood to her elbows, her front spattered with it. She paused half a dozen paces from Denan. "What?"

"Do you think you can get Garrot to stop this attack?" Denan asked.

Magalia's mouth opened. Closed again. "What does Garrot have to do with—"

"He's the Master Druid," Larkin said.

"That can't be," Magalia said. "He was training to be a

merchant under my—"

"He came after you," Larkin said. "Into the forest—he and his brother, but his brother didn't make it. Garrot made a deal with the wraiths."

"The wraiths!" Magalia looked between Larkin and Denan. "He would never—"

Larkin gripped her hands. "Magalia, you have to stop him."

The fight drained out of her. "How?"

"Make him see that the pipers aren't the enemy," Denan said. "The wraiths are."

Magalia shrugged helplessly. "I can try."

CHAPTER

MAGALIA

Nearly five hundred women gathered to listen to Larkin. They were blood-splattered and bandaged. They kept glancing toward the front—where the opposing sides of their families had been killing each other.

"You want us to fight our own fathers and brothers?" a woman asked.

"No," Larkin said. "I want you to knock them on their arses, then stand before them, proud as the dawn, while Magalia tries to talk some sense into them."

"What if they won't listen?" another woman said.

Larkin pulled herself up onto the first branch of a tree. "Once, we were taken. Forced away from everything we ever knew and loved. But it did not break us. We learned to forgive. We learned to love.

"Now, we face another reaping. Only this time, our past would try to steal us from our future. No matter who wins, *we* are the ones who lose."

She shook her head. "I say to you, no more! We are not our fathers' daughters. We are not our brothers' sisters. We are not our husbands' wives. We are our own. Warriors who fight for what's ours!"

A cheer rose up, the women lifting their magical weapons.

"It's time to make them see—we don't need saving."

Another cheer. This one louder than the first.

"Sisters of my soul," she cried. "Will you fight?"

They roared, weapons lifted to the sky. Larkin dropped from the tree to the ground beside Alorica and Magalia.

"That was beautiful," Alorica said dryly.

"Shut it," Larkin grumbled back.

"I thought it was well done," Magalia said, but her gaze didn't leave the assembled Idelmarchians.

"Captains," Larkin said. "Spread your women out behind the pipers. We're going to relieve them." The captains left to see it done.

"And what do we do when our past won't listen?" Alorica said under her breath.

"Then they leave us no choice." Larkin fought to keep her voice even. "We will defend what's ours."

Sick anticipation twisting her insides, Larkin formed up in the center of her line. She opened her sigils until they buzzed like angry bees. She looked up and down the line, watching the captains move their subordinates into place.

"Larkin," Denan called from atop a boulder above her. "You're out of time."

Down the hill, the Idelmarchians and mulgars charged.

"Alamantians, withdraw!" Denan roared.

One of his men played a sharp, short note three times. Captains echoed the command up and down the line. The women took the places of the retreating pipers—just under five hundred where over two thousand had stood before. The nearest women on either side were four strides away. Such a sparse line wouldn't hold against an initial charge.

"I'm no warrior," Magalia said. Indeed, she had no sigils.

"Stay back until I call for you," Larkin said.

Magalia nodded nervously.

Larkin glanced back at Denan, the feel of his chapped lips still raw against her own. His words from minutes ago echoed in her ears, *"I understand this is a battle you have to fight alone, but that doesn't mean I won't be ready and waiting to help in any way I can."*

Taking a fortifying breath, she faced the oncoming horde. Each step brought the battle closer. Brought with it the rank sweat-and-blood stink of warfare. The cries of those pierced and battered down. The sight of hands crusted with blood that lay thickest between the fingers.

"Helms!" Larkin cried.

The women pulled off their helmets, their faces exposed, their hair shifting in the brisk wind. Some of the Idelmarchians faltered, slowed. Others continued. She waited as she had with Tam at the previous battle.

An Idelmarchian soldier's ax slammed into her shield. She shifted her arm, so his blade glanced to her left and thrust her sword up and in. He fell.

Ancestors, he wasn't her enemy!

Another soldier took his place, his face twisted with hate. He was tall, so tall he peered down at her. He took her in. Her long red hair. The softness of her cheeks. His expression shifted to concern. He hesitated and took a step back. "A woman?"

Similar cries were heard up and down the line.

"Copperbills, pulse!" Larkin shouted.

Five hundred women pulsed. A concave burst of golden light slammed into the Idelmarchians and threw them back half a dozen steps. They shook off the impact and gaped at the women. Larkin knew how surreal they must look, backlit by burning fires, their hair shifting with the smoke and wind.

Larkin risked a few steps in front of the line. "We, the daughters of the Idelmarch, demand this bloodshed stop! I will speak with Master Garrot. Bring him to me!"

Idelmarchians blinked up at her in shock. They lurched to their feet and glanced among each other as if searching for a clue as to how to proceed.

"Maylay?" A man staggered to the empty space between the two armies. His gaze fixed on a girl with short blonde hair. "Maylay!" He staggered toward her.

"Stay back!" Larkin barked. She couldn't risk losing her entire line to weeping reunions. If they were scattered, Garrot would divide and conquer them.

The father stumbled to a stop and stared at Larkin.

"Hold the line!" she called to her copperbills.

"Girls." A man with hair shot through with gray motioned frantically to them. "Come here. Hurry. We won't let them hurt you anymore." The other men seemed to latch on to this. Some of them eased forward.

"You come into the forest and slaughter our husbands," Larkin shouted. "The fathers of our children. All because you have believed the Black Druids' lies! You have aligned yourselves with mulgars and wraiths because of these lies."

"I know you, Larkin of Hamel. I know how you betrayed your own people to become a piper whore!"

Larkin searched out the voice she wished she didn't recognize. Horace Beetle climbed a nearby tree—a boy she'd once freely given kisses to. It felt like a lifetime ago.

"If she's a whore," Alorica cried, "then so am I."

"And I!"

"And I!"

The cry echoed up and down the line.

"Alorica?" Her father stepped forward, his hand extended toward her. "You've been enchanted, child. Come away with me."

"More lies," Alorica said, her voice shaking. "The pipers took us because they have no daughters of their own. Only sons to fight the mulgars you've aligned yourselves with!"

"Come away from there," a druid with silver inlay on his belt said.

"You will do as you are told," said another man.

He motioned, and a few of the braver men followed him a couple of steps forward. Larkin signaled again. The woman shifted into fighting stance—shields held before them, weapons cocked back.

"You're enchanted," the same man pleaded. "Please, girls, come away from the beasts."

A Black Druid spurred his horse to the front lines. "What are you doing?" he cried. "Fight!"

The Idelmarchians called out the names of their daughters and sisters, begged them to come to them even as the druid lashed them with his whip.

"Steady." Larkin paced before her army. "We do not give way. We do not give in. We do not go quietly. We stand steady and inescapable as the dawn."

"Hello, Larkin."

Dread skittered up and down Larkin's spine. She forced herself to turn. To face Garrot atop his massive bay horse.

"Magalia," Larkin called without daring to take her eyes off him.

His gaze shifted behind Larkin. All the color leached from his skin. "Mags?" he whispered.

She stepped up beside Larkin. "Hello, Garrot."

His horse danced beneath him. "Come away from there. I'll protect you."

"I don't need protecting." Magalia tipped her head to the side. "Tell me you didn't make an alliance with wraiths, Garrot. Tell me you haven't allowed yourself to be deceived. Tell me you're not that big a fool."

His brow furrowed, his breaths coming faster. His gaze landed on Larkin. "Is this because of her? Because of her lies?"

Magalia shook her head sadly. "You hurt her, Garrot. The gentle boy I knew could never hurt anyone."

Garrot pointed at Larkin. "She belongs to the wraiths!"

"She's the Alamantian princess," Magalia chided. "She belongs to herself. As do I. As does every other woman here."

Hurt flashed across his face. "I risked the forest to bring you back. Jonner and I both did. Only one of us returned."

She winced.

He nudged his horse forward, his voice deadly. "I control the wraiths. I made a deal with them to bring you back and end the threat of the pipers once and for all. Nothing will stand in the way of that. Nothing."

"*I* will stand in the way of that," Magalia said.

The two glared at each other, the tension so thick Larkin could taste it. She longed to wipe away a drop of sweat running down her temple but dared not move.

"You think you control the wraiths?" Larkin said. "The wraiths only want one thing—the utter destruction of mankind. They will turn on you and rend you to pieces. And they will not stop. Ever."

Garrot studied her a long moment before dismounting. He slowly made his way toward them until he was close enough to hold his hand out to Magalia. "Come with me. Come with me— prove you can—and I will call off my armies."

Magalia hesitated, turned back questioningly to Larkin.

It could be a trick—a way to whisk Magalia away from harm before he ordered his army to attack. Only Larkin didn't think they would obey him even if he ordered it. "Any woman who wishes may return with you, Garrot, but you will take none by force."

"How do we know you are not under enchantment?" someone cried from within the druids' ranks.

Larkin signaled for the women to release their sigils. "Ask them for yourselves."

The magic slipped back into the copperbills, though it remained ready to be recalled at a moment's notice.

Garrot ground his teeth. "It's a trap," he murmured. He turned back to his men, his body tensed to shout.

Magalia grabbed his hand, his shoulders, took his face between her palms. "Look at me. See me. The only trap there has ever been has been from the wraiths."

Garrot softened. Larkin saw it then. The love he had for Magalia. The love that had caused him to risk the Forbidden Forest, as Larkin had for her sister. Only unlike Larkin, Garrot had returned empty-handed, save for his brother's tooth and an unholy bargain with the wraiths.

"I should have waited," he choked. "I should have waited for you, Magalia, but I've fallen in love with another. She's having a child and ... and it's too late for us. But it's not too late to save you." He wrapped his arms around Magalia.

Larkin flared her sword, but she couldn't attack him without risking Magalia. Garrot dragged her back as she struggled and cursed him. Larkin followed half a dozen steps before she paused, not daring to draw any closer to the Idelmarchians.

"Attack!" Garrot shouted.

A handful of men charged, but then paused when they realized the other men weren't following.

"You want us to kill our own daughters?" A man hauled himself up a tree. Kenjin, Alorica's father. He'd dragged her from her home to face the crucible in Hamel. "We came here to free them."

Garrot's head whipped from side to side in disbelief. "They made themselves our enemies when they turned against us!"

Kenjin's gaze narrowed. "It sounds like you're the one who turned against us."

"The girl," a thousand mulgar voices thundered in unison—

perhaps the first time Larkin had heard them make a sound.

Every mulgar turned, their gazes locking on Larkin. Idelmarchians warily backed a pace or two away from the mulgar units they'd been fighting beside moments before.

"Bring me the girl. Kill the rest," the mulgars said.

As one, the mulgar turned on the Idelmarchians. Shocked, the Idelmarchians fell back, rallied, and braced against the attack. Their organized rows and ranks turned into a melee.

Of all those mulgars, the dozen nearest arrowed for Larkin. And at their head ... At their head was what was left of Talox.

Magalia screamed. Garrot thrust her behind him. But Talox paid them no mind as he shot past them, aiming for Larkin.

Oh, Talox. Oh, my dear friend. She'd promised him if she ever faced him, she'd end his existence. But Denan's words echoed in her head, *"You're not ready to face an ardent yet. Run."*

Heart twisting in her throat, Larkin sprinted for the safety of her line as Talox bore down on her. *It's not Talox. It's the monster that killed him.*

Two steps before she reached safety, Talox tackled her from behind. She hit hard. Her lungs froze with the shock of it.

"Larkin!" Alorica took a step toward her, only to be driven back by one of the mulgars with Talox. The line buckled under the furious assault. Pipers rushed up from behind to assist. Talox cinched a rope around Larkin's hands and hauled her toward a knot of mulgars.

"I have her, Master," he said, his voice hollow.

Larkin threw her head into his chin so hard she saw stars. She kicked her heel down his shin and stomped on his foot. Pipers and Idelmarchians fought the mulgars, slaughtering them. Larkin thought she heard Denan's voice.

"Here, Master," Talox said. "I am here."

With a roar, Garrot barreled into Talox, knocking them both to the ground. Larkin rolled free and ended up in a bush, jammed against a tree. She coughed, her ribs singing with pain. She crawled out and came face-to-face with Garrot.

She yelped and jerked back.

He grabbed her hands, knife sawing through her bonds. "I still think you're a traitor, but I promised Magalia I'd save you."

"Nesha?" Larkin asked.

"Fine, no thanks to you."

So he'd bought their lie, then. Good. No time to feel relief. Garrot grabbed her arm and hauled her to her feet. All around them, mulgars fought Idelmarchians. A thick knot of mulgars shot down the hill toward them.

"Larkin! Larkin, this way." Maisy motioned to them from the heart of a thicket.

"Maisy?" Where had she come from?

Larkin looked behind her, at the mulgars bearing down on them.

"Hurry!" Maisy disappeared in the thicket.

Larkin started after her.

"You want to follow a madwoman?" Garrot cried.

That made her decision. "Stay behind, then." Larkin pushed through brambles.

Grumbling, Garrot followed her.

Two dozen steps and innumerable scratches later, Larkin stumbled from the thicket into a clutch of dozens and dozens of mulgars. She flared her weapons, but none moved to attack.

Maisy stood among them, her expression lost. "I tried to warn you. So many times, I tried to warn you, but you never listened."

A pit yawned open inside Larkin. She turned to run back into the brambles, but Talox hacked into view. She and Garrot were surrounded. But still the mulgars made no move to attack.

She glanced up the hill to her left, where the pipers and copperbills fought side by side with the Idelmarchians—too far away to hear her scream for help over the din. Maisy had lured them here, far from where Denan could help.

"Oh, Maisy, what have you done?" Larkin said.

Maisy sang.

The beast comes. The beast takes.
That which he takes, he breaks.
That which he breaks, he remakes,
And then a beast like him awakes.

The song. Maisy had been trying to warn her all along. But Maisy wasn't a mulgar. Nor was she a wraith. "What are you?"

"One of their daughters," Maisy said.

Like Larkin was.

And then Larkin smelled it. The mineral rot of the grave.

Garrot's head came up. "Wraiths."

Before them, the Wraith King appeared.

CHAPTER 36

ANCIENT MAGIC

Larkin swallowed hard against the sickness rising in her gut. The mulgars took a single step forward. And then another. She and Garrot were forced back to back. Ramass held out his hand for them to halt. All that stood between her and three-hundred-year-old evil was her sword and shield.

Talox's words echoed through her. *"You don't defeat a wraith—not alone."*

Three hundred years to her scattered few lessons. It was not enough. It would have to be.

"Is it me you want?" she mocked. "You sack of bones bound by shadow?" Fighting wasn't the only thing Tam had taught her. He'd also taught her how to defeat her fear.

Ramass finished forming, his gaze shifting to Garrot, who went suddenly still. "I gave you everything, *Master* Druid. Power. Knowledge. Magic. And still you broke our bargain." He closed his fist.

Garrot choked and clawed at his chest, at the poison spreading toward his mind. "No! No!" He collapsed, writhing.

Larkin hated Garrot. Loathed him. And yet her sister loved him. Larkin hated her sister, but she loved her too.

Gah!

Larkin charged, if for no other reason than to silence her tangled thoughts. The wraith swung at her. She blocked with her shield, the impact sung all the way down her bones. She gritted her teeth and held steady.

"Don't let his blade touch you," Tam had said.

Both hands braced behind her shield, she danced back. Ramass swung his sword, the shadow-wreathed blade aiming for her exposed legs. She shoved her shield down and deflected the blow. But not before a second blade appeared in the wraith's other hand and thrust toward her face.

She jerked back, the blade slicing through her thick hair, a hank slithering down her shoulder.

Ramass could have taken off her head. He'd pulled back. He wasn't trying to kill her. He was trying to wound or capture her. A little less afraid, she swung from the left. He deflected. Her sword skittered off his darkened blade and glanced off his arm, shadows pouring forth. She kicked his chest. He fell back, one hand over his injured arm.

She rolled to the side and killed three mulgars at once with her magic sword. Her blade stopped just short of Talox, who looked at her with hollow emptiness.

She pulsed. The wave knocked him down, along with mulgars a dozen deep, and stunned a dozen more. She sprinted past Talox's prone body, rushing up the hill where a pocket of Idelmarchians slaughtered the sluggish mulgars left and right.

She concentrated on her sigils. Her magic had grown much stronger, but that had been her third pulse of the battle. The buzzing in her sigils had lessened. If she pulsed again, she would lose her ability to form her sword and shield.

"Larkin!" Her head came up at the sound of Denan's voice.

He'd caught sight of her at some point and fought his way toward her.

Half a step behind him, Tam stopped and sighted down his bow. "Down!"

She dropped flat. He loosed. But then the shadows surrounded her, like the wraith had stopped suddenly but his robes had not.

Ramass flipped her onto her back and straddled her, pinning her arms at her sides. Ancient hate and malice and barbed thorns coiled around her, hauling her back into nothingness.

It was different this time. For the hatred and malice was not all Ramass's. Some of it was hers—malice born of pain and betrayal and loss.

Larkin's malice mixed with the wraith's. Dark, twisted joy writhed within her.

No. She would not be taken by the shadows without or the malice within.

She pulsed her magic. All of it. A shield of light thrummed out of her. The shadows screamed and writhed. She fell upward and out, landing in a jumble of bones and senses seared raw. She choked in a breath and reached for her magic but only found a thread that dissipated in her fingers.

She darted to her feet but froze at the sight of Ramass's sword wavering before her face. He lunged. She crossed her arms before her defensively. Instead of taking off her head, the sword sliced her forearm. She froze in shock, waiting for the pain and the poisonous shadows to infect her.

They didn't come.

She risked taking her eyes off the wraith to glance at the wound. Clean, red blood sheeted from her bent elbow, but there were no black lines.

"Blood of my heart, marrow my bones," the wraith whispered. "You are the one we've been searching for all these years."

"She's too strong now to force her through the shadow." Hagath appeared behind Larkin, her shadowed sword trailing along the ground, killing everything it touched. "She must accept it willingly."

They flanked her. Larkin wasn't sure which wraith to keep her eyes on. "I will never come with you!"

"All mortals have a price, my king." Hagath's gaze shifted to something behind Larkin.

Hagath moved toward her. Larkin tensed—she couldn't outrun her, and her magic was too weak to fight—but Hagath slipped past her. So, too, did Ramass and every last mulgar.

Only Maisy remained behind, her arms wrapped around her as she rocked back and forth. "Can you hear him? The beast is coming for you."

Gasping, Larkin whirled as they charged up the hill toward Denan and Tam.

Denan.

No.

Not him.

Never him.

She opened her sigils wide, but her magic was a ribbon of useless light—not enough to forge her sword. She searched the dead and found an ax and shield, which she hauled from the hands of an Alamantian. She charged uphill toward where the wraiths fought against Tam and Denan.

Shadows pulsed, knocking them both down.

The wraiths had pulsed. Ancestors, none of them had even known that was possible.

The wraiths paused over Denan and Tam, their swords poised.

"No," she screamed. "No!"

Behind the men, Alorica took Tam's discarded bow and drew back. The sacred arrow flew through Hagath's center and out her back, shadows trailing like a dark comet. Even as Hagath dissipated, she thrust.

Ramass thrust.

Half a dozen steps back, Larkin could see the blood bloom across Denan's side—blood that was already turning black. A mulgar grabbed Alorica. Another held a sword to Tam's throat.

Larkin dropped to Denan's side, half sobbing, her stolen weapons slipping from her hands as Ramass looked on. She managed just enough magic for a needle-thin dagger that she sliced through the straps of Denan's armor. She ripped his shirt, revealing a cut along his left ribs the length of her hand. A cut edged in black, lines branching out like thorns beneath his skin.

"No," she gasped. "No, no, no, no, no."

Denan stared at the wound, and then his eyes slipped closed. "No one lives forever."

"No." She glanced into his eyes—the eyes of her heartsong. "It can't end like this."

Denan's hand slid up her cheek. "Larkin …"

"I will give them all back." Ramass's whisper slithered up her spine.

Jaw gritted so hard one of her teeth chipped, she lifted her face to the Wraith King.

Ramass stood before her like a boy offering his sweetheart a rotten apple. "Come." His voice echoed oddly, as if a hundred voices whispered instead of one. "And I will give back all I have taken."

Around them, the black lines drained from the mulgar faces. And not just the ones around them. All of them. Mulgars staggered. Gasped. Collapsed. Wept and screamed. Laughed maniacally. The ones holding Tam and Alorica dropped to their knees.

"Give them back," she said. "Like you gave Maisy back?" All madness and grief.

Maisy wiped a black tear from her cheek. "Look at his wound, Larkin."

Poison faded from Denan's skin. The mulgars might be beyond saving. But Denan ... Denan wasn't.

Tam pushed to his feet, but he made no move to end Ramass. "Larkin ..." His voice sounded like a broken little boy's.

Larkin's and Denan's gazes locked. Untold emotions channeled between them—foremost among them, love.

"Their words are poison," he said firmly. He reached up and laid her hand overtop of his, then pulled back, leaving his sword hilt in her grip.

Heart pounding in the cage of her ribs, she closed her eyes and forced down the terror and the dread. The wraith had the power to save Denan—how could she refuse him now? But if she took his foul bargain, if she went with him, all their hopes would die in Denan's stead. And Denan would never forgive her. Ancestors, was she strong enough to let him die?

No.

She was the heir of the Curse Queen. She remembered what the woman had taught her. Fighting the wraiths didn't mean accepting their shadows. It meant driving them back with light.

She would defeat the wraiths. She would save Denan. And if not ... Ancestors, if not, she would rather have him die proud of her than live ashamed of her.

She opened her eyes, tightened her grip on Denan's sword, and thrust. Ramass reeled back, his hands flaring. As his shadows writhed, he looked at her.

"Never," she ground out. And then the Wraith King was gone, his ashes holding his shape for a moment before blowing away.

Dread filled Larkin to overflowing, making her so heavy that her legs cut out from beneath her. Ancestors, had she just condemned Denan to the worst kind of death?

Denan glanced at the dead and dying around him. Without the wraiths to drive them, the remaining mulgars tried to flee and were slaughtered by Idelmarchians fighting alongside pipers and copperbills. Talox was nowhere to be seen.

The battle was over. They'd won. Idelmarchians and Alamantians had fought side by side. And yet Larkin had lost everything.

Maisy stood over Larkin, more black tears streaking down her cheeks.

"Can I save him?" Larkin begged. "Is there a way?"

Maisy backed up a step and then another. "Magic black. Magic white. Magic binding up the night." She turned and ran.

"What does that mean?" Larkin screamed after her. "Tell me what it means!"

Denan's gaze slipped to something behind her. Tam and Alorica standing over them, their expressions grave.

"Did Hagath cut you?" Denan asked his friend.

Tam shook his head.

Denan nodded in relief. "Bind it. I still have a few hours—enough to arrange terms of cessation with Garrot."

He had maybe an hour until the pain overcame him.

"Magalia!" Larkin tried to push to her feet, her head whipping frantically. "Magalia."

Denan gripped her arms, holding her in place. "There isn't anything for her to cut off. There's nothing she can do."

"Magalia," Larkin wailed.

Wincing, Denan wrapped his arms around her and tucked her head into the crook of his neck. "Shh, Larkin. Quiet, my little bird."

She couldn't have come this far, accomplished this much, and lose Denan. None of it was worth it if he wasn't here to share it with her. She gripped his armor. "No! It will not end like this. There has to be a way."

"If these are my last hours, I would spend them with you in peace, Larkin. Please."

A sudden image of Eiryss weaving magic to form an orb that pushed back the shadows flared in Larkin's mind. She'd watched Eiryss weave the magic a hundred times—she had the scars on her arm to prove it.

"Magic binding up the night," Maisy had said.

Light to bind the shadow.

Working on instinct, Larkin gathered all her magic. Enough for a small sword and nothing more. Pulling out of Denan's arms, she wiped her nose and glanced at the crowd gathering around them.

"Alorica!" Larkin commanded. "Flare your magic."

She started. "What?"

Larkin pushed to her feet, catching sight of five more copperbills around her. "Flare your magic. Now!"

After a moment's confused hesitation, they obeyed. Doing as Larkin had seen Eiryss do, she grasped the edge of their shields. The magic felt warm, soft and hard at once. She tightened her grip and pulled. The magic came free like molten glass in her hands.

Alorica gasped.

With a thought, Larkin changed the shape into a long strand, like a dangling ribbon that gleamed a faint blue.

"She can't do that," Tam gasped. "It's men's magic and a lost art, besides."

"Not for the Valynthians," Denan said. "Their women wielded the magic and their men fought."

Valynthians—Larkin's people. She took the magic from another copperbill. And another. Six in all.

"What are you doing?" Denan asked.

She closed her eyes, her memories of Eiryss playing out behind her closed eyes. Eiryss wove the strands in a familiar pattern. Dray played the music behind her.

Larkin hummed Dray's tune, got it wrong, and started again. Catching on, Tam took out his flute and played. Larkin wove the magic as she'd seen Eiryss do, the slight variation in color making it easy to tell which strand went where. Between

Tam's music and her fingers, she made an orb.

"The forest take me," Alorica murmured. "How did she do that?"

Someone shushed her.

Larkin moved the orb toward Denan's side. The words of one of Eiryss's poems came to mind. She sang it, her voice rough, the notes all wrong.

Light through dark and shadow pass,
Then tighten and trap the poison fast.

"Larkin," Denan gasped. "What are you—"

She pushed the magic into his side, his blood sticky and slick beneath her fingers. The shadows inside him were sharp-edged thorns clawing forward. Her orb slipped past them. She shifted the weave, tightening it to become impenetrable. It flared once and then steadied.

"Wh-What have you done?" Denan asked.

She concentrated on the shadows as they niggled against the barrier she'd created. Those shadows bristled, sending a phantom ache through her limbs, but the thorns spread no further. One breath out, then in again. She pulled the orb, drawing it out.

Denan writhed away from her. His head thrown back, he screamed, the sound raw and primal. She froze. He panted, gasping. "No. You're killing me."

Tears smarted her eyes. "I have to draw it out."

Denan gripped her wrists. "It's part of me." He shook his head as if even he didn't understand. "If you pull it out, you'll kill me."

Slowly, she released her hold on the magic, gasping in relief when it remained in place.

"It's contained," Larkin said. *For now,* a nasty voice in her head echoed.

Denan peered at the wound, his hands freezing cold against

her wrists.

"You— That's not possible." Tam knelt beside him. He traced the edge of the wound. "They aren't moving."

The three of them exchanged glances.

"Can you do it again?" Tam asked.

Larkin swallowed. "I-I think so."

"Then do it for me."

Larkin knew that voice. Hated that voice. She whipped around, a too-thin sword clenched in her fists.

Garrot wavered on his feet, lines of black visible on his collarbones. He had perhaps an hour left before the shadows reached his eyes and he was lost.

"How many men are dead because of you?" she hissed.

He deserved this. This and so much worse.

He spread his hands, the lines stark against his palms. "Nesha will never forgive you if you let me die."

How dare he use her sister against her—again! She took a step toward him.

Tam gripped her arm. "Kill him now, and the fighting may start all over again." She tried to wrench free.

"Think." Denan grimaced as he pushed to his feet. "Do this, and the Black Druids are at *your* mercy."

She shook her head in disbelief. "He destroyed my family. He murdered Bane!"

Gripping the back of her neck, Denan rested his forehead against hers. "I know. I know he did."

"There are so many others I can save," she whispered. "People who will be dead because I took the time to save him."

"Larkin," he whispered.

She shook her head. "You can't ask this of me."

"You're a princess, Larkin. You do what's best for your people. Always."

She pulled away from the warmth of Denan's embrace and stared at Garrot. "The war is over."

"Yes," Garrot said.

"From now on, we work together." Her voice trembled.

"To defeat the wraiths," Garrot agreed.

"Your people will make the pilgrimage to the Alamant to have their curse removed," Denan said.

Garrot's eyes widened. "That's possible?" Before any of them could answer, he staggered, his hands going to his neck. His eyes and veins bulged as the shadows writhed up his neck. "Yes. Anything you want. Please."

Behind him, one of the Black Druids dropped, his whole body jerking. He sat up, his eyes fully black. Tam shoved a sword into his neck.

The first step was the hardest. Larkin gathered magic from the copperbills, weaving the magic into an orb while Denan and Tam played.

Light through dark and shadow pass,
Then tighten and trap the poison fast.

She pushed the magic into Garrot's skin.

CHAPTER

ALWAYS

*L*arkin stumbled through the mist, rain seeping from her hood to run in freezing streaks down her back. Darkness fell, bringing with it the scent of death and the grave. It grew stronger with each step she took. Until she ran blindly.

A sound behind her. She slammed into something and fell back. Above her, a body swayed, turning. She didn't want to look. Couldn't look away. His face pale and dead, Bane looked down at her. "I can't die for you twice, Larkin."

She staggered to her feet and backed away from him, only to bump into another body. Talox, his eyes black. "It'll be your turn soon."

She turned and fled, running until she reached the edge of a ravine, a frothing river rushing far, far below. The updraft blew at her hair. She turned as the Wraith King slipped from the shadows.

Ramass reached for her, one gloved finger trailing down

her cheek. "Every mortal has a price." It was not the wraith's horrible voice that said it, but Denan's.

Larkin gasped awake to early morning. She wrenched herself up, away from the sweat-soaked sheets. She drew her knees to her chest and panted, letting herself orient to the simple elegance of Denan's bedroom—*their* bedroom now. Through the magical barriers, the White Tree gleamed opalescent gold in the dim morning light.

Denan lay beside her, one arm over his face. She longed to curl up beside him, feel the impossibility of his body—all hard softness—against her own. But he slept so fitfully, when he slept at all.

Letting him rest, she slipped soundlessly from the bed and tugged on a long tunic. She left their room, padded down the stairs of their hometree and through the main room. Not far above the water, the training platform jutted out.

She took a long staff from the hooks embedded into the tree and centered herself. She went through the motions Tam and Denan had been working with her on—slowly at first, perfecting each movement before she increased her speed.

Not long after sunrise, Denan appeared at the entrance. He watched her a moment and then left, returning with a pitcher of water and two gobby fruits. Still, she didn't stop until she was too tired to picture the faces of the dead.

She slumped down beside him, drinking directly from the pitcher. She wiped her mouth and tore into the gobby.

"What is it?"

Her first instinct was to shrink away from him. But she had made that mistake with Nesha once. She wouldn't make it again. "I saw Bane and Talox dead. A wraith hunted me. And when he caught me, the wraith was you."

"Oh, Larkin." He wrapped an arm around her.

She considered all she had risked. All she had lost. All she might have lost but didn't. "They died for me. Why? Why is my life worth more than theirs?"

"It has nothing to do with worth. It has to do with love. They laid down their lives because they loved you and they loved me."

"I can never repay them."

"You can make their sacrifice worth it."

She rested her head on his shoulder. "I didn't find the ahlea amulet."

"We will."

"The wraiths are still out there."

"We will defeat them."

"How?"

He kissed her temple. "The same way we have always faced the darkness: together."

She sighed, pushed herself up, and held her hand out to him. "The delegation from the Idelmarch should be arriving in a few days. We have a lot to do to prepare."

He allowed her to pull him up, but instead of letting go, he tugged her until she stumbled into him. He pressed his lips against hers. The kiss tasted of the sweet tartness of the fruit, with an undercurrent of salt from her lips. He deepened the kiss, which started a low fire in her belly.

She pulled back. "We don't have time for this. And I'm all sweaty."

"I'm a prince. We have time for whatever I say we have time for."

She tried to wriggle out of his arms. "At least let me shower."

"Certainly." He swung her into his arms and stepped up to the edge of the platform.

She squealed and kicked her feet. "Denan! What are you doing?"

He looked at her, perfectly serious. "Giving you a shower."

Then they were falling, dropping through crystal clear water, pulsating fish darting for cover all around them. She flung out her limbs, which wrenched her from Denan's arms. She swam for the surface. Light rippled through the plants around them, indicating Denan had touched down at the bottom.

She risked a glance to see him arrowing toward her. She broke the surface, took a gasping breath, and swam for the edge of the tree. Hands wrapped around her waist from below, rolling her under him.

Denan grinned at her, clearly thinking he'd won. She flared her magic and pulsed, sending him shooting away from her.

He skidded like a skipped stone across the water, bellowing, "Cheater!" before he sank.

She pulled herself out of the water, laughing. His head popped up, and he glared at her. She laughed harder. His eyes slid down her wet tunic, her bare legs, and his gaze turned hungry as he swam toward her.

"You're not sweaty anymore," he said as he climbed the length of her.

She trembled inside. She was so grateful for this man. For letting her be sad. For making her laugh. For letting her fight when she needed to fight. "Thank you. For coming for me."

He kissed the palm of her hand. "Larkin, I will always come for you."

THE END

Turn the page for exclusive bonus content of Amber Argyle's bestselling novel, *Of Ice and Snow.*

AMBER ARGYLE

OF ICE AND SNOW

Fairy Queens 1

"A captivating series!"
– Jennifer A. Nielsen, author, *The False Prince*

Cut off from the help of the other clans and dodging raiders, Otec must become the warrior he was never meant to be. By his side is a foreign woman stalked by a dark, mysterious magic. Together, they race to save his family and his people.

1

Pushing aside the thick brush, Otec eased into the shadows of the ancient forest. Branches scratched at him like a witch's fingernails. He tried to ignore the itch that always started under his skin when he found himself in a space that was too tight. Soon, midday had darkened to twilight under the impenetrable fortress of leaves.

"Where's the lamb, Freckles?" Otec asked his dog. "Go get her, girl."

Freckles perked her ears and sniffed the air. They hadn't gone more than a half dozen steps before she stiffened suddenly and burst forward, right on the heels of a squealing gray rabbit.

Otec shouted at her, calling her back. But Freckles was already out of sight. Even his own dog wouldn't listen to him. Grumbling under his breath, Otec continued following the spoor his sheep had left earlier that day.

Finally, he spotted an out-of-place patch of white under some brush. He knelt down and parted the angry thorns, then took hold of the lamb's neck with his shepherd's crook. She bleated pitifully and struggled weakly to get away. Her face felt feverish under Otec's palm as he held her still. "Easy now, little one."

He gently took hold of the animal's front and back legs and hoisted her over his shoulders, her wool coarse against his always-sunburned neck. And though she wasn't that heavy, the burden weighed down Otec's shoulders.

Heading back the way he'd come, Otec didn't bother to call for Freckles—she'd get bored or hungry and come along eventually. Just when he could see the way out of the forest, something warm and runny slid down the left side of his chest. He glanced down to see himself covered in sheep diarrhea.

Otec swore—he was wearing the only shirt he owned, so it wasn't like he could change. He set the lamb down and jerked his shirt off, careful not to smear any of the excrement on his face. Then he tossed the shirt into a bush. The thing was worn so thin it was nearly useless. Besides, after he spent an entire summer in the mountains, his mother always made him a new shirt.

The shadowy breeze crawled across his skin. Shivering, he took hold of his shepherd's crook and was about to pick up the lamb again when something out of place caught his eye—a splash of red in a square of sunlight. It was far enough away he could cover it with an outstretched hand.

Squinting through the tangled limbs all around him, Otec automatically quieted his steps and moved at an angle toward the strange shape and color, hoping the lamb he had left behind would remain quiet. As he came closer, the color shifted and he could make out a pair of bent legs clad in black trousers with a bright-red tunic. Strange clothing.

Otec pushed aside some brush and saw a figure bent over something. Even at fifteen strides away, he could see that the face was fine featured with deeply tanned skin, enormous brown eyes, and thick black hair.

He knew two things at once. First, this wasn't a man as he'd first suspected—but a woman wearing men's clothing and sporting hair so short it barely touched her ears. And second, she was a foreigner. What was a foreigner doing on the edge of the Shyle forest?

She was close to Otec's own age of twenty, and she was almost pretty, in a boyish sort of way. But what intrigued him most was how engrossed she was in what she was doing, the tip of her pink tongue rubbing against her bottom lip, and her brows furrowed in concentration.

That concentration stirred something inside him, an uncanny sense of familiarity. Something about the forward bend of her head, the intensity of her gaze, sparked a deep recognition. He shouldn't be watching her—should be moving the sick lamb to the village, but he couldn't seem to take his eyes away. Eager to see what she was doing, Otec moved as close as he dared, coming to the edge of the shadows and peering at her from behind a tree.

A sheet of vellum was tacked to a board on her lap. Her hands were delicate, beautiful even, as her fingers worked a bit of charcoal in what seemed a choreographed variation of long and short strokes. Bit by bit, the drawing began to take shape. It was of Otec's village, which was spread out below them. Surrounded by the crimson and gold of autumn, Shyleholm was nestled deep in the high mountain valley. This foreign woman had somehow managed to capture the feel of the centuries-old stones, cut from the mountains by glaciers, rounded and polished for decades before they were pulled from the rivers by Otec's ancestors.

She had depicted the neat, tidy fields of hay set up against the harsh winters, even managing to give a hint of the surrounding steep mountains and hills. But what she hadn't captured was the chaos of wagons and tents set up on the far side of the village. They were a little late for the autumn clan feast, but Otec couldn't imagine any other reason for them to be there.

After his five months of solitary life in the mountains, the mere thought of the mass of people set Otec's teeth on edge. Already he could hear the incessant noise of the crowd, feel the eyes of hundreds of other clanmen who, when they found out he was the clan chief's son, expected him to be the leader his oldest brother was. The warrior his second brother was. Or the trickster who was his third brother.

They learned soon enough not to expect anything at all. When Otec wasn't in the mountains, he was carving useless trinkets or playing with the little children who didn't know he was supposed to be more. To them, he was simply the man who brought them toys and tickled and chased them when no one was looking. And that was enough.

The woman's darkened hands paused. She set aside her drawing and twisted the charcoal between her fingers. Wondering why she had stopped, Otec looked past her and saw another foreigner with the same strange clothes and dark features climbing the steep hill toward her.

Just as the man crossed under a lone tree, an owl stretched out its great white wings. It was easily as long as Otec's arm. He'd never seen its like before, white with black striations. And stranger still, it seemed to be watching the girl.

Still in the shadows, the man spoke to the girl drenched in light. "Matka, what are you doing out here?" He had a strong accent, his words flat and blunt instead of the rolling cadence of native Clannish.

Matka didn't look up at the man, but Otec noticed her shoulders suddenly go stiff. "I can't—can't be around them, Jore." Her accent was milder.

Jore rubbed at his beard, which clung to his face like mold to bread. "You have to. For both our sakes."

The charcoal shattered under Matka's grip. She stared at the destruction, surprise plain on her face. "This is wrong, Jore. I can't be a part of it."

"It's too late, and we both know it." His voice had hardened—he sounded brittle, as if the merest provocation could break him.

She tossed the bits of charcoal and rose to her feet, her gaze defiant. "No. I won't—"

Jore took a final step from the shadows, his hand flashing out to strike Matka's cheek so fast Otec almost didn't believe it had happened. But it had, because she held her hand to her face, glaring fiercely at Jore.

She opened her mouth to say something, but Jore took hold of her arm. "I'm your brother—I'm trying to protect you."

All at once Otec's sluggish anger came awake like a bear startled out of a too-long hibernation. He forgot he'd been eavesdropping. Forgot these were foreigners. Forgot everything except that this man had hit her—a woman, his sister.

Otec burst into the brightness. The man saw him first, his eyes widening. Matka was already turning, her hand going to something at her side.

A mere three strides away, Otec called, "How dare—" He came up short. Jore had drawn shining twin blades, and the ease with which he held them made it clear he knew how to use them.

"Who are you, clanman? What business do you have with us?"

"You hit her!" Otec's voice rumbled from a primal anger deep inside his chest. His hands ached to strike Jore. Ached to wrestle him to the ground. But Otec held no weapon save a weathered shepherd's crook—he'd left his bow tied to Thistle's packsaddles when he'd gone in search of the lamb.

Jore surveyed Otec, his gaze pausing on his bare chest. Otec had forgotten he'd thrown his shirt away, too. "Who are you? I haven't seen you before." Jore said.

Otec raised himself to his full height, a good head and a half taller than this foreigner. "I am Otec, son of Hargar, clan chief of the Shyle."

Jore stepped back into the shadows, his swords lowering to his sides. "You do not know our customs, clanman. I am well within my rights to discipline my younger sister."

"It is you who do not know our customs," Otec said, barely restraining himself from charging again.

Jore jutted his chin toward Matka. "Come on. You've caused enough trouble for one day."

For the first time, Otec met her gaze. He saw no fear, only sorrow and pity. He wondered what reason she would have to pity him.

She turned away and followed after her brother without looking back. Feeling a gaze on him, Otec glanced up to find the strange white owl watching him with eerie yellow eyes. The bird stretched its great white wings and soared off after Matka.

The strange trio was halfway across the meadow when Freckles came panting up to Otec's side. She plopped on the cool grass, her tongue hanging out. "Didn't catch that blasted rabbit, eh?" Otec said to her, anger still burning in the muscles of his arms.

It was then that he noticed Matka had forgotten her drawing. He picked it up. He'd never seen anything so fine, since clanmen didn't waste valuable resources on something as extravagant as art.

Otec traced the lines without actually touching them. With a few strokes of charcoal, Matka had managed to capture his village—to freeze it in time. Simply by looking at her drawing, he felt he knew her. She saw details other people glossed over. She felt emotions deeply. And she saw his village as he saw it.

Otec remembered the lamb with a start and hurried back to the forest. After settling her back over his shoulders, he called out commands to Freckles, who circled the scattered sheep, gathering them together. Otec fetched his donkey, Thistle, from where he'd tied her to the trunk of a dead tree. He led her toward the paddock to the west of the clan house, where he lived with his parents, his five sisters and eight brothers, and three dozen members of their extended family.

At the thought of them all crammed into one house for another never-ending winter filled with wrestling and lessons with axes and shields, Otec had a sudden urge to command his dog to drive the sheep back into the wilderness, to live out the winter in his mountain shack or under the starry sky. But of course that was impossible. The hay would already be laid up for the coming winter. And his mother would never allow it, even if he was nearly twenty-one.

As he unlatched the gate, Otec expected someone from the house to come out and greet him, or at least for his younger cousins and siblings to help bring the sheep in. The boys and girls were always eager for the toys he carved over the summer. But no one came, so he herded the flock into the paddock by himself and tied his donkey in one of the stalls.

He went to the kitchen door, rested one hand on each side of the frame, and called inside. A thin whimpering answered from upstairs, something not unusual in a house bursting with children. Grumbling, Otec tied up his dog outside the door—dogs were strictly forbidden inside, except for after mealtime when the floor needed to be licked of crumbs and spills.

Following the sound, Otec walked through the kitchen and the great hall, then climbed the ladder to the upper level. The sound was growing louder—someone crying. He finally pushed the door open to the room his five sisters shared. Sixteen-year-old Holla was huddled on one of the two beds, her wild blond hair a matted mess. She was his favorite, if for no better reason than because she talked so much he never had to. But also because she was the kindest, most gentle person he'd ever met.

At the sight of Otec, she pushed to her feet and ran to him, then threw herself in his arms. He grunted and stumbled back, for Holla was not a waifish girl. She sobbed into his bare shoulder—luckily the side that hadn't been covered in diarrhea.

He rubbed her back. "What is it, little Holla?"

"I'm not little!" she said indignantly. Some people found her hard to understand, for she often slurred her words. Before he could apologize, she lifted her tear-stained eyes with the turned-up corners and the white stars near her irises. He always thought she had the prettiest eyes. "I can't tell."

Otec guided her onto one of the two beds and held her hand. "Remember what Mama always says—'Never keep a secret that hurts.'"

Hiccupping, Holla nodded solemnly. "I can tell you. You never talk to anyone."

He winced. Not seeming to notice, she leaned forward to whisper in his ear, "I was waiting for Matka to come back—she always has pretty drawings. But Jore told me to get away." Tears spilled from Holla's eyes again. "I froze and he called me an idiot, and ..." She paused, her sobs coming back. "He pushed me and I fell."

The rage roared to life inside Otec. It took everything he had to shove it back into the damp dark where it came from. "Who is he? Where is he?"

Holla wiped her face. "One of the highmen from Svassheim. They're camping out on the east side of the village."

In his mind's eye, Otec saw the dozens of tents in that direction, and he realized they were different from the clan's tents. "All highmen?" he asked. Holla nodded. "So the clan feast?"

"Cancelled."

"What are they doing here?"

She shrugged. "Hiding from the Raiders."

"Raiders! How—" Otec checked himself. Holla wouldn't know the answers—they would frighten and confuse her too much. And right now, he needed to deal with one problem at a time. "Where is the rest of the family?"

"The highmen offered to feed the villagers the midday meal to repay our kindness." Holla's eyes welled with tears again.

With a trembling hand, Otec tried to smooth her wild hair. Sweet, perceptive Holla. "I brought you something."

She sniffed. "A carving?"

He suppressed a smile that his attempts to distract her had worked so easily. "It's not quite finished yet. I want it to be perfect." She nodded as if that made sense. "If you promise to stay here, Holla, I'll give you the spiral shell I found on the mountainside."

She gave him a watery grin. "All right."

"Stay here." Otec pressed a kiss to her forehead and left the clan house at a trot.

It was ominous to see the village so empty. There were no women perched in front of a washing tub. No men chopping wood or cutting down hay in the fields behind the houses. No children tormenting whatever or whomever they could get their hands on.

Otec rounded the Bend house—second largest home after the clan house. Another enormous owl, just like the one from earlier, was perched on the roof. Otec wouldn't have paid it any mind at all, except he was surprised to see two such birds in the same day, and away from the shadows they normally dwelled in. He would have studied the bird a bit longer, but he had more pressing matters to deal with.

On the other side of the home, a crowd had gathered. Hundreds of mostly clanwomen and children intermixed with hundreds of highmen and an equal number of highwomen—all of them under thirty years old.

For once, the familiar, sick feeling he had whenever he was confronted with a crowd failed to turn his stomach. Instead, anger simmered just beneath his skin.

If you've enjoyed this preview, order your copy today!

Visit http://amberargyle.com/fairyqueens/ to order.

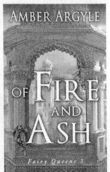

ACKNOWLEDGEMENTS

Thanks go out to my amazing editing team: Charity West (content editor), Jennie Stevens (copyeditor), Cathy Nielson (proofreader), Elissa Strati (proofreader), and Amy Standage (proofreader); and my talented design team: Michelle Argyle (cover designer), Julie Titus (formatter), and Bob Defendi (mapmaker).

My everlasting love to Derek, Corbin, Connor, Lily, and God.

ABOUT THE AUTHOR

Bestselling author Amber Argyle writes young-adult fantasies where the main characters save the world (with varying degrees of success) and fall in love (with the enemy). Her award-winning books have been translated into numerous languages and praised by such authors as *New York Times* best sellers David Farland and Jennifer A. Nielsen.

Amber grew up on a cattle ranch and spent her formative years in the rodeo circuit and on the basketball court. She graduated cum laude from Utah State University with a degree in English and physical education, a husband, and a two-year-old. Since then, she and her husband have added two more children, which they are actively trying to transform from crazy small people into less-crazy larger people. She's fluent in all forms of sarcasm, loves hiking and traveling, and believes spiders should be relegated to horror novels where they belong.

To receive her starter library of four free books,
simply tell her where to send it:

http://amberargyle.com/freebooks/

OTHER TITLES BY AMBER ARGYLE

Forbidden Forest Series

Lady of Shadows
Stolen Enchantress
Piper Prince
Wraith King
Curse Queen

Fairy Queens Series

Of Ice and Snow
Winter Queen
Of Fire and Ash
Summer Queen
Of Sand and Storm
Daughter of Winter
Winter's Heir

Witch Song Series

Witch Song
Witch Born
Witch Rising
Witch Fall

Printed in Great Britain
by Amazon